Heart Over Heels

S.M. AFREEN

BLUEROSE PUBLISHERS
India | U.K.

Copyright © S.M Afreen 2024

All rights reserved by author. No part of this publication may be reproduced, stored in a retrieval system or transmitted in any form or by any means, electronic, mechanical, photocopying, recording or otherwise, without the prior permission of the author. Although every precaution has been taken to verify the accuracy of the information contained herein, the publisher assumes no responsibility for any errors or omissions. No liability is assumed for damages that may result from the use of information contained within.

BlueRose Publishers takes no responsibility for any damages, losses, or liabilities that may arise from the use or misuse of the information, products, or services provided in this publication.

For permissions requests or inquiries regarding this publication,
please contact:

BLUEROSE PUBLISHERS
www.BlueRoseONE.com
info@bluerosepublishers.com
+91 8882 898 898
+4407342408967

ISBN: 978-93-5989-171-2

Cover Design: S.M Afreen

First Edition: February 2024

*To anyone who's struggling to follow a path,
maybe it's time you make your own.*

1
AVERY

Being an American kid in a British boarding school is a sport. And although I'm an athlete, I was struggling with it.

My life had so far brought me to a place where I was sitting in my aunt's office, her judgmental eyes trained on me as she went on lecturing about how things were different here than in America.

"Students here don't just waste their time on parties and games, you have to be really dedicated if you want to keep up with the pace of the curriculum," Asami told me, looking over the rim of her glasses. Now that I was looking at her up close, I realized that she really resembled my dad. She had a pair of plump lips that enhanced her delicate features. Her eyes were just like my father's except they didn't hold the same look of understanding and warmth in them.

Even though she was my dad's sister and it was technically a very close relationship, I had never met her before this. I was in America and she was all the way here in England. The only reason I had to come here was to escape the humiliation of repeating my junior year after failing, although a part of it was to try out my luck in the soccer scene over here. Now I was thinking things were far better when I didn't know her personally, because it was causing me a great deal of guilt to not like the woman my dad grew up with. Her aura was so cold I almost considered wearing a jacket the next time I came here.

"I know you have some excuses, but even so I expect you to try harder and not fall behind like before." Her tone was linear, with no emotion or care carrying the words.

It took all my strength not to let my emotions get the best of me. As always, she had implied that my dyslexia was an excuse for me to be lazy and laid back with my studies. If I had a dollar for every time someone passed it off as an excuse, I would own a freaking soccer club. Or football, as they call it here.

However, as hurt and nervous as it made me feel, I wasn't going to sit here and listen to this old taunt again.

"It's not about making excuses. I work twice as hard to achieve the same results as others. Just because you can't see the effort doesn't mean it's not there. " I said, showing none of the humiliation on my face.

"It might not be, but it doesn't mean I'm going to let you use it to justify your failures. I can't let you get comfortable with that story." That '*story*'. As she said that, she looked at me like she saw right through me. Like she caught me red-handed, using my condition as an excuse. Yes, *using* it. It's horrible to even think about, I don't know how she managed to convince herself it was okay to say it. It was humiliating enough for me that I failed a whole class and all my classmates went ahead without me, and now she was here trying to make sure I don't ever get over my failure.

"You won't let me get comfortable, that's for sure." I scoffed and looked away. I couldn't shake the feeling that she had already made up her mind about me, and no matter what I said, she wouldn't truly grasp the daily battle I faced.

This was my first time in her office as it had only been three days since I came to England, and yet she hadn't even asked me if I was feeling okay after moving to a whole new country alone. She hadn't even considered how low I was already feeling after having failed in my junior year and being left behind by my classmates. It had left me feeling miserable for weeks on end before I decided to come here, but of course, Asami didn't give two shits about it. She didn't even ask me if I had breakfast today. Which I didn't by the way, because I had already been running late before she even called me to come here and now I had to listen to her lectures before I ran to my class.

So basically, I was hungry, nervous, and lonely but she felt like this was the perfect time to remind me of my weaknesses. I didn't even feel like I was related to her. She was worse than an unrelated unknown bully of a teacher.

And yet she looked offended by my response, I don't even know why. I was the one who had the right to be offended here. "And that is exactly the kind of attitude you should change here."

Still not looking at her, I said nothing. There was no point, she already had a prejudice against me in her head, and if I said anything it would only hurt me more because she would either ignore it or misunderstand it. She might be the head of the department here, but if she couldn't give me basic respect and decency, I had no obligation to be nice either.

"I know your sport is more important to you than your studies, and your main reason to come here was to play football and possibly get selected for a national level club, but let me tell you, I don't think that is as impressive as you think it is." God, she just keeps getting worse and worse with every word.

"Sure you can play for your team and even play inter-school matches, but if I ever see you falling behind on your studies, I won't hesitate to inform your parents and make them change their mind about your ambitions." She tried to threaten me but my mind was scoffing at her words. She thought my dad finds it degrading that his daughter wants a career in football, but she doesn't know just how much he encourages me for that. Just because she is vain and shallow, doesn't mean my dad is, too.

I said nothing else except a confident "Sure." with a casual smile.

I could tell it was absolutely pissing her off that I didn't look affected by her degrading remarks or heavy threats. Even if it *did* hurt me inside, I was not one to show it on my face. I wouldn't give her the satisfaction. She already thought she was the queen of the world just because she had always been good in academics and holds a doctorate. Nevertheless, if she can't respect other people's skills and achievements, I definitely won't respect hers.

"Your first class starts in ten minutes." She told me, looking at her watch. "Better not be late for your first class."

'Better not insult me again or I won't hesitate to trash your office' I thought, and got up from my chair, giving her a big smile which seemed to upset her more. Oh, how I love that annoyed scowl. I could already tell it was going to give me a great deal of pleasure to piss her off any chance I got.

Asami gave me a map of the school marked with the classroom I was supposed to go to, and after a good twenty minutes trying to figure out the directions, I gave up. I think I should have mentioned I can't make sense of maps in my head, but admitting a weakness in front of a woman who just invalidated my feelings was a huge no for me. I had too much trust in my future self to think I'd figure it out if I tried hard enough, and that trust was finally crumbling with every passing minute I spent in the school corridors. The classes had started ten minutes ago and all the students were already in their classes, which meant I wasn't going to find anyone around me to ask for directions.

I was walking around the corridor with a map in my hands, looking at the room numbers, when I heard the sound of rushed footsteps which stopped right behind me. I turned around and realized I was being a roadblock for the boy who was also running late for his class. *Thank the heavens, maybe he can tell me where my class is.*

"Are you new here?" His voice was deep and boyish, and it was unusual for me to hear his British accent so casually.

I guess it'll take me a month before I start thinking this is normal.

"Yes, can you tell me where this class is?" I said, holding the map in front of him.

He looked at the map and then back at me. His tall stature stood much above mine, and I had to look up just to meet his eyes. The eyes that had incredibly thick and long lashes, which immediately gave me a feeling of envy. His lightly tanned skin and sharp features made him look presentable, but his messy dark brown hair told me he had just woken up ten minutes ago. Which clearly explains his rash appearance in the corridor.

He smiled, and I don't know if it was just me or his face, but the smile didn't feel warm and welcoming. There was a sparkle in his eyes like he was amused by my question. His smile radiated menace.

"Sure." He turned around in the direction he was coming from and pointed towards the end, "There."

I looked in the direction of his finger but when I turned around to thank him, he was already running towards his class again. Which made sense since he was also running late.

I started my walk in the other direction, turning around again to see if he got to his class and saw him standing outside a door in the middle of the corridor. Just then, he turned and looked at me, giving me the same playful smile before he disappeared into the classroom.

It took me approximately three minutes to understand why he was smiling so much. That stupid, jerk of a guy told me the wrong directions. When I reached the door he pointed at, I realized it was a spare classroom that was being used to store extra tables and chairs. It was completely devoid of any living being. I let out a low curse and walked back into the corridor. *What a douche.* Was it costing him a fortune to just tell me the right directions like any decent person would do?

I looked at my digital watch and realized I was now running twenty minutes late with no idea of how to get there. I decided instead of wasting my time trying to make sense of the map, it was better to just walk around and sneak into every classroom until I found the right one. I stepped into seven classes while asking "Is this grade 11 Math?" and had seven teachers frown at me for being careless before I walked into the right one.

The teacher, an old man with glasses on his nose and a marker in his hand, looked at me. Well, I guess I can't exactly call him old, but he looked like he was in his late forties at least. Math can make you look weary and old earlier.

"Yes, are you Avery Kai?" He asked me, and I found it strange that he already knew my name.

"Yes," I replied, still standing in the doorway. It was a bit awkward, so I glanced around the classroom to avoid his gaze but a shocking revelation came over me as I spotted the guy from the corridor. He probably read the shock on my face and found it amusing because he leaned back in his chair, flipping a pen in his hands with a smirk on his face.

He was going to the same class as me?

"Well, I'm Mr. Becker, your math teacher." My attention was drawn back to the man in front of me. "Miss Asami told me about you and she mentioned you might be late since you're new to this building."

Oh. So she knew it wouldn't be easy for me to find the classroom and still chose to give me a map. Probably wanted to teach me to 'try harder'. *I hate that woman.*

"Yeah, I'm sorry, I couldn't find the classroom," I told him and then glared at the Corridor guy. "I couldn't find anyone to show me the classroom."

He seemed almost proud of being the reason behind my delay because he replied with an innocent smile. *What a jerk.* I rolled my eyes and looked back at Mr. Becker.

"Well, half the class is over but I'll let it go since it's your first day today." He said. "But you won't be let off next time, so try to get up earlier."

I nodded as he dismissed me before I walked into the classroom to find a seat.

The front seats? Taken. Middle row? Taken. I went ahead and-

Great.

The universe seemed to enjoy my misery because the only empty chair I saw was right in front of Mr. Jerk. He looked up at me as I approached the chair, the satisfied grin still pasted on his face.

After shooting a sharp glare in his direction, I settled down in the seat, immediately making myself busy with taking out my books.

"Took you long enough." I heard him say.

I turned around to face him. "Yeah well, I ran into a jerk on the way."

"You literally had a map in your hands," He deadpanned.

"Well, it didn't really help me all that much."

He raised his eyebrows in mock amusement. "Well then maybe it's about time you learn to read a map."

I threw him a bitter look and sat back straight. The way he said it reminded me of the way Asami always tells me to just try harder. I hated people like him. Just because it was supposedly an easy task, doesn't mean everyone can do it easily. I decided to ignore him and his stupid comments as I opened my textbook.

"Oh, I forgot to mention." Mr. Becker suddenly faced the classroom, turning away from the board. "You are not meant to change your seating arrangement after the first day, so please remember your seats."

I resisted the urge to let out the groan that was building up in my throat. The whole year right in front of this idiot on my back? The Universe was having quite a fun day today.

Dorm 208. This was the room I was supposed to spend my junior year in. I had come here before when Asami was showing me my allotted room, but there was no one else in there except a huge suitcase on the bed. I wanted to tour the football ground they have here but now that the first day of classes was over and everyone went off to rest after lunch, I decided to postpone my tour and get some rest instead.

Putting in the code and entering my dorm, I was met with someone hovering above their suitcase to find something. When the girl heard the door opening she turned around, throwing a pair of socks back into the suitcase.

"Oh hey." She smiled. "Avery, isn't it?" Her deep blue eyes were sparkling with affability and the voice that left her pink lips was soft and feminine. She had smooth blonde hair that fell over her shoulders and almost reached her waist.

Damn, she's pretty.

My eyes left her gorgeous hair and went back to meet hers and that's when I realized she was still waiting for an answer. I blinked quickly, dragging myself out of the hypnosis. "Yeah, how do you know?" I don't remember meeting her in the morning and I didn't even introduce myself yet.

"Mr. Becker introduced you in Math class, dumbo." She chuckled. The desk on her side of the room was already littered with thick books and the pen stand held a variety of pens along with other study supplies. "I was just unpacking my suitcase, where do you think we should keep our socks?"

If there was anything I learned from my Japanese side of the family, it was how to organize and keep things tidy at all times. I had already put away most of my belongings in the closet so I had pre-decided locations for everything. "I put them all here, so if you do that as well I think we can officially call it our sock drawer." I pulled open a drawer in the closet which had my rolled-up socks sitting in a neat line.

"You unpacked already?" If her reaction was anything to go by, she was quite impressed by my well-organized closet. All my winter clothing was stacked on the right side- sweaters, jackets, and oversized cardigans. My casual flowy dresses hung in the middle and all my pants were on the left. I have yet to receive my soccer kit from the school but I already made space for it on the bottom right corner. My soccer cleats were sitting beside the empty space on the left. "Shit, you're so much cleaner than my last roommate."

"You say it like it's a bad thing." I never had someone curse at how clean my room was.

"But it's actually the best thing ever." She laughed and went back to her suitcase to bring her socks. "Why didn't I see you at breakfast?" She asked while rolling up each pair of socks so she could fit them in the drawer beside mine.

"Because I skipped." I went and sat down on my bed.

"You skipped?" She looked at me with a horrified expression on her face. "And then you directly had lunch at three?"

I nodded. "Yeah."

"How were you even walking at that point?" I was barely handling myself by the time lunch came around but I didn't say anything. "You know that's not good right?"

"I woke up too late." I was a bit embarrassed but the way she was concerned made me feel better. At least *someone* here cares about me.

"Wow. You're eating every meal with me from now on." She ordered before closing the sock drawer.

"That's very nice of you but I don't want to crash in between your friends, what if they don't like me?" I was flattered by how sweet she was, but forcing myself into a friend group was just pitiful.

"My friends?" She laughed. "Girl, I don't *have* any friends. I spend most of my time either in my room, library, or going through all my classes. At least I'll have a table partner if you eat with me."

My mouth fell open but I'm not sure if she noticed how flabbergasted I was with that information because she casually went back to taking out more clothes from her suitcase. When I saw her in my room, there was a small part of me that was intimidated because I expected her to be the queen bee of the school. With how pretty and sweet she was, she could be ruling the sorority in America. "So you're telling me you're a loner?"

"Ouch, that's harsh." She put her hand on her chest and acted like she was hurt. "But yeah, everyone kinda thinks I'm boring. But anyway, enough about me. Where are you from?"

It was hard to imagine how anyone could call her boring so I focused on answering her question instead. "Uh, I'm from California."

"I thought so. Your accent is so American." She folded her arms on her chest and leaned back on the closet. "What brings you here?"

"Soccer." I lied. Telling her that I came here because I failed junior year and was too embarrassed to stay in the same school seemed like a bad idea. She was the first person who had been so nice to me here and I really didn't wanna mess it up by disappointing her. "I mean Football." It wasn't a complete lie though because I did choose England so I could get more opportunities with soccer.

"You play Football?" She asked with a gush of amusement, which somehow felt like an achievement.

I smiled proudly. "Yeah, it's what I wanna do in my life. Become a Football player."

"Wow." Her big eyes were admiring me like I was impressive. No one had ever appreciated my passion like that, especially someone who was personally inclined towards academics. "So the coach selected you for the team?"

"Yeah, he had a talk with my previous coach and they decided I can play within the school teams. My practice starts tomorrow." She was listening to me with such attention that it didn't make me feel silly for getting excited over something as small as my first practice.

"That's so cool, I'll always attend your matches."

My heart warmed. Many of my friends back in America never cared about supporting me on my matches or even appreciated the sport, and yet here she was- a nerdy girl who I just met and who had zero interest in sports- telling me she will willingly attend and watch all my matches.

"I would love that." I smiled as I checked my digital wristwatch- it was 05:23 P.M. "So when do we have dinner?" I wasn't exactly hungry right now but I needed to know about the next meal so I knew how much time I could waste before I go.

"At seven or seven-thirty. We just have to be finished before eight." She was now putting her clothes on the hangers.

"Two more hours." I plopped down on the bed and scrolled on my phone, going through the highlights of the latest match in the Premier League.

The early September breeze was slightly more chilly than it is in California, so I put on my hoodie before Mia and I headed towards the dining hall for dinner. We reached at seven fifteen, so there was quite a bit of a crowd but we managed to find an empty space for ourselves by the corner of the room.

"Oh, there you are, I've been looking for you!" A boy came walking towards us, clearly talking to Mia.

"And I've been trying to avoid you." She responded with a sigh.

The boy was kinda tall and was wearing a varsity jacket with an 'M' embroidered on it. With his ruffled hair and sharp jawline, he looked like the textbook version of a high school jock.

"Look, I got something for you." He fished his hand into his pocket and took out a small blue flower. "I saw it earlier and it reminded me of your eyes."

With that handsome face and the athletic thing he had going on, I'm sure any girl would have melted at the gesture, including me. But except for a small smile that betrayed its way out of Mia's lips, she displayed no gratitude. "Was I the first blue-eyed girl you came across? Because I'm sure you would be willing to do this with many others."

The boy laughed, shaking his head. "You're cute even when you're skeptical."

"Mason! Come on, I'm hungry." Another voice came in from behind us and then a boy appeared, a tray in his hands. He was too tall for me to notice him straightaway, but when I lifted my eyes I was met with an urge of irritation. It was the Corridor guy. As soon as he recognized me, his irritated expression turned into an amused one. "Oh hey, new girl. Congratulations on finding the dining hall on time."

Whoever he was, I was sure I was going to spend my time avoiding him and his annoying remarks. "Thankfully, not everyone in this school is a jerk like you."

"Come on, you can't always blame me for your lack of intelligence." His smug smile was so annoying I could punch it off his face right now if I wasn't scared of Asami hearing the news.

The thing about Dyslexia is that any comments about your intelligence hit you straight in your heart, triggering your anger in a way nothing else can. He might not know about it but the effect it had on me was certainly the same. Before my anger reached an even more explosive stage, I decided to leave this conversation.

"Is he friends with you?" I asked Mia.

"Noah? Nope." Mia answered. "Neither of them is my friend." She added and with that, Mason's smile was instantly replaced with a frown.

"Then let's go, I can't stand his presence for another minute." I held her hand and dragged her away, leaving them both in their own company.

"Not like I was enjoying your presence either." He called after me.

After reaching our table, I put my tray down and gulped down half of my water bottle in one go. "It has only been a day and he's already getting on my nerves," I thought out loud, trying to forget any encounters I had with him today. There was risotto and fried chicken on the menu and I wanted to enjoy every bit of it without the thoughts of some annoying guy disrupting my peace.

That night, I had planned to call Ella and tell her all about my first day as she asked. Since she was in California, she had to pick absurd times just so she could call me when I was free. It had only been three days but I already received about ten calls from her, asking me how I was managing things on my own. As my big sister, she had always looked after me and now it was driving her crazy to know I had no one to help me around.

'Too tired today. I'll call you after practice tomorrow.' I texted her, the light from the screen illuminating my face in the dark.

'No problem. Get plenty of rest! <3' She texted back almost immediately and I smiled.

Even if I live alone thousands of miles away, I could always count on her to pull me up from any problem I fall into. Taking the step to move to a new continent was difficult, but with the care and concern she had for me, I knew I'd never feel alone.

2
NOAH

Reasoning with a ten-year-old was a difficult task as it is but when that ten-year-old happens to be my very own sister, it was futile.

"You can't just punch someone in your class," I told her as we were walking out of the principal's office. I had been called to report to the office in the middle of my class so even though I was grateful for skipping the rest of it, I still had to talk some sense into her.

"Was I just supposed to stand and watch them bully my friend?" she asked, her mighty words being carried by the feathers of innocence.

"I never said that," I replied. Even though this was the second time she had me reporting to the principal's office, I still can't say I'm not proud of her. I admit she has always been a bit of a troublemaker, but I loved the fact that she never tolerated a joke at someone else's expense. Despite her mischiefs, she always made sure no one was ever left behind. The last time I was here, it was because she had gotten into trouble for sneaking an abandoned kitten into her room without the warden's permission. Someone on her floor heard meowing coming from her dorm and had snitched on her. However, the teachers thought the calico kitten was indeed very cute and she now roams the campus as the school's official pet.

Count on a Turkish person to rescue and domesticate any cat they set their eyes on.

I turned to her and she was looking at me with her small squinted eyes, like she was disappointed in me for saying she shouldn't have punched them. "I mean, just report them to the teachers next time, okay?"

Her eyes relaxed and she nodded, walking towards her class with her small hand in mine. It had been years since I last saw my mom, but every time I look at Deniz I recognize the same warmth and charm I remembered from my childhood. She doesn't remember our mother just from her memory because she was very little when our mom died, but she did look at her pictures enough to know that she looked like her. Same brown eyes with gorgeous lashes which makes her face look angelic. Curly brown hair that was always falling onto her shoulders in bouncy rivulets. Her small pink lips carrying a smile beautiful enough to make anyone's day.

I smiled at her and tousled her hair, to which she responded with an annoyed groan. "Don't mess it up, I don't want it to get frizzy." She quickly became busy flattening it down with her hands.

"God, you're already so vain" I laughed.

"I'm not vain, I just want to look presentable without being told there's a nest on my head." She replied, which kinda made me angry to think anyone would ever say that to her. Her hair is so pretty, why would anyone be mean enough to say that?

"Tell me who said that next time and I'll punc-" I stopped when I saw her eyes going big like she just caught me saying a curse word. "I mean, I'll report them to the teachers." I corrected myself.

She put a hand on her mouth and giggled. "There's no next time, I already made my point very clear."

Making her point clear would have definitely included a healthy dose of roasting and sarcasm from her end, so I knew I didn't need to worry about it further.

"Can I watch your practice today?"

"Don't you have to complete your homework?" I asked her and she pouted in defense. "I'm not going to save you the next time you're called in for not completing it."

"I'll bring my books to the ground and do it there." She asked, looking at me with her big puppy eyes. "Please?" Her pout was getting more sad by the minute.

"Fine." I can never say no when she's making that face. "But don't get too distracted and focus on your homework, okay?"

"I will!" She nodded sincerely.

I told her to grab her books from her dorm while I went to pick up my training kit from mine. It was my first training session in junior year and I couldn't wait to finally get back on the field.

For a regular junior year student in the Summerfield Institute, we only get thirty minutes of PE sessions per week. Which- for a hyper-athletic guy like me- was very sad and depressing. This was initially the reason why I joined the out-of-hours school sports club when I was in 5th Grade. I had been playing football way before that, ever since I was old enough to start playing outside but my dad only realized my potential when someone in our neighborhood told him I was too good to only play in the streets. After the death of our mom, Dad got quite busy with running our Turkish supermarket back in Liverpool, so he thought it would be best if Deniz and I enrolled in a boarding school, living with friends around us at all times. He also wanted me to focus on my game, and Summerfield had one of the best coaching opportunities for that. Our school sports club has links to sports clubs in the north of England and our city's football club plays in the second division in the premier league. For a small boy with a big dream like me, that was huge.

When she was alive, my mom loved football and was very proud of me for taking it seriously. And although Dad has never directly said it to me, I believed that was the reason he supported me so much even after Mom's death. He never pressured me over grades, he was happy even if I got a C. I was so grateful to him for letting me be passionate about whatever I liked and ever since he enrolled me here, he had never doubted me for a single moment. He isn't worried about what I'd do if I don't make it as a footballer because he is absolutely convinced that I will. That belief has eventually led me to be confident and assured in myself too.

When I was in 9th Grade, after playing intra-school matches for four years, I finally got selected to play for the official school team during inter-school competitions. It was my first time playing at a higher level outside our sports club, against real competitors with real audiences cheering for their schools. Since we were all high schoolers, we were supposed to play in unisex teams until we turned eighteen, and I slowly got used to sharing the field with girls as well. Ever since then, I realized the value of playing for a team, to do everything you can to avoid disappointing your teammates and all the people cheering for you in the stands. To wear a jersey with the name of your team and represent it with your skills. To belong.

But today, as I walked onto the football field for our daily practice, expecting the familiar sights and sounds of our pre-training routine, I witnessed the most unlikely events being unfolded right before my eyes.

Avery Kai- the girl who couldn't even navigate our classroom yesterday- was wearing a scrimmage vest and doing warm up exercises. My steps faltered, eyes fixed on her, a lingering question mark hanging in the air. Was she here to play or did she lose her way again? I calculated the possibilities.

The girl, all five-foot-four of her, whom I witnessed grappling with our classroom layout just yesterday, now adorned a football jersey on the field. Twin French braids danced around her face as she executed high knees, and beneath her scrimmage vest was the unmistakable training kit of the Blue team. Yup, she was definitely here to play.

"Oi Noah!" Mason called me from afar.

I waved at him and was about to join him in the middle of the ground, but my name must have struck a bell in her mind because she immediately looked up and met my eyes with a dash of annoyance.

"You again?" The distaste on her face was loud enough to be heard across seven continents.

"You play football?" I asked her, the stupidity in my question clear to me even as I said it, considering she was currently warming up in her team's kit.

"No, of course not." She denied my implication with a pretentious smile. "I came here for a tea party."

I rolled my eyes. "You can never talk nicely, can you?"

Her eyes traveled down to my training kit and then back at me. "You're not in my team, I don't have to be nice."

"And yet some people do it for the sake of being civil."

She considered it for half a second before shaking her head. "Nah, I don't think you deserve that."

I scoffed, annoyed by her attitude. "Keep up with your attitude new girl, good thing I get to beat you when the games start so you can see where you stand."

The fire that ignited in her eyes at that moment felt like a reward. "I have a name." She said slowly and sternly, not a hint of intimidation in her voice.

Even though I remembered her name from when Mr. Becker introduced her to the class, it gave me great pleasure to act like she was too easy to forget. "Oh yeah, what was it again? Maybe I'll remember it when you actually do something worth remembering."

Without waiting for her response, I walked off toward my team answering Mason's call. I had never seen her playing so I didn't have any rightful reason to challenge her but even so, I had a feeling I won't have to regret it any time soon. Even if the Blues give us a fair competition in the future, I doubt she will play any part in their wins. In fact, I'm sure it'll take her at least two months before she's even included in the playing eleven. There wasn't much she could do to prove me wrong while sitting on a bench.

"What were you guys talking about?" Mason asked me as I reached our side of the field.

"About how I'll beat her when the first match day comes around."

"Damn, she's got you all riled up." He laughed.

"I'm not riled up. She's just annoying."

"Whatever, dude. Just don't go too far. She's roommates with Mia and I don't want to be in her bad books." There he comes with his endless pining for Mia.

"How do you even know that?" I looked at him a little too uncomfortably, not sure if it was okay to call your best friend a stalker.

"Don't look at me like that, Chloe told me!" He explained quickly before I could even get my thoughts out. Chloe was a midfielder for the Yellow team, the most social and chatty member of our team. "We were discussing her before you came, apparently she heard the Coach saying she was a good catch. She used to play for her school when she was in America."

"A good catch? Her?" I knew I shouldn't underestimate someone based on their appearance, but she just looked too nimble to actually make a difference in the game.

My thoughts were disturbed by a loud shrilling whistle before Coach Martinez came up on the halfway line, clapping his hands to gain the attention of everyone on the ground. "Gather 'round everyone, I've got news to share." He yelled while gesturing at us to stand in front of him. The air buzzed with anticipation as the team gathered, cleats scraping against the turf. Whether it was yellow or blue, all twenty-eight people from our sports club gathered around him for the meeting. Coach Martinez stood at the center, a stern figure amidst the sea of eager faces.

He was very fit for a fifty-year-old, with gray hair and stubble on his face. Having him on the ground was by far the best service Summerfield Institute offered, his joviality and skills making him the perfect coach for us. Most of us called him the Jugen Klopp of our school. "I want to introduce you guys to a new member of our sports club family." He said and gestured toward Avery to come stand next to him.

She hesitated to step ahead. "It's okay, I'm-"

"Oh come on, they need to know you." He insisted, making her reluctantly step forward, her determination visible despite the uncertainty in her eyes.

"This is Avery Kai, a very talented midfielder." He patted her shoulder as she stood there with a closed smile on her lips. "She has come here all the way from America, to pursue her dream of making a career in football."

My curiosity sparked. I had seen the intensity in Avery's eyes during our encounters, but I never imagined she harbored a passion for football. Taking such a huge step to pursue your passions takes a great deal of confidence and belief in your skills, and if she managed to make this move, I was itching to know how she executes it on the field.

However, the revelation didn't have the same effect on everyone because Jack, a defender from our team, scoffed at that. I wasn't really surprised because he had always been an arrogant person but Chloe wasn't going to let it slide and threw him a hard glare. She could never tolerate it when anyone from her team looked down on the ambitions of another and she always made sure to call them out on it.

The coach must have noticed the little interaction because his voice raised a tad bit higher for his next words. "Avery's got skill, and I expect you all to treat her like one of your own. Welcome her to the club, folks!"

A few nods and half-hearted claps greeted Avery, but Jack, the team skeptic, crossed his arms with a smirk. I knew him enough to know that if I saw her with his eyes, she seemed like just another face in the crowd, a regular girl who wouldn't pose a threat on the field. He was a big muscular defender and she was relatively much smaller to give him any challenge. Nevertheless, his conceited act of arrogance gave a tinge of irritation to me as well.

Coach Martinez, with a knowing glint in his eye, threw a challenge into the air. "Now, we're not just going to welcome Avery with words. Let's see her in action." He suddenly looked at me, his attention catching me by surprise. "Noah, I saw you had a little talk with Avery when you stepped on the field, late as usual." I really thought he wouldn't notice considering there were more than twenty players on the ground, but as always he had taken note of my unpunctuality for the hundredth time. "I'm sure that calls for a penalty." Avery looked at me with her eyebrows raised, almost recognizing Coach's intentions. He turned to her again. "Avery, you're up for a little one-on-one with Noah here."

The coach's challenge hung in the air, a palpable tension building on the football field. Avery and I exchanged glances as the coach hollered again, "Avery you're supposed to head for the goal and Noah, you have to stop her before she gets a chance."

Gladly accepting the challenge, I stepped on in front of the net, and Avery, undeterred by the skeptical glares, stepped forward as well ready to prove herself. The football field transformed into a stage where uncertainty met possibility, and I couldn't help but feel the stirrings of excitement in the air. It was a clash of expectations, a collision between doubt and potential.

Now that I was facing her head-on, I couldn't deny that my initial reaction was a subtle underestimation. After all, Avery was much shorter than me, and the idea of her outplaying me seemed unlikely. The smirk on my face was an unintentional expression of that doubt. And yet, no matter how much I looked, there was not a sliver of fear on her face. Her determination was evident in her eyes and when I recognized her confident stance, my amusement shifted to intrigue. Maybe there was more to her than met the eye and I was dying to find out.

The ball started rolling, and the challenge was underway. Avery, swift on her feet, navigated the field with a finesse that caught me off guard. I quickly tackled her and took possession of the ball but running past her was still a challenge as she matched my quick movements in a focused sync. I pushed the ball to the side to throw her off but she swiftly reached over and took the ball, making me desperate for a tackle again. As I got busy trying to match her dribble, she sidestepped and weaved with a grace that defied her stature. In a blink, she was past me, the ball neatly threaded between my legs.

The collective gasp from the onlookers was a testament to the surprise that echoed within me. Avery had just nutmegged me, and I stood there, momentarily stunned. I could only look over in defeat as she sprinted towards the goal, kicking it straight to the back of the net. Considering the moment, I had thought she would celebrate my humiliating loss but after the unexpected goal, she just casually stood with her hands on her waist. My self-esteem crumbled into a thousand pieces at my feet. Her silent victory was way more humiliating than a loud one.

"And that is why the football field is not a place for underestimation." Coach told us in a lighthearted timbre, almost as if he knew the outcome.

Avery turned to me, finally milking her triumph. "Your defense is full of holes today. You might need a patch-up."

Embarrassed as I was, I still tried to shake it off. "Oh please. I'm just giving you a chance to shine since you're new. It's called sportsmanship."

"Whatever helps you sleep at night." She said simply and walked off, joining her own team for individual practice.

Even though I'd never admit it to her, I had indeed underestimated her skills, and it was a lesson learned on the field. From that moment, I knew not to judge a player by their height. Avery's agility and quick thinking were assets I hadn't anticipated.

Note to self: next time we hit the field, keep an eye on Avery Kai. The girl's a surprise package, and cautious respect should be the strategy when facing her in the games ahead.

The dining hall was a haven for hungry athletes after practice, and I was finally glad to escape the field where Avery just introduced me to a very humbling session. The taunts of my teammates followed me all the way to the dining hall, where I was now seated in peace, enjoying a good Shepherd's Pie. Mason was the only person at my table, as we both scarfed down our meals, savoring each mouthful.

However, I was unaware of a brand new presence joining us, which came to my attention only when Mason elbowed me from the side. I looked up in response and saw someone standing in front of me. Everly Campbell.

"Hey, Noah." She said in her sugary sweet voice. She was wearing a pink frill top and a green pleated skirt. Her nails were perfectly done and her blonde hair was sporting soft curls today.

"Hey," I replied with a small smile and continued with my food.

"I was wondering if I could eat dinner with you?" She had a tray in her hands and I knew she wasn't expecting a no. No guy would ever say no to dinner with Everly, but let's just say I was not in the mood for her company today.

"Uh, I'm almost done," I said and shoved half of the pie in my mouth. An uncomfortable air surrounded me, and I was probably the only person who could feel it.

"Oh." She said and glanced around, pretending to look for another place to eat but I knew she was just looking around to see if anyone heard that.

When she made sure that no one was around to witness the rejection, she turned to me again. "It's okay, see you later." She continued her walk to another table nearby, the one with all her rich friends.

"You're cold," Mason told me.

"No, I'm just hungry," I replied, not wanting to initiate any conversations about her or our shared past.

3
AVERY

After the unexpected win against Noah, pure adrenaline and triumph were running through my veins. Coach told us to split up according to our teams, and the players wearing their yellow vests went on their way. As I approached the side my team was on, a girl came toward me with an energy that matched her vibrant physical presence.

"That. Was. Awesome!" She exclaimed, her friendly energy making me forget I was meeting her for the first time. She had an easy way of carrying herself, radiating both confidence and approachability. "I love it when the underdog beats the lion."

I laughed, feeling instantly at ease in my new team. "He's supposed to be the lion?"

"Well, yeah. I know you're new but you should know Noah Yildiz is like, a prodigy or something." She said. Her bright personality matched her appearance- her hair a radiant shade of ginger, cascaded in loose waves in her ponytail, catching the sunlight and creating a warm halo. Freckles adorned her face like constellations, scattered across her cheeks and the bridge of her nose. Her hazel eyes held a mischievous glint, hinting at a sense of humor and a penchant for lighthearted mischief.

"So I've got myself a nice little rival." I chuckled. *Prodigy? We'll see.*

"And I'm going to enjoy this drama from the sidelines." She smiled. "I'm Leah by the way, I play midfield too."

"So we're basically partners on the field."

"Damn yes, we are." Leah looped an arm through mine, and we embarked on what felt like a guided tour of the football battlefield. "First things first, let's get you acquainted with the lay of the land."

She effortlessly weaved through the players doing their drills, introducing me to each member with an enthusiasm that made it seem like we'd been friends for years. "Avery, meet Fred, Ellie, and oh, there's Kyle."

"Avery, right?" Kyle turned his attention to me, his eyes assessing but welcoming. "I saw the stunt you pulled just now, and I don't want you to get all cocky but Noah's no slouch on the field. If you can handle him, you've got potential." He was yet another towering man, but his aura radiated maturity and kindness.

Still processing the compliment, I stammered a bit. "I, uh, well, I'll do my best. I'm here to learn and contribute."

With an encouraging smile, he placed a hand on my shoulder. "That's the spirit. We've got our first match coming up, and I want to see what you've got. Work hard in training, and let's make that debut something to remember."

I offered a tentative smile, still grappling with the concept of being part of this seemingly close-knit team. Leah, sensing my hesitation, nudged me with her elbow. "Kyle's the best captain ever. Trust me, you'll love him."

The training drills and exercises started and I couldn't help but notice how different it was compared to how it felt back home. This time my passion had stakes. This time I wasn't just participating in my hobbies but there was a sense of responsibility in my game here. A responsibility that regarded my own self and how I could move on from my failures with a new path of my own. With my first day of training, I embraced the mix of emotions as the heartbeat of a journey about to unfold. Each step forward was a chance to discover not only the dynamics of the game but also the resilience within myself.

But even with the motivation brewing inside me, there was one thought that kept lingering in the back of my mind. Was this the best decision I could ever take or was it yet another mistake that would lead me down the path of disappointment?

I was officially done with my first week of school and things were finally settling into place. I was making it to classes on time and my schoolwork had been going fine so far. The beginning of the school year is usually the time when I can easily catch up with my studies because it's all introductory and easy. I know I will start to struggle the moment we hit the fourth week but until then, I was enjoying the smooth sail.

The two friends I had made so far couldn't be more different. After living with Mia for a week, I learned that she was a huge bookworm and liked to stay on the calm side of chaos. She is pretty humorous and funny, but only around people she is comfortable with. It seemed I had somehow managed to cross that border because she really liked telling me all about the recent book she had read. Of course, I had no problems with that because it meant I got to hear drama without having to read. When she was not reading, she usually busied herself with solving math equations that no one asked her to do. Personally, I couldn't imagine seeking thrills by just sitting at a table for hours but to each their own.

Leah, my other friend, was the person I looked for whenever I was bored in my room and Mia was occupied with her huge book tower. Leah turned out to be as outspoken and voluble as Mia was shy. On top of that, she was as competitive as me, and now we had a nutmeg competition going on between us at all times. I've gotten her more times than she has gotten me, but I still never let my guard down because I know she isn't one to sit down and accept defeat.

As the new Monday approached, I was in yet another math class, playing with my pen while nodding so I could manage to keep my brain awake. After about twenty minutes of trying to pay attention to the theorem Mr. Becker was babbling about, my efforts were shattered when I suddenly felt my chair shaking. I tried to ignore it and didn't think much of it at first but I had to give up my attempts at concentrating on the class when the shaking just didn't stop. I looked down and realized there was a pair of feet tapping away on the footrest below my chair- fidgeting, I'm sure- because of the boring class. The pair of feet evidently belonged to Mr. Jerk on my back, who was seemingly too tall to rest his long legs on his own footrest.

Not wanting to look at his face for another moment, my mind came up with the excuse that turning around and telling him to stop would only gain the attention of Mr. Becker. So instead of telling him off, I decided to kick his foot below my chair, hoping he would be smart enough to get the message.

"Ouch," I heard him whisper with some additional curse word that I didn't quite catch. Even though getting back at him did give me a sense of satisfaction, I showed no emotion on my face as I continued looking forward like nothing happened.

Recognizing the little commotion, Mr. Becker stared at us momentarily while saying something about the theorem he was teaching, but then continued his speech ignoring our little exchange. But the moment he raised his marker and turned toward the board, he started shaking my chair again, clearly doing it out of spite this time.

Even though my first instinct was to turn around and yell at him, being in the middle of a class stopped me from following my passions. Instead, my annoyance manifested itself in a much harder kick than the last but this time he quickly retracted his feet, making me directly hit the footrest. A loud CRASH echoed in the silent room startling everyone, which unfortunately also included a very annoyed Mr. Becker. Startled by the noise myself, I sat up straight, acting like I didn't just destroy school property.

I heard a gleeful chuckle coming from behind me which cracked up my anger, making me snap around and glare at him immediately. He looked back at me with a raise of his eyebrows as if to say *'What are you gonna do?'*. Before I could even respond, our fierce eye contact was broken fast enough by a loud, "Avery and Noah, WHAT IS HAPPENING back there with you two??!!" from Mr. Becker.

Noah quickly stood up and pointed at me. "She was the one who broke the chair."

Shocked at the accusation, I stood up and faced Mr. Becker, "Sir, he kept disturbing me by tapping his foot on my chair!"

His eyes went wide hearing the blame. "It was just a bit of harmless fidgeting and I wasn't hurting her, but she still kicked my foot in response! How is that fair?!"

I had just turned around to tell him it was *obviously* his fault for bothering me in the first place when I heard Mr. Becker shout, "ENOUGH!"

Startled by his loud voice, I immediately turned around and looked back at him, a little nervous.

"You do know you both are at fault here?" He took off his glasses and frowned at us. "Noah, it was wrong of you to disturb her while she's trying to focus and Avery, it was wrong of you to kick him instead of politely asking him to stop."

His fair judgment left us no room to argue any further, resulting in us standing quietly and putting on our most innocent faces hoping it would convince him to cancel any repercussions he had in mind.

However, it quickly became clear our tactics weren't going to work because he was still frowning at us, eyes glaring with disappointment. "Detention, both of you." He ordered, his voice stern and serious. "You're solving ten extra sums before leaving, right here in this classroom." Considering Mr. Becker's hard and unchanging glare, both he and I decided not to challenge him with any more complaints.

"Now sit down and listen to the rest of the class in silence if you don't want more trouble." He put his glasses up on his nose again and turned away, continuing with his lecture from where he left off.

"Thanks for the detention idiot!" He whispered behind me as we sat back down.

Is he seriously blaming me for this? You can't just fidget on someone else's chair and get away with it.

"*Shut up and keep quiet if you don't want him to get more pissed, this is all because of your stupid habits anyway!*" I wrote on a piece of paper and threw it back over my shoulder.

Ten seconds later the same paper ball landed back on my table.

I opened it up and saw his scribbled handwriting right below mine. "*And what about YOUR stupid habit of overreacting at everything?*"

I wasn't going to engage in a verbal war so I crumbled up the paper before aiming for the dustbin near the door. I watched it fly across the room and exhaled a grateful sigh when it landed right inside the bin because I wasn't willing to hear another lecture about littering in class.

The rest of the day went surprisingly well when Noah decided to mind his own business and just as Mrs. Welson ended her lecture on Thermal Properties of Matter, I was relieved as ever and started packing up my notebooks to leave the classroom. But fate wasn't going to let me off yet as Mr. Becker chose that exact time to walk into the classroom, carrying some papers in his hand.

A silent groan built up inside me as I realized I had forgotten all about the detention. I turned around and glared at Noah, reminding him it was his fault we were stuck here for another hour. "Don't look at me like that, you were the one who kicked me," he said, making me roll my eyes to the back of my head.

As the rest of the class got dismissed, Mr. Becker came toward us and handed us two papers. Taking one glance at it, I immediately knew it was gonna take me a day and a half to solve them and certainly not an hour.

"You can leave as soon as you finish all these sums. I'll be in the staff room, so give it to me before you leave." He said before leaving us in our misery.

Slowly, the noisy classroom turned into a silent one, all the benches now empty and deserted. Noah picked up his paper and got up from his seat, sitting in the one beside me. "Are you aware that you overreact at everything?"

He seemed just as annoyed with being held back as me. "Oh, this wasn't overreacting," I told him. "Just be glad I don't believe in violence because your face is looking very punchable right now."

He laughed, not even a real one but a short patronizing laugh. "You really think you can threaten people with the body of a twelve-year-old?"

His tone was condescending but I can also be realistic. "I can manage to break your nose at least."

"I would love to see you try."

"Would you?" I narrowed my eyes and he realized pushing it too far might end up in *some* casualties.

He cleared his throat. "Anyway, can we at least solve these together so we can get out of here?"

"Bold of you to assume I'm going to help you." I shifted and looked down at my sheet in false confidence, knowing full well it would be a miracle if I solved even one of them correctly. Nevertheless, I wasn't going to help someone like him either.

"Well, then *I'm* not helping *you* either." He announced and turned a bit away, staring at the paper while flipping the pen in his hands. And with that, we sat there in silence trying to finish the paper before the other.

After a good twenty minutes of racking my brain for theorems and formulas, I finished the first sum and basked in the joy of my momentary victory. I wasn't sure if I did it correctly but a win is a win. By the time I finished my second sum, I stopped caring whether I was even using the right formulas and only focused on finishing so I could get it over with. Since doing mental math was like dancing on a tightrope for me, I was calculating the multiplication on the paper. Suddenly, the sound of pen tapping filled my ears and hijacked my brain. I tried to ignore it and continue with my calculations but there it comes again.

Tap, tap, tap, tap. It was a steady beat.

I didn't even have to look to know it was Noah tapping on the table with this pen. Being his desk neighbor for a week now, I had learned he couldn't sit still without doing some sort of fidgeting. He was probably doing it absentmindedly while thinking about the sums. Nevertheless, it was getting on my nerves.

"Can you stop that?" I snapped.

"What?" He turned immediately.

"The pen tapping. Can you stop that?"

"Oh." He looked at his pen like he just realized what he was doing. "So you're allergic to *any* kind of fidgeting."

"And you're allergic to letting others live in peace?"

He scoffed. "Do you always think you're the boss of other people or is today something special?"

"Well it's the first time I've met someone as annoying as you, so I guess it *is* something special," I replied.

He rolled his eyes and went back to solving his paper. After several more tries at concentrating, I peeked over at his side to see how much he's done. I might have talked a big game and told him I wouldn't help, but with each passing moment, I was starting to realize this was impossible to do alone. Looking at my watch, it had been almost an hour since school ended and I was still nowhere close to being done. Math is even worse for me than words in weird fonts. Looking over at him, I calculated how much damage my dignity would have to take if I asked him for help. He's looking at the paper with his eyebrows knit together, desperately trying to figure something out. As much as I hated myself for doing this, I was now desperate enough to seek help.

I cleared my throat to cover some of the embarrassment. "Uh, how many did you solve?"

He looked over, his concentration broken by my voice. "Uh," he rubbed the back of his neck. "Just two."

"I did three. Show me yours, maybe you did the ones I missed." I held my hand forward.

He looked at me with narrowed eyes, like I asked for his social security number. "Why should I? You weren't gonna help me."

Sigh. *Is he always this petty?* "Quit being a baby. The only way we can get out of here faster is if we work together."

"Oh that's funny, it sounds exactly like something I said an hour ago but someone was being too moody to cooperate."

I rolled my eyes. "Whatever, I'm willing to cooperate now."

"Well, that's too bad because now I want tax." His skeptical face gave way to a malicious smile.

"Tax?"

"Yes, tax. Get me a pack of Jaffa Cakes from the vending machine and we have a deal." He held out his hand like a real businessman.

"You're actually serious?"

"Of course. I deserve something sweet after working with someone bitter like you."

I looked at his hand and then back at him.

He read my expressions like a hawk. "But of course, it's fine if you don't want to, I'll just run out alone afte-" He started taking his hand back and I hurriedly grabbed it before he had the chance to take his offer back.

"No, fine! We have a deal." I shook his hand and he shook it back with a pleased smile. A moment passed while looking into each other's eyes and even though it was a silly deal, it felt strangely momentous. "Just get me out of here."

4
NOAH

The new girl had spent a total of one week in my vicinity and other than embarrassing me on the field, now she had me wasting my time in detention. I could have been in my room playing video games on my smuggled Nintendo Switch, but no, I was sitting in an empty classroom facing a daunting task instead – trying to solve the impossible math problems to earn our ticket out of this academic purgatory. We are sitting side by side at our tables, working together to finish this and head out. We decided to pool our mediocre math skills, but after what felt like an eternity, we'd only managed to conquer four sums. We have been trying for the past hour, and somehow she turned out to be worse at math than me.

"You know we could have avoided this if you weren't petty and kicked my leg," I said, giving up on my current sum and doodling a ship instead. A sail might look good on this. Do big ships even have sails? I don't know. Mine does.

I could feel the heat of a deadly glare in my direction so I tore my eyes away from my sailing ship and looked on my side.

"I only did it because you kept disturbing me."

"Disturb you? I was minding my own business."

"Oh, please. You were tapping your foot like you were auditioning for Riverdance."

"So? I was just tapping, not summoning an earthquake. You overreact at everything."

"*I* overreact?" She said with a finger toward herself, seeming offended. "You intentionally kept doing it out of spite. Who's the petty one here?"

"It's still you." I didn't care if she was right, I was still too pissed to agree with her. I tossed my pen on the table and sat back. Even with our joint efforts, this was a struggle. "This is hopeless. How would we get out of here?"

She mumbled some curses and went back to her paper, desperately trying to solve something in her notebook. Just three minutes had gone by after our argument when we both heard a soft knock on the door. I looked up and saw Liam standing at the door. His blonde hair was neatly brushed back and he was wearing a navy blue sweater. Avery seemed like she didn't know him and I was a bit confused by his appearance as well. Liam, the epitome of studious behavior, in detention? Something was fishy.

"What brings you to the dark side, Liam? Detention doesn't seem like your usual scene." I asked him, and he smiled.

"I just don't think the new girl should be wasting her time in detention." He replied kindly and turned to her. "Avery, right?"

"Yeah." She gave him a hesitant smile.

"Need any help with those sums? Maybe I can help."

Avery and I exchanged glances, the unspoken agreement hanging in the air. Desperation had a way of forging unexpected alliances. Since she was technically the one he asked, she was the one who had to answer.

"Um yeah, we do need help. That's very sweet of you." She said, "We did four, but I don't understand any after that."

"We? I did three and you copied." I remind her.

"I helped you with the formula in the second one."

"Where would I be without you," I said and she rolled her eyes.

He smiled and walked in, gladly taking a seat beside her and looking at the paper. It took him around five minutes to understand how they're solved and then he picked up Avery's pen and started scribbling in her notebook.

"Tell me when you're done so I can copy," I told them and Avery raised her eyebrows at me. "What? We had a deal. You're not getting out of here without me." I reminded her.

"Fine, you can get your Jaffa Cakes for at least solving three." She said and returned her attention to Liam's attempts in her notebook, slowly getting more and more invested in the process of solving.

With the passing minutes, our boring detention turned into an unexpected rendezvous for equations, with Liam and Avery huddled together over the math problems, their pencils dancing across the paper like synchronized partners. I sat at my desk, bored as hell, not wanting to be a part of this impromptu math class. Liam's explanations were met with nods of understanding from Avery, and their combined focus created a bubble that left me on the periphery. Glancing down at the doodles on my notebook, I added some unruly waves under my big sailing ship. I leaned back in my chair, trying not to get distracted by their babbling, but my attention kept drifting back to their animated discussion.

"I understand it so much better now! Thank you so much!" Avery said and Liam smiled at her, the permanent smile that was refusing to go away in her presence.

"Ah, no problem. You guys were stuck here for almost two hours, I'm glad I could help." Liam's usual indifference was replaced with overflowing sweetness and smiles, and as much as I had no concern for this situation, it just seemed weird to me. I have known him for three years, why did his whole demeanor change in the span of a week? He had never helped anyone get out of detention before. Nevertheless, help had finally come my way so I accepted it without further thought and started copying the sums in my notebook.

"I appreciate it." She smiled.

"See you tomorrow then?" He asked, pumping up on the friendliness.

"Sure... Of course," Avery replied with an equally friendly answer but there was a hint of doubt in her voice, like she was surprised at making a friend so quickly. He said his goodbyes while leaving the classroom and then it was just the two of us again as I scribbled down the notes.

"Looks like your pretty privilege got us out of here," I said.

"Pretty?" She sounded surprised at the implication. "I'm sure he was just being nice since I'm new." She said, depreciating herself.

"That would make more sense," I said, covering up the fact that I accidentally called her pretty since appreciating her beauty sounded too much like flirting to me. Sure, she was pretty, but I didn't want her to think it had any effect on me.

It didn't seem to bother her though, almost as if she believed it herself and I almost felt bad for taking back my compliment. *Why do pretty girls never know they're pretty?*

When I was done, we went to the staff room and handed our notebooks to Mr. Becker, who looked at our notebooks and gave us an appreciative nod. After receiving the declaration of our freedom, Avery got me a bag of Jaffa Cakes as she promised before we parted ways to finally get some rest in our comfortable dorms. It was one hell of a boring detention with Miss Angry but sitting in my dorm while playing my video games, I was glad to have gotten Jaffa Cakes out of it.

I trudged into the bustling dining hall, my shoulders slouched from the weight of a long day that seemed to stretch on forever. Detention had been a drag, and football practice hadn't been any easier. Mason was still in the room doing some economics homework he missed so I decided to have dinner early since I wanted to jump into my warm cozy bed as early as I could. The dining hall was buzzing with chatter and clinking cutlery as the elementary students had their meals, earlier than the seniors since they had their curfew at eight. I scanned the room for a familiar face, and my eyes lit up when I spotted Deniz sitting with half a dozen of her friends at a corner table. Being the life of the party, as usual, she was entertaining her friends with her humorous chats.

With how busy I am between classes and football, I barely get time to hang out so I took this as an opportunity to share a meal with her. Approaching her table, I gave a smile when she looked up, her face immediately lighting up at my sight.

"Abi, what are you doing here so early?" She asked, her brow suddenly furrowed. "Are you tired?"

I always found it surprising how she was so caring and thoughtful even at her young age. Always checking up on me and Dad, even though she was the youngest. "You could say that," I replied with a half-hearted chuckle, running a hand through my disheveled hair. "Detention and then football practice. I'm beat."

Deniz's expression softened, and she pouted sympathetically. "Well, at least you're here early. Let's eat together." She excused herself from her group of friends and we settled at a different table, just the two of us sharing a meal like we used to do at home.

The canteen was serving Shepherd's Pie today, which added more substance to the homely feeling. Not that we make Shepherd's Pie at home, but being a combination of meat and bread, it was close enough to the Turkish food I grew up eating at home. Our mom used to make the best Turkish meals, always on call with my Grandma to learn her culinary secrets. After she died, Dad tried his best to make good meals, and to his credit- he really was a very good cook, but it was just never the same as eating our mom's food. She used to make it with some sort of motherly love spell that made it the most delicious thing on the planet.

"How's your studies going?" I asked her as she was trying to cut through the pie with her knife and fork. I reached over and cut it for her, gaining a happy smile from her end.

"It's good." She shrugged. "But more importantly, how's your practice going? Who's that new cool girl?" She piped up, suddenly excited in our conversation.

"New cool girl?"

"Yeah, the one that nutmegged you that day. She did it so quick and smooth, it was amazing!" She recollected that memory with a lot of joy.

"You're talking about Avery? When did you-" I remembered suddenly. "Oh. You were there that day." Sigh. So even my little sister saw that embarrassing sight.

"Of course, I saw everything and it was really funny." She giggled. "You should have seen your face when she went past you and scored."

"So you're taking her side over your own brother?" I asked her with fake betrayal in my voice.

"No, I'm taking the side of football."

"Touche." There was nothing else I could say when she was genuinely supporting the one who outsmarted me. "But you won't be cheering for her too long."

"Is that so?"

"Our weekly matches start on Saturday, and it will be the first time she faces me in a real match."

Her eyes lit up again. "Really?" She asked and I nodded. "I can't wait to see you and Avery face each other in a match! It's gonna be so cool! I'll bring all my friends."

I sighed, realizing that I couldn't escape the Avery fan club, even within my own family. "Yeah, it'll be cool when you realize you betrayed your brother for a mediocre player." Even though I knew it was far from the truth, something in me wanted to win the favor of my sister.

"She's not mediocre." She defended her. "You're just jealous that someone else can be as good as you."

"As good as me?" I laughed. "You'll see when the weekend comes around Deniz, we will all see." Even with the confidence dripping in my words, I had already decided not to overlook her strengths. Looking all tough in front of Deniz was what I wanted to do, but inside my heart, I knew underestimating Avery again would be a huge mistake. As we finished our meals and went back to our dorms, the confidence I exuded was beginning to fall heavy on my shoulders. The match was still five days away, but a voice inside me told me to rise up on my practice. My laid-back days were over, and now I wanted to come back with a newfound passion, a passion to rise above Avery and show her she would have to stand next to me if she wanted to shine just as bright.

5

AVERY

The aroma of freshly fried fish and chips wafted through the air as Mia, Leah and I sat at our usual spot in the bustling dining hall. All the classes of the day were over, meaning we were all starving for a fulfilling lunch. If there's one great thing about moving here, it's getting the original fish and chips without the effort of finding a good British restaurant. Apparently, it's only on the menu on Thursdays, but a week's worth of waiting was nothing when the food was as good as they make it here. The three of us eagerly dug into our meals, savoring the crispy texture of the fish and the golden perfection of the chips.

Mia, however, couldn't help but bring up our study habits like always. She set down her fork and looked at me and Leah with concern. "Have you guys started preparing for the test tomorrow?"

"What test?" Leah asked, her mouth full.

"The Chemistry test! Mrs. Jones was telling us about it at the end of the class!" She always seemed more worried about our grades than we could ever be.

"Oh did she? I was too distracted after the whole beaker incident." It was my first day in the chemistry lab and Mrs. Jones asked me to pour some water in the hot beaker. I forgot to check the temperature of the water before pouring it in, and the beaker ended up shattering because of thermal shock. I was very embarrassed but luckily Mrs. Jones didn't yell at me since I was new. Then she asked Noah to bring another beaker, and he bumped into a table corner and dropped the beaker which shattered way worse than mine. It was a sad day for the beakers but the sight of an embarrassed Noah getting yelled at by Mrs. Jones was worth it.

"It's *tomorrow*," Mia emphasized the urgency.

"But I'm tired now." I drawled. "I'll study right before the test tomorrow. We have plenty of time."

Leah, engrossed in her plate, glanced up and shrugged. "Yeah, me too. It would be fresh in our memory that way. We might even score more than you." She winked at Mia.

Mia's eyebrows furrowed in disbelief. "You can't be serious. This is important. We need to do well on this test, they all add up at the end of the year."

"Relax, Mia," I said, shoving a bunch of fries in my mouth. "We've got it all under control. We'll study a bit before the test. It'll be fine."

Mia sighed, knowing our laid-back attitudes all too well. "You guys should take it seriously. Chemistry isn't something you can cram in one night. It requires understanding."

Leah waved her hand dismissively. "We'll be fine. Besides, we have our first match on Saturday. We need to practice for that."

"Exactly." I nodded in agreement.

Mia slumped back, finally accepting her defeat. "You guys make me stressed. I don't know how you can perform well in the match if you're stressing about a failed test."

"We won't fail," I reassured her. "It's just two chapters."

"I hope so." She replied wistfully. "But if you guys decide to change your mind, I'll be in the library okay?"

"Okay Mia, we'll come if we get time," I told her and she seemed to ease up a little. She continued her slow process of eating, cutting extremely small pieces of the fish with the patience of a sage. She was exactly like Ella when it came to studies, always stressing about it days before it was due. I was used to reassuring Ella about my tests, and I was now using the same tactics on Mia.

A small part of me was indeed worried about the test, but I had studied the same chapter a year ago when I was in America. I might have forgotten some parts but surely I would be able to pass a little test right? Besides, I was too excited for the upcoming match to care about anything else at the moment. It was a mix of excitement and fear, my doubt and confidence mounting in my heart in equal parts. It had been a rough couple of months ever since I failed, and I was finally returning back to the field with a newfound ambition at a brand new place. It was a moment big enough to disassociate me from everything else. After all the changes that I brought upon myself these past few weeks, a soccer game would definitely be the perfect thing to cheer me up and get me back to my real self.

The students of Summerfield Institute weren't blessed enough to enjoy a two-day weekend, but we did get the advantage of sleeping in late because our Saturday classes always started at ten. It was just a bunch of random classes for teachers who weren't able to finish their portion in the past week, and they ended pretty early to give us space for extra-curricular activities- one of them being football. Leah had told me that the football scene was big here, that even students from other extracurriculars fill the bleachers and enjoy the afternoon being spectators of the live matches. We weren't exactly professional football players but the fact that the matches were received with intense amounts of attention, the pressure was sure to spike.

It had been a few months since I played against a team, and there was no denying my nervousness for today. But if there was one thing I couldn't stand- it was my form getting mediocre. So far I have gotten through a lot of things- failed tests, embarrassing moments, high school drama, anything. But I know the minute it starts to affect my game, I will lose all sense of my self-esteem. It crushes me to think that I can get bad at the thing I'm most passionate about, and if I can no longer lead my life with it, I'll crumble.

People might tell me that it's just the first match and I can manage to take a few hits before actually rising up. And to those people, I say *sure, you might be right*- but maybe I wouldn't have been this much worried about the results of the match if *someone* from the other team hadn't riled me up in advance. Noah was supposed to be the top player on his team, and if I could somehow manage to drive my team toward victory while also crushing his humongous ego, it would be the best debut I could make in England.

But to make that happen- I had to be willing to put in my best work. This meant that the few extra hours of sleep I could have gotten on this fine Saturday morning had to be sacrificed with an early alarm- waking me up in the wee hours of the morning to get some solo practice on the football ground. Well, by wee hours, I meant seven O'clock. Mia groaned as my alarm went off and I quickly shuffled around my desk to turn it off.

"It's Saturday, what are you doing?" She dragged sleepily and buried her head under the blanket.

"Sorry," I said in a low voice. "I'm going for practice."

As I waited a whole minute without any response, I realized she had already fallen asleep, not bothering to receive the answer to her question. It took me about ten minutes to braid my hair into two French braids and then another ten to find my training kit in the darkness of the curtained room before I was on my way toward the dining hall to fill my empty stomach with a breakfast sandwich. It was expected for the dining hall to be empty at this time but it still gave me an odd feeling to be sitting here without the usual hustle-bustle of students. Instead of getting a coffee, I grabbed an apple and headed out, taking my time to munch on the apple while roaming the campus on my way to the locker room.

The empty girls' locker room gave me the same spooky vibes as the dining hall- maybe even scarier- and I rushed to change into my training kit before running onto the field, escaping the imaginary monsters hiding behind the lockers. But before I could reach the safety of the field, I bumped into something, my face planting on something robust. I shrieked, spooked out by the sudden presence of an unknown obstacle in front of me, but my panic subsided when I heard a familiar voice.

"Why are you screaming?" The annoyed voice said and I immediately knew who it belonged to.

"Oh." I opened my eyes, feeling a little embarrassed at my misplaced terror. "It's you."

"Scared much?" Noah snickered, fully dressed in his training kit just like me.

"What are you doing here at this time?" I had expected to be completely alone when I decided to come here but now I had to share the field. Bummer.

"Same as you." He shrugged. "Getting some last-minute practice."

"Aw, you're that scared of me?" I said in a patronized tone.

"You wish." He scoffed. "I do this before any big match, rain or shine. I gotta say though, I didn't expect you to be the hardworking type."

I wasn't sure if I should have taken offense to that, but it did make me feel a tinge of hurt that he would assume I was lazy or unambitious. "Well, you know what they say. Hard work beats talent." It sure sounded corny but it was one of the truest quotes out there.

"Do they? I bet they'll say 'Noah beats Avery' next."

A chuckle left my mouth before I could stop it and I surprised myself by laughing at his lame comeback. "Arrogant much?"

"Nope, just practical about how things would work out."

"You wish, bumblefoot. We'll see it soon enough."

"Sure thing, Captain America." He performed a salute and I playfully rolled my eyes before stepping onto the field. Something about the excitement of my first match stopped me from getting angry on this fine day.

The dew on the grass crunched under our cleats with a satisfying sound as we both parted ways to different parts of the field. It was like we had an unspoken agreement to take sides and then we both started setting up our courses for practice. I picked up the stack of cones and started arranging them in a zig-zag pattern, making up small gateways to pass the ball accurately. I practiced short controlled passes for a while before I started hearing the rhythmic sounds of the ball being kicked and then hitting a target two seconds later. I looked over at Noah's side and saw a line of targets set at different angles and distances. He had a row of balls lined up in front of him and was hitting every single target with pinpoint accuracy. He kept changing the kicks- using the inside, outside, and instep of both feet.

I hadn't ever asked him or anyone else which position he plays, but now it seems pretty clear that he's a striker. We both have different responsibilities in the game- I see the field with a strategic lens, orchestrating plays and facilitating transitions, while he views it as a canvas for goal-scoring opportunities, constantly seeking spaces to exploit and capitalize on. Now that I know how we both differ in our games, it gives me a slight sense of recognition- what to expect and how to steer him away from a victory that I want for myself.

It was time. The crowd was on the bleachers and I was standing on the right side of the field. Or maybe it was left, I don't know. That's not the point. The point is, the moment I've been waiting for since I came to England was finally here. My first match on English soil. Shirts of Blue and Yellow were standing on the field waiting for the kick-off. I could see Noah standing on the other side and an expected thought found its way to the surface- if he won't be able to score in the first game, I'll be the happiest girl here.

More than half of the student body of the Summerfield Institute was on the bleachers, blue and yellow colors mixing in the crowd. It felt serious. It WAS serious because Leah had told me the weekend matches and their results directly influence the selection process for the school's official team in inter-school tournaments. If someday I wanted to play for an actual English football club, I had to start by making it in the school's team first. Coach Martinez was standing outside the touchline and the fear of disappointing him injected a rush of motivation inside me. I want to leave a good impression on him. He didn't hesitate to include me in the team right away instead of benching me for a few weeks, and I wanted to show him it wasn't a wrong decision.

Breathe in. Breathe out.

The referee's whistle pierced through the field, and just like that I was back on the field with a team around me and a ball at my feet. It didn't matter if my teammates weren't my friends yet or if the ground I was playing on didn't feel familiar- all that mattered now was the game.

The moment my head was in the game, all thoughts of success and failure went flying out the window. All that was left occupying my mind was following the ball and creating opportunities that would hopefully lead us to a goal. It had been a long while since I felt this rush running through my veins, and now that it was- I was charged like a battery left on the plug for too long. Brimming with energy and potential, ready to spark into action like a coiled spring released at the touch of a button.

"Good evening, ladies and gentlemen! I'm Luke Carroway, everybody's favorite commentator, and I'm thrilled to be here bringing you the live coverage of Team Blue versus Team Yellow." The voice broadcasted on the speakers, with the crowd around the field bustling with noises and excitement. "The game has started with quite a quick start, with some attempts to score from the Yellow team, but the Blue team seems determined to protect their end." Mia was sitting in the front row wearing a blue shirt and a blue scrunchie securing her ponytail, cheering and clapping for me and Leah. I could tell she had never been to a football game before, so her support was really making me happy. Even if no one knew me there yet, her presence was enough to make me feel confident and seen.

"As the game goes on, it seems like the Blue team have adapted a defense strategy, although it seems like their supporters want to see them making a go for the goal,"

Kyle had told us to focus on our defense since the Yellow team had a tough attacking line-up and all of us executed his strategy sincerely. Kyle hadn't actually advised us to stay in the defense, but with their tough attacking line-up, the Yellow team was so desperate to score first that we had to stick on their side of the field for the first thirty minutes of the game.

Kyle had chosen me to be the attacking midfielder, which meant I was constantly keeping an eye on the front of the team, who were currently jogging around in the middle of the field. I could tell they were also getting bored after not getting any passes and wanted to receive an opportunity for an attack.

Well, I won't let it be long before that happens.

As I was trying to figure out an offense, there was a sudden shift of action happening in the midfield. "Oh would you look at that, Mason Wilson has snatched away the possession from Fred Smith and passed it on to Jordan

Clarke, there seems to be a bit of a struggle to take possession as both teams are pushed together on the right end to carry out their own tactics." Luke was quick to pick up on every detail.

I rushed toward their goal, positioning myself just ahead of our defenders, who were trying to corner Jordan and waiting for him to slip up so they could get the ball. Jordan passed the ball to Mason on his side, and now he was surrounded by our defenders too.

Mason was trapped on the left wing with three of our defenders, and a few feet away from him was Noah. He was standing right in front of the goal, a few steps behind the defender but just a step ahead of Harry, making sure he didn't accidentally score offside. Our goalkeeper Ellie had her eyes pierced, ready for any unexpected attempts and Noah was doing the same. Assessing the area for any possible hurdles, his eyes fell toward the back and spotted me. For a second, our eyes met and there was a hint of a smirk coming up on his face as he realized the tension, but suddenly the movement on his left alerted him as Mason had managed to dribble through our defenders and had now moved forward. In an instant, Noah returned his attention back to his teammate, snapping back into the game in the blink of an eye.

"With that quick instep from Mason the attack has gotten ahead, we might be close to witnessing the first goal of the match as Mason has carried the ball forward with the defenders at his heel, he has two options to choose from in front of the net and an instant to decide,"

Mason could either take the shot himself or pass it on to Noah, but since his angle was a bit too risky he passed it to his right where Leah leaped ahead to block it. However her attempt was just a second late as it reached Noah an inch away from her feet, and quick as a flash, his foot claimed the ball.

Luke's voice went up by several decibels as he got excited to announce the recent exchange, "NOAH YILDEZ STRIKES TOWARD THE GOAL AND-"

My heart drops.

There was a sudden cheer from the crowd but as quick as the applause, the cheer died down in an instant as the cries of disappointment filled the ground instead. The thud of the ball echoed in my ears. I blinked and registered the moment- the ball had bounced off the bar.

A shout came out from the commentator box. "OFF THE POST! A CLOSE VERY ATTEMPT executed by the golden striker but the shot was in fact not on target and the ball has deflected back to Leah,"

The next few seconds went by in a rushed blur.

The second Leah received the ball, she noticed me standing just outside the penalty area, and quick as a flash she passed the ball toward me. I received it and took a sharp turn, sprinting towards our side of the field while trying to steer it away from the opposition. I looked around for Blue shirts as I ran ahead, guiding the ball forward with Jordan at my heel.

"And it's-" Luke paused, and even though I couldn't see him, I could tell he was squinting at the ground to recognize the player. Despite his hawk eyes, he wasn't able to announce my name because this was my first match and there was no way he could know of my existence. "Uh, so the new midfielder is running towards their goal, as the Blue team's formation quickly changes into an attack, a counterattack to be specific, led by the- uh okay, Avery, Avery Kai everybody!!!" It seemed he had finally scanned the list of players on his table and connected the dots. Cheers erupted from one side of the audience, as we were speeding through the midfield and quickly taking our places for the formation.

"And the ball is passed on to Kyle, who is now trying to dribble past James, and oh- Travis has received the ball and moving further along on the right wing, there's a quick pass to Avery who passes it on to Fred and- GOOAALLLL!!!!! A QUICK AMAZING SWIPE TO THE LEFT OF THE NET, and Ben was just a second late to catch that speedy strike! There wasn't a second wasted in receiving the pass and shooting it past the goalkeeper, a very quick and thrilling goal by the Blues!!!! Right in the 38th minute just before half-time, the Blue team has commenced the point system with a fantastic goal by Fred and a very tactical assist by Avery!"

Fred came running to throw me a high five, celebrating the first goal, and without even intending to, my eyes went straight to Noah, who was standing way back in the midfield registering quite a shock. Startled like a deer in headlights, he blinked with a bewildered expression, not quite believing that the counterattack was initiated by me. His eyes met mine and I recognized a fire in his eyes. A fire so bright I could feel the heat travel across the ground, and with good reason. I took off with the deflection of his failed attempt and stole their first goal with one of our own. I might have taken a moment to feel pity if I wasn't so absolutely ecstatic about conceding against his team.

His usual smirk was completely washed off his face and replaced with a scowl, and the smile I gave him was nothing less than a punch in his gut. I tore my eyes away as if he was too irrelevant to look at, and turned towards Ben who was now placing the ball on the ground to start off another play.

80 minutes went by, and there had been quite a few attempts to get an equalizer from the Yellow team, though none of them found their way into the net. Every time I came across him while playing, he looked away and acted like wasn't just about to lose dignity when the final whistle sounded. One time he even got the shot right on target, but our goalkeeper Ellie was too quick to save it, and the disappointment on Noah's face was as delightful as ice cream on a very hot day.

"Hey, do you need a map to find the goal? Here's a hint, it's that big net at the end of the field." I told him when he missed another shot, to which he looked at me with loud annoyance and walked past me without saying anything. Can't blame him. What do you even say when you're so close to losing after running your mouth so much?

"The referee has given an additional 5 minutes of overtime, but dare I say, it doesn't look like the scoreboard is going to take any more advancements since the first goal before halftime," Luke commented, tiredness lining his voice. The crowd had already started to disperse as all the students were probably going off towards the canteen, but Mia was still glued to her spot, smiling and waving every time I saw her.

And truly, no other advancements were made on the scoreboard, which meant I had managed to successfully crush Noah's ego and win my first-ever game in England. The final whistle echoed across the stadium and the Yellow team was left sighing in defeat. Noah started his walk toward the locker room and I couldn't help but feel like I conquered an empire. The football field had become our battleground, and I was reveling in the sweet taste of victory.

"You did it!" Leah ran up to me and gave me a spirited high-five. "You won your debut!"

"Well, I have *you* to thank for giving me the pass from the deflection." I smiled, it was sweet that even though it was a victory for the whole team, she was particularly happy about mine because she knew how much it meant to me.

"Oh come on, you're too humble."

Suddenly there was a pat on my back and I turned around to see Kyle with a huge grin on his face. "Well played, Avery. I knew you were a good addition to the team."

One after the other, all the members of our team came up to congratulate me, members I hadn't even talked to before this match. The feeling of being an outsider was slowly fading away, leaving a sense of belonging in its wake. I may have been selected in the team from day one but it was now that I won the favor of my teammates. Not only was it a victory in the face of doubt but it was also the beginning of camaraderie in my lonely struggle.

As me, Leah, and Mia were walking toward our table with dinner trays in our hands, I was happy as a clam. After the match, we went to the girls' locker room and took a good long shower, where I changed into my favorite baby pink sweatshirt and black yoga pants. I don't usually wear this sweatshirt on just any normal occasion, but today was a special day and the shirt had won its right to be worn.

The dining hall was bustling with chatter, half the audience, and all the players were now cramped altogether having their dinners. Fred was especially impressed with my play and assist, so he gave me his muffin as a token of gratitude for giving him a goal in the first game. The rest of the team was now slowly becoming my friends, and I could already feel the sense of belonging one feels when they are part of a team. I was no longer just a teammate, I was a *member* of the team.

"No offense but I was really pissed at Kyle for not benching you at first, like we do with all newbies," Ryan said while stabbing cherry tomatoes and cucumber on his fork. I don't know how he was opting for a salad after such a tiring game, I assume he's a health nut. No heavy dinners or something. "And then I learned never to judge our captain's decisions again."

I smiled and ate the pasta off my fork. We were sitting with some of our team at the table, which could only have six people max.

"Well, I couldn't risk you guys bullying me off the team." Not that they would ever actually bully me for anything. They were all really nice, not like some of the cocky American jocks I was used to.

Speaking of cocky American jocks, that's when I noticed Noah and company walk into the dining hall- freshly showered and scrubbed- taking up all the space with their egos even after the result of the game. Well, let's just call them cocky *British* jocks now.

One thing I couldn't deny was if Noah's hair was tousled perfectly when it was dry, it was even more flattering when it was damp. You could tell how they would arrange themselves into a controlled mess that would add to his physical charm. Mind you, only physical, because his selfish habits were anything but charming. But since we're talking about the physical charm, I didn't think sweatshirts with shorts looked good until I saw it on him. He gave out a certain boyish allure that only girls would understand. He was towering above the rest of his friends just a bit, his confidence making him stand out from the crowd. As much as his arrogance repels me, he does have the kind of look that can make any girl swoon over.

After ten minutes of them choosing their food and walking to their tables, he happened to pass by our table and I found it physically impossible not to acknowledge his defeat.

"Well, well, look who's eating humble pie today," I said loudly and he paused, undoubtedly catching my remark.

"It's just one match, Avery. Don't let it get to your head." His attempts to sound unaffected were betrayed by the slight touch of insecurity in his voice that I'm sure no one else could pick up on.

"Oh, trust me, I won't. But it's not every day I get to witness the great Noah Yildiz take a tumble on the field. I can practically see your ego deflating from here."

Brushing it off, he tried to appear more calm. "Everyone has their off days. Yours just happened to coincide with my middling performance. It was just beginner's luck." He said, his words dismissing any efforts I made today.

"Learn to hit your shots on target before telling me what it was." My smile was honey poured over sugar.

I know I hit the right spot because I could visibly see him lose some of the confidence he came over with. For a soccer player, missing perfect shots and hitting the crossbar probably held the same amount of mortification as voice breaks for a singer. Maybe even more. Embarrassment and humiliation, with lots of cursing from the crowd.

"Everyone misses once in a while and everyone wins once in a while too. If you win the next match, then I'll know it wasn't just a fluke."

Fluke? Even though he was the one who took the loss, it was me who was starting to get frustrated by his remarks.

"Fluke? A fluke Noah? Seriously, how petty do you have to be to deny someone's hard work and call it a fluke?" If I looked into the mirror right now, I would definitely see smoke coming out of my ears.

And yet he seemed utterly unaffected by my anger. Maybe even satisfied. "Enjoy it while it lasts, Avery. This is just the beginning." He answered casually and walked to his table like he didn't just flip a dangerous switch in my head.

My jaw dropped at his attitude. "Oh, I'm counting on it. This is just a preview of what's to come." I said loudly to his back as he conveniently ignored my presence and when I looked back at my table, Mia was sliding Fred's gifted muffin in my direction. "Eat something sweet. You look like you can murder him right now"

"Oh, I just might." The pasta suffered my wrath as I fiercely stabbed it with the fork with more force than necessary and stuffed it in my mouth. Good thing there was plenty of distraction on my tray because at this point only food could distract me from the infuriating entity that was Noah Yildiz.

6
Avery

The world is one wicked place. One day you're on the top of the world, and the next you're being pushed into the ground.

That's what I felt when I looked at the results of the Chemistry test on Friday. The test had ten questions and I had only gotten two correct. My hands had a slight tremble as I saw the glaring red "F" at the top of the page.

I had failed. Again. My body felt hot as I slumped back into my chair, shoulders sagging with disappointment.

We gave the test a day before the match, so even though I walked out of the classroom with a not-so-good performance, it wasn't on my list of priorities at the time, given the anticipation for the match. But the circumstances had changed since then and now I was facing the consequences for being heedless.

Mrs. Jones looked at me from above her glasses while handing me the paper, staring with such an intensity that could cause a chemical reaction on its own. "Failing your first test isn't a good sign, Miss Avery." Her eyes trained on me with a look that told me I should stop being lazy with my studies. Before I came here, I desperately wanted to impress the teachers so I wouldn't go through the humiliation I experienced with my past teachers. And yet, here I was after my test, already giving Mrs. Jones a reason to see me as a failure.

"Better than last year, Yildiz." She walked past and gave him his paper, which apparently had better results than mine.

As if I needed another reason to make this more humiliating. For some reason, I didn't perceive Noah to be the studious type. Maybe it was my distaste towards him that stopped me from having any positive thoughts about him in the first place, but getting good grades in Chemistry, of all things? That ought to prove his intellect.

Trying to get his better-than-mine grades out of my mind, I looked over at Mia a few benches ahead of me, who met my eyes right then and held up her paper- an "A+" was scribbled at the top. I smiled and gave her a thumbs-up. She had been preparing for it a week before, and just because I had a bad result it didn't mean I couldn't be happy for my best friend.

Looking around the classroom, I observed the students and realized everyone seemed quite happy with their results. I glanced back at my paper. *Am I the only one who failed?* This was our first test and the portion was so small. I still failed. The big heavy clouds that loomed over me the whole past summer came back to threaten me again. Ever since I started high school, my grades had never gone above a 'C' and I was starting to think maybe it was just too much for a stupid person like me.

A lump formed in my throat and it was suddenly hard to swallow. I put the test back on the table and leaned back in my chair, looking outside the classroom so I could focus on something other than the disheartening thing in front of me. Crying in the presence of even a single person has always been embarrassing to me, and right now I was surrounded by sixty other people. The tree outside the window looked a lot less full than it did when I first came here and the early effects of winter could already be seen in the pile of orange leaves on the ground below.

Suddenly I heard a shuffle behind my desk, which was followed by a voice that distressed my already troubled nervous system. "Uh oh, chemistry isn't your strongest suit, is it?" Noah had leaned over and had managed to witness my humiliating result before I could hide it. "Good thing you're an athlete. Maybe you should consider a career in something less brainy."

There was no energy in me to come up with a comeback, so I just turned around and glared at him. He went back and sat on his chair, showing me his paper- a "B". Not exactly an amazing score but at least he managed to pass it. In my head, I debated over a response to his mean comment. However, if I said anything, my voice might break and let him know how close I was to breaking into a cry. And of course, I would never let that happen.

"Leave me alone," I told him, my eyes reflecting that I was in no mood to joke.

He looked taken aback by my lack of a sarcastic response, but I knew he wasn't going to let it go until he got a reaction out of me. "Okay, I'm sorry I hurt your feelings by implying that you're stupid." He said, and before I could even wonder where he found this surprising compassion, he followed with an extremely hurtful addition. "I thought you already knew." Maybe in his head, he was just trying to have one of our usual feuds, but this time his sarcasm cut way deeper than it should have.

I bit my lip, trying to ignore Noah's taunts. On the list of the most hurtful things you could say to me, implying that I was stupid was in the third spot, right after lazy and naive. I tried my best to maintain a neutral expression but his tone and words were cutting their way deeper into my barely-managed mental state. It reminded me of each ignorant person I met who had ever implied that I was dumb-witted and dense just because I struggled in some aspects more than others. I already struggled with spelling and memorization, and Chemistry took me thrice the amount of practice. I admit it *was* my fault for not preparing enough, but if it was someone without Dyslexia, they still would have passed this easily without studying for it. Like all my other classmates did.

I felt my eyes sting as the tears I was holding back began to well up in my eyes, betraying my will to appear unaffected. After realizing I was failing at maintaining my usual impervious mask, I turned back around and sat straight, ignoring him and his snide sarcasm. I closed my eyes and ducked down, my palms over my eyes, desperate to fight back the overwhelming tears. I knew I needed a good cry to calm myself down, but my dorm would be the right place to break down, not the classroom. Not in front of everyone and certainly not in front of Noah.

After a good five minutes of distracting myself from the current situation, I sat up straight and started listening to the class with a heaviness in my chest. I just have to get through three more classes, and then I can go. I can go back to my dorm. Although, I wish I could go home. I wish I could go back and start over and avoid failures altogether.

The Skype ringtone played along as I sat in front of my laptop, waiting for Ella to pick up. I hadn't found time to call her since coming here, just a few texts here and there telling her that I was fine and settling in properly. I missed home- having my friends and family around, and not having to stress about managing everything on my own. I hadn't mentioned it in any of my calls with my parents though, because it was my decision and they were already being supportive by letting me carve my path in my own way. I told them I was happy and enjoying every bit of boarding school. but today I needed something. I needed the warmth of my family, I needed advice from my sister. Even if she yelled at me, I'd take it.

When all of your family members are professional academics, it's hard to ever let go of the academic guilt completely. My dad, Dr. Benjiro Kai is an Orthopaedic Surgeon, meanwhile my mom, Dr. Emily Morgan is a veterinarian. Ella is in med school as well, becoming a doctor just like our parents, which makes me the only one in the family who wasn't following the usual academic path. I wanted to study the same subjects my family did so I could feel like we all had something in common even if I was always the odd one out. Maybe having the same major would somehow make me feel like I'm not so different after all. So even after failing once back in America, I decided to choose it as my major again when I came to England. I didn't always score well, but still, my family never made me feel miserable about it.

Being from an Asian family, it could have been a great cause of shame for them, but luckily my family was very understanding and supportive. They motivate me to do well in school, while also wholeheartedly supporting my ambition for a career in Football. When I failed junior year, I cried for two days straight and had a very intense breakdown. I felt like they would be ashamed of me, I felt like I embarrassed them in front of everyone they knew. However, after already seeing my miserable state, Dad, Mom, and Ella didn't blame or taunt me even once. They often saw me struggling with my studies, but it was me who decided to choose Life Sciences as my major even after knowing I struggled with it. And even though I struggled with the spelling and words, I started to find it extremely interesting.

The ringing stopped with a bubbling sound and I finally saw my sister on the screen. She looks more like our mom, with golden brown hair and pretty green eyes. If my features were soft, hers were sharp. Her chiseled nose was much different than mine and made many people wonder if we were actually real siblings. Her hair was in a messy bun and she was wearing a Stanford University T-shirt, probably studying at her dorm, per usual. Ella goes to Stanford University, which makes it even more embarrassing to tell her that I was failing my tests all over again. She was one of the most dedicated, hardworking students I had ever seen, and then there was me, a dyslexic child who failed simple tests and was only dedicated to one sport.

"Hey, I was just thinking of calling you. Didn't you have a match on Saturday?" She asked straight away.

"I did, and guess who bagged an assist in the only goal of the match?" Thinking about the match brought up my spirits again, but I was still hiding my academic misery behind my athletic achievements.

"I can't even say I'm surprised, I expected no less from you." She was smiling, and it eased a bit of the heaviness in my heart. Unintentionally, a sad smile came up on my face and almost immediately Ella's eyebrows furrowed together.

"Is everything okay? Did you have dinner?" It was a simple question but it caused a flutter in my chest and a tiny lump in my throat. Other than Mia, not a single person here had asked me that question even once, even though my aunt was literally in the school. She never cared about my well-being, she never asked me if I was doing fine, and she never cared about anything more than the grades on my tests. I wasn't aware how untended it made me feel until Ella brought it up. As the youngest person in my house, everyone was always looking after me at home, and now it's like I'm suddenly left here alone to fend for myself.

I cleared my throat so my voice wouldn't come out all weak and frail. "Yeah I did, I had carbonara ravioli. Do you know they even have fish inside the ravioli here!"

"That doesn't sound good to me. You know I don't like seafood." She made a queasy face as if she could smell the fish.

"You're half-Japanese Ella, you should be ashamed of yourself." I always tried to convince her to keep trying different Sushis whenever we went out to eat, but she always rejected them because apparently she could smell the seafood and it threw her off.

"Says the girl who never wears a kimono during our New Year parties."

"It's not a jet-set rule to wear one. We don't even go to the temples anymore." I responded and Ella snickered at the memory of our last visit. I broke my arm when I was trying to run down some stairs in my kimono, and the long cloth got tangled in my feet, making me tumble down the stairs like a barrel. I stayed at home from practice with a fractured arm for weeks.

"Does Asami give you any special treatment over there?" She asked me, opening a bag of Hot Cheetos. Oh, how I miss Cheetos.

"Special? If anything, she treats me worse. I don't know what she has against me." But the thing is, I *knew* what she had against me, I was just too embarrassed to say it out loud. All of the faculty knew I was Asami's niece, which made her very conscious about her image. Dr. Asami Kai, aunt to the lousy dumb student Avery Kai? Surely her image was stained. She wanted me to leave sports and focus on my studies so I could be worthy enough to be related to her.

"Oh you know she's very narrow-minded," She waved a hand dismissively. "I don't want you to take it personally okay? She thinks academic success is the only success that matters." She told me, certainly having a clue as to how rude she can get.

"She is right though." I sniffled. "I already failed once and wasted a whole year of my life." The panic in my chest was rising again.

Sensing my nerves, Ella quickly jumped to the rescue. "Who said it was a waste? It was because of this initial 'failure' that you decided to study in England, right? And who knows what the future holds for you there? Failures are temporary Avery, just as long as you grow from them and move forward. If you keep looking at yourself like the girl who failed her junior year, you will never become the girl who came back stronger and became an amazing soccer player." I didn't know how but she always knew what to say whenever I was going through moments of doubt. She was the one who got me through the failure and now she was picking me up all over again. Do all big sisters have this superpower?

I looked at her with a hesitant expression, unsure if I should even trust myself that much. Trust that I will actually get over this and not mess up again. What if I get too confident and end up failing again? What country would I escape to this time?

"What if I can't?" A few tears escaped my eyes and I rushed to wipe them.

"You WILL, Ave. Didn't you absolutely ace your first match?"

I nodded, looking at my lap.

"You probably practiced extra hard for it, didn't you? Even though nobody asked you to?"

I nodded again. "I did."

"See, I knew it before you told me because I know you're not lazy." How did she even know I was blaming myself for being lazy? "You just pay more attention to stuff that you care about and block out the other things. Just try to give more time to your studies next time and you'll get over this, okay?"

Her reassuring words settled a raging storm of emotions inside me and I slowly felt myself coming back.

"Now come on, tell me about your new friends. We haven't talked in ages." Her trust in me was phenomenal, I didn't even know how she believed in me that much when I didn't have any tangible proof of being capable- no records, no achievements, except a few good matches. Nevertheless, it always made me happy. It made me feel like I could actually do anything. Achieve anything. Because Ella thinks I can do it.

"Well, Mia, my roommate, is currently sleeping with her head on the Physics textbook, so that will tell you a lot about her," I said. "And then there's Leah, I met her in my team. We don't have many classes together, but we always hang out outside of classes and matches. They are both basically my permanent table partners during meals."

"Ahan," Ella devours another handful of Hot Cheetos. "So that basically sounds like you got your Ron and Hermione in your own little version of Hogwarts."

"I guess so." I chuckled. Harry Potter was a huge part of my childhood, and part of the reason I was excited to come here. "Because Asami sure can take on the role of Umbridge."

Ella gasped and put a hand over her mouth in mock offense. "Wait till I tell Dad about that!"

"You can, I don't care, it's not my fault his sister acts like a meanie. The other day she gave me a map to find my class, *a map* Ella! Even after knowing it's hard for me to make sense of it! I feel like she enjoys watching me struggle."

"Well, then you got all the more reason not to take her seriously." She said, "She's doing all this intentionally." Thank God she never expects me to be a goody-two-shoes.

"And then there was this guy, I asked him where my class was and he told me the wrong directions!"

"He did not! What did he even get for doing that?"

"I know right? But don't worry, I got him back by defeating him in our match on Saturday. He's supposed to be one of the best players in our school but that defeat certainly deflated his ego a little bit."

"Best player in the school? Sounds like an arrogant piece of work."

Our conversations went from checking up on each other to talking about all our recent adventures, and slowly we got lost in our chats until we realized it was almost midnight for me. I had missed talking to her and sharing laughter, and after she gave me all the updates about Mom and Dad, we decided to call later since I had to go to sleep. I woke Mia up from her impromptu desk nap and told her to sleep properly before changing into my pajamas and snuggling inside my blanket. After the emotional roller-coaster of a day- I went to bed in a much lighter mood than I thought I would, with a newfound hope to get back up from every new challenge that tried to throw me down.

7
NOAH

The common room elicited much cozy vibes as Mason and I were sprawled on the couch, lounging off after our tiring day being engrossed in the glow of the TV screen. A few other friends were watching with us a while ago but now that it had gotten late, the common room was empty except for Theo hunching over the coffee table, scattered with papers and textbooks, attempting to make sense of his math homework.

"Noah, do we have any snacks?" Mason asked, his eyes still fixed on the screen.

"Yeah, I think we have some crisps in the cupboard," I replied absentmindedly and got up, withdrawing some snacks from our common snack pantry.

On my way back to the couch, my attention was drawn to Theo's focused efforts on the homework. "Theo, you want some?" I offered a bag of crisps in his direction.

"No, I'm good." He looked up from his notebook. "Can't distract myself until I finish this."

We didn't really get much homework in the past few days which made me wonder what he could be working on that called for so much concentration. Curiosity getting the better of me, I leaned over to glance at Theo's work. "What's that you're working on?" I saw a bunch of numbers on his page which looked like our homework from last week. "Still tackling that math homework?"

Theo sighed, running a hand through his hair. "Yeah, man. Dyslexia's making it a real pain. Hard to wrap my head around these problems."

If the problems were hard enough for me, I couldn't imagine how hard they would be for someone who struggles with a disorder. "Have you talked to the counselor about it? She might be able to help."

He nodded. "Actually, I did, and she gave me some visual strategies to work with. I was used to being the only one in the counseling but now the new girl has joined in too."

"The new girl?" I echoed a hint of surprise in my voice. There had been no other 'new girls' in our grade except her and it was quite a shock to know she was in counseling.

Theo nodded again. "Yeah, Avery." Even though I knew it could only be her, hearing her name still made my breath freeze for a second. "She's cool, helped me out a bit. Turns out she's dealing with some dyslexia too."

I felt a knot tighten in my stomach. *Avery struggles with dyslexia.* My expression shifted, a sudden realization dawning on me.

A recent memory resurfaced in my brain as my gaze absentmindedly fixated on the paper in Theo's hands, the memory of mocking Avery for failing her Chemistry test. It was quite a simple test and I had acted on my resentment from losing the match to make fun of her, not knowing the truth behind her result. I remembered how her voice was quieter than usual and how she ignored my comments instead of firing back like she usually did. I had felt quite surprised when she didn't hit me back with an equal insult and I remember feeling a hint of guilt creeping up in my heart when I saw those dull eyes that day, which I decided to ignore out of pure ignorance.

"Avery?" I repeated, my voice quieter than before. "The girl Mr. Becker put me in detention with?"

Theo nodded, oblivious to the internal turmoil his words had caused. "Yeah, that's her. Really smart and nice, you know?"

My mind raced, connecting the dots. The reason she couldn't make sense of the map the first day, the reason she couldn't solve the problems in detention, and now the reason she failed her Chemistry test. It was all because of one sole reason, the reason I had failed to be sensitive with her. Avery, the girl I had underestimated, the girl I had made fun of, all because of my ignorance. The same girl I had teased about her struggles, the girl whose dyslexia I had unknowingly mocked. My chest tightened with remorse.

"I didn't know she was dealing with dyslexia," I admitted, partly replying to Theo and partly saying it as an explanation to myself for my previous behavior.

Theo shrugged, still unaware of the internal struggle I was facing. "Yeah, she isn't open about it. Said it makes things challenging, but she's determined to overcome it."

Guilt crept over me, and I couldn't shake the memory of her expression in the class, the vulnerability I had failed to recognize.

As I threw the bag of crisps at Mason and sank back into the couch, the guilt lingered on my shoulders, a heavy reminder of my previous ignorance. I remembered the hurt in Avery's eyes, the unspoken pain I had caused with my thoughtless comments.

"I feel bad," I mumbled to myself, thinking back to the classroom encounter. "Really bad."

Mason, finally tearing his eyes from the TV, looked at me with a furrowed brow. "What's up?"

I shook my head. "I made fun of her yesterday, Mason. I basically called her stupid when I didn't know she was dealing with dyslexia. I feel like a jerk." I rested my head back on the couch.

Mason's expression softened. "Well, maybe now you know better. Just talk to her, apologize. People make mistakes, man."

I nodded, realizing that understanding others was crucial, especially when it came to the struggles they faced. As Mason and I continued watching the sitcom, I made a mental note to apologize to her, vowing to be more considerate in the future. I thought I was fine as a person but I had a lot to learn about empathy and the importance of not making assumptions about others.

With how quickly Mrs. Jones was going along in her syllabus, I was desperately trying to cover at least one chapter of Chemistry today, when Mason's incoherent yelling started again.

"I said cover ME you dumbasses, Adam already had a cover! I'm dead now you morons, DEAD!" He was yelling into his earphones, clinging to a Nintendo Switch in his hands. Our school doesn't allow us to keep or bring any video game consoles, so our dorm was the only place we could openly play our games. The warden can't get mad at what he doesn't know.

"Mason, can you keep it down please, I'm trying to study here," I told him, but the intense volume on his earphones stopped him from hearing my voice. I rarely ever saw him studying so it wasn't a surprise that he was using the school-allotted study hour to play video games. He took up humanities as his major, precisely because he didn't want to give much time to studies and focus more on football instead. I wanted football to be my main focus too, but not taking up any STEM subjects would have been a risky thing to do for a guy like me. Our family wasn't doing well when it came to finances, so I didn't want to put all my stakes on something that could turn upside down at any moment. The chances are slim, but many athletes lose their careers because of an awful injury or controversial matches and press. Being a professional athlete wasn't the most secure career out there. Besides, I had no problem understanding the concepts of science. Even if it wasn't my end goal, it was interesting to study nonetheless.

Tired of being invisible, I threw my pen at Mason and he finally looked up, taking off his earphones.

"What?" He asked, a bit too loud after wearing his earphones for too long.

"Can you stop yelling? I'm trying to study." I showed him my textbook.

"I can try but you never know." He put his earphones back on and returned to his game. "You have a whole library to study, but there's no gaming room for me." He yelled, adjusting back to the high volume.

I sighed. *Can't argue with that logic.* We can't take our consoles out in the open anyway. Well, never mind. No one can stop a gamer from yelling profanities when they're playing. I decided to pack all my notebooks and head to the library where I could study in total peace without the constant stream of curses floating around the room.

Our library was huge and extremely quiet, one of the most peaceful and calm places on our campus, free from all the chaos of the high school students. I went to the chemistry section and looked around for the book I needed. I found it in the corner of the shelf, my luck playing out in my favor as I realized it was the last one left on the shelf. I glanced around and saw that people were mostly studying in groups, which meant almost every round table had a bit of whispered chatter going around it. Since I was studying alone, I chose the long table in the middle of the room. Even if someone else wanted to sit here, the table had like 20 seats, so I could still be seated alone and study in peace.

I had just started getting into where I had left off when I saw Avery walk into the library with a bag on her shoulder. My heart played out a weird rhythm on her appearance. She walked toward the Chemistry section as well, looking at the shelf with her brows knit together. I looked down at the textbook in front of me. I had taken the very last one.

Since I didn't want to get kicked out of the library for yelling loudly to get her attention, I quickly tore a piece of paper from my notebook and scribbled my message.

'*I took the last one, maybe we can share?*'

I crumpled it up and threw it in her direction, both feeling accomplished and scared at the same time.

My silent prayers of not making her angry betrayed me, as the paper ball hit her on the head and fell on the ground in front of her. She rubbed her head and immediately looked around to see who threw it, her confused expression turning into extreme distaste when she saw me sitting in the direction of the throw. She was probably thinking I did it just to annoy her, so I gestured with my hands and mouthed '*Pick it up and open it*'.

With a disgruntled shake of her head, she picked it up with an annoyance that didn't leave her face until she read it. I was expecting a book to be hurled in my direction or that maybe she would leave the library, but she seemed awfully calm and collected as she considered it. Yes, she was actually considering sitting next to me and studying together. Her lips went into a pout as she looked at me and then back at the note like she was contemplating how this would work out.

Now, I wasn't one to be affected by the rejection of others, but the seconds she took to come to her decision were directly proportional to the number of breaths I was unknowingly holding.

I was still looking at her with my raised eyebrows when she nodded to herself, crumpled up the paper, and threw the ball into a nearby dustbin.

Well, I expected worse.

Going back to my textbook, I felt a continuous river of guilt flowing through me over being such a jerk that she refused to even accept a joint study session. I don't even blame her, the way I've been insulting her ever since she came here, I deserv-

The sound of the chair scraping against the floor snapped me out of my thoughts as I saw Avery taking the seat beside me and putting her tote bag on the huge wooden table.

Oh.

"Honestly? I didn't expect you to agree to a study session." I whispered.

"I'm only here for the book, not a study session." She replied in a low voice.

As she opened her notebooks and shifted the Chemistry textbook in the middle so we could both read it, I sat back in my chair and glanced in her direction. Her usually braided-up hair was in a high ponytail today, a few of her loose bangs framing her face in a pretty way. For the first time since I knew her, I noticed a gentle dusting of freckles on her nose and across her cheeks, our close encounter unveiling a layer of her beauty I hadn't appreciated before.

"Look, I..." I started nervously, as her attention left the notebook and landed on me. "I know I was a jerk about the test, I'm sorry about that."

Her face displayed a mix of surprise and confusion, like hearing an apology from me wasn't on her list of 'things that might happen' by a far mile. "You're sorry? Why are you sorry?"

"Well, maybe I realized I don't know everything. And maybe I feel kinda guilty."

"Guilty? For what exactly?"

I don't know if she was okay with letting me know about her struggles, but I supposed I couldn't apologize properly if I didn't tell her the truth. "I want to apologize for making fun of you before. I didn't know you were struggling with dyslexia."

Her eyebrows went up like she could have expected anything except for an apology. "Oh. So it's about that." She nodded slowly, unsure how she should react. "How did you know?"

"Theo told me," I replied with a grimace. It felt wrong to know something she didn't want anyone to know, but now that I did, I couldn't lie to her and continue being ignorant either.

"I see," She said and nodded again before waving her hand to dismiss the conversation. "It's okay, I get it. Chemistry isn't my strongest suit."

"No seriously, it wasn't okay and I still feel guilty. If you want, I can help you study. We can figure this out together before the next test."

"Why would you do that?"

"Because guilt is heavy?" I didn't want her to think I had any other intentions because I really didn't, all I wanted was to help her pass the next test and kick this guilt out of my system.

"Well, I *do* need some help." She flipped the page over to the chapter she wanted to study. "But don't confuse this with the beginning of a blossoming new friendship. You feel bad and I need help, let's keep this professional because you're still as annoying as a pebble stuck in my shoe."

I sighed with relief as a smile appeared on my face, grateful for the shift to our usual squabble. "Perfect."

8

AVERY

When I realized Noah was the one who took the last book, my first instinct was to throw a book at him. But then I considered how badly I was struggling with Chemistry, and how I probably wouldn't get anywhere if I kept putting my ego above my needs. Studying with someone who had passed the test sounded like a better option than studying alone, especially considering how it turned out the last time. At this point, any help I was offered should be welcomed with open arms. Even if it's from Noah.

"So, what topic do you want to start with?" He asked me, flipping through the pages of the textbook.

"Well, for starters, I can never remember which way the periodic trends go. It's like a never-ending guessing game."

He flipped some more and landed on the chapter, keeping the book in the middle so we could both see properly. "Hmm, let's see." He focused on the text, coming up with a simpler way to make me understand the pattern. He took out his glasses from where he had hung them on the neck of his T-shirt and put them on, making his whole aura change from a sporty jock to a wise nerd.

"Okay, so," He suddenly nodded, like the glasses gave him some geeky superpowers. "Let's just say electronegativity is like a game of tug-of-war. Fluorine always wants to pull the electrons closer because it's greedy. The bigger atoms are like the chill teammates, not bothered by the tug-of-war. Does that help?"

I focused on what he told me and tried to put it in theory. "Yeah, that actually makes sense." I nodded slowly. "I'm starting to see the patterns."

"See, Chemistry is all about finding those patterns." He nodded and went on to the next trend, coming up with another creative way to explain ionization energy.

Slowly, as the minutes went by with our explanations and discussions, the panic I was feeling before started to settle down. The overwhelming sense of not being able to understand started to wash off, and I felt like I finally caught up with a train I was missing.

In the quietness of the school library, Noah and I were still huddled over the chemistry textbook, our notebooks sprawled with equations and diagrams. Noah, now with a pair of glasses perched on his nose, was engrossed in explaining a particularly tricky concept.

"So, you see, when these molecules bond, it creates a more stable compound," He explained, gesturing to the diagram in the book.

Focused on the lesson, I nodded in understanding. However, as I glanced up from the textbook, something caught my attention- one of the strands of his messy hair was falling over his forehead, adding a princely charm to his already handsome face. The realization hit me unexpectedly, and I found myself studying him for a moment. His glasses- the ones I saw him wearing for the first time- accentuated his features and the touch of nobility it gave him hadn't escaped my notice.

"Are you following, Avery?" Noah asked, probably noticing my distracted gaze.

I blinked. "Uh, yeah, totally. Molecules."

He chuckled, not catching onto the subtle shift in my attention. "Alright, let's move on to the next section."

I shook my head from the distracting thoughts of his appearance and tried to focus on the topic instead. I was *not* going to pay attention to his distractingly good looks again because he was still an annoying jerk under all of that. Giving me a tutoring session out of guilt didn't exactly count as a good deed done out of kindness. I would be dead before I ever consider him a decent human being.

Nevertheless, the fog of confusion was finally lifting over my head, giving me a clear view of the topics I was previously struggling with. With a bit more practice and hard work, I was sure I could face the test with more confidence than before.

Staring at the question paper went much differently that Friday than the last time I was sitting there. This time, I was mentally ticking off the questions I could do and the ones I couldn't, and the right-to-wrong ratio was looking much better than before. It wasn't exactly a huge jump from my previous state, but it was a start. A good start.

The next day, I woke up early in the morning and left for the football field, the Saturday morning solo practices almost becoming a ritual for me. I changed into my training kit and left my bag in the locker room, walking onto the field with an apple in my hand.

Unfortunately, my solo practice was sabotaged once again as I saw Noah out on the field, juggling a ball for God knows how long. He was earlier than me this time.

He heard footsteps and looked up to see me joining him on the field, which didn't have any effect on the ball switching places at his feet because his footwork was still insanely controlled even if he wasn't looking. A pang of envy hit me as it was the type of ball control I hadn't mastered yet.

"Why are you always here?" I said, taking a bite of my apple. "Can I never catch a peaceful moment without you hovering in the background?"

"That's what I get after being nice?" He said playfully, tiny clouds of vapor leaving his mouth in the cold morning temperature. "How did you find the test?"

"I found it well Professor Yildiz, thanks for the help."

He smiled at my gratitude.

"But since you only did it out of guilt, I won't call it being *nice*." I know it was decent of him to at least apologize and make it up to me, but his initial behavior still made me feel insecure and guarded.

"Fair enough." He returned his attention back to the ball, which was still alternating between his feet.

A thought suddenly came to my mind and I realized I had to get it out before it worried me further. "Uh, Noah..." I called again.

Sensing the tension in my voice, he caught the ball as it came up and turned to me. "Yeah?"

"Can you not mention it to anyone? Uh... About me being dyslexic?" It wasn't something to be ashamed of, but I already knew how it goes when the whole school knows your weaknesses. Some bullies mock you for having it, and the teachers often use it to give you lectures on being lazy. I had already gone through the bullying and the mocking and even though the chances of it happening were slim, I didn't want to risk it again.

"Oh." He nodded, his eyes holding a softness that told me he understood my sensitivity on this topic. "Don't worry. You're not really the topic of my conversations." The usual sneer was pasted on his face again. Even though he said it with a roguish careless attitude, somewhere in my heart I knew I didn't have to worry about him betraying his words. He might act smug all the time but I had a feeling he was quite sincere under all that smoke. The fact that he apologized bore witness to that.

A grateful smile fought its way out of me as I acknowledged his good faith. Walking away to start my own practice, my steps halted when he called out my name.

"Oh and Avery?"

I turned and posed a silent '*What?*' through an inquisitive tilt of my head.

"Just so you know, it doesn't change how I see you on the field." His words were honest, not a tiny touch of mockery lacing his voice.

It was a sentiment I hadn't expected, and my heart warmed at his words. It might have been quite a simple thing to say, but it meant a lot more to me. Not many people in my life saw past the dyslexia, and I knew many people who treated me differently because of it. Either invalidating my struggles or acting like I needed extra pity. It was refreshing to be seen without the weight of judgment or pity.

"As a threat?" I asked, unable to come up with a heartfelt response. As much as I appreciated his thought, thanking him just felt like taking it too far.

He laughed and dropped the ball on his feet to start another juggling marathon. "More like an inconvenience."

Once again, I was in the middle of a match, standing on the halfway line as I saw the Yellow team's midfielder push the ball forward past our defenders.

"And James has once again found the opportunity to strike the ball as he is advancing from the left wing, Team Yellow is making the effort to gain possession, it seems like a hard call for him because he has passed the ball back to their halfback, there seems to be a bit of hesitation as the defenders are covering quite a lot of ground in their space." Luke went on, and the audience fell silent as everyone got busy following the progress of the game.

Just as their halfback was trying to pass the ball to their forward, Kyle ran forward and received it quickly, and that's when I started running backward, still facing him in case he decided to give me the pass. I glanced around me and noticed both Harry and Fred were surrounded by Blue midfielders, and I was still figuring out the formation when Kyle shot the ball toward me. I received it with my right foot and instantly started running forward, spotting Leah on the right wing and giving her a pass before the defenders could predict my next move.

"An attempt has been made as Avery passed the ball to Leah, there is a chance to make a shot but Leah has passed on the ball to Will, and SHOOT! Ben caught the ball right in the middle of the net, an attempt was made but the goalkeeper stopped yet another goal with his mighty hands. The Blues will have to regroup after that missed opportunity."

There was a collective noise from the bleachers as our striker missed the opportunity for a goal.

My eyes went back to Noah, who was already looking at me with a gleeful smirk. It was almost like his whole focus during these matches was to make sure my efforts were always wasted.

Filled with a newfound urge to wipe that smirk off his face, I returned my attention to their goalkeeper, who was just about to resume the play. Instead of a subtle kick-off, Ben shot the ball with all his might, and it went flying across the field to their side. He must have caught on to my intention of stealing possession as quickly as I could. Not a slow player, I see.

Across the field near the penalty box, Noah received it with an insane first touch that immediately stopped the high-speed ball at his foot. There was another cheer in the crowd as he passed it on to Mason.

"Mason has received the pass from Noah, who has an incredible first touch by the way, but there seems to be no open opportunities to score the goal. Mason is face-to-face with Kyle, who is just a slip-up away from gaining back the possession, but Mason seems to be determined to score today, the tension is increasing in the penalty box- Mason has passed the ball back to Chloe, Chloe to Will, and the ball has found its place back to Noah- OH quick as a fox Noah has pushed forward, a quick pass to Mason and Mason is going forward, is it going to be an attempt- and OH MY GOD a last minute pass to Noah- AND SCOREEE!!! The high assist was received by Noah and thrown into the net with a volley, striking right past the goalkeeper and changing the scoreboard to 1-0!!" Luke and the crowd were thrilled to witness that undeniably spectacular goal, but it was gushing fire in my veins whenever I looked at the scoreboard. I wasn't usually a very competitive person, but whenever Noah was in the equation, it felt like a full-fledged war. An ego battle that I couldn't afford to lose.

The referee blew the whistle and Ellie kicked the ball from our goal post, and the game started again with a different nature altogether. I couldn't let him off the field without scoring at least an equalizer. However, even with my strong determination, twenty minutes went by with some casual passes and runs, both teams not making much progress in terms of an opportunity.

"It seems like the Blue team is making up for that goal by gaining more possession, they haven't let the Yellows have possession for more than five minutes." I could sense the tension in our team as they desperately tried to keep the ball in our control, trying to gain ground on the right side of the field. Their defenders were following close, either blocking with their bodies or trying to slide in to get the ball, it seems they were getting impatient because of our constant possession too.

I looked at Leah who had the ball at her feet and three defenders in front of her. Leah was known to play recklessly and make the move whenever needed, so their defenders were making every bit of effort to carefully focus on her spontaneous movements. Our eyes met right then and there was a brief moment of understanding before she passed the ball over to me, immediately running forward to receive a pass if needed.

"OH there goes an advancement from the Blue team, as their playmaker Avery Kai is running forward from the midfield, a formation seems to be uncovering as she goes on, Jack running behind to keep up, trying to take the ball and-"

OHHHHH!

There was a huge gasp from the crowd as I was thrown forward, my feet twisting over and my cheek crashing over the ground. *That bloody asshole!* He made an obvious foul, kicking my feet instead of the ball as I was getting closer and closer to the end.

I clutched my foot and sat up straight, brushing off the grass and dirt from my cheek. Matthias, our referee, came running over and pulled out a yellow card from his shirt pocket. Jack was standing there with his eyes wide open as Matthias held the card above his head. Someone give this guy an Oscar because he really was acting like he didn't just deliberately launch me off the ground.

"That looks like a pretty painful foul, to be honest. Avery Kai was knocked down by Jack Wright, and her team is making sure she is well enough to play further. A direct free kick awaits this turn of events, as a warning is given to the Yellow team for their very obvious foul. The Blue team ducks into a circle as they decide who is going to take the shot."

We were on the right wing, just a few feet away from the penalty box, so it was an excellent chance to score an equalizer. Luckily, I had just been practicing my aim and shots before the match started, albeit in the presence of an annoying Noah. I don't think the confidence was coming from a bad place when I said, "Maybe I can take it?" out into our little gathered circle.

Kyle, our captain, stood straight and looked back at where Matthias was standing. His eyes followed an imaginary line from where I fell, straight to the net. I could see the mental calculations on his face as he considered the angle and space. "I mean he stopped YOUR attempt, Avery. They are starting to realize just how much of a threat you can be. Maybe you should take this opportunity to bag your debut goal and scare them further." He winked, looking at me with a truckload of belief and trust.

The team dispersed and took their positions on multiple potential passing spots. Leah stood a few feet away on my left, and Kyle, Fred, and Harry went further on the left, standing one after the other from the front to the back. I took my place behind the ball and studied their players. Their goalkeeper Ben was standing with his arms and feet spread out, trying to look bigger and covering more of the net. Jack, that asshole, was standing a bit on my left, and three other defenders were standing in a straight line making a wall. I looked beside me and there was Noah, as he had positioned himself ahead of his defenders, in case he had to receive a pass or deflection. His jaw was set, and his gaze was intense, a mix of determination and anticipation etched across his face. His usual confidence was replaced with a bit of caution and his seemingly casual posture masked a readiness to respond, a resolve not to be caught off guard again.

I liked that.

I looked at the net and took a few steps back, racking my brain with all the different ways this could go. I couldn't come up with any particular strategy. The only thought in my brain was that I *had* to nail it.

Someone in the crowd yelled, "Bend it like Beckham!" and it was like my brain was ready to do anything you would push it for. I closed my eyes and took one last breath.

Yeah, maybe I should.

The tension in the air was palpable, and the stadium fell into a hushed silence as the referee's whistle pierced through the atmosphere. I took one last look at the wall of defenders in front of me and started the jog, mentally calculating the height and curve I should give so it would go past the wall. My left foot stood directly next to the ball and I hit the ball with my right, low on the side, and lifted it up to execute the ideal curve I was looking for. Time slowed as I stared at the ball- which took off to the right before curving to the left- the defenders taking a jump in my slow-mo sight, as it went up and around them towards the goal. It seemed their goalkeeper was expecting it to stop at the wall if his rather shocked face was anything to go by. I could tell he didn't expect me to go for a curve. He was just a second late as the ball swished past him, crashing straight into the back of the net as time went back to its natural speed and the crowd erupted with a cheer.

It went in.

Not only did I somehow pull it off, but the speed and curve turned out to be so perfect it made the other team open their mouths in astonishment. And Noah, well I was immensely satisfied to see that he stood there with an absolutely dumbfounded expression. I stood in a state of awe as my teammates came around me and hugged the breath out of me, yelling their praises above the sound of the crowd to congratulate me on my first goal for the team.

"I can't believe you pulled that off, little Becky!" Leah said while high-fiving me, her excitement more than doubling mine.

"And I can't believe I saw that legendary kick with my own two eyes," Ellie said, her arm around my shoulder. A celebratory moment like this was rare for me because of my position in the mid-field, and I was only involved in the assists more than the goals themselves. I cherished every bit of praise that came my way.

Kyle, our captain, came running from his place in our defense and patted my back in such a proud and appreciative way, it diminished any self-doubt I might have had about my worth as a soccer player.

"You're going places, kid." He said, much like a big brother.

"Places like maybe the school's official team?" I asked with a sneaky grin.

He laughed and patted my back again as he ran back to his place, his demeanor changing from casual to focused as Ben started another kick-off.

My heart and mind were no longer blaring alarms in my head, as I felt a lot better now that the scoreboard was tied. Not completely at rest though, because it was just half-time and a conclusion still awaited us in the next half.

9

NOAH

I watched as the ball sailed through the defenders, curled, and then, against all expectations, found the top corner of the net. It was a goal so epic, so beautifully executed, that for a moment, time itself seemed to stand still.

I stood there, dumbfounded, my eyes fixed on Avery as she raced away in celebration. The cheers from her teammates and the crowd engulfed the stadium, but all I could hear was the pounding of my own heart. How did she pull that off? It was a level of skill and finesse that I hadn't anticipated, and astonished was an understatement for what I was feeling now.

Mason sidled up to me with a laugh and threw his arm around my shoulder. "You messed with the wrong girl, Noah," he said, reading the shock on my face like an open book.

I tore my gaze away from Avery's jubilant celebration to look at Mason. "What the hell just happened?" I muttered, still trying to process the unexpected turn of events.

Mason chuckled, clapping me on the shoulder. "Avery happened. That was one hell of a goal, man. You've got to give credit where credit's due. First, she won the match, and now she scored a jaw-dropping goal for her debut. At this point, she has more rights to flex than you do."

I gave him the most indifferent look I could manage, completely hiding the urge to applaud her skills with the rest of the crowd. "Are you on her side or mine?"

He lifted his arms in a way that said *you never know*. "I might have to switch sides if she keeps being such a boss."

Despite the fact that it was my rival who had scored against my own team, I couldn't help but appreciate the artistry in her technique, each curve and dip of the ball was a testament to her exceptional skill. It wasn't just about the goal; it was about the beauty and mastery with which she had achieved it. In that moment, I found myself not just a competitor on the field but a spectator, appreciating the magic that unfolded when Avery unleashed her skills.

As she took position for another kick-off, the sunlight met her brown eyes and radiated a charming glow. Mixed with the brightness of her happiness it made her shine in an alluring light among the others. For a moment, her eyes met mine, but they quickly went over as if acknowledging my presence would ruin the beautiful moment she was having.

As wholesome as the moment was, we were the one who conceded the goal and now we will be spending the rest of the game to make up for it.

"Seventy minutes into the game, it's hard to tell if there will be any changes on the scoreboard, both the teams have fallen into a back-and-forth rhythm after the last attempt by Chloe went straight into the hands of Ellie." Luke was going on, as the game settled into a slow rhythm.

Twenty minutes ago we had almost conceded, but Avery met my eye just past the half-line and raced ahead, determined to sabotage our attempt. I managed to pass it to John, who was going straight for a goal when it met Ryan just near the penalty mark and it got passed on to Kyle. They have been controlling the possession since then, not giving us any chances to create an attack.

But I wasn't going to settle with that.

After a bit of tackling, our midfielder Camila got the possession and immediately passed it on to me, me who was planning to carry it forward like my life depended on it. Well, my ego definitely did.

"Camila to Noah, the way Noah has shot forward with the ball it seems an attempt will be made, Mason and Chloe running parallel to Noah- OH a tackle by Kyle, Noah's is tryin- OH WOULD YOU BELIEVE THAT, the Blue captain has been NUTMUGGED by Noah, who isn't taking more risks and has passed on the ball to Chloe, Chloe to Henry, Henry to Noah and there he is taking off with the ball again- Mason has received a quick pass- it's back to Noah AND THERE IT GOES IN THE BACK OF THE NET!!! What a way to break the deadlock! It was Noah with that stunning strike, ladies and gentlemen! After a slow interval, Team Yellow's golden striker has scored another tactful goal, and the scoreboard now stands 2-1 for Team Yellow!!"

I breathed a sigh of relief after what felt like the most intense five minutes of my life, after which I was choked by Henry and Mason who jumped on top of me, cheerfully celebrating my goal more than me.

I glanced toward Avery at exactly the right time to catch the roll of her eyes as she blew some hair out of her face. She didn't try to hide her distaste as she looked at me the way one would look if they ate a much overripe banana.

I threw her my most cheerful smile, as I finally, *finally* had a step ahead of hers.

The rest of the game went by with two more attempts by the Blue team, one of which was stopped by Ellie, and the other simply didn't hit the target. The final whistle blew and the crowd cheered, finally for the Yellow team as we all celebrated. Losing the first game against Avery had left a hole in my heart, which was now completely refilled with the stuffing of victory and triumph.

The Canteen was bustling with life as everyone filled in for refreshments and snacks. I, for one, went straight to the vending machine. There usually aren't many people near the vending machine during meal hours, but right now I see someone trying to get a chocolate bar drop down into the box. Someone who was still in her football kit, trying to hit the machine to make it drop. What a pleasant sight.

"The machine doesn't serve losers," I said, as Avery turned around, the messy bangs almost hitting her eyelashes.

She rolled her eyes, unaffected. "At least we went down with a goal. Losing a match without scoring any goals is just sad." She replied, referencing our first match together.

"Like I said, it was beginner's luck," I replied, coming in front of the machine to put in the money. "As proven by our victory today."

"You are insufferable." She said, watching me push the button for a bag of crisps. "How come you aren't getting Jaffa Cakes? I thought it was your drug."

"Well, the victory was sweet enough, now I want something salty."

To my surprise, I heard her laugh. A laugh that was not just pleasing but downright adorable.

"That's so tacky."

"Hey, can you not laugh at me? I am trying to bring you down."

She laughed even more. "Well, sorry, but your attempts to bring me down are just too hilarious, especially when it's over something I'm hella confident in."

Hella confident. Is it just me or is her American accent kinda cute? I had never found it cute before but now it was growing on me. Her accent, once merely a background detail, now seemed to paint the conversation with a unique charm.

It's because she's the first American I've met. Nothing else.

My bag of crisps dropped in the dispenser, and I bent down to pick it up.

"Hey, help me get my chocolate bar too! I've been trying so long, and the stupid machine ate my money."

I smiled. "Fine, I'm feeling generous today." Vending machines aren't that heavy if you compare it to the weights I was used to lifting in the gym, so I just tilted the machine a bit and shook it, until the chocolate bar wrestled free and dropped down on the dispenser as well.

I picked it up before she did.

"You're welcome," I said as I handed it to her.

Our post-match conversations had become quite a source of joy for me and I had no intention of abandoning our little meet-up until I saw a pair of blue eyes glancing at me from behind Avery. Recognizing who they belonged to, I got a sudden urge to flee before they started walking in my direction.

"Anyway, so... See you in class," I said hastily and walked away.

It was a shame that I had to leave early on a day when I had all the right to brag about my victory, but after such a good match, the last thing I wanted was to ruin it with a conversation with Everly. Deep inside, I knew I had to stop avoiding her and sort it out, but in order to do that, I needed to sort out my messed-up feelings first.

"She looks so cute with her hair down," Mason whispered to me in English class, looking at her across the classroom with heart eyes.

"Quit stalking." I rolled my eyes.

"This is the only class I have with her, let me adore her in peace."

"She is just one flirt away from giving you a restraining order. When are you going to stop trying?"

"Easy for you to say, Everly's boyfriend."

"Ex." I reminded him.

"Whatever, you just don't know what it means to yearn for your love. You like a girl and boom- she instantly becomes your girlfriend. Some of us have to go through a yearning phase." He told me like it was a law of nature.

"I only ever had *one* girlfriend!" I objected in a whisper, taking offense to the way he talked about me like I was a flirt.

"And that one girl was Everly. That's like catching the golden snitch and gaining 150 points at once." He said and leaned back in his seat, returning to his favorite activity- adoring Mia.

I shook my head and looked back at Miss Olivia, who was seriously overexplaining some poem by W. B. Yeats. If he were here, he'd be shocked at how a teacher went deeper into his poem than he ever did. Miss Olivia looked like the kind of woman who had dozens of cats at home and probably no love life, even though she was always looking pretty in her floral tunics and dresses. It just seemed like she was done with everything in the world.

Right now, she looked like she was almost about to cry when there was a knock on the door. All the bored students immediately turned towards the door, desperate for any kind of distraction.

Mrs. Jones came inside, and whispered something in Miss Olivia's ear, who nodded and gestured for her to go ahead.

"Your chemistry test papers are back, and I have to distribute them back right now as I won't be able to take my class today. My son has a recital in his school and I have to be there." She handed the stack of papers to Mia, who always sat in the front. "Pass it back to everyone, they are in order of your seating arrangement."

I might have imagined it, but in front of me, Avery stiffened up just the slightest. Like she was bracing herself up for whatever the paper was about to tell her. Strangely enough, I found that same anticipation in my heart too. For some reason, I didn't want to look at the same disappointment on her face that she had last week. Not the tears that were on the verge of falling down. This time, I wanted to know she did well.

The passing papers reached her as she kept her test and passed the rest to me, our eyes meeting for the tiniest of seconds. I kept my test and passed the rest to Kyle behind me. My eyes were still trained on Avery, and the way her shoulders relaxed made my heart sigh in relief.

In a heartbeat, she turned around, her eyes holding a sparkle much brighter than the stars.

"I passed!" She exclaimed, the paper in her hands showing me a 'C' at the top.

Absolutely nothing could have stopped the huge smile that immediately formed on my face. Not even the part of me that found Avery annoying. "See, I told you could do it." The old Noah who would have tried to hurt her by taking the credit for helping her was suddenly not responding. In his place, a much considerate Noah was making sure she knew she was capable of doing it all along, she just needed the right push and a bit of practice.

Her eyes went down to my table. "No way, you aced it!" She said, with equal excitement.

That's when I realized I hadn't even looked at my paper yet. A big red 'A' was scrawled at the top. I was so curious to know her grade, that I had almost forgo-

Wait, A? I did a double-take. I got an A? Never in my life had I scored this much before. Mason was definitely going to call me a traitor, I broke his 'never ace the tests' rule. Jogging my memory back before the test, I guess I did pay more attention to the test than I usually did, so I could have helped Avery better.

"This is new," I said with a surprised laugh.

"I know right? Turns out we are an academic weapon together."

I smiled. "So should I expect you in the library more now?"

"Maybe. If I can tolerate you." She said, and turned around, showing her test to Mia who was glancing back from the first desk. Mia raised her eyebrows at the result and gave her a thumbs-up, a huge smile on her face. I glanced at Mason who was still looking at Mia, also displaying a huge smile.

For the rest of the class, as Miss Olivia uncovered several more revelations, I was busy uncovering one of my own- Avery Kai's happiness was affecting me more than I would have liked.

10

NOAH

Plates clinked, and lively chatter surrounded us as the students got together for breakfast, the November wind starting to get cold and chilly in our campus. I was scarfing down a bowl of oatmeal, as Mason was busy panicking for a test he had today.

"You had the whole day yesterday, are you seriously blaming me for not 'letting' you study? I didn't hold you back from touching your books, you know?" I told him, adding more milk to my oats.

"You weren't studying, so it made me not want to study either. I do what I see others doing, I need a vibe." He said and despite his complaints, he still didn't seem worried enough. I have never seen him genuinely stress out over his studies, and it didn't matter anyway because he somehow managed to pass every class even if it was with a below-average grade.

As he delved into the details of the exam, Avery and Mia entered the crowded dining hall, scanning for an available table. After filling their trays, they finally settled on the table beside us. Not a purposeful choice I assume, given the fact that neither Avery nor Mia could stand the both of us. Mason gave out a heart-struck grin when Mia sat close by, piping out a cheerful "good morning" to which she politely nodded.

"Say what you will about Kai, but I, for one, am thankful for her arrival. Mia never used to attend matches before, and now she never misses any because of her. At least if she sees me being good at something, she won't think I'm such an egghead." He says wistfully.

"Don't carry such hopes my friend, it doesn't look like you're her type." I would guess Mia has a very specific type, the kind that studies STEM subjects and prepares for a test a week in advance instead of leaving it till the last minute like Mason was currently doing.

He shook his head with a smile, "Too late, my heart's carrying plenty."

Looking away from Mason's yearnful glances, I noticed someone approaching our table. Someone with pretty blonde hair gracing her shoulders in soft curls and a flushed face from the morning cold. The one person I didn't want to encounter this early in the morning.

"Hey Noah, hey Mason," Everly said, setting down her tray and taking a seat at our table, not even asking for permission this time.

"Hey," Mason replied with an awkward smile, looking over at me to find me looking down at my bowl, equally awkward.

"Hi." I managed to say.

I wasn't sure if I even had any feelings for Everly anymore, but I couldn't help being awkward whenever she was around because she was the only person I had ever liked or dated. And uh, kissed.

I think it would be the right terminology to call her my ex because even though she hasn't fully accepted it yet, I did break things off before our school ended last year. I hadn't wanted to, because I genuinely did like her, but something I overheard accidentally bothered me too much to stay with her.

I had been exempted from the football practice that day, with a small injury to my knee, and I had thought about surprising her in the dining hall to have lunch. I always had practice at that time so we never had the chance to share a lunch. I was almost at her table when some words from their conversation stopped me from joining them.

"We had a burglary yesterday." Her friend was telling her while eating a salad for lunch.

"That's awful! Do you have any idea who could've done it?" She had asked.

"Not yet. We are asking around for any sightings though."

"Have you suspected that immigrant family that lives next door? I mean, immigrants can be so sketchy. You never really know what they're up to." She said, not aware of my presence behind them. My eyes widened, and I couldn't believe what I was hearing. It shattered some part of me inside, as I stood there listening to their conversation unable to move or think about speaking up.

"Oh, that makes sense. They always seem so out of place." Her friend continued.

I felt a knot forming in my stomach. I was an immigrant myself, and the fact that Everly was so quick to generalize and make negative assumptions based on someone's background hit me hard. I had always tried to assimilate, and my accent often masked my immigrant status, but it hurt to discover that she held such biased opinions and harbored such discriminatory views. Would she feel embarrassed to date me when she realizes I'm an immigrant too?

When my dad, Deniz, and I first came to England, we wanted to start a new chapter. My dad wanted to give me better opportunities for football and to give Deniz the choice to do anything she wanted to do because she was the one who was affected by our mother's death the most. It still hurts me to remember little Deniz not eating anything for weeks, crying silently on her bed every night before sleeping. She was too young to understand the concept of death, all she knew was that she missed her mother, who was just not coming back. The mother who used to come running at the slightest inconvenience was just not coming back no matter how much she cried.

My dad opened a Turkish supermarket in Liverpool, and we started a new life. One of our neighbors told us about Summerfield Institute, and how they have a a great track record of developing talented players. He told them that the Institute invested a lot in their sports programs, as well as having strong ties with the local football club. My Dad thought it would provide me a great pathway to get noticed by scouts and possibly move on to higher levels of play. Deniz followed me here a year after that since she was getting lonely at home and wanted to be around me more often. Since English wasn't my native language, I used to struggle when I first joined school. Not that I struggled with communication, because my old school was English medium as well so I was able to speak fluently. But my accent was different and I wasn't as confident as I am now, so it took me a while to sound like an Englishman.

Moving away from the place where my mother had been, leaving behind her memories, accepting the fact that there would never be a future where she would be a part of it, it was all too much. Then it was the whole moving and settling in a new country, learning new cultures, and trying to fit in. It was enough to deal with. Piling my studies and practice hours on top of that? Initially, it was too much. My dad was working a lot to give us a good life and Deniz was still a little kid who missed her mother- my heart often worried about them more than it worried about me.

It first started to show in my studies, when I started failing my tests and was constantly falling behind on schoolwork. During those times, football was my only escape. I couldn't bother to pay attention to my studies because all I wanted was to be out on the field, surrounded by my teammates and living in the constant thrill of a game. Being so busy and engrossed in the passing and dribbling and tackling and running towards the goal with a ball at my feet that it pushed any negative thoughts out of my brain. The moment I stepped onto the field, all other thoughts stepped aside to make way for the game I needed to play. I started to make friends in the team, I started to belong. To belong in a team, who I could now call my friends.

Hearing Everly say these words about immigrants made me fall back to those years when I was trying to fit in. She had a rich background and had only joined our school a year ago, so there was no way she could have known where I came from. I wondered if she would feel ashamed to be with me when she found out I'm from a working-class immigrant family as well. Her dad is the owner of a big jewelry business, so I'm sure her class is much above mine. I didn't think it was important, until now. Now I knew how she felt about the immigrants and the working class, and it made me feel inferior like I would always be lesser. I'm no expert in love, but I know that's not how you're supposed to feel in a relationship. If I'm embarrassed about my background in front of her, I don't think she would be the right person for me. After a lot of debate with myself, I realized that I deserved someone who accepted and respected every aspect of who I was. I decided I couldn't be with someone who held prejudiced views, even if unintentional.

"Your last match was amazing," Everly said, snapping me back into the present.

"You saw it?" was the only stupid response I could conjure up. Of course, she saw it, the whole school saw it, it was our own personal premier league.

She gave me a weird look, a result of my stupid response. "Why wouldn't I?"

Mason was almost grimacing, the way I was acting like a deer in headlights.

"I mean..." I cleared my throat, "I mean you're a day scholar, I thought you went back home after school." When we were dating, she always stayed back for my match. Like a true sports girlfriend. I don't know why she would do that now.

"No." She said, cutting through her pancake. She doesn't seem to be catching on to my awkward energy, thank God. "You thought I wouldn't stay for your games just because we aren't together?"

"Kind of..." I said, avoiding her eyes by staring at my bowl of oatmeal like it was the most interesting thing on the planet.

"Well, just because we aren't together, it doesn't mean I can't still support you." She said. All of this was now making me uncomfortable because I didn't know how to look at her as a sincere friend when I knew she would not have respected me if she just knew my background better.

"I guess," I replied because I really didn't know what else I was supposed to say. I might still be attached to the memory of her since she was my first girlfriend and all, but I didn't want to confuse that with having feelings for her.

"Sure, you're the only person who has ever dumped me, but that doesn't mean I'll be a complete bitch about it." She smiled sweetly, all honey and sugar.

"I appreciate that." Was all I could say.

Her best friend Lucy joined us at our table, and the rest of the meal went by talking about random things. When my eyes wandered towards Avery, I wasn't surprised to see her usual company- Mia, Fred, and Leah. But escaping my gaze before, I realized there was one other person at her table today. Liam. He was smiling at Avery as she laughed about something he said, a very specific glint in his eyes. A spark that showed admiration. It was a look I recognized. As amusement rose in my head over that potential pairing, some other strange feeling rose in my stomach. I looked at the empty bowl in front of me. Was there something in my food?

After a rough and tiring week, Mason and I decided to dedicate our Sunday to video games, playing on our Nintendo, completely engrossed in our own world. The common room was peaceful and empty because the students either went to their homes or took the bus to the city, the usual ritual for our high school boarding students. Playing in the common room with our Nintendo out in the open was a risk in itself because our school doesn't allow us to bring or keep consoles on the premises. But since it was a holiday and even the teachers were busy, we took the liberty to come downstairs and enjoy it in the open well-lit common room, with some snacks and the TV playing a sitcom in the background.

"Stop fooling around, hit the one on the left!" Mason yelled at me, maneuvering his character out of my radar.

"Come on, it's so fun to see you cry when you get knocked out of the arena," I responded, still going after his character in the game.

"I'll show you, you-" He paused immediately and from the corner of my eye, I could see him sitting up straight all of a sudden.

"Hey, why aren't you-" I was going to ask why his character suddenly stopped moving but when I looked at him, he didn't have his console in his hands anymore. He was looking at me with a panicked expression and from how close I was, I could see his Nintendo hidden behind the cushions.

So there's someone behind me.

I realized we got caught and slowly turned around, expecting to see our warden- Mr. Wilson- at the door. He would be mad about the consoles for sure, but if I just apologized, I was confident he would let me go with a warning or the promise that I would take it back home on my next trip. I was playing it on a holiday anyway, so it's not a big deal.

But when I turned around, the person standing there wasn't Mr. Wilson, it was someone much worse. Someone who would blow this little mistake into a full-blown felony. Our unbeloved Miss Asami.

Shit.

She was standing at the doorway with her arms folded across her chest, glaring at me with the energy of two hundred suns. I looked at her furious eyes and back to my Nintendo, which was probably going to witness arrest and imprisonment.

R.I.P.

"Are you not aware of our school policies Mr. Yildiz?" She asked, in a tone much harsher than sandpaper.

I stood up and faced her. "I am." There wasn't much else I could say. She caught me red-handed.

"And do you know how we deal with such violations of the policies?"

Violations? Seriously? It's a video game for God's sake.

But despite my irate thoughts about her overreaction, I had to answer her in the most patient and respectful way possible.

"By giving us a warning so we don't repeat the mistakes next time?" I tried to be positive, but we all knew there was nothing positive about the woman in front of me. Still, I thought, what's the harm in trying?

"No. We deal with such violations by confiscating the item that you weren't allowed to bring here in the first place." Her voice was firm and unmoving. Clear in its message that no other arguments will be taken into consideration.

"But it-"

"Hand it over Mr. Yildiz." She said, her hand spread out in front of me.

I looked back at Mason. He gave me a helpless look and shrugged, wordlessly telling me that there was no point in debating.

I sighed and handed it over, my precious Nintendo landing in the hands of the evil queen. She tilted her chin up and took it, staring at me one last time.

"I will hand it to your father the next time he's here for the Parent-Teacher meeting." She said and looked back at Mason. He shifted in his place, desperately wishing his Nintendo would stay out of her sight.

"It's your responsibility to inform the faculty when a pupil is breaking the rules. I better not see students covering up each other's mistakes next time." She said to him firmly. "Anyway, have either of you seen Mr. Wilson? I came here to have a word with him but can't seem to find him."

"We haven't seen him either," Mason said. So it's Mr. Wilson's fault for disappearing and letting this joy-stealer enter our lands.

"Very well. I'll call him. You guys better behave." And with that she finally walked away, my precious Nintendo in her evil hands.

I turned towards Mason and we both let out a heavy sigh.

"My responsibility is to protect my friends, not to rat them out to the police." He said, sitting back down on the couch and pulling his Nintendo out from behind the cushion. "At least we still have mine."

"I'll have mine too," I said and sat on the couch opposite him. "I'm not gonna sit here and wait for my dad to show up. The next meeting is probably after three months at least."

"So you're gonna arrange a heist and get it back from her?" He asked with a ton of disbelief like I just suggested we go to war with the government. "What would you say when your dad's here and your Nintendo isn't in her office?"

"It's not an office. It's an evil lair of confiscated objects. I bet she won't even remember my Nintendo being there." I said, already planning my heist.

"Dude, you could get into trouble."

"Only if I get caught." I could do anything to get my Nintendo back. "And anyway, it's unfair that she just confiscated my stuff without even giving me a warning or a strike. She can't just do whatever she wants."

"Uh, counter argument- she does." He reminded me.

"Counter counter-argument- then I can do whatever I want too," I said and laid down on the couch, my day suddenly empty without my video games. The weather was so cold and the common room so cozy, I might just fall asleep right there. "I'm sick of her overbearing attitude. She's Avery's aunt, isn't she? I guess overreaction runs in their DNA."

"You say you don't like her and then you mention her a hundred times a day."

Is that true? I mention her that often? "Only because she gets on my nerves."

"So you're really gonna steal it back from her?" There was a hint of concern in his voice, like he was worried if I get caught I'll be thrown into Asami's dungeon.

"Watch me."

"Noah the freedom fighter?" He laughed, laying back on the couch himself. The curtains were drawn and laying down in a dark heated room was as good as it gets.

"Noah the freedom fighter," I repeated and closed my eyes.

From laying down for a quick rest to our eyes falling shut, it barely took five minutes before we both fell asleep into a peaceful afternoon nap.

11
AVERY

The soft hum of music played in the background as Mia and I lounged in our cozy dorm room. Even though it was a weekday, we had no classes because the faculty was busy attending the memorial of some guy who established our institute. The coaching staff counted as faculty, so our training was canceled as well. The room was filled with a comfortable vibe, a sanctuary away from the hustle and bustle of our school life as we decided our plans for the day.

"What's the time?" Mia asked, lying on the floor while painting her nails with a light shade of peach.

"Eleven-six," I responded while shifting my body to a more comfortable position on the bed.

"Hmm. Let's make plans after we submit the assignment."

She wasn't even done with her sentence when my eyes widened and I sat up straight, a sudden realization washing over me.

"Oh my gosh, the biology assignment! I completely forgot about it." A very sudden change from my previous comfortable state, my heart was now threatening to break free from my ribs the way it was thudding through the walls.

"You *what?*" Mia seemed more scared than me, her academia-related fears coming true in real life.

"Asami would be here any second, I can't let her lecture me again!" I scrambled to my desk, frantically searching for my notebook and pen. I hastily flipped open my biology textbook and started jotting down notes. The urgency in my movements was evident as I mumbled to myself, trying to recall the key points for the assignment.

"Cell division, mitosis, meiosis... I can't believe I let this slip my mind." I was desperately trying to write it all down, still wondering how it got pushed back to a corner in my head. Not being able to turn in *any* other assignment would have been fine by me, but when the assignment was given by Asami, it was like my life depended on it. She was always super strict with her work, marking my whole paper in red whenever it didn't quite meet her expectations. If she can be that bitter when I wasn't able to do it perfectly, imagine her reaction when she realizes I didn't do it at all.

"You won't be finished on time, why do you always procrastinate till the very last second, Ave," Mia said, watching me write in a desperate hurry.

My handwriting was hopeless at this point, not only was I hurrying through the words, but my dyslexia made sure I was getting certain letters twisted and wrong every once in a while. I didn't even bother to check back as I kept writing in an attempt to finish before Asami came to collect them at noon.

"Is it my fault there are lots of other interesting things to do besides completing your hand-written assignment? What is up with you Brits and hand-written assignments anyway, ever heard of a PDF?" I missed submitting assignments the American way, copy-pasting paraphrased bodies of text, and then hitting send right before the deadline. The satisfying 'whoosh' of the email being sent and then the 'click' of flipping the laptop closed.

"If you were done with it on time, we could have spent our day doing *other* interesting stuff. Like maybe going out to the city since we don't have classes today. The bus leaves at eleven thirty and now we can't go." She rested her chin on her palm, sulking.

My head flipped up. "Going to the city you say? Which city?"

Mia sighed. "London. But don't get your hopes up now, we can't go until you're done."

"Unless," I said, with much eagerness in my voice.

"Avery, no." Her order came out stricter than my parents.

I glanced at the digital watch on my wrist. "See, there's only about forty minutes till noon, which means it's impossible to complete this paper on time.

Even if I try, it'll be terrible and you don't want to disrespect this beautiful subject by hurrying through it, do you?"

"There comes your elaborate scheme."

"So I say, let's just hold off on this assignment until the evening, and go enjoy our day out in the city while we can." I ended, my tone stable and steady despite the anticipation bubbling inside me.

"But how would you submit your paper then? You *know* if you don't submit it on time she won't accept it later no matter what you say." She really seemed more worried about this situation than me.

"Well," I got up from my study table and put my arm around her shoulder, "Leave that to Avery Kai. Let's just go and enjoy our London stroll. Rest assured, my paper will be on her table tomorrow morning when she checks them, whether she likes it or not."

It was inarguably the right decision to go on our little London adventure trip because that whole afternoon was spent in pure bliss. The cute sidewalks with the infamous red telephone booths, the amazingly delicious chocolate strawberries from the Borough Market, and the enchanting sight of the ginormous Wembley Stadium were more than worth it to skip the boring handwritten assignment for. Leah, Mia, and I took the bus from our school to the city, which was a delightful experience on its own. I was starting to build a fondness for the places and people here, even if sometimes my heart missed the comfort of my home. My new experiences were slowly building a different place in my heart, a whole new sense of familiarity and love for this new part of my life.

However, the not-submitted assignment was still looming over my head, so I completed it the moment we got back into our dorms. Mia was freaking out over my elaborate plan, but I just had to reassure her like a soldier going into battle and give her hope for my return.

Sneaking into a HOD's office at midnight seems like a very bad thing to do, but it's not bad if I'm here because of the consequences of trying new experiences. Right?

Personally, I really think they need to invent actions that don't result in such consequences. But nonetheless, Avery Kai knows how to deal with them.

As I carefully turned the doorknob, the door creaked open, revealing the silhouette of Asami's neatly organized workspace. I looked around the corridor one last time before sneaking in and closing the door behind me, finding myself in complete darkness. Turning on the lights would surely alert the warden so I turned on my phone's flashlight and started my search. Asami was too disciplined for her own good, so I knew she wouldn't be here anytime before seven in the morning. Yes, I was supposed to submit it by noon, but she won't even get to know I submitted it late because my assignment will be right here on Asami's table when she comes in here tomorrow morning.

The thundering clouds were warning against heavy rain, with a few droplets already falling down outside the window. I made a mental note to get this done quickly and go back before a thunderstorm starts up.

I tip-toed my way toward the table until I realized they didn't have wooden flooring over here. There was no risk of squeaky floorboards when the flooring was done with marble tiles. Replacing my stealthy walk with a normal one, I reached her table and shuffled through the stack of papers, checking to see which one was supposed to be the assignments from 11th Grade. I found it on my third try and a rush of achievement went through me. Lifting the first few papers, I put my own assignment in the middle of the stack. I won't be around when she will be checking the papers later in her office, but for some reason, I still didn't want my paper to be the first one she checked.

Another flash of thunder rattled the windows with its sound, and I could hear the rain falling with much more force than before. *Dammit.* Our dorm building was across the campus, which meant I was most likely going to get drenched by the time I reached there on my way back. I should have at least kept an umbrella before leaving for my quest.

After successfully adding my paper to the pile, I was ready to go back when I heard the doorknob twisting, followed by the door creaking open. My heart rate shot up as I quickly ducked behind the table, praying it wasn't the warden or worse, Asami herself. I crawled under the table and sat there, waiting for the lights to be turned on and wondering if the table was giving me enough cover. I held my breath, not wanting to make *any* sound that would alert the visitor.

But the lights never turned on and I didn't hear any loud footsteps. What was going on? Was it a thief? In an HOD's office?

I was busy wondering if I accidentally involved myself in a burglary when a pair of feet appeared in front of the bookshelf on the right side of the room. I squinted hard to see who it was, but there was no light to determine the identity of this mystery person. Judging by his trendy sneakers, he surely wasn't an adult, and his hushed attempts at searching through the drawers told me his intentions were not any nobler than mine. Quiet as ever, I crawled out from under the table and stood up, folding my arms across my chest to observe what this person was trying to achieve. He made sure to check every single drawer and shelf before he turned around and that's when I was met with the most high-pitched scream I ever heard. I stepped back into the darkness and clutched my chest with a gasp, equally scared by the sudden loud scream. There was a strike of lightning outside the window, and the illuminating flash finally revealed who this high-pitched screamer was.

What the hell was Noah doing here?

"Oh my God, SHUT UP YOU ABSOLUTE DWEEB!" I whisper-yelled while hitting him over the head, absolutely enraged that he probably alerted the whole building.

"Bloody hell Avery, why did you sneak up on me like that?" He said through his quick breaths, his hand over his chest in a dramatic stance.

"I was just standing here!" We were both whispering with the intensity of a full-blown argument.

"Yeah, in the midst of utter darkness in a deserted office at midnight! I didn't exactly expect you to be here, or anyone for that matter." He was pissed, probably because I witnessed his girly scream.

"What are you doing here?!" I recalculated my escape plan and realized I needed to get out of there before the watchman rushed over here to check who it was. He must be halfway here already.

"I came here to get my Nintendo back, Asami confiscated it." He replied and quickly went back to his search, sliding past me and checking the drawers on her table now.

"That is such a corrupt thing to do," I said, shaking my head as I watched him shuffle through the drawers.

He turned around and said, "Well you aren't exactly here to clean up her office at this time, are you?"

Busted. I remained silent as I had nothing to say to defend my name.

"That's what I thought. You have no right to act all holy when you're here stealing something as well." He went back to open another drawer.

"I'm not stealing, I just came here to submit my assignment." How dare he accuse me of stealing?

"Submit?" He turned around again mid-shuffle, looking at me with an arched eyebrow. "I didn't know assignments were submitted to empty dark offices past midnight."

I rolled my eyes. Not bothering to respond, I saw as he opened the last drawer on the desk, immediately jumping a bit out of excitement.

"Found it!" He picked it up from where it was on top of like eight other consoles, putting it on the table and closing the drawer.

"She has so much confiscated shit in there she will never notice that my Nintendo is missing. I bet she won't even know the differenc-" We heard a thud outside the room and he stopped abruptly, looking at me with wide eyes.

My eyes were staring back with the same amount of vigilance as we realized someone was coming up the corridor. We could hear the loud footsteps, the footsteps of someone who just heard a noise in the office and was coming here with full determination to expel whoever it was.

"What do we do?" He said as we both started looking around, looking for a way to get out because running out the front door was not an option right now.

My eyes fell on the window behind the table, and I quickly went over and slid it open. The rain was pouring down heavily at this point, but getting drenched in the rain was not my concern right now. If Asami finds out I sneaked into her office at night, she will never stop babbling about it for a whole decade. Both in front of me and my family. Maybe even the neighbors.

I glanced at Noah with an urgent look and climbed out, shielding my head from the water as he followed me out in an instant. We closed the window shut so whoever came looking for us, won't find any opening for a supposed escape.

It was risky to hide under the window, so with an unspoken mutual understanding, we took a run for it. A swift, rapid, speedy run towards the nearest building we could see. Whoever it was back at the office would first check the whole room before even considering opening the window- if it would even cross their mind. And if by some miracle they happened to look outside the window right now, the heavy downpour was so intense they probably wouldn't be able to see past ten feet. I was sure it would affect the visibility, especially at night.

Our hands shielding our eyes and our feet never stopping, we ran and ran without looking back. Good thing we were both athletes because running against the direction of the rain was not an easy task. We reached the boys' dorm building and quickly ran inside, heading towards the common room. It was dark and deserted at this time, a stark difference from how common rooms usually looked during daytime. As soon as we reached inside, we closed the door and doubled over, catching up on lost breath. We were both drenched from head to toe, our clothes clinging on to us as water dripped all over the floor.

Somewhere in the middle of pants and sighs, my eyes caught his and there was this silent sense of acknowledgment about what we just did. A smile came upon his face that lasted for a millisecond before it turned into a laugh, and before I knew it I was laughing too, the thrill of the last five minutes finally catching up to us. There was a spark in his eyes at that moment that only pushed me into a bigger fit of laughter whenever our eyes met.

Each glance that we exchanged triggered another round of giggles until we were clutching our sore stomachs from all the laughter. After five full minutes of pure adrenaline bliss, his eyes met mine with a different light shining in them. "We just pulled off the heist of the decade."

"Do you think they saw us?" I asked, still giggling.

"Nope, I don't think so. The watchman is a lazy bloke, so he would probably just assume the sound came from somewhere else and give up." He replied, which reminded me of the sound in question.

"Yeah, he can assume it came from the girls' dorm since it sounded like a little girl coming across a spider." The memory of Noah's high-pitched girly scream sent me into another fit of laughter.

"It was a totally reasonable reaction!" He defended, running a hand through his wet hair, shaking off the excess water.

"Yeah, a reasonable reaction for a six-year-old," I said as more giggles came my way.

"Whatever. You totally looked like a ghost standing there in the dark." He took out his Nintendo from his pocket and turned it on. "Come on, please turn on. I don't think these things are waterproof."

As he whispered prayers for it to turn on, the light from the console suddenly illuminated his face in a soft glow. His hair was still falling over his forehead, damp and lustrous, as he kept pressing different buttons to make sure they worked. It was dark in the common room as well, but him standing there with that busy expression on his face was indeed a good sight. With every flicker of lightning, his charm got more and more impossible to avoid. The boy was cute, can't deny.

"All good." He finally said, looking up at me with a smile that reached his eyes.

Shy about getting caught, I wiped the adoring expression off my face and started walking towards the door.

"Where are you going?" He asked, putting his Nintendo back into his pocket.

"The girls' dorm? You were lucky enough to be dropped off right at your dorm building, but I still have to get back to my room. If the watchman starts a roll call, I'm dead." I went ahead and opened the door. He pushed past me and exited the room before I could even take a step as if I was holding the door open for him.

This guy. I followed him outside.

"Relax Kai, no one's starting a roll call. The watchman will just think it was the thunderstorm or whatever."

"Okay, but I still need to go bac-"

"Wait a minute! Just wait here, I'll be back." He shushed me and suddenly ran toward the staircase. "Don't go anywhere!" He said before disappearing into the night.

Although a bit confused, I waited for a full three minutes before I heard footsteps running back down the stairs. Noah appeared again, this time with an umbrella in his hand.

"Here take this."

Where did he even get it this quick?

"As if this would help after already getting caught in the rain," I said, but took the umbrella from him nonetheless. I didn't want the force of the rain slowing down my steps again.

As I opened the umbrella and started walking toward the exit, his voice called me again.

"Wait!" He said, and came up behind me, taking off his jacket. "It's really cold." Since one of my hands was preoccupied with holding the umbrella, he held the jacket at my back so I could put my arms in one by one and then came back in front of me. He adjusted the zip and zipped it all the way up, not letting any air reach my damp clothes. I doubted anything would keep me warm when my clothes were already drenched but the extra piece of thick fabric really calmed the shivers coming up my spine.

"Don't forget to return it to me, it's my favorite jacket, okay?" He said, and I blamed the cold wind for the shiver that went through my body at his smile.

And just like that, I ran out into the rain again, running towards the building which was just a few yards away from me. As I ran up the stairs and pulled the umbrella down, I glanced back toward the boys' dorm. I don't know what I was expecting to see when I turned around but there he was, looking at me from his spot on top of the stairs. He waved a hand and I did the same, signaling that I reached my destination safe and sound. As the breeze distracted me with its harsh chill, I quickly turned and ran towards the stairs- towards the heat, dryness, and comfort of my room.

I took off his jacket which was frankly quite big on me and put it near the window before drying myself and changing into a fresh pair of my woolen pajamas.

The unexpected encounter had sure surprised me, but what surprised me more was the feeling I got when I looked back and saw him standing back there at the dorm. The heist, the escape, the laughter, and the care- all of it left me feeling warm and fuzzy inside as I snuggled inside my blanket, the smile refusing to leave my face until I fell asleep.

12

AVERY

"Why does he always have to be so flirty, it's annoying," Mia said, as she reached her assigned seat before our Chemistry class and found her favorite chocolate bar on the table. Without even a note or any indication of the mystery chocolate Santa, she knew it was from Mason. No other person in the whole class would know her preferences, not even me, but Mason was attentive enough to know everything. Her words make it sound like she didn't like the gift, but she was holding a smile and her fair cheeks hid a tinge of pink.

"He's annoying? Is that why you're happily snacking on the chocolate he left for you?" I asked her. She always talked like Mason was a huge flirt who shouldn't be trusted, but ever since she had been attending our games and got to know him better, her demeanor had changed the slightest bit. Deep past her fears of being fooled by his potential insincere flirt, I knew she adored his efforts too.

"I mean, why is he always after me when I have made it clear that I don't like him back?" She said while taking a bite.

"Maybe because you haven't made it clear that you don't like him."

"I really don't!"

"Your flushed cheeks say otherwise." I teased. Let's just say I enjoyed this denial of feelings from her side because she really tried her best to not be flattered and yet her blushed face betrayed her act every time. Yesterday, she saw Chloe flirting with him during practice and her efforts to stay calm when her heart was bursting with jealousy were hilarious.

"Well, then you claim to hate Noah but his jacket in our room says otherwise too." She fired back.

"It was raining! And it's just a jacket which I'm going to return anyway." I pointed my finger at her and emphasized, "It doesn't mean anything."

Thank God Noah hadn't arrived yet because I would have died of embarrassment if he heard this conversation. I don't even want to imagine the ego boost he will get high on if he even minutely gets the idea that I *might* like him. It wasn't true of course, that guy was insufferable, but even hinting at that possibility was a threat. Even thinking about it was unacceptable. I didn't want to cross that topic within a sixty feet radius.

"Sure it doesn't." She said lightly and turned around as Mrs. Jones entered the classroom.

"It really doesn't," I whisper to her one last time before walking a few steps back to my assigned seat.

Sure, running away from the office together while it was raining was fun and adventurous, and sure, Noah gave me his favorite jacket so I wouldn't get cold, but it doesn't mean either of those actions melted my heart through its icy covering. He was my rival on the pitch, and he was going to stay that way.

Almost as if he was conjured by my thoughts, Noah walked into the classroom, his eyes still puffy while carrying his backpack on one shoulder. I would say his messy hair was a result of waking up late, but his hair was always tousled anyway. Maybe no one told him about hair gel or hair brushes yet.

Good, I thought. I was roasting him in my head which was a healthy sign. I hoped someone would advise him about a hair gel, because if he looked nerdy with flattened gel hair, maybe I wouldn't have to make an effort to *not* pay attention to him.

"Mr. Yildiz, stop arriving late to your classes." Mrs. Jones said without looking up from her textbook, like it's part of her routine to say that.

"Yes ma'am." He replied like it was a part of his routine as well and sat down behind me, shuffling through his bag to take out his textbooks.

"You catch a cold yet?" He asked when Mrs. Jones turned towards the whiteboard.

"No," I replied, still looking forward at Mrs. Jones' back.

"Damn. So you're playing the match tomorrow?" He made an effort to sound disappointed.

I turned and looked at his slightly surprised face. "Playing the match and getting selected for the school team, yes I'm doing both."

His eyebrows went higher and his eyes held a spark as he looked at me like he was impressed by my determination. "That delusional?"

"No. That *confident*."

"We'll see." He replied casually and leaned back in his chair, stretching his feet and folding his arms over his chest. Something captivated me, holding me back from turning toward the class as his gaze was locked on me. He tilted his head slightly, a challenge written in the lines of his expression. The room seemed to shrink around us as the moment stretched, a prelude to the impending battle. I could see the specks of golden in his brown eyes as the sunlight fell on them, and something else that wasn't quite as obvious. Something soft that was hidden behind the roughness of his words and the intensity of his gaze. Something positive. Almost like admiration.

A cough from Mrs. Jones pierced the silence between us, breaking the spell. I tore my gaze away from Noah, redirecting my focus to the class, nodding at her like I never lost a part of her lecture. I didn't realize when my heartbeat started beating fast, my breaths speeding up like they were competing in Formula 1. For every speech of confidence that left my mouth, there was a huge boulder of doubt creeping up behind them. Ready to fall over and crush me in an instant.

The reason I talked a big game before a match wasn't to convince others of my ability. It was to convince myself. To tell myself that I could do it, no matter how unlikely the consequences made it seem. It had worked in my favor all these years, every time I faced a challenge, I told myself I could conquer it. And conquer it, I did, up until this moment when the challenge was no longer just winning a match, but an opportunity to show Coach Martinez just how determined I was to join his team. I was hoping the utter confidence would work out this time too.

Winning a place in the school team wasn't just a desire anymore; it was a commitment I had made, and the challenge in Noah's eyes only fueled my resolve.

The sun had barely kissed the horizon when my eyes flickered open, the weight of the impending match settling heavily on my chest. Even without an alarm, my body woke me up for my solo practice, almost like it remembered my match-day routine better than myself. Today was the day that would determine my spot on the official team for the inter-school competitions, and the gravity of the situation hung in the air like a thick fog. It felt weird not to play for my old American school anymore and prepare myself to get selected for my new abode.

I swung my legs over the edge of the bed, my mind already buzzing with a mix of excitement and nerves. Inter-school competitions in England were a different ball game than in America, and I couldn't shake the anxiety that came with the heightened level of competition. I never got this much nervous before, because honestly not many people love soccer in America, it's more of a football country. American football. But people take soccer seriously here, which means I had to be ten times better than I was in America to get a spot on the team.

Will I be able to do it? Can I trust myself with this? What if I lose?

If I don't get selected, what am I supposed to tell Ella? Yesterday when I called her, she was one hundred percent sure that I would get in, but let's be honest, I'm the only person she has seen playing soccer. She thinks I'm great but chances are, it's only because she doesn't know just how amazing and talented others are. She hasn't been to England and she definitely hasn't seen my teammates. Can I really trust her judgment?

All the nervous thoughts had me paralyzed for about ten minutes before I realized it was close to hitting 07:30. I usually reach the football ground fifteen minutes from now, so I put on my hoodie and quietly left the room with my kit bag in my hand.

The lunch lady who had recognized my matchday traditions at this point only had to look at me once before she handed me a tray with my usual sandwich before going back to reading her book. It felt strangely nice to be recognized by her, it meant the feeling of being foreign was washing away and I was slowly becoming a part of this school, where the teachers and staff remember me as their own and not as some outsider or a tourist. I couldn't see the cover of the book she was reading, but it must've been boring because she was already half asleep. In her defense, this seems like the most boring job ever.

I settled down with my tray and was almost done with my sandwich when the doors opened and someone walked in. The cologne reached my senses before his appearance did and I immediately knew who it was.

"Fancy meeting you here today instead of the ground." Noah greeted, ruffling his disheveled hair. He had his kit bag in his hand just like me, clad in a comfortable hoodie and shorts. I suddenly remembered his jacket that was still sitting in my room but I was in no mood to return it so soon, with how comfortable and warm it was.

"Only because I got late. I have no interest in sharing a meal with you first thing in the morning." As I picked up my apple and took a crunchy bite, Noah went toward the lunch lady to pick up his tray.

Even though I made my preferences very clear, he still picked my table out of all the empty ones and settled down in front of me.

"Why were you late? Nervous much?" He said it in his usual teasing tone, not realizing he actually hit the target with his assumption.

"Always a bit. Keeps me sharp." I admitted, still not letting it slide as a weakness. "You?"

"Nah, just excited to see you try and keep up with me." He picked up the can of coffee from his tray and opened it, his bright smile still intact.

I rolled my eyes and took another bite, which brought his attention to the apple in my hand.

"What's the deal with the apple anyway? You're the only person I've seen taking pre-match apples instead of coffee." He tilted his head to the side, genuinely curious.

His question struck me with a bit of surprise. *Has he been noticing my habits?* "I'm caffeine sensitive. No coffee for me. Apples are my fuel."

"So, you're a health nut?"

I shrugged, "More like I don't want to be jittery on the field. Apples give me energy without the jitters."

He nodded, registering the information like it was crucial. "So this is your version of a pre-match caffeine boost, without the caffeine." He took a sip of his coffee, his eyebrows immediately falling into a relaxed state.

"You can say that." Expecting Noah's company during breakfast didn't cross my mind by a far mile, but now that I was living this reality, it wasn't such a bad experience. Our solo practices had become an unspoken culture between us, a shared experience that was slowly becoming something I looked forward to. Having someone on the field during solo practice wasn't such a bad thing, especially when the competition gives you motivation to perform better.

We walked our way toward our respective locker rooms, before finally stepping foot onto the field. As usual, we parted ways and set up courses for our drills, tirelessly going at it until our muscles screamed with finesse.

I stood at the center of the soccer field, the air heavy with the weight of anticipation. The stadium roared with the collective voices of supporters, each cheer and applause resonating through the crisp evening air.

Luke's voice echoed from the speakers, our irreplaceable commentator back at his job. "Good evening, ladies and gentlemen, the stands sure look as cheerful as ever as almost all of our school is here to either support their friends or diss their rivals, some of them doing both."

The gravity of the moment sank into my bones. I could feel the eyes of the coach, the expectations of my teammates, and the undeniable pressure to prove myself in this defining moment. Mia was here to cheer me as always but this time I noticed someone else cheering us on with a little blue flag waving in the air. It was Noah's little sister, cheering for our team instead of her brother's. A smirk came across my face- it sure feels good to steal fans from your rival.

Noah was standing opposite to me, looking ready as ever to give his best. I noticed something was different with his positioning today, until I realized he was playing midfield today. This was the first time I had seen him in a new position and I sure wanted to see how he would cover that responsibility. Jack was in defense per usual and I made a mental note to steer clear of him during the match. He had played an awful foul on me during our last match and I really didn't want to be on the receiving end of his tactics again. I wouldn't put it past him to injure me while tackling and I wasn't willing to spend my time on the bench especially when the inter-school matches were just around the corner. Sure, I didn't know if I was going to be selected but I still wanted to be in my best form in case the opportunity presented itself.

I heard the shrill whistle of the referee and quickly passed the ball to Ryan behind me, and the much-anticipated game finally commenced.

The first twenty minutes passed with us playing on the attack while the other team gave us a pretty hard time going any further than the halfway line. I was going in and out of our formation, desperately trying to create opportunities as our opposition maintained a strict wall of defense. The cards seemed to be dealt the wrong way this time as our usual strategies were switched, where the Blue team with the strong defense was trying to score and the Yellow team with a strong attack was defending their goal.

"Oh what a lovely sight, the midfield has become a battleground, with both teams fiercely contesting possession. Every pass, interception, and shot on goal carried the weight of each player's dedication and training. With this match carrying the weight of our school's official team selection, each player is pushing themselves, as the ebb and flow of the match seem to mirror the pulse of the spectators, a collective heartbeat racing with anticipation." The audience was indeed loud today as almost all of the school joined, so they could decide which one of us should represent our school with mutual discussion. We just love to be judges, don't we?

Noah was dominating the midfield with his presence as I tried to take the ball forward, which resulted in me standing face-to-face with him, his eyes sparkling with the determination to sabotage my attempts. Learning from my time dribbling past him during my first practice, I executed the same moves but this time he had already caught on to my tactics. He blocked my right foot with his left and pushed the ball further, running after it as I found myself tripping and falling onto the grass. He hadn't touched me at all, but the speed of his dribble had twisted my ankle and tripped me before I even realized what happened. As he passed the ball to someone else, he turned around and saw me getting up.

"I'm sorry, did I hurt you or just your pride?"

"Oh, you'll see."

"Filtering through the Blue defenders, the ball is slowly reaching the penalty area, Chloe with a pass to Mason, and with a strong sh- and OHH, the agony of a missed chance! Frustration for Team Yellow as the ball narrowly misses the goal. The game is restarting with a kick-off and Team Yellow seems determined to make up for their missed shot."

"Looks like the pass was unlucky." Noah's pass getting denied at the last moment was giving me more joy than it should have.

"Oh please, talk to me when you can keep your feet on the ground."

Gritting my teeth on his condescending comment, a competitive fire burned in my eyes. Before I even hit the grass when I fell, I knew he wasn't going to let it go.

Sparked by a new motivation, I received the ball from Fred and passed it forward to Harry, who went running past the halfway line to their side.

"The Yellow team's attempt at their defense-splitting passes to the strikers has resulted in them losing the possession, meanwhile the Blue team is running ahead with the determination to score a goal."

I ran forward and received the pass from Harry, carrying the ball forward to the right wing when I noticed that Hannah was just in the right position to score. She signaled in my direction to give her the pass and I went forward, dodging the attempts of the defenders.

"Jack with his defensive strides trying to stop the attack-

OH wait wait we have Avery here, and she GETS THE CROSS IN! It's towards Hannah, AND THAT'S A BREAKTHROUGH! Hannah Wilson has scored a spectacular straight shot RIGHT PAST THE

GOALKEEPER! And the scoreboard changes in favor of the Blue team, what a fantastic goal!"

Through the goal celebration, I felt heat coming in my direction and discovered the angry glare Jack was throwing at me for crossing him. His gaze was scary like he wasn't going to accept his slip-up as his eyes demanded revenge. I shook my head, not wanting to get intimidated by that asshole when I saw Noah, who looked genuinely disappointed to have conceded a goal.

The rest of the first half went into some attempts from the Yellow team but none of their tactics worked as our team had formed a strong wall near our penalty box.

And just like that, with one goal in our favor, it was half-time.

A few changes from the Yellow team had shifted the air of our game, as I saw Noah back in his usual position as a striker. Turns out his team needed his targeted shots more than his midfield dribbling, and he was now standing happily near our penalty box. Determination fueled his stance as we waited for the whistle, and I realized their desperation for an equalizer would be playing against us now.

The adrenaline surged as the referee's whistle pierced the air, signaling the second half. My eyes flickered with determination as I sprinted into action, not letting Noah's confidence or Jack's intimidation affect my game.

Team Yellow took in an offensive formation, their forwards charging to our side with such a pace that left most of our defenders confused and tired.

"As the match progresses, moments of brilliance unfold. Chloe is executing a breathtaking give-and-go, showcasing not only her individual skill but also her understanding of teamwork. The Yellow team seems determined to score this time, not letting the tactical Blue defenders have their way," Luke's commentary was making the whole audience tense and exhilarated at the same time.

"And here comes Chloe giving a pass to Mason and- THERE IT IS! Team Yellow breaks the deadlock with a spectacular goal! An amazing back-heel executed by none other than Mason Williams! And with that, Team Yellow scores an equalizer in the 67th minute of the game!"

Dammit. They did it.

The sudden change in the game made me lose some of my confidence from the first half as I ran back to the halfway line, prepared to meet this new challenge with equal efforts of my own.

"As you can see, the scoreboard is 1-1 as of now, let's see the last few minutes go by as the game takes an exciting turn for both sides! This is the perfect time to make your bets guys! Get going!" And with Luke's remark, the crowd erupted into cheers, appreciating the offensive prowess displayed.

I could feel the panic building inside me as each minute passed, making me more and more desperate to try for another goal before the last whistle. The pressure of getting selected came over me again, as I found myself struggling to make sense of the current dynamic of the game. All logic left my brain when I thought of getting rejected by the coach during the selection and an unknown force took over me as I made the decision to change the position of the game myself.

The tension in the stadium reached a crescendo as the clock ticked down. Determined to make an impact, I executed a perfectly timed slide tackle, dispossessing my opponent and initiating a swift counterattack. I glanced around, trying to find any gaps in their defense, but since I hastened in running over, I disrupted our formation and found myself cornered by two defenders with no one to pass to. As I maneuvered the ball around and ran forward, I found myself face-to-face with Jack.

Luckily, I knew his weaknesses when it came to the game so I tried to dribble past him from his left side but unfortunately, he called the shot and stopped me in my tracks, kicking my ankle intentionally while making it seem like he was trying to kick the ball. The impact was sharp, and I crumpled to the ground, clutching my foot in pain. He made it look like routine play and continued forward but the referee had seen my injury and blew the whistle on my fall.

"Ave, are you okay?" Leah ran over to me, her voice growing serious when she saw me wince in pain.

"I don't know." I tried to move my foot but the pain was fresh and it hurt even if I clutched it too hard.

"Are you okay?" Kyle came up beside me, his eyes full of concern.

"It's just... It's hurting." I told him.

"Do you think you can play?" He asked and I realized with a thud of my heart that I won't be able to continue the match this way.

"I..." I considered lying, maybe if I tried hard enough I could pretend like I was fine. But when I tried to get up, putting my weight on my foot sent a sharp pain through my leg and I immediately held on to Leah for support.

"I don't think I can play." My voice was barely above a whisper, my hopes crashing as I realized my chances of getting selected went down the drain.

"It's fine, get some rest. Don't worry about it, it'll be fine." Kyle tried to calm me down but I already knew the consequences of an injury.

Leah tried to help me reach the benches but I refused and pushed her away, telling her it was just a sprain and I could walk by myself. As I crossed the field, Noah was standing on the left wing, and for a split second, our eyes met.

Maybe it was just me but in that small moment, I saw something in his eyes that I had never seen before. Concern? Worry?

But that moment barely lasted for a second before the referee blew the whistle and the game started again, a new substitute taking my place in our formation. As I sat on the bench, a wave of sorrow took over me, the excitement I was feeling just this morning turning into a numbness that muted my surroundings. The pain in my foot was sharp, but it was the sting of self-blame that cut deeper. I had ignored my team's tactics to fulfill a goal of my own, getting so desperate in my attempt that I recklessly invited my own downfall.

The loud cheers of the audience snapped me out of my thoughts, as I looked up at the scoreboard and realized Team Yellow had scored yet another goal. A spectacular bicycle kick by Noah Yildiz which sent the crowd roaring at his finesse.

By the time the final whistle sounded, I had fallen into a deep sense of misery, stuck in the cycle of loathing myself and enraging over the cruel scheme of Jack's play. It was my fault that I rushed over but it was his fault for intentionally causing me harm in a way that would affect my matches in the future. With each passing minute, I was falling into a deeper pit of turmoil, holding myself up just enough until I could leave the attention of the crowd and lose myself in a long overdue breakdown.

13

NOAH

The sound of the final whistle pierced through my ears as I celebrated the goal with my teammates, everyone coming over to hug me while the audience cheered like crazy.

But even in that moment of glory, in between the hugs from my teammates, there was a little prick in my heart that I couldn't quite understand. Like there was a looming urgency blaring alarms in the back of my mind but I knew I needed to check on it. My eyes instinctively went toward Avery, who was crushed by the defeat, sitting on the bench with a potentially bad injury.

Could she be the reason for my unease?

As I prodded my heart for more answers, it asked me a question instead. *How was I supposed to be happy when a girl who had everything in her to win this match was sent off because of a cruel foul?*

Everyone on the ground was either exchanging post-match high fives or going off toward the locker rooms but my mind was constantly bugging me to check up on one certain girl. I scanned the whole ground and realized the girl I was looking for wasn't hard to spot, she was the only one limping, walking towards the girls' locker room with Leah on her side. Leah was holding her slightly to help her walk, and from the looks of it, it didn't look like a small injury.

When I saw the foul, everything in my body was screaming with concern. I knew how important this match was for her, and I knew how badly she wanted to win, but everything went plummeting down when that asshole decided to intentionally harm her. And even though seeing her in pain and walking off the field was somehow difficult to watch, I couldn't do anything about it. Henry, our captain, was not exactly a sweet person, and if I called Jack out for the evil foul he committed, Henry would have sent me off for not standing with my team. But looking back at it, maybe I should have said something. To hell with Henry and his punishment, I really should have said something. It shouldn't have mattered if I was sent off or benched for another ten games, because the agony she was facing at that moment was way beyond anything else I could have cared for.

There was a fleeting moment where she looked at me, her eyes displaying anger and hurt, and all I wanted to do at that moment was to run over there and get her to safety. The game left my mind for a second as I was filled with this strong urge to pick her up and call the nurse. Check if she was okay, and ask her if she was in pain. I wanted to tell Matthias that it was intentional, I wanted to punch Jack for ruining her important day and potentially ruining her chances of getting selected for the school team. The chances that she very well deserved, way more than him. He did it on purpose, he targeted Avery on purpose because he knew damn well she was a threat to his spot on the team. He knew the coach would see her shining potential and kick him out because he was terrible at maintaining the team's strategy anyway. Always going out and doing things for his own glory rather than the team's.

"There was a crazy hit!" Mason jumped on me from behind, Henry and Chloe coming over and gushing about the goal as well.

"You pulled a Ronaldo dude, that was crazy!" Chloe exclaimed.

I was aware of how astonishing the goal was, I shocked myself with it, to be honest, but the happiness wasn't quite striking me as much. Yes, it was cool, but it was mostly because Avery was no longer on the field, which gave us way more possession than we get when she's on. Footballers are supposed to take advantage of such situations, but when the person concerned was Avery, it fell in bad taste for sportsmanship.

"It just happened," I said, shrugging off Mason from my shoulder. The match was over and it was time to get off the field and deal with real life.

The chatter from my teammates was blurred off into a white noise, as my eyes were trained on the girls' locker room, wondering if she was doing okay. I followed Mason and Henry into the boys' locker room, a dark cloud of worry still looming over my head. This was the first time the beautiful combo of an amazing goal and stunning victory didn't make me happy. I couldn't be happy until I knew how she was. I couldn't move on with my day until I checked up on her.

Not wanting to waste much time, I took a quick shower and ran back out, deciding to act on my worries and wait outside the girls' locker room. I don't know why but I don't think I can be at peace until I see her. Maybe it was just guilt for not calling Jack out when he committed the foul, but I needed to know how she was. She was happy and excited about the match, confident as well, and rightfully so. If Jack hadn't played dirty, she would have won without a doubt.

I was leaning against the wall when Chloe walked out of the locker room, her ginger curls damp from the shower. Her steps halted when she noticed me, confusion written in her eyes.

"Is Avery in there?" I asked, getting straight to the point.

She looked back at the door. "Yeah, she seems low. Everyone left the room but she's still in there. I don't know if she's okay."

"So there's no one else inside except her?"

"Yeah?" She replied.

"And she isn't changing or anything, right?" I asked, just to be careful.

"No, she hasn't changed yet. Why are you grilling me with these weird questions?"

"Just making sure no one throws a shoe at me when I go inside," I said and walked into the locker room, making my footsteps intentionally louder so she would know someone was coming.

There was no sign of Avery but I could hear sniffles coming from somewhere in the room.

"Avery?" I said, not sure where the sound was coming from.

"Go away!" She yelled, but even her harsh words couldn't manage to sound strong as a quiver shook her voice. At least the direction of her voice gave me the location of her hiding spot. In three quick strides, I passed the rows of lockers until I was standing at the last one and there she was.

Sitting on the ground, her back against the locker and her knees drawn up to her chest. She hadn't changed out of her kit yet, her boots still covering the injury of her foot. I could tell she hadn't even thought of checking it yet. Before I could even take in her current state, she lifted her head and looked at me. Her eyes were red and puffy as more tears fell down her cheeks. She was shaking.

My heart sank.

Seeing her like this sent a rush of alarm in my body like there was something deeply wrong with the world and it needed to be fixed immediately. Her usual strong and confident demeanor was nowhere to be seen, a picture of vulnerability taking its place. As she met my concerned gaze, there was a rawness in her eyes I had never seen before. The eyes that always held fierceness and resilience were suddenly empty of any such defenses. The same boldness that once irritated me was now the only thing I wished to see on her face. I hated seeing her like this; it was like seeing Superman without his cape.

An overwhelming feeling came over me, a feeling that told me to hold her and wipe the tears from her face, and tell her that she didn't deserve to feel this way because of a stupid guy. To tell her she was far too powerful to be affected by an injury. It was an urge so overwhelming, that nothing in the world could have stopped me from acting on it. And, truly enough, nothing did.

14

AVERY

The walls were closing in on me and I was having a hard time dealing with the mess. All my fears from this morning came true the moment Jack kicked my foot. Not only did I lose the match, my ankle was probably injured. If my ankle is injured then forget the inter-school matches, I won't even be able to play inside the school. Leah and Kyle tried a lot to calm me down. They said it wasn't my fault, they believed me when I said Jack did it intentionally, and they kept saying it doesn't mean I lost my chances of getting selected either. But the problem was, even they knew it wasn't true. I could see it in their eyes. Their eyes held a hint of doubt like they were secretly worried their reassurances would soon disappoint me even more. They knew what happened was a pretty big mishap, and that my rash decision could count for a negative point in my favor in the eyes of the coach.

My breaths came in ragged gasps as I sat on the cold floor, my back pressed against the lockers. The stinging pain in my foot matched the ache in my chest, both throbbing with the weight of failure. I replayed the scene over and over in my mind—the crucial moment in the match when I made that impulsive decision. The decision that ended with Jack's cleat making a painful connection with my foot. The decision that left me questioning my abilities, my worth, and my place on the team.

I came here for this. I came to England for my dream, I came here for Football. Imagine the torment if I couldn't even get selected to play for our school. Imagine being good at one thing and still not being able to achieve a small milestone in the journey of that ambition. Not only was I falling behind in my studies, not only falling behind my former classmates but now I was falling behind in my game too. This was the last thing holding me together and now it was shattered as well.

There's actually nothing I can do properly. No matter what, I always fail.

I always fail. I always fail.

The reality of that phrase was settling in as it kept repeating in my head like a broken record.

It was getting hard for me to respond to Leah and Kyle's positive talk so I told them I was fine and that I just needed to be alone for a while. Thankfully, they respected my emotions and left, even though I could see the hesitance in Leah's eyes until her last step toward the door. I could sense that she wanted me to tell her to stay, she didn't want to leave me alone, but there was nothing else I deserved more than this pitiful solitude. Now I realized, what I needed was not some alone time. What I actually needed was to figure out what was wrong with me. How could I never manage to get ahead when everything in me was always desperately trying not to get left behind? I needed to know if I could ever manage to become a worthwhile person or if I was always going to be a loser like this. If I knew the answer, maybe it would be easier. It would be easier to accept defeat because I never expected to win.

If I knew I was always meant to fail in everything then I would never try. And if I knew I was always meant to win then I would never stop. It was just hard to be in this middle zone, where I kept trying to become better and yet always ended up disappointing myself.

And now, as if it couldn't get any worse, Noah walked in with all his winning glory, witnessing my sad pitiful state that I wished I could still erase from his memory.

"I said go away!" I said, trying my best to maintain my natural voice that was still betrayed by sobs. "I'm not in the mood to hear about your f-fantastic goal."

Just this morning I was running my big mouth and telling him how I'll win a place in the team. Now I was sitting with an injured foot in an empty locker room, crying a river of failure. His presence was only contributing to my humiliation. I wanted to disappear, I wanted to run away, I wanted to do anything except stare into his eyes as he looked at me with... wait, concern?

In all my past experiences with him, all the times he held annoyance, fury, challenges, or arrogance felt like a distant memory as I witnessed a flicker of genuine concern in his eyes, an emotion I saw in his eyes for the first time. My heart calmed down a little as I read his soft eyes, the eyes that told me he had no intention to bring me down.

"I'm not here to brag about anything." He said softly, taking a step in my direction. "Are you okay?"

His words hung in the air, and I wanted to scoff at the irony of the question. Of course, I wasn't okay. But Noah, with his sincerity, made me consider the possibility of being okay again.

"I'm fine," I said, wiping a tear with the back of my hand. But even as I said it, it was like my body refused to lie as more tears started falling down. Tears with much more intensity than before. With a silent thud of my heart, I realized I didn't want to lie about being fine anymore, I just wanted to accept my defeat and cry over it. No more pretending to be strong, no more holding it all in. I wanted to let it all go, accept my incompetence, and grieve over it.

It was like he understood the silent battle going on inside my head as he approached slowly, gentle as ever as if afraid I'd shatter at the slightest touch. He sat down beside me, his presence shifting from a mere interference to gentle reassurance. "Hey... it's okay," He said, his voice calming.

I had nothing to say at his generous act of compassion, I just did what I could at that moment- cry, cry, and cry some more as his attempts to comfort me were making me feel more vulnerable.

"Hey, please, please don't cry. Is your foot okay?" He reached for my foot, his touch gentle as he began to unlace my cleat. "Let me check if you're hurt."

He carefully took off my sock and I winced, a fresh wave of tears threatening to spill as he examined my ankle. "... it looks blue. Does it hurt?" He looked at me expectantly. I could tell he wanted me to say no.

I nodded slowly as I looked at my foot, I hadn't even thought of checking it yet. There was indeed a blue patch and it looked like it was going to swell pretty soon.

The sight of my injured ankle reminded me how I wouldn't be able to play all over again, and the suffocating feelings returned. More tears started falling as my body started to shake again, my mind racing with thoughts of failure. The sobs racked my body, each one a release of the pent-up frustration, disappointment, and self-blame.

I was so lost I didn't even notice when Noah got up and sat beside me, pulling me into a hug. The smell of his shampoo was overwhelming as always, blanketing me with a feeling of safety and validation as his warmth enveloped me completely. My breath hitched, and I clung to him as if he were an anchor in the storm of my emotions.

"Hey it's okay, it's not a big injury. We get injured like that all the time. It will get better in just a week or two, why are you crying?" He was rubbing his hand over my shoulder, comforting my shaking form.

"It's not t-that." I cried, finally letting my emotions flow out of me. "What's the point even if it gets better? Coach still wouldn't select me for the team. I couldn't prove myself to him." The sobs were escaping without my permission, vulnerable and weak.

"Who said that?" His voice was a source of stability in my stumbling state.

"I know that." His hoodie was getting soaked with my tears. "I was so stupid I thought I would win. But I failed. I failed again. I failed just like always."

It was like my words were a message for him to hold me tighter, because the more vulnerable I got the more he hugged me into a sense of stability. "You weren't stupid. You were admirable. And your confidence wasn't misplaced, believe me."

"You just don't know." Even though his words were sincere, somewhere inside my head a voice was telling me that he was only saying it because he didn't know about my past failures. He didn't know I failed a class, he didn't know just how far back my connection with failure goes.

He whispered words of comfort, his voice a soothing balm to my wounded spirit. "Avery, it wasn't your fault. These things happen in the game. You're not a failure."

But I felt like one. Coming to England with dreams of proving myself, only to end up injured and defeated. Maybe he should know the reality of my setbacks. Maybe if he knew how useless I was, he wouldn't try to console me with these words. I pulled away from him, wiping my tears with the back of my hand. I was one hundred percent sure I looked like an over-steamed dumpling right now but I didn't care.

"Do you know why I came here?" I asked him, his eyes looking back at me with the need for an answer. "It wasn't all about football. I failed back in the States." I confessed, my voice shaky. "All my classmates went ahead without me and I was the only one left behind."

Noah looked at me, his eyes unwavering. "We all stumble, Avery. It's how we get back up that matters." I expected him to look at me differently after knowing that, or at the very least I expected him to seem staggered when hearing about my big failure but he acted like it was no big deal. It was strangely comforting. He took my hands, holding them to make sure his warmth calmed down the shakiness. "Yes, maybe you failed a grade but it doesn't mean that will be your reality forever. You're not defined by one mistake. You're defined by how you pick yourself up after."

"But it wasn't just one mistake." I looked into his eyes, desperately needing to hear his words even as everything in my body rejected the idea of holding myself valuable. "I thought I could make a fresh start, match the pace with my classmates this time, but I'm just repeating the same mistakes again." It was like I wanted to tell him all my faults and all my weaknesses so he would finally believe just how useless I was. Maybe he would stop telling me all these nice things if he knew my sad reality. "And now, I've probably ruined my chances of making the school team too. Everyone will go ahead to play without me and I will be left behind again. Just like last time. Just like every time. I'm not worth anything, Noah." The last sentence came out way rawer than I meant it to be and his hands fiercely tensed at my words.

"Avery, you deserve to be here. You're worth everything that comes your way." His words were stern and unmoving, not betraying any hint of doubt. "Nothing is ruined and you're not going to be left behind. You deserve a spot on the team just as much as anyone else. Jack might have a flashy kick, but you have heart, determination, and skill. I'm sure our coach isn't blind enough to miss that."

His words reached a dark corner in my heart and for the first time since the match, a glimmer of hope ignited within me. I nodded, wiping away the last traces of tears.

Noah smiled, a genuine, comforting smile that reached his eyes. His hands left mine as he massaged my ankle gently, taking away some of the pain. "You'll get through this, Avery. And you'll be stronger for it."

As numb as my face felt, I couldn't hold a tiny smile from escaping my lips. "Thank you. You are..." *So wonderfully kind, compassionate, downright amazing.* "Tolerable."

The playful change in my tone visibly relaxed him, and a certain warmth found his eyes at the sight of my smile. "Geez, don't say thanks, Kai. Makes it sound like we are friends." He looked at me a second longer before reaching into his bag and taking out a water bottle. "There's supposed to be seventy percent water in a healthy human body and you probably cried out sixty."

He handed me the bottle and it suddenly occurred to me that I was actually very thirsty. Having an emotional breakdown right after playing a full match sure was exhausting. I gratefully took the bottle and chugged almost all of it, the cold water washing down my throat, moistening all the dry organs inside me.

"Avery?" Someone said and we both turned in the direction of the voice, discovering Mia and Leah standing beside the lockers, looking at us like they saw snow in March.

Leah was quite surprised to see Noah sitting beside me when I clearly told her to leave me alone a few minutes ago, but Mia was looking at me with a specific glint in her eyes. A glint that said 'I knew it.'

My eyes went wide and I started shaking my head at Mia the minute a smile came upon her face, warning her with my eyes not to embarrass me in front of him.

Noah seemed unbothered. "What kind of friends are you? Leaving your friend alone when she's going through a crisis." He said it casually like he didn't care about 'the crisis' but just wanted to say something to shame them. And just like that, the same old unbothered Noah was back. Like he wasn't just stroking my back a minute ago or hugging me until my panic attack went away. He stood up and picked up his duffel bag, walking towards them.

"Anyway, I filled in for your friendly duties." He looked back at me. "Take a shower Kai, the match ended an hour ago." And with that, he walked out of the locker room, leaving me with Leah, Mia, and their contrasting stares.

"How's your foot?" Leah asked, examining it herself.

"I think it's sprained. Noah said it'll get better in a week or two." I told her.

"I *knew* there was something going on, I could smell it from a mile away," Mia said enthusiastically and that's when Leah caught up to the situation.

"Something what?" Leah asked her.

"I thought you hated Noah? Why was he tending to your injuries after the match?" Mia ignored her question and asked me another.

"There's nothing like that Mia, shut up!" I got up and opened my locker, taking out some clean casual clothes.

"You sent everyone away when we asked if you were okay," Leah said slowly like she was uncovering a mystery and was about to reach the conclusion.

"She did?" Mia asked, surprised but somehow still not surprised.

"And then we find you here with *him*." Leah continued.

"We did!" Mia ended, as they both looked at me with proud expressions plastered on their faces.

Their know-it-all stares made me feel exposed like they were looking at all the secrets I kept hidden inside my head. My cheeks went pink, but I'm sure it's only because of all the crying. *I swear* they have it wrong.

"You both are *so* dramatic." I turned around to hide my red face and went inside the stall, finally taking a shower. A good long shower after a tiring match and lots of crying hits different. I came out feeling lighter and better. Mia and Leah were on their phones, so it seemed like the embarrassing topic of Noah was thankfully out of their heads now.

"Guys I'm hungry," I said while stuffing my team kit and cleats into the duffel bag.

"No shit, me too." Leah joined and got up from the bench, already walking toward the door.

"I heard we have Mac-n-Cheese today," Mia said and followed Leah outside.

I silently let out a breath of relief at the change of topic. They might have forgotten about the Noah thing, but it seemed like it was going to take up some permanent space in my head. I was so far deep in my inevitable breakdown, but somehow he managed to pull me back. On the list of all the people who could have made me feel better at a time like this, Noah was the last. He sure was first on the list of people who could push me into a rage. But not this.

And yet, his warmth still calmed me long after he let go, and I no longer felt a crushing sense of defeat. I mean, yes I lost the match, and yes I injured myself, but if I let myself fall into a hopeless pit of despair then I won't be able to get out of it. I have been there before. I have been hopeless before. And as a long-term resident of that place, I know it doesn't do me any good, especially when what I need is to stand back up and try to be better. This isn't the end. Not being on the school team left a big hole in my heart, sure. But that doesn't mean playing intra-school is any less of an achievement. I will keep playing. I will keep trying. As long as I have football, I haven't lost anything.

15

NOAH

"Mia texted me! Do you see that?" Mason showed me his phone screen, where I could see a text from Mia that read 'Congrats on your win'. The dining hall wasn't quite full on this blissful Sunday morning, as most of the students went to the city to spend the weekend. The only people that were left behind were the members of the sports club, too tired and hungover from yesterday's match to do anything except lounge in our respective common rooms.

"Wow, when's the wedding?" I asked him, and he quickly took his phone back.

"Fine, maybe it's not a big thing, but it *is* big to *me*. The more she sees Lily flirting with me the less she ignores me. Does it mean she's jealous?" He asked, all smiles and rainbows as he looked back into his phone.

"Maybe. But I don't understand girls. First, she acts like she doesn't like you, and then she gets jealous when someone flirts with you. What's up with that?" I returned to my bowl of Rigatoni, clueless to the things that went on in a girl's mind.

"That's how girls work, Mr. Yildiz. Knowing Mia, I can tell she's too shy to admit she likes me even to herself, let alone to *me*. So until she comes to that realization, I think I'll just bask in the knowledge that she got jealous and be happy until she decides to make a move." He looked over at Mia who was sitting two tables away, and she smiled at him for a millisecond before returning her attention to her friends. That one millisecond probably gave Mason enough happiness to last the whole day.

If you asked me about this a few days ago, I would tell you I don't understand why or how he can admire someone so much that even the slightest bit of attention from her can make his whole day. But now as I caught sight of Avery, and now that she gave me a small smile, I knew how. I could see how a small smile from someone could make your whole day, almost as if their happiness fueled your own.

But the blissful moment lasted for just a second more before Coach Martinez stepped into the dining hall with a notepad in his hands, looking around the room to make sure the members of our club were there. He nodded to himself as he realized all the students from the match were already gathered here, so he could save his energy by addressing all of them in a single place.

Only, he wasn't here to address, he was here to announce a lineup.

"In my hands, I have the list of the players who are selected for the school team ahead of our inter-school matches. Whoever is called, please report to the ground after breakfast."

This roll call was something I was familiar with. When I first started playing here, I used to get nervous during the roll call, and rightfully so because I didn't get selected the first year around. But after that initial year of rejection, I got selected the second time around, and ever since then, the uncertainty that came with these roll calls was a stranger to me. Because after that, I was always confident about getting selected. And yet, even though I have been getting selected for the last two years and there was no reason for me to be dropped this year either, a queasy feeling still found its way into my stomach and settled there. I surprised myself as I suddenly found myself wishing for a particular name to be called out, against all odds. A name that maybe a few weeks ago would have annoyed me or a name that I would have actively wished wouldn't get selected.

The roll call began with Coach Martinez raising his voice so that it reached every corner of our big dining hall.

"Kyle Evans," A few claps erupted from the students for the captain of the Blue team, who was obviously going to be selected.

"Henry Fisher," The captain of the Yellow team received a smaller amount of applause as his captaincy wasn't the most adored.

"Diana Davis, Fred Smith, Ellie Walker," With each name he took, a few claps followed, the friends and supporters of each player cheering them on for getting selected.

"Mason Williams," Again, obvious.

I looked over at Avery, who was unaware of my gaze and was listening intently to each pause he took before announcing the names. Despite her panic attack in the locker room yesterday, her eyes still shone with a bit of hope. She still hoped that the Coach would look past her mistakes and recognize her for her talent. She hoped that maybe, she still had a chance. But with every name being taken, the hope in her eyes diminished, like a candle light flickering in the dark.

"Noah Yildiz," My name snapped me out of my thoughts, as our table clapped for me. I looked around and smiled, grateful that I was selected this year too, although I had no reason to think I wouldn't. After the little applause, my ears tuned back to the Coach's voice and my eyes went toward Avery for just a second more. She was waiting so intently I wanted to snatch the note-pad from the Coach's hand and announce her name myself.

"Ryan Morris, Harry Hughes and..."

The room fell silent in anticipation as he paused. My breath was stuck in my throat and it threatened to stay that way until Coach spit out the last name.

"Chloe Lewis." He ended.

The breath Avery let out was just a bit short of a sigh. She nodded and looked down, moving the pasta on her plate with a fork with no intention of eating it. Even though I couldn't see her eyes clearly from here, I had a feeling she was pushing back a few tears. My heart went down with a sigh as well, and I realized I was waiting for her name to be called almost just as much as she was.

"But that's just ten," Jack spoke up from beside Henry, a troubled look on his face. "And why wasn't I called?"

It was then that I realized that his name wasn't taken either. He had been so confident about getting picked, and his face said all the things he was feeling loudly. Shock, anger, betrayal. He looked at the Coach like it was his birthright to get a spot on the team and the Coach just committed a felony by not giving it to him. Maybe it was wrong, but the news pleased me more than it should have. He might have been my teammate all along, but he never played like one. I never felt the sense of camaraderie from him that I felt from my other teammates. I could have been more connected with a street cat than I was with him.

As if answering Jack's question Coach continued, "I currently only want these ten players to attend the meeting. We ought to have a discussion before we go ahead. Meet me on the ground after..." He looked at his wristwatch. "Fifteen minutes." He gave us all a nod and left behind a mix of happy students who got selected and a bunch of disappointed ones who did not.

"I'm not going to let this go. How can he not select me after I literally made us win the game today?" Jack was visibly fuming, we could expect to see steam coming out of his ears any minute now.

"There's still a spot left. Maybe he wants to consider someone else too." Mason said casually, not catching up on Jack's anger.

"If it's that stupid girl, Avery, I swear to God..." He said, rubbing his forehead.

"What about her, huh? I don't see anything wrong with Coach selecting her." An edge of irritation entered my voice. The way he took her name like it was hurting him to say it made me want to punch his face.

"Seriously Yildiz? She's a rookie! She probably doesn't even know what she's doing, everything she's done so far could be a fluke." He stabbed his fork into the pasta and stuffed it in his mouth.

"Or maybe her continuous 'fluke' is actually her hard work and skill." My eyes never left his face as I said my words sternly.

He glared at me for a second before pointing his fork at me. "You better not say all this bullshit to the Coach." He warned me.

"Or what?" I wanted to laugh at his attempt to intimidate me. He might be buff and big, but that doesn't scare me even a bit. If he thought I was going to sit here and let him tell me what to do then he was severely mistaken.

He nodded and slowly lowered his fork, meeting my defiant stare with a firm one of his own. "You better watch out." He went back to using his fork like a utensil instead of a weapon.

"I don't need to." If he said anything after that, I didn't hear it because I picked up my tray and went to sit at a different table. Mason and Theo picked up their trays and joined me as well, a nervous look on their faces.

"Dude, I've never seen you like that. What's the matter?" Theo asked.

"His arrogance and pride is the matter." I ignored the knowing gazes they were exchanging, clearly not missing the fact that this was about much more than just his ego.

Later in the day, we gathered on the ground as the new official team of the Summerfield Institute. Seven of us were the same players as before, but there were three new additions to our team. Ben had been dropped from the Goalkeeping position, and Ellie was selected to be our goalkeeper this year. Oliver and Garret had been dropped to bring Fred and Ryan to the team. Other than that, the rest of the team was all here, except for Jack. Which I was wholeheartedly grateful for.

"I know it's unusual for us to have a meeting like this ahead of an inter-school match." Coach Martinez started, standing in front of us as we all stood in a line. "But I believed it would be better if all members of the team could weigh in on this decision."

We all knew what decision he was talking about before he even clarified, but what we didn't know was *who* he had chosen to stand against Jack.

"As we know, despite being new, Avery Kai has proved to be valuable for her team so far." He said, and it was like the nervousness that had been building up in my stomach since breakfast was finally starting to disappear. Coach did realize her potential, and even if he seemed hesitant to include her in the team right now, I was happy to know that at least he was considering it.

"However, you must have noticed that I also redacted a valuable defender from joining us, and I need to consider what you all think about the importance of having Jack in the team."

Well, I, for one, didn't see any importance in having him on the team, but I had to be patient and listen to his whole speech before stating that.

"I want you guys to consider this matter thoroughly, so I will present some facts in front of you." He continued. "As we know, Avery Kai plays midfield and Jack Wright plays defense. Avery is a new member, and she has never been to any inter-school matches in England, which might affect her performance. It also means that it might take some time for her to adjust to the new atmosphere, and she might also lack the bonding that is needed for a good team. On the other hand, Jack is familiar and already has a bond with the team, but some of his mistakes in the past have caused us to lose some matches."

I see the others nodding along to his words, considering the facts before coming to a conclusion.

"I am torn as to whether it's more important for us to recruit new talent, or rely on the familiar skills of our old teammate." He looked at us, each of us still looking confused about the decision. "There's also the fact that losing Jack would mean we will lose an important part of our defense system, meanwhile recruiting Avery would mean we can strengthen our midfield and make our attack formation stronger than before. I have observed Avery's playmaking, and I have to say I was pretty impressed before yesterday's match." His face twisted into a frown. "Yesterday I saw her ignoring her team's formation and going for the goal herself, which caused her to injure herself. It was a pretty reckless move if you ask me, and it affects her chances of being selected."

I looked down. I knew why she was reckless, and I also knew it was not something Avery usually does. She was tense and anxious about the outcome of the match, and Coach was still thinking that the injury might have been accidental. It might not have been a part of their strategy, but the decision she took was definitely going to result in a goal. It wasn't her fault Jack tripped her intentionally, and it surely wasn't her fault that she was now sitting on the bench with an injury. If Jack had done it just a few inches ahead, it would have been a penalty which was actually good for her team, which meant it would have been

Jack who made a bad decision, not Avery. She was just in the wrong place at the wrong time.

"I want to hear what you guys have to say about this situation. I will consider each and every one of your opinions." He finished, looking at us to start a discussion.

Henry raised his hand and Coach gestured at him to speak. "I think if we don't take Jack then it might weaken our defense. We all know how strong Oakwood's Defense is, and it's always hard for us to get through it to score. I think we should also prioritize having a strong defense like them."

His argument immediately crossed with mine and my hand instinctively went up. "I don't think we should be focusing on copying other teams' strategies, I think we should be recognizing the abilities of our own players and create our strategies according to that."

There weren't any strong agreements to my point but Mason nodded like he was on board.

"But I don't think we should be taking in a newbie," Ryan said. He plays defense as well, so he and Jack are pretty close. Of course, he'll take his side. "She just moved here from America and we are going to take her in the official team? I think it's too soon. We should let her play intra-school for a year before we consider taking her the next year."

Coach nodded at his input and it immediately set my nerves on fire.

"She isn't a newbie in football, she is only a newbie in England," I said to Ryan and turned to the Coach. "How are we supposed to bond as a team if we are not even giving her a chance to be in it."

It seemed like I was the only one taking Avery's side so I elbowed Mason on his side and he immediately stood straighter.

"Yeah, I also think team-building is not an issue and we should give her a chance." He said. "I got you, lover boy." He whispered to me.

I glared in response. "This has nothing to do with her."

"Sure." He winked.

I rolled my eyes and realized Chloe was also nodding in agreement. "As a midfielder myself, I recognize her skills in playmaking. I have often seen her mapping out possibilities and acting on it in an instant, I think she would be an asset to the team. And honestly, I don't think team building would be an issue because she's very friendly and nice."

I let out a sigh of relief, grateful that I wasn't the only one taking a stand for her here.

Coach nodded with narrowed eyes but it still seemed like he liked Jack's arguments better.

"Noah, you seem to have a strong opinion about Kai." He said to me, which made me feel a bit exposed like I was caught red-handed while doing a robbery. Which was a bit weird honestly, because I wasn't doing anything secretly or holding an ulterior motive.

"Because I believe Jack isn't a good team player sir."

"Seven out of ten people here think that Jack is actually helpful for the team. I really want to know how Avery can benefit us more than him?"

I had about a hundred answers to that question, but I thought of voicing the most important ones.

"As a striker myself, I think she has every ability to control the flow of the game before it comes to m-"

"Did you see her ruining her team's play yesterday?" Henry asked with a condescending tone like he was suggesting she didn't know what she was doing. "She injured herself and gave our team an opportunity to score. It would be a problem if she did that to our own team some day, during a much more serious match."

I hesitated for a moment if telling everyone about his intentional foul would be okay, but then his 'warning' in the canteen crossed my mind and his arrogance frustrated me all over again. Who does he think he is? Why should I protect his image when he didn't hesitate to injure a player?

"About that Coach." I turned to him, looking away from Henry because his Jack-obsessed words were starting to piss me off. "Jack intentionally kicked her foot when she was right outside the penalty box, which means *he* was the one who would have created an opportunity for them to score if he just had been a few inches ahead."

"Later on in the game he gave you the assist for the goal you scored. How can you say it was a bad move?" Henry looked offended.

"Yes he did and yes I scored from it. But why was he in our attack in the first place? Just like yesterday, he has often changed our game plan by doing something completely selfish and had cost us many goals in the past. He's a defender but he's often jumping around in our attack. If we're gonna have a hole in our defense anyway why not just invest in an actual midfielder who would improve our offense."

Coach nodded. "Noah, do you actually take the responsibility for that decision? You're the only one who's pushing that far, so I want to be sure that you're confident about her."

I thought about it for a second. *Is it worth it?* Would it come back to me if she ever messed up in our games in the future?

But then her words after the match flashed in my head and I remembered just how badly she wanted this. I remembered how many times she gave me a run for my money and created multiple assists for her team. She wanted a place in the team so bad. And she deserved every bit of it.

"No one knows the capability of a person more than their rival. She plays against me pretty much as my clear enemy, and one thing it has taught me is that she shouldn't be underestimated. I believe in her skills to the point I'm willing to take responsibility for her performance. If she ever messes up, you can bench me for the rest of the year and bring Jack in." I said confidently, turning heads in my direction. Most prominently, Mason's.

"Dude!" He whisper-yelled, clearly not liking the idea of me sitting on the bench.

But Coach was looking at me with a conclusive stare, and I took it upon myself to match that stare with a confident one of my own. He was looking for a hint of doubt, any sign that I might have spoken too much or oversold her abilities, but he couldn't find anything. I meant every word I said, and I knew I would never have to worry about getting benched because I knew Avery would never take her spot lightly. I know if she was given the chance, she would prove herself to the Moon and back.

"Does anyone else have the same belief regarding Jack?" He looked at me a moment more before switching to look at the rest of the team, but no one spoke out after that. Putting their own spot at risk for a selfish person like Jack was inherently too much to ask. And even Henry wouldn't put that much trust in him.

"Maybe we can take her in as a substitute?" Chloe spoke up and everyone turned to her. "If Coach isn't sure about her then we don't have to keep her in the line-up. But she would definitely be useful if someone's injured or has a yellow against them." She suggested the middle ground.

Coach nodded slowly, considering the idea.

"And if Avery does well, we can bench Jack too," I added.

Coach nodded one swift nod. "Fine then. I believe we have come to a conclusion."

Everyone else nodded, as a picture of Jack sitting on the bench was already giving me a deep sense of satisfaction.

"I'll inform Avery about the decision and she will join the additional team training from tomorrow." He said while writing something down in his notepad, which was most probably her name. "Run two laps and then we'll start with some drills." He blew the whistle and everyone dispersed, warming up their hands and legs for the practice.

"You took a massive risk there, mate," Mason said, bending down and stretching his legs.

"It's not a risk if I know she won't let me down," I replied, my heart letting out the biggest sigh of relief as I thought how happy she would be when she got to know she was selected for the school's official team. Even if it was as a substitute.

16

AVERY

"Don't tell Dad about this," I said, nervously playing with the hem of my sleeve.

"I won't, but even if you tell him he's not going to be mad you know?" Ella said in a low voice. Her roommate was sleeping so the lights in her room were off and she was wearing headphones. It was quite late in America, but I could see her properly since the light from the laptop was illuminating her face.

"I know. It's still embarrassing. One of the biggest reasons for me to come here was football, and guess what? I couldn't even get selected for the school team." Tears were threatening to make an appearance again, but I didn't wanna cry in front of her. She was always so strong and put together, it was getting embarrassing to be always losing my shit at this point.

"You've been there four months, give it a rest. Playing for a school club is a big thing, maybe they just don't take new students right off the bat." She tried to console me.

"But they've seen my game already. Am I that bad?"

"Not being great doesn't equal being bad. Mia sends me your videos sometimes. I've seen how good you are. Yes, not being selected feels like a defeat. But you shouldn't start doubting your ambitions because of that." It was like she read my mind, I was wondering if I even deserved to dream about playing for a club one day. "Things take time. You really need to stop blaming yourself. Believe me, if I thought you were slacking off I would've told you that straight away."

"I believe you." And I really do, but it's hard to believe her words even if she said it with certainty. The constant blame I've often heard from people and how it's always because of my 'laziness' has taken a permanent spot in my brain. Now whenever I'm not able to achieve something, I always think it's because I slacked off.

"Anyway, did you see Daisy's pictures? After all those years begging them for a cat, *now* they get one." She started scrolling through her phone looking at pictures of Daisy, the cat our parents got last week. They sent the pictures to our family group, which honestly made me miss being home. There was a picture of Mom petting her on the couch and a picture of Dad lifting her up to let her see outside the window.

"They should put up a cat tree and those hanging seats by the window. I bet Daisy will love all the bird watching." I was very excited about having a pet cat, even though I hadn't seen her in real life. I counted down the days when I would get to pet her, probably six months from now.

"I'm gonna bring her so many treats when I visit home next weekend," Ella said, squealing a little. Ella and I both shared an undying affection for cats, and Daisy's arrival got us both excited even miles away from home.

"Don't get too many though, I bet Dad is already spoiling her as we speak." A huge part of me envied Ella right then, for being able to visit them easily and often. She could visit every week and whenever she wanted and then here I was, I only had the option to visit them twice a year.

She yawned a big yawn and the light from her laptop highlighted the tiredness of her eyes. "You should sleep," I told her, even though I wanted to keep talking for an hour more. Talking to her always made me feel closer to home.

"Yes, I'm kinda tired. I'll call you soon, okay?" She yawned again, her eyes heavy.

"Good night!" I ended the call, shut the laptop, and laid down myself. It was a Sunday morning so we had no classes and breakfast wasn't served for another two hours. As I tried to rest, my mind refused to settle down and kept going through everything all at once. Failing my junior year, coming here, failing my tests, missing my family, not getting selected, all of it. I wondered if it was worth it to make such a bold move after all. I imagined what it would be like if I never came here. I won't be able to achieve much in terms of football, but I will be home. I wasn't achieving much here anyway. Despite what Ella said, I couldn't help doubting myself. What if it was a mistake? What if I actually don't have what it takes? What if taking such a big step for my dream was a bad choice after all?

Monday morning, I was sitting in the Physics class, absentmindedly drawing doodles on my notebook, when a crumpled-up piece of paper flew in and landed on my notebook. I glanced in the direction it came from and saw Liam giving me a smile. Before he could notice the redness on my cheeks, I looked down and opened the note- which made me smile even bigger.

'Excuse me, have you lost an electron? Because you are positively attractive.'

A chuckle left my mouth and I looked toward the window on the left, where Liam was giggling as well. I looked back at the paper- am I seriously receiving cute notes from my crush?

"So cheesy." I jumped from the sudden comment that came from my right and saw Noah standing beside me reading the note in my hands. He must have arrived just now and stopped on his way to his seat when he saw me blushing. He had his backpack on his right shoulder and his left hand was in his pocket.

"When did you-"

"Just now, when you were busy with the task of staring at the paper." He went around and sat on the seat behind me, shuffling in his bag to take some books out.

"It's not cheesy, it's cute." I turned around and whispered.

"Whatever you say, cheeseball." He raised his hands in surrender, still wearing a mischievous grin. I rolled my eyes and turned my attention back to Mr. Evans, determined to concentrate on the lesson despite the newfound butterflies in my stomach.

"Should I, or should I not?" I wondered aloud, lying on my bed as Mia was busy doing her homework.

"Should you what?" She asked, looking up from her textbook.

"Go for the training." My ankle was still positively sprained, but it wasn't bad enough to give me trouble while walking. At the same time, I wasn't sure if playing more with my left foot would actually make it worse.

"I think Coach can tell you the answer to that. At least show up to the training." She answered.

I pushed a pillow down on my face. "But I'm so embarrassed. I don't feel like facing everyone there. Especially Noah. I was so confident about getting selected I didn't hesitate to run my big mouth before the game. What if he makes fun of me?" I looked at her from under the pillow.

She sighed. "Well, then at least you learned not to talk a big game before you actually win. I think you should go. How long can you even avoid him, he will eventually catch up to you."

I threw the pillow aside and sat up, still debating it in my head. "What if I injure my ankle more?"

"Your teammates would know that better than me, don't you think?" She pushed.

"You're so mean." I picked up my duffel bag and started stuffing it with my soccer stuff.

"I just don't want you to skip practices just because you're embarrassed for not getting selected Ave. Sometimes we don't achieve things on the first try, and that's okay. How do you expect to get selected next year if you just give up like this today?" She went back to writing something like she didn't just deliver a solid motivational speech.

Suddenly there was a loud banging on my door followed by "Ave? Ave!! Open the door!"

I opened the door and Leah stormed in, fully dressed in her kit.

"Why aren't you on the ground?!" She asked like she was my mom and just found out I was skipping classes.

"I was just about to come." I showed her my fully packed duffle bag.

"Was she?" She asked Mia.

I could have expected my best friend to take my side but no, she just shook her head and ratted me out. Leah folded her arms and gave me a stern look.

"Well I'm coming NOW!" I slung the bag over my shoulder and marched out, waiting for Leah to follow me.

When I reached the ground, everyone was already done with their warmups and was busy practicing some passing drills. Since Coach Martinez was busy talking to Noah on the far end of the field, I just started my lap around the ground without informing him first. However, when I reached the end of the field where Noah and Coach were standing, he noticed me and called me over.

"Yes, sir?" I asked, a bit out of breath.

Noah was standing beside him, and when I reached over, the corners of his mouth tugged up, with a hint of amusement in his eyes. That little shit, he's probably basking in the fact that I wasn't selected. Coach cleared his throat and brought my attention back to him.

"I might be quite a casual coach but I don't tolerate tardiness when it comes to our official team members." He said, looking me in the eyes.

Official team members? Confused, I glanced between Coach and Noah, my mind racing to figure out what I had missed, but Noah was still looking at me with that smile like he couldn't hold in his amusement.

I mustered a nervous smile. "Um, Coach, I'm not on the team."

"Oh wait, did I not inform you?"

That one sentence caused an explosion in my body, my heart suddenly racing like it was a car in fast and furious. "Inform about?" I faltered, not letting myself get too far ahead. Maybe he's talking about something else, there has to be an explanation.

"We have taken the decision to select you for our school club." My hand went up to cover my mouth, still not being able to believe his words. "As a reserve, for now." He added quickly as if he didn't want me getting too happy about that. But that didn't affect my excitement because it still meant I was a part of the team, even if it was on the bench. It was still better than not being a part at all. "Welcome to Summerfield Football Club." He patted my back.

"Are you- Did I really-"

"Yes, you did. But that also means you have to attend the extra training and take out an additional hour from your day." He informed.

"Of course, why wouldn't I, thank you so much for selecting me, I-"

"You earned it kid." He said and gestured his hand toward Noah. "Noah here said-"

"Uh sir, aren't we getting late for the practice?" Noah added hastily, looking at this watch like we were running out of time. Even though the training had just started ten minutes ago.

Interrupted, Coach looked down at his own watch. "Oh yeah, the training. I should check on the others." He turned to me again, this time saying something completely different. "Do your best kid, I'm counting on you." And with that, he went off to yell at someone else about their passing technique.

"What was he-" I started to ask what he was saying, but Noah interrupted me again just like he interrupted Coach.

"So you did get selected. I'm glad." He said it like he just found out about my selection. Maybe Coach actually forgot to mention it to the others, just like he forgot to inform me about it.

"Thank you." I was so happy I didn't know what else to say.

"How's your foot?"

I looked down and moved it a bit. It hurt slightly. "I guess I have a sprain." I looked back up at his face and smiled. "But it's okay. It'll get better if I keep playing with it."

"I'll get better if I keep playing with it?" He repeated the same sentence with a new tone of his own, a tone that suggested that the sentence was stupid. "Are you even wearing a brace?"

"... was I supposed to?" I asked sheepishly. I hadn't even thought of doing that. "But you said it'll get better in a week or two."

"Yes, if you put on a brace." He said it was the most common knowledge on Earth. "Maybe even before that if you are careful."

"Is it my fault you didn't mention it?" I wasn't going to let him act like I was stupid, even if it was actually true. "I don't get injured often." I defended myself. In fact, this was the first ankle injury I had. I didn't know Jack back in America so I was all good.

"You're so-" He stopped himself, his eyes telling me something had suddenly crossed his mind. "Wait here." He went running towards the touchline, rummaging through his gym bag. Moments later, he returned, brandishing an ankle brace.

"You can't just play like that without support." He knelt down and took off my shoe before taking off my sock as well.

"What are you doing?" I protested, my face starting to feel a bit hot.

"Stay still, you need to wear a brace." He said, his movements deliberate as he expertly positioned the ankle brace around my injured joint. "Tell me if it's too tight."

I winced slightly as he secured the brace, but the added support brought me instant relief. "That's it, I think that's enough," I told him, and he gently locked it up.

A ton of relief and gratitude washed over me, but I didn't think I could even express it without sounding too nice. Being nice to him just felt weird.

"Wear this while playing for at least a week." He said. Carefully, he put my shoe back on my foot, as the brace sat perfectly snug inside the shoe. "You're such a noob with injuries."

I tried to stay calm but something inside my chest was fluttering uncontrollably. I tried to tone it down, believe me, but the sight of Noah kneeling down and carefully tying my shoelaces was not helping. How did he go from getting on my nerves to absolutely flattering me by pulling something like this so casually? I was actually having a Cinderella moment in real life and the Prince was none other than Noah Yildiz. Who would've thought?

He definitely had no idea the amount of thoughts and feelings that just went through my head and heart in the span of two minutes, because he just stood up and looked at me expectantly like he wanted feedback. I blinked. Oh right. The brace. The ground. My injury. I shook my head out of its trance and focused on the feeling of my foot. I moved it a little bit to test out the flexibility. Actually, it did feel better to move it now, more easy. The brace was supporting my ankle and gave it a lot of relief from the mild pressure.

"It feels... better." I moved my foot in circles, just to make sure there were no weak spots. "Thank you."

"Well, you're my teammate now. I have to deal with the consequences." He started jogging towards the rest of the students, calling me after him. "Come on now Captain America, we got lots to do."

A chuckle left my mouth as I saw him excitedly jogging toward the others. So he was my teammate now? One thing led to another and I reached a bigger realization- I was eventually going to be playing for the school? Against other schools? The whole reality of the situation hit me, and I felt a thousand times better than I did yesterday. Being on the bench still meant I could get lots of chances to play, even if it was not full-time.

I couldn't help but feel grateful for the turn of events. Just moments ago, I doubted my decision to come to England, questioning if my dreams were too far-fetched. Now, as a substitute on the official school team, I realized every step had been worth it. This was my chance to witness my dreams slowly materializing, and I was ready for the journey ahead.

The little snowball of my ambitions had finally tipped off the edge and the more it went down the mountain of my dreams, the more it would grow. There was hope for so much more and the questions that went through my mind in the morning finally had answers.

That taking bold steps for your dreams was never a bad choice. It could never be. Because no matter how slow or small, eventually, you will be where you want to be if you never stop trying.

17

NOAH

"I don't wanna go to the city today," I said after fifteen minutes of Deniz insisting I go. I was just passing through the grounds to get some snacks from the vending machine so I could just stay in my room and play video games all day but then she caught me having a good lazy time and came up with a plan to ruin it.

"But I finished my box of Turkish Delights two weeks ago. You've been saying you'll get them next week but you never go." She made a puppy face, her eyes all big and soft. There wasn't much she asked for, so that face only made an appearance once in a while.

"Fine." I could never hold being stern with her, she always managed to cave me in. Me and Dad alike. We can never say no to her. "What do you want?"

Elementary schoolers weren't allowed to go outside the school premises without their parents, so Deniz had a habit of giving me a list of all the stuff she wanted from the city. We do have some snacks available in the school, but she likes the traditional Turkish snacks that we don't get over here. I would prefer to buy all her snacks from our own shop, but it was all the way up in Liverpool and going there every other week was practically impossible. I was thankful for London being a big, diverse city because I could always find whatever she wanted over here as well.

"The same box of Turkish Delight you got last time. It was so good and had four different flavors!" She clapped her tiny hands as her lips turned into the cutest smile.

"Okay." I tried messing up her hair but she swatted my hand away. "Mason's going to London today, guess I'll go with him."

"Yay!" She squealed and ran away, joining her friends on the ground to resume her game of tag.

I wasn't really in the mood for a trip to the city today, but since Deniz had been asking for those candies for so long, I thought I might as well just get it. I could easily sacrifice ten other Sundays just to make her happy. When I went back to our room, Mason was already all dressed up in his casual outfit- a green and white T-shirt with denim jeans. He was brushing out his hair when he noticed me walk into the room.

"You look like you're going for a Celtics game," I said, landing down on my bed.

"And you look like you're going to spend the day alone in your room." He replied, putting down the hairbrush and turning to me.

"Before you try to insist, yes. Yes, I am coming too." I got up and looked into the mirror as well, making sure my hair wasn't too messy. Of course, I liked it messy, but there was a certain line I never wanted to cross. There was a difference between looking effortlessly cool and straight-up untidy. I checked myself out with the dark green T-shirt and black pants I was wearing, and with how good it was looking, I didn't think I needed to change.

"Are we taking the bus?"

"No, I'm taking my car." He said, getting the keys from his nightstand drawer.

I groaned. "But it's a Sunday, and there will be so much traffic."

"Geez, you don't even need to wait to turn into a forty-year-old man, you already sound like one." He said and walked out the door as I followed him out with much less enthusiasm. I didn't get to laze around in my room all Sunday, but now that I had to go, I tried to tell myself maybe a day out in London wouldn't be so bad.

As we were walking by the school bus stop, someone called out Mason's name and we both halted to see who it was. It was Lily, waving her hand at Mason with the biggest smile on her face. As we started walking toward the bus stop, I mentally prepared myself for the cheesy flirting that was going to be thrown toward him any moment now. Lily had been dropping hints about liking Mason for a long time, but with how much he was obsessed with Mia, he never responded with more flirting.

As we approached the bus stop, I saw some other people waiting for the bus and that was when I realized this impromptu casual meeting was probably going to turn into some seriously interesting drama. Avery and Mia were among the boarders, standing at the stop in absolute boredom as they waited for the bus. Avery was busy doing something on her phone but Mia saw us coming.

"Where are you guys going?" Lily asked Mason.

"London," Mason replied, looking over at Mia who was standing beside Lily. "Hey." He smiled at her. Mia smiled back, a tinge of irritation hidden beneath the surface.

"And I see you don't have a date?" She asked, the flirt in her tone too obvious to miss.

"Not yet." He said with a smug smile. "But maybe I'll have one in a few minutes."

I- being Mason's best friend- knew that his flirting was backhandedly directed at Mia, but it seemed no one else besides Mason and I realized that piece of context. Since he was technically talking to Lily, it might have looked like he was flirting with her back. Lily thought he was about to ask her for a date and Mia was conveniently looking far away at some random tree with an irksome expression. Mia must have thought her emotions were hidden well under the rug but her jealousy-fueled annoyance was too loud to ignore. Even though Mia was clearly angry, the only effect it had on Mason was in his smile getting bigger. He was looking at her annoyed face with a truckload of satisfaction as she tried to ignore his knowing gaze. For the first time in history, Mia was jealous over Mason. It needed to be documented and preserved because it wasn't short of a miracle.

"Then why don't you ask her out?" Lily said, and it honestly gave me second-hand embarrassment over how clueless she was. If it was any other girl except

Lily, maybe I would feel bad for her. But since she was one of the meaner girls, I'm not ashamed to say I was enjoying this situation.

"I don't know, she looks kinda mad right now." He tilted his head at Mia, who finally turned and met his eyes. She understood what was happening and a hint of relief covered her face but there was still a bit of anger left behind.

"No one is mad. You can ask out whoever you want." Her words were saying 'Go ahead' but her face was saying something else. She was simmering with anger at the thought of Lily going out with Mason but we all knew she wasn't going to display that.

Avery was starting to get distracted from her very important scrolling session because she was now looking up from her phone and listening to the conversation as well. Standing there in a yellow sundress, the vibrant color accentuated her features in a way that her usual football kit never could. Her hair, usually confined in practical French braids, was now flowing freely down her shoulders, the sunlight falling on her brown hair giving it a honey-golden glow.

Mason leaned down to meet Mia's eyes. "You look cute when you're angry."

"I'm not angry." She replied angrily.

"Are you going to London as well?" He asked her, seeming very much pleased at her jealousy.

"Yes." She replied

There was a pause, and at that moment they looked at each other like they were the only people in the world. "If you keep looking at me like that I'll have no choice but to ask you for a date." He flirted out of habit for the millionth time in history.

Now, as the person who already had plans with him today, I would have revolted at his sudden decision of going on a date, but since it was Mia we were talking about, I knew there was no way she was actually going t-

"Then maybe you should." Mia replied with a little bit of anger mixed with a little bit of certainty.

I had to double-check my hearing senses to make sure Mia really said that. Did she really give him permission to actually ask her out on a date? First jealousy and then the subtle hint of flirting, Mason was going to faint if this goes on any further. Beside her, Avery looked just as shocked as me, her eyes wide and her mouth turning into a proud smile. But the most startling reaction was given by Mason- he physically took a step back as if he thought Mia was being possessed by a ghost.

"And you will say yes?" He asked again. Lily had finally realized what was happening and she wasn't too happy about how this conversation was going. But in his defense, the whole school knew about his huge crush on Mia so she kinda brought it on herself.

"Maybe." It was a vague one-word answer but it made Mason go feral.

"Will you go out with me?" Mason asked finally, two years' worth of hopes and dreams filled in his eyes.

"Yes." She replied, a subtle hint of blush on her cheeks.

Avery was short of exploding into a happy firework the way she let out the biggest smile. Lily was disappointed to witness this flirtation right in front of her eyes and I was feeling invisible because Mason just ditched me for a date. I cleared my throat to get Mason's attention and he looked back at me like he just realized I was still there.

"Oh, um." He leaned closer. "Can you take the bus today?" He whispered to me, his eyes pleading.

Maybe I would have thrown a best friend tantrum if it wasn't the absolute love of his life agreeing to go on a date with him after two years of chasing, but since this was the day he has been dreaming of- I say, "It's fine, I'll manage."

I'm imagining something similar happened with Avery and Mia because they whispered something to each other as well. At long last, after abandoning their respective best friends for an impromptu date, Mia and Mason went towards the car parking lot. Mason was looking at Mia like he still couldn't believe what was happening, probably struggling to accept that he was actually living out his biggest dream.

"Well, well. Looks like Mason and Mia are a thing now." Avery said, bringing my attention to her as she stood next to me.

"Took them long enough." I sighed, the realization of being left behind finally settling in.

Avery and I exchanged glances, the mutual disappointment apparent on our faces. It was our usual Sunday city trip, but the absence of our companions felt like a break in tradition.

"I don't want to stay in my room all day." She told me, like canceling her plans for today was off the table, even if her partner was now busy with her own plans.

"I have to pick up something from the city too." I replied.

"So we're actually going together then?" She asked, still unsure if we should trust ourselves to take a friendly trip to the town. "Because I don't know if I have it in me to spend the whole day with you without throwing up."

"Well, maybe you should carry a sick bag because this is really happening. Unless you want to spend this beautiful Sunday rotting in your bed, of course." Even if my words were unbothered, somewhere in my heart I wanted her to come along. As hardly as I maintained a façade of annoyance and indifference in front of her, deep down, I found a sense of satisfaction with how things worked out. Going out with Avery never occurred to me even in my wildest thoughts, but now that it was happening, I couldn't deny the little pinch of happiness it gave to my heart.

"Fine." She sighed. "I'd rather take this trip with you then go back to my room and waste my pretty outfit. Consider yourself tolerated for today."

"Oh, what an honor." I said dramatically before rolling my eyes, as she returned my sentiment with a grumble of her own.

And yet, beneath the grumbles and the eye rolls, there was a part of me that secretly welcomed the opportunity. I couldn't deny the fact that spending time with Avery, no matter how much we bickered, was strangely enjoyable. There was a certain energy between us, a dynamic that kept things interesting. And recently, I found myself craving for it more often than not.

We stood at the bus stop for a couple more minutes, scrolling on our phones and mostly avoiding any conversations. Eventually, the bus arrived and we filed in. Neither Avery nor I had preferred sharing a seat with the other, but when we boarded and searched for some peaceful solo spots, we realized that the seats were pretty much all taken. Deciding that it was better to tolerate each other rather than sitting with an almost stranger, we finally decided to sit together. The back seats were always the ones to fill in first, so I sat down in the second row and Avery settled down beside me.

"What are your plans?" She asked me.

"Getting candy for my sister is the top priority, and then maybe some food?" I told her. "What's yours?"

She shrugged. "I was just planning to explore the city more, so I'm fine with anything."

"Okay then, guess I'll show you around."

There was a bunch of yesterday's newspapers on the back of the front seat that someone probably left behind, and Erling Haaland was on the front page. Avery took them out to read the headlines. She took a second longer than usual before saying, "Damn, I wish I get to see him play one day."

"It's just a two-hour train ride to Manchester, you know. You can go and watch the next time we have a holiday." I suggested, and there was an excited glint in her eye. She said something about the MLS not being as good as the Premier League, which then led her to an unstoppable lecture about how the football culture in America differed to the one in England. Soon enough, I found myself not following her words as my eyes got busy in appreciating something other than her animated rants. The yellow sundress she was wearing and the free-flowing hair that framed her face had an undeniable charm, and in that moment, I couldn't help but feel a sense of admiration for Avery's versatility. Her usual sporty demeanor had transformed into something softer, more delicate. The sunlight played off the fabric of her dress, casting a warm glow over her. It was as if I was seeing a different side of Avery, one that I hadn't fully appreciated before. Her loose hair kept falling on her face swept by the wind, and she kept pushing it back whenever she was saying something.

I never really liked bus rides, with all the noise and people inside. But the more we got lost in the conversations we had, the more I started to forget the people around us.

And as I was nodding along to another one of her rants, a strange whim erupted in my chest and surprised the living daylights out of me. I found myself hoping for traffic. More traffic than any other day of the year. The slower we get there, the better.

18

AVERY

The bus ride with Noah wasn't as agonizing as I had thought, but nevertheless, I came out thirsty and tired from that extra-long bus ride. I had been talking for the whole ride non-stop as Noah just nodded at everything I said, and it got me craving something cold to moisten all the organs in my body that were probably drier than the Sahara desert at this point.

"Can we get drinks before we continue?" I suggested, just as Noah climbed down the bus after me. "I think I might die if I'm not provided with a frappe in the next ten minutes."

"Well, if it's a matter of life or death, I suppose I can spare a few minutes for your hydration needs." He said, taking the lead toward a particularly busy street. "There's a nice Cafe over here just five minutes away. Let's go there."

"Well, let's see what you call a 'nice Cafe', Mr. Guide."

Noah and I walked through the smaller streets with him guiding the way. Sunday was actually proving to be a sun day because the streets were really illuminated by the bright sunlight. For a gloomy and dim city, London was giving out much cheerful and sunny vibes today, which made this California girl really happy. It was kinda rare here in England, but I loved the days when we had the sun out in the open. My sunscreen finally had a job to do, and I made sure to use plenty. I even kept one bottle in my bag so I could reapply it after every two hours.

Originally, I wanted to hate this outing and loathe Noah's company on a fine day like today. But somehow, being spontaneous with our day was actually giving me a far better feeling than going through a predictable routine. After lots of walking where I gazed around at the beautiful storefronts and the cobblestone sidewalk, we reached the Cafe. The words 'Brewtopia Cafe' were beautifully written in a brown and beige theme, and there were flowers in hanging pots right outside the storefront. It was a small aesthetic Cafe on the side of an aesthetic cobblestone street. A good enough place to visit with someone you don't particularly like.

"It's so beautiful," I said, gaining a smile from Noah. "Maybe the place will compensate the company," I added before he got too arrogant about his choice.

The aroma of freshly ground coffee beans enveloped us as we stepped in. The atmosphere was inviting, with the hum of conversation and the gentle clinking of cups. It was the first time I had been to a Cafe in London and the sight was not at all disappointing. There were faux brick walls that had beautiful flowering creepers hanging on them and the low-hanging bulbs on the ceiling looked like little fireflies in the brightness of the sun. We walked toward the counter, looking at the menu and deciding our drinks.

"Hi, what can I get you?" The girl behind the counter chirped with a bright customer service smile.

I was looking at the menu behind her, wondering if they had anything without coffee. I really wanted a frappe, but I didn't want to-

"Do you have any decaf options? My friend over here can't have caffeine." Noah spoke before me, making my head snap back in his direction.

Did he just read my mind?

I was trying to make sense of how he could possibly have known about my caffeine sensitivity, when my brain went back a few weeks before to one of our pre-practice conversations. I remembered how we came across each other in the canteen, and how I told him that I avoid caffeine because it makes me feel jittery. But it was weeks ago, and I hadn't expected him to pay attention, much less remember it weeks later.

"Sure, we have decaf." She told him.

I turned to him, my face displaying every bit of astonishment I was feeling. "How did you-"

"I pay attention." He said it like it was the most normal thing to say and not something that would absolutely send my heart shrieking and running down the lane.

"Can I take your order?" The barista's shrill voice took me out of my trance, which instantly made my cheeks feel like the surface of the sun.

"Uh, yeah, I'll take a white mocha frappuccino, thank you," I said hastily.

"White chocolate frappuccino, Decaf." She nodded and typed into the computer before looking at Noah for his order.

"Caramel Macchiato for me." Noah smiled.

"Sure, your drinks will be ready in a few minutes."

As we paid for our drinks and took a seat at the back of the cafe, my mind lingered on the fact that Noah had remembered my dislike for coffee after all these weeks. It was a small detail, buried in the midst of our banter and occasional clashes, yet he'd held onto it. A timid smile played on my lips as I glanced at him. His attention seemed absorbed by the phone in his hands, and for a moment, the usual distaste between us took a backseat. The revelation that he paid attention, that he retained those subtle nuances, left me genuinely surprised. I was supposed to hate him, I was supposed to find him annoying, why did he have to remember one tiny detail and set my heart on fire?

"I wonder what Mason and Mia are doing." He wondered, still looking at his phone.

Before he could witness my embarrassingly admiring eyes staring at him, I quickly averted my gaze, pretending to be engrossed in scrolling on my phone.

"Date stuff," I replied casually.

He looked up from his phone. "Aren't *we* doing date stuff as well?" He held a snarky look in his eyes, like he was just teasing me with it but somewhere inside my chest, my heart did a cartwheel.

"Ew, don't say it like that. People might think we are a couple." As much as he had managed to dismantle my whole defense system, I still had to act like our forced togetherness wasn't bothering me at all.

"And that would be a major shame."

I tried not to pay attention to the fact that we truly *were* also doing date stuff because if I went any far with my imagination I was going to turn into the human version of a tomato. Sharing a bus ride, getting coffees together and then having plans to explore the city. I told myself this little date situation didn't count because neither of us had any feelings for each other, and we were only doing it because we had no other choice.

After ten whole minutes of agonizing proximity with Noah, the barista called for our drinks. Thankful for abandoning our date-y location, I quickly walked over and took my drink, heading toward the door without so much as letting my eyes fall over on Noah. As we left the café, the chilly breeze tugging at our coats, I found myself resisting a smile. We were sipping on our drinks as we walked through the streets, our steps slow and peaceful as we navigated without any sense of urgency or purpose. Perhaps Noah and I were an odd pair, but in the heart of London, surrounded by the vibrancy of the city, I couldn't deny that the unusual day had its own peculiar magic. And in that moment, I couldn't help but admit that maybe, just maybe, spending time with Noah wasn't as bad as I had initially perceived.

We walked all the way to Borough Market, my favorite place in all of London. Noah suddenly went out of the way and I raised my eyebrows at his act of abandoning me on the sidewalk. But then he located a trashcan to throw his cup in and I realized I had finished my drink as well. I followed and threw my empty cup, the white mocha frappe making me feel a thousand times better than before. The cold coffee was even more gratifying in the rare afternoon heat, which kinda reminded me of the coffee runs I always had with Ella back in California. Simply reliving this little activity wrapped me in a blanket of familiarity, and I felt like this was actually where I should be. Spending a fun afternoon in the city, having coffee and random conversations after getting selected for the school team with my friend. Er, teammate.

While I was browsing all the shops and the different traditional goods from the many countries, Noah walked into a little Turkish shop and got some candy for his little sister, along with a small packet to keep for himself.

"Aren't you hungry?" Noah asked while looking at his watch, which showed- umm. My dyslexia made it hard for me to read his analog watch properly so I brought out my phone, which showed me it was 02:47 PM. Thank God for digital clocks.

"Yeah, it's almost lunchtime. What do you recommend to eat here?" I asked, looking around at the stalls and restaurants. The diversity was crazy here because there were all sorts of cuisines. Spanish, Indian, Arab, Chinese, Italian, Thai- you name it, they have it. There were lots of options for seafood as well, but I wasn't really in the mood for fish today. Glancing around, I saw a lot of stalls for fresh produce and cheese as well. My mom loves trying out stuff from different cultures and she would have actually loved this place.

"Well," He looked around and pointed toward the path on the right. "I usually eat from a Middle Eastern shop over there. Have you had Middle Eastern food before?"

I gave him a piqued look. "Obviously I have, I didn't live under a rock. I love Falafel." Come to think of it, it has been a long time since I had Arab food and I was in the mood to have something fulfilling anyway. "Let's go, where is it?"

His unbothered demeanor quickly changed to reveal a very happy and excited one when I agreed to go for a Middle Eastern cuisine. I knew he was Turkish and it probably meant a lot to him to share his culture with anyone, I just didn't think it would give him the same amount of happiness even if it was with me. As we walked toward the street Noah had pointed out, I came across a crowd I hadn't really experienced here until now. They were mostly tourists, people from all over the world who came here to enjoy the diverse collection of food. Scared of getting lost in this labyrinth of people, I made sure to walk close to him so I didn't lose his lead. But his quick tall strides made it hard for me to catch up and I instinctively caught his hand, making him slow down as I followed him through the streets.

Surprised by my sudden touch, he turned around and glanced at our hands, a subtle smirk coming up on his face.

"I didn't know you were into hand-holding in public. Trying to make a statement?" He said sarcastically but still not letting go of my hand.

"Oh, please, it's called trying not to get lost in a crowd. Unless you want to play Marco Polo every five minutes."

"Whatever you say, tiny human."

Surprisingly, he didn't pull away or react negatively. Instead, a warm smile played on his lips as we navigated the crowded market hand in hand. I couldn't help but appreciate the ease with which we moved through, no amount of awkwardness or uneasiness betraying me as my heart told me I could trust the boy in front of me. It wasn't something I had ever thought of, his hand in mine, but now that it was happening, his company was too comforting to complain about.

Miraculously enough, it felt almost natural to be hanging out with him, I didn't have to be conscious or act more sophisticated than I was- the way I sometimes had to be with Liam. With him, I had to reach his level of British sophistication in order to be likable. But being with Noah was effortless, I could be as rude and sassy as I wanted and he could happily do that back. At least I liked that much about him. He knew how to take a joke and throw it back.

After following him through half the market, we reached a wooden storefront. The name 'Levant' was written in a calligraphic font that resembled the Arabic scripture. The tantalizing aroma of freshly prepared Levantine cuisine wafted through the air as Noah and I stepped into the warmly lit Palestinian restaurant. The ambiance was inviting, with intricate Arabic patterns adorning the walls. An elderly man was sitting behind the counter, and behind him, a younger guy was rotating the meat.

"Selam Khaal!" He greeted the elderly man with a bright smile and the uncle returned it with a delightful one of his own.

"Ah, Noah, it's been long." The old man said in a heavy voice, and it was instantly clear that these two had known each other for a long time.

"I got busy with school." He replied, looking pleased to meet him.

"How's Demir and Deniz?" He asked Noah and he told him a detailed description of what was going on in their lives recently, how his Dad's business had gotten better the past few weeks, and how Deniz was now the social butterfly of her class. They caught up on some stuff for a full five minutes before I accidentally coughed and Noah realized I was also there.

"Oh, Avery, this is Uncle Hassan, he owns this shop." He finally turned to me, and Uncle Hassan gave me the most warm welcoming smile. "He is from Palestine so he knows all the original Levantine recipes better than anyone. I come here with my Dad and Deniz whenever he visits London."

The way Uncle Hassan greeted me so lovingly it was hard to believe I was meeting him for the first time. "Such a sweet girl you are." He said to me, and I felt like I was praised by my own granddad. "Is she with you?" He asked Noah. "Your girlfriend?"

The quick change in the color of our faces was identical and he hastily denied the suggestion as quickly as he would deny a murder. "No, no, she's uh, she's my teammate- yeah she plays in the school with me." He replied fast as a Ferrari.

"Ah, I see." He nodded with an edge of allusion. "Going out for lunch with a singular teammate. Totally normal." There was an edge of tease in his words and Noah acted like he didn't quite catch it.

As the silence was getting more awkward by the minute, I looked to my side and realized Noah had long departed from the uncomfortable conversation, going through the menu like it was the most interesting piece of literature- written by Shakespeare himself. Well, I was right there with him ignoring that conversation because I had no interest in discovering what we were.

"Have you had Fatayer before?" He asked me. "Arayes?"

Since both of those things were absolutely new to me, I shook my head and he gave me a smile in return. "So I get to introduce you to all this?" He was practically jumping in excitement as delight filled his voice. "Then I think we should also get the Nabulsi Cheese, it's a specialty of Uncle Hassan. I bet he's the only person in all of England who knows how to make it."

He went off on a detailed rant about all of the things on the menu and carefully selected some dishes that he thought I would love. The way he was so delighted to introduce me to his cultural food made me feel all warm and lovely inside. There was just something about learning a person's culture and the way it makes them feel so happy and seen. I was grateful to be the one he was introducing it to, even if we didn't have any history of being close. I always enjoyed introducing my friends to Japanese cuisine back in America, and it felt nice to be on this side of the conversation for once. His happiness was so contagious it was transferring over to me and I found myself smiling softly- listening to him talk about all the things his Mom used to make and how it still reminds him of home whenever he eats here.

A realization dawned on me, that beneath the rivalry and the occasional clash of personalities, I secretly had a growing appreciation for Noah's company. Perhaps our dynamic was shifting, evolving into something beyond the constant exchange of snarky remarks. In that cozy corner of the restaurant, surrounded by the comforting hum of conversations, I found myself slowly savoring the unexpected amity that had sprouted between us.

The unexpected charm of his company, the lively streets of London, and the sarcastic remarks that had initially grated on my nerves had all woven together into an experience that was, dare I say it, enjoyable.

19

NOAH

As we sat down to eat, I explained each dish as it got served to the table, sharing stories of family gatherings and the significance of the flavors. Avery tasted each dish, savoring the unique blend of spices and textures, and soon the table that was filled with Levantine dishes half an hour ago was now spread with empty bowls and plates, as Avery and I were sitting at the table sharing a Knafeh to end the meal.

"I didn't know you could add cheese to a dessert," Avery said, enjoying a mouthful of the crispy juicy Knafeh.

"Cheesecake?" I reminded her.

She looked up for a second as if she just realized Cheesecake was indeed made of cheese. "Oh yeah, I forgot about that." She swallowed the bite. "I can't believe I forgot about Cheesecake, I used to have it every week!"

"The American in you is getting left behind." I laughed, scooping up more Knafeh on my fork.

"You were right, this cheese is unlike any other I had before."

I smiled. I didn't know how to explain it but whenever she praised the food, it felt like a personal win. I had nothing to do with it- heck I didn't even know how to make it- but just the fact that she was appreciating my culture made me happy beyond words. Avery's words resonated deeply with me, considering many people ignore or even downright deny my culture, but she was genuinely acknowledging it.

"My mom was from Nablus, she used to make it at home." The smile sat on my face stubbornly, refusing to go away. "Eating here reminds me of the food she used to make." Even as I talked about an unachievable reality, something about that memory was refusing to make me sad. She was looking at me with depth in her eyes, and I smiled at her so she knew I was not upset. Yes, I miss her every day and I wish I could still have her presence in my life, but it doesn't take away the fact that our time together was still filled with happy memories. Memories that always brought a smile to my face.

Just when it looked like she was about to ask me a question about my mom, I spoke up. "Wait a minute," I held up a finger. "Let me get take out for Deniz before we go, it'll take time." I got up and walked back toward the counter where Uncle Hassan was busy solving a sudoku on a newspaper. I ordered a shawarma take out- no pickles, and no turnips, just how Deniz likes. When the cook got busy with preparing the food, I returned back to our table, grateful for the change in topic.

"Where did Mia tell you to meet up later?" I asked. My instincts stopped me from continuing our last conversation before I even realized it. It wasn't that I didn't wanna talk to her about it, it was just that something inside me told me to stop and change the topic. The last time this topic came up, I was severely hurt by the indifference Everly showed. She never had any regard for my background, so I never mentioned it either. If I ever accidentally talked about my culture, she used to get embarrassed and change the topic, like it was embarrassing that I didn't exactly 'belong' here. It was like she was only happy with me as long as I behaved a certain way, a way that completely hid my background and ethnicity. It had made me feel so insignificant for so long that now I avoided mentioning it to anyone, even when she was not around. And hiding my roots had now become an involuntary response.

"Near the London Eye." She replied, wiping her mouth with a napkin.

"Let's get going then, it's a thirty-minute walk from here." I got up from our table and started heading out but the sight of Avery not following me out stopped me from going any further.

Instead, she was looking at me with a strange expression that suggested she wasn't too happy about my plans. "What is with you Europeans and walking? Do you guys not have subway here?"

I shrugged. "We do, but walking is just nice."

Not giving me an answer, she stared at me like it was unacceptable to say that and waited for me to change my decision. "Or we can take a bus, sure." I added with a chuckle.

And that was when Avery finally got up, satisfied with the idea of not having to take a thirty-minute walk. We greeted Uncle Hasan one last time as he gave us a warm smile, before stepping back out into the sunlit streets and finding a bus to the London Eye.

The sun dipped low on the horizon as the four of us returned to the school gates, our impromptu trip to London coming to an end. The chatter of the city still echoed in our minds as we approached the familiar entrance.

"I can't believe you actually went on with him, you refused to go with me last time." Avery was busy complaining to Mia all because she went on the London Eye with Mason. Mason, however, was unbothered as he was happily holding Mia's hand like he didn't want to waste a single second of their proximity.

"Only because he insisted and held my hand the whole time," Mia responded.

Avery opened her mouth but then closed it, holding herself back from whatever she was about to say. "You're right, I'm not holding hands with anyone, I didn't wanna go *that* bad."

"We'll see how you feel about that when it's-" Mia was about to take a name but Avery glared at her which immediately made her stop talking and give her a smug smile.

What was that about?

We reached the girls' dorm first so Mason could drop Mia at her room like a gentleman and I could deliver the goods to Deniz. Inside the common room, Deniz was sitting with a couple of her friends playing Monopoly on the floor. "Deniz?" I called for her but she was too busy rolling the dice to pay me any heed.

"Just a minute." She replied with a glance in our direction, which quickly turned into a double take when she noticed Avery standing beside me.

"Avery!" She left the dice on the board and ran towards us. *What do I have to do to get the same reaction from her?* "Didn't you get selected for the school team?"

"You'd think I was invisible or something," I muttered under my breath.

"As a bench player, sure I did." Avery laughed but her gratefulness was apparent even in her self-deprecating joke.

Deniz squealed, clapping her hands super fast. "I'm gonna watch all your matches, *even* if they're in other schools."

My eyes went wide in surprise. "You never went out for *my* matches?" I protested but she just gave me a disappointed look.

"I've seen you play a thousand times Abi, I know what you'll do before you even do it. Avery is unpredictable."

I scoffed, "So this is what I get after getting you a shawarma from Uncle Hassan's shop?"

She immediately looked at my hands- the bags of candy and shawarma- and narrowed her eyes. "Does it have pickles and turnips?" She asked finally.

"No, I told him to make it your way."

A flattering smile came up on her face as took the bags from my hands before giving me a tiny hug. "Okay, then I'll watch the matches for you too."

"Did you have dinner yet?" I asked and she stepped back to shake her head. "Then wash your hands and eat first before playing Monopoly or you guys will end up playing it all night."

"Yes sir!" She replied and ran off to gather her friends to join her in the dining hall.

Turning away from her cute little antics, I looked back just in time to catch the soft look Avery held in her eyes before she quickly looked away. That one tiny spark that went off in my heart was enough to make me smile. "Are you coming to practice tomorrow?" I asked her before leaving.

"Of course I am, someone has to kick your ass."

"We're on the same team now," I reminded her.

She smiled, her smile that now had the power to make my heart beat thrice as fast. "Doesn't mean we can't have a nutmeg contest."

20

AVERY

Wearing my new practice kit for the first time, I geared up for my first training session as an official player of the Summerfield Institute Football Club. All the other members had left the ground after the general training and now it was just the members of the football club who had to go through another set of rigorous training. Coach Martinez had told us to pick up the stack of cones and line them up, putting them close so that we could only make quick and short passes through them.

The players scattered to grab cones, and the familiar routine of setting up the training course began to make me feel at ease. As I stood in front of my own training course, I realized Noah was standing right next to me, our eyes exchanging glances as Coach Martinez waited for everyone to finish.

"Looks like we're in for some dribbling drills." He said, the barely hidden challenge peeking through his words.

"Ready to see who's the true dribbling champion?" I challenged, our competitiveness taking the best of us whenever we came around.

"Oh, you're on, Avery."

As the rest of the team set up the cones, Coach Martinez explained the drill and demonstrated a few quick dribbles through the course. "The key here is control and speed. Use the inside and outside of your foot to maneuver through the cones. Let's see some precision, team."

All of us took our positions behind the cones, anticipation building. Coach Martinez blew his whistle, signaling the start of the drill.

Players weaved through the cones, the sound of soccer balls tapping against the grass creating a rhythmic melody. Coach Martinez moved around, offering pointers and encouragement. "Good, good. Control is crucial. Keep those touches close. Avery, nice work on the footwork!"

Racing through the cones like my life depended on it, I shot a triumphant glance at Noah, who was determinedly navigating through the cones.

"You might be good, but don't think I'm letting you win!"

A laugh escaped my lips as I turned around to dribble the other way around. "Bring it on!"

The training session continued with the team honing their dribbling skills, the cones becoming a dance floor for soccer balls, and determined players. Coach Martinez watched, pleased with the progress, and the players, despite the challenge, found joy in the camaraderie of training together.

"You should eat more protein, you play for the school now!" Leah told me as she added another piece of chicken to my plate from the buffet dish.

"You already gave me an extra egg 'for the protein', how can I eat all this?" I looked down at my plate- two omelettes, three pieces of chicken, and a side of rice. This was like twice the amount of food I usually had.

"You're going for extra training now, you need more energy and muscle. I don't care how but you *have* to finish it." We walked over to our table and I sat down with an unwilling fresh motivation to gain more muscle.

"Wow, that's a lot for a girl." I knew it was Liam before he even appeared in front of me, lowering his plate on the table as he sat down opposite me. He eyed my plate and snickered, and I felt a hot dose of embarrassment rush to my cheeks.

"For a girl?" Leah looked over at him with a twisted expression. "I didn't know girls are forbidden from eating whatever they want. Is this a new rule?" She was pissed at his weird remarks yet again and I elbowed her in the side before she could start a full-blown argument in my defense.

"I was just saying." He laughed and picked up his spoon, not catching on to Leah's deadly glare.

The doors of the hall opened and a loud group of boys walked in- Mason, Noah, Henry, and Jack. All of them held the attention of almost all the girls in the dining hall, but two of them were focused on our table. Almost accidentally, Jack caught my eye and turned away like he just looked at a rotten set of bananas. Mason spotted Mia at our table and walked over, driving my heart insane with the fact that he brought Noah over with him too. He took Mia's hand and gave it a kiss like he was a duke and Mia was a princess and we were sitting in the dining hall of the freaking Buckingham Palace.

"We have space here, why don't you sit with us?" Mia asked him.

"I was going to, even if you didn't ask." He replied and went towards the buffet with Noah on his side.

Leah leaned into my side and whispered into my ear, "I bet Noah isn't a food shamer."

I rolled my eyes. "How do you know? Maybe he is." Liam didn't catch on to our secret conversation but Leah's distaste for him was no secret anyway.

"Are you guys together now?" Liam asked Mia, carrying on the conversation at our table.

"I think so." Mia blushed. Although Mason and Mia haven't explicitly talked about being in a relationship, it's pretty much official ever since their date in London. The same date that caused me and Noah to spend the day together, but I'd rather not think about that. Every time I think of that I get this weird urge to spend more time with him, to know more about him and it disappoints me that I can't just go and actually do that. Every time he walks into the room, I feel a bit of flutter in my chest and every time he leaves, I feel disappointment filling my heart. It was like eating a snack for the first time, like spending that one day with him had left me wanting more. When his conversations are soothing and his company wholesome, it's definitely not something you can get enough of.

Noah and Mason returned to the table with a tray full of food and Leah gave me a look like she was about to take the unspoken competition between Liam and Noah a whole lot further. She cleared her throat. "Noah, do you think Avery is eating too much?" She asked him and it was all I could do not to get up from the table and hide behind a couch.

He looked confused by the question but nevertheless, he took a good look at what I was eating and gave a shake of his head. "You need to be eating more if you are gonna train more."

Leah looked back at me with an 'I told you so' face and I just shook my head in defeat. Liam and Noah seemed to be busy with their food, and I couldn't be more grateful for their complete ignorance toward Leah's competition.

"Oh, by the way, Miss Asami was looking for you," Mason informed me in the middle of enjoying his second omelette.

"Oh yeah, I forgot to mention, she saw us outside and told us she wanted to have a talk with our new 'teammate'," Noah added, focusing on picking up the last spoonful of rice from the corners of his plate which kept escaping the spoon. How the hell do boys eat this fast?

I let out a sigh. "She probably wants to discuss my new schedule now that I'll be taking extra training." I was already exhausted from the amount of nagging she was going to unleash once she caught me happily going for the training. Joy sucker.

"You aren't doing bad at school, I don't think she should be concerned," Noah said, finally scooping the rice up with the help of a butter knife.

From my side of the table, a clear snicker erupted and everybody turned to see Liam chuckling. "That's if you consider twelve out of twenty a good score."

Noah turned from his seat a little bit to glare at Liam and Leah rolled her eyes so hard I was wondering if it hurt. He saw their expressions and chuckled again. "Chill guys, I'm just joking." His comment had actually struck a sensitive cord deep inside my head, but I tried not to let it upset me too much. I knew how much work it took for me to even score that much but at the same time, I knew Liam won't understand all that. After all, it feels like an excuse when I say that out loud.

Nevertheless, I mentally prepared myself for the confrontation that was waiting for me in Asami's office.

"Why didn't you ask me before agreeing to the offer from Mr. Martinez?" She was looking at me over the rim of her glasses, her elbows on the table with her hands clasped together.

"Because it was what I wanted in the first place?" I felt infuriated by how she was talking to me like she owned me but I tried to suppress it and talk politely. Why was I supposed to ask for her permission? My parents are happy with it and so am I, but she just has to make things complicated by pulling her rank and relation on me.

"But did you consider your grades before making such a decision? Did you consider how it's going to affect your grades even more?"

I resisted the urge to roll my eyes. Is that all she thinks about? Does she know there's a whole world outside the papers she marks every day? "I don't think I'm doing that bad, I'm improving."

I could see the scoff coming long before she let it out. "This is your improvement?"

It was getting harder and harder to maintain my politeness when she was pushing all my buttons in such a condescending tone. "Yes, it is. It did take me twice the amount of effort to achieve what other students have, but it doesn't mean I didn't work hard for it."

She nodded slowly, realizing that I wouldn't be taking the bait. "I see. Did you talk to Ben about this?"

Her 'discussion' was getting more ridiculous by the minute. Why wouldn't I tell my dad? "Of course I did. And he was happy about it."

She nodded some more before pushing her glasses back up on her nose and opening her laptop. I suppose that's her way of ending the conversation. "Just remember, if you fail any more classes I won't hesitate to take you out of the team." She looked at me. "You can't play if any teacher from this school is against it, don't forget that."

I tried not to take her threat seriously but it frustrates me to admit that I believe her. She won't miss any chance to force her wishes on me and I'm pretty sure she's already looking forward to it. I know she will enjoy snatching my passion away from me to push me into academics, just like she always wanted. I decided not to give her the satisfaction and sat up straight, not showing any signs of being intimidated. "Of course." I smiled.

She looked at me a second more before nodding and waving her hand. "You can go."

Even though her petty discussion dropped my spirits a bit, I walked out of her office with a new revelation- I don't care if my passions don't align with hers, from now on I'm going to put all my efforts and energy into something I actually want to achieve. I worked too hard to get here and I'm not letting anyone take that away from me.

It had been three days since I started doing my extra training, and now I was pretty much getting used to my tiring schedule. Out on the training ground, all the players were running off to the locker rooms after our regular practices and Coach Martinez was calling all the team members toward the center of the ground.

"Alright boys and girls, listen up." Chloe was the last one to join the group and then he started again. "Our first match would be against Silver Oak High, and it will be a charity event."

Everyone was nodding so I started nodding too, but I had no idea who or how good the Silver Oak players were.

"The match would be held on their ground so it will be an away game for us. Since we won't have the home advantage, I want you guys to focus on the strategies and formation." He looked at Jack. "I don't want anyone to be going against our plans, and I thought I should mention that a week before so everyone will get it in their heads by then."

"Today we will be practicing shielding the ball and long pass control. Break down into pairs, and Matt, give them a ball each." He ordered his assistant, who came running with a bag full of balls and passed it on to us. Six balls for six pairs.

I was paired with Fred who was also a midfielder and we practiced having control of the ball without letting the other person have it. Whenever he managed to touch the ball, we switched sides and then he was the one trying to shield it from me. Since Fred was my teammate in the Blue team, it was easy to get along and do the drill. I was kind of dreading having to practice with Jack, but he seemed to be avoiding me just as much as I was avoiding him. I was happy with that.

Next came the long pass drills, and Coach switched up the pairs before the drill. I was praying with all my might not to get paired up with Jack and my prayers were answered when Coach ended up pairing me with Noah. I was half relieved, half annoyed. I haven't ever practiced drills with him before.

"What are you gonna do first? Shoot or receive?" He asked, holding the ball in his hands.

"I'll shoot." I took it from him and placed it at my feet as he ran all the way to the other side of the field. I was standing just ahead of the penalty spot and Noah was all the way across- near the other end. Coach blew the whistle and we both started passing the ball and then ran a few feet toward the side to change the angle and receive the next pass. After a while, we reached the opposite ends of the field diagonally, and a pass from this angle would have to be the longest and strongest for it to reach him across the field. I hit the ball in his direction with all my might, and there was a second where he predicted the landing before he ran up to reach the spot and received the ball with his thigh, before juggling it to his feet. The shot was way too powerful to be received in a single touch, but he received it perfectly and took it forward like it was no big deal. Seeing him as a teammate for the first time and nailing each of his drills, I realized it wasn't so bad to be playing with him after all.

The moment when you take a shower and change back into comfortable clothes is ethereal. I changed from my cleats to a light pair of flip flops and my hair was still drying in the cold breeze of the evening. The sun had set and I was walking towards our building with Chloe and Ellie when I saw someone getting out of the Library and crossing our path. My palms felt hot when I realized it was Liam.

I'm in my dumb flip-flops dammit.

He saw me and gave a quick smile, before walking over and joining us. Chloe and Ellie said their hellos and then went on walking, leaving me and Liam standing there alone.

"How was your practice?" He asked, a bright smile on his face.

"It was good, I'm a bit more tired than usual but I guess I'll get used to it," I replied, trying not to feel too embarrassed about my appearance.

"Um, I heard you like stargazing?" He asked, confusing me with the sudden mention of the activity.

"I do, yeah."

"Then, what do you say we meet up on our roof tonight? Just you and me, looking at the stars." He said and my heart started running a sprint.

"Like a... like a date?" I asked, just to make sure I was not getting the wrong idea.

"Yeah, like a date." His handsome boy smile was melting my heart as we spoke.

"Sure, I'd love that." Even if his presence was igniting my chest with the speedy flutters, I tried to sound casual.

"See you tomorrow then." He smiled and walked past me, leaving me to manage my heartbeats on my own.

I have never had a crush ask me out before so it was utterly new and an absolutely delightful feeling to experience this. Chloe and Ellie were long gone inside the building so I skipped all the way behind them, excited to tell Mia about my first date in England.

"And you said no right?" Mia was actively trying to rain on my parade when I spilled the conversation I had five minutes ago.

"Of course not, I said yes!" Honestly, I was expecting her to meet this information with the same amount of enthusiasm as I had when she said yes to Mason but she was not following my mental script.

She put down the pen on her table and shook her head. "I told you before, that guy is a douche, he changes girlfriends like he changes clothes."

"So? I've had an ex before too, I'm sure he's not as bad as you think." I defended.

"He's friends with Jack, how good can he be?" Okay, that information kind of stung me like a bee but I wanted to ignore that and stay in my ignorant bliss. He was nice to me when I was new and he helped me with homework when I was stuck in detention because of Noah. He couldn't be as bad as Jack right?

"Are you coming for dinner or not? I'm starving!" I changed the topic before she could convince me further and she got up from her table with a sigh.

"Don't come to be with your broken heart later." She said before walking out the door and I happily followed because there was no reason for her to be worried. Liam has been nothing but a good friend to me ever since I joined the school, and it was hard to believe he would ever intentionally hurt my feelings. If he wanted to hurt me, why would he ask me out on a date? Although the fact that he was friends with someone like Jack kept nagging in my head, I still tried to convince myself he couldn't be as bad as him. Liam knows I like him back so he would never disrespect or look down on me like Jack does. He's not the kind of person to look at girls like they're playthings.

Right?

21

NOAH

Sitting in front of the TV while doing my math homework had become a tradition for me at this point, my brain refusing to work without the background music of the TV shows and the constant chatter of the people around me. Mason was sitting right beside me, surfing through the channels and shoving his hand in a packet of crisps. I was engrossed in my math homework when the door swung open and a hint of surprise filled my eyes. It was Avery, walking into the boys' common room with purpose in her eyes. Her scent told me it was her before her appearance did, which was quite gorgeous if you ask me. She was wearing a Burgundy sweater dress with black yoga pants, the color brightening up her skin as her dark-colored hair fell down in an elegant flow. Did I mention she was gorgeous?

She didn't notice me on the couch and went straight toward the stairs, her hair bouncing with every step she took. Assuming that she must have visited the common room to find me, I thought maybe I should save her some time and grace her with my presence.

I shut my notebooks and went after her, stopping behind her right before the stairwell. The sound of my footsteps was quite loud, and she turned around and saw me before I reached her.

"You know losers aren't allowed in this building," I said to her, finally catching up.

She looked at me, her eyes going up and down.

"Then how come you live here?" She looked annoyed by the fact that I was here, which didn't make any sense because I literally lived here. And didn't she come here to see me?

"Cut the crap, what do you want?" *Why is she here so late at night?*

"What do you mean 'what do you want'? I came here to see someone." She said and then studied my expression as I slowly realized I *might* have misunderstood the situation.

Great. Totally not embarrassing.

The slow gears of her mind finally clicked and a cheeky grin formed on her face.

"Oh poor soul, you thought I was here to see you?" She said, in a much clear patronizing voice. "Did you forget the world doesn't revolve around you or should I remind you again?" This time sweetly, totally soaking up my embarrassment.

Not having anything to say, I just rolled my eyes. "Whatever."

"See you later, loser." She said and started climbing the stairs, leaving me with a hell lot of curiosity at the bottom. My mind started racing with all of the guys she could possibly be meeting, and I couldn't manage to come up with many. But then a light bulb went off inside my head as I remembered the time when we came back from our London trip, and how Mia had almost mentioned a guy before Avery interrupted her. Who was she going to mention?

Who is she seeing this late at night?

She's in our building so it must be a boy.

She's dressed too nicely to be visiting Dylan, so that means...

DOES SHE HAVE A CRUSH?

The revelation sent the air out of my lungs, and I knew I wouldn't be at peace until I knew what was going on. When I leaned over the railings and looked up, I could see Avery going up the stairs. I decided to keep watching to figure out which floor she was going on, but time went on and her steps never halted as she kept going up and up and up. I was still watching when she ran out of floors without stopping anywhere and then finally went straight to the roof.

The roof? Of the boys' building?

Is she meeting someone on the roof? Who else could it be if it's not me? I know I'm not exactly her friend, but I haven't seen her talk to anyone much except me, Dylan, or Liam. But she couldn't possibly be seeing Liam right? With how much of a douche he is?

Should I go? It wouldn't be safe for her to be on the roof at this time, right? Maybe I should go. After a good five minutes of contemplating, I started running up the stairs, panting and struggling for each breath until I finally reached the roof.

When I started getting closer, on the last flight of stairs, I could hear two people talking faintly. I reached the top stair and there they were, Avery and Liam, standing near the railing. I didn't know what they were talking about but apparently, it was very funny because Avery kept smiling that cute smile of hers and Liam was looking at her like she was the most precious person in his life. *What a douche.* I sighed as I realized how Avery must be falling for his lover-boy act. I would believe he actually felt like that too if I didn't overhear his conversation in the boys' locker room the other day.

"How far have you gone with that American girl?" Jack asked Liam. I was behind the wall of lockers so maybe they didn't notice me. Even if they did, Avery was not exactly my girlfriend so they had no reason to hesitate. Everyone knew the tussle me and Avery had since the beginning of our school year.

"Well, we're texting." He replied, looking at his phone. Obviously texting Avery.

"You haven't kissed her yet? Nothing at all?" Jack insisted. Considering Jack's dating habits, not only is he a douche himself, but he encourages other guys to be a douche too. And since Liam wasn't that far away from the douche lifestyle, I could easily see him following Jack's terrible footsteps.

"It's just been like a month bro, chill," Liam had replied.

"A month? I think that's long enough for a kiss at least."

"I don't know. She seems like the sensitive type."

"Or maybe you are the sensitive one." Jack laughed an obnoxious laugh. "You have no game if you can't kiss her by next month."

What the hell?

"Wanna bet?" Liam asked.

Betting over a kiss? What a douche.

"Ten pounds," Jack said. "I bet you're too soft to do it."

"Watch me," Liam replied, with a challenging smirk.

Disgusting.

Looking back on that memory, I thought Avery would be clever enough not to give him what he wanted. I didn't know about her love life much, but one thing I did know was that she doesn't take shit from anyone. Especially not from douchey boys like Liam, I'm certain. But she was looking at him with those lovely eyes, and I realized she had no reason to push him away. How would she know he was a douche when he was acting like the most sincere guy on the planet.

Even if I put that conversation aside, there was something else punching my gut telling me I needed to stop this. I didn't like the idea of Liam being with her for God knows what reason. I just knew he couldn't.

I looked back at them, as Liam had a tender hand on her face, softly pushing the hair away from her face. He was looking at her softly like his feelings for her went deeper than the Grand Canyon. Well, too bad I know about his bet.

As I heard some footsteps on the floor below, I froze. If I get caught sneaking in the stairwell, it would take ten weird minutes to explain the situation and I really didn't want anyone telling me I was just being jealous. Because I'm not. I just don't want Liam to win his stupid jerk bet, that's all. Isn't it?

A door opened on the floor below and the sound of the footsteps disappeared behind it. The coast was clear.

As I stepped back, my eyes fell on the emergency bell at the bottom of the stairs. The whole purpose of the emergency bell was to alert the warden in the case of any threat, and right now, Liam was looking like enough of a threat to Avery. But if the warden came here and caught her in the boy's building she could get into trouble as well. As a matter of fact, this wasn't exactly a real emergency so I could be punished by the warden for ringing the alarm myself.

Amidst the war waging on in my heart and mind, I glanced back at the happy couple on the roof.

Would I get in trouble?

I probably would, but when I looked back at Avery and Liam, my heart told me the trouble would be worth it. Back on the roof, he was leaning in as Avery was closing her eyes, and that's when all my thoughts were thrown out the window as I ran down the stairs. Broke the seal. And rang the alarm.

22

AVERY

It was a cold chilly night and I was fidgeting with the sleeve of my sweater while looking up at the stars. Usually, stargazing takes up all of my attention and I get lost in trying to find all the constellations, but today my mind was distracted and I was beyond nervous. If there was anyone else here with me, I would have been fine- but Liam's presence on this silent roof was constantly kicking up my heartbeat.

"There's Draco." He pointed towards the left side of the roof. "Right beside Ursa Minor."

The smell of his cologne was strong and heavy. I looked in the direction of his finger and watched carefully. After a few seconds of recognizing the stars and connecting the dots- while my brain kept malfunctioning because of the close proximity- I spotted the constellation. A smile escaped my lips- I had never seen Draco before.

When I turned back to him with my content smile, he was already looking at me with the same soft eyes as always. Only this time it was more intense, like it carried a message. And I might not be perfect at reading messages but it was quite clear what his eyes were telling me.

My heartbeat froze as he was leaning closer, I closed my eyes-

A loud high-pitched alarm went off in the distance and we jumped apart. Liam quickly glanced toward the stairs and then back at me- the panic in his eyes too evident to miss. Was he panicking about the emergency or was he panicking about getting caught?

"What's going on?" I exclaimed, the loud blaring making me wince from the voice.

"I have no idea," Liam replied, his eyes scanning the rooftop. The emergency bell went off which meant that the warden would be here any minute and if I got caught, I was definitely going to be punished.

Panicked by the situation myself I decided to run downstairs and try to possibly leave before George reached the premises. I was so focused on reaching the lobby that I didn't pay attention to any of the students coming out of their rooms, some kinda panicked, and some just annoyed about the alarm disrupting their sleep.

Just two more flights of stairs. I told myself as I almost reached the bottom, skipping two or three steps at a time. Quick as a flash, I reached the lobby, running toward the door of the building. However, the moment that was supposed to be my triumph quickly turned into a moment of horror as I saw George looking around frantically and my steps screeched to a halt at his sight. In his panic-stricken attempt to spot the threat, he didn't seem to notice me standing right in front of him, and for a moment I found myself looking around with him too. When I actually paid attention, I realized I hadn't come across any dangerous or emergency situations in my whole journey from the roof to the lobby either. Soon enough, I found myself just as confused as George, trying to find the threat.

However, after searching the lobby for any signs of distress, his eyes finally fell upon me and my whole body went still, like making no movement was somehow going to make me invisible. I slowly turned around, expecting to see Liam behind my back, but there was nothing behind me except the vast flight of stairs that I just descended from.

Did he abandon me on the way down?

But I was pulled out of my confused thoughts fast enough when George spoke up, addressing none other than the girl in front of him. "Were you the one who pulled the alarm? What's wrong?" He sounded genuinely concerned about my well-being but I didn't know how to answer him, considering how close I was to getting caught when he finally realized that I was not supposed to be here.

"Uh, I- It wasn't me." I was still trying my best to be invisible, like being still would make him forget about my presence.

"Then what is it?" He asked as he went toward the stairs and -thank freaking God- came across another student on the stairwell. Maybe this guy would have an explanation.

But upon looking closely at the guy coming down the stairs, I realized it was... Noah?

Trust him to be there in a messy situation.

"What happened?" George asked Noah.

"What happened?" He asked him in return, parroting his words.

"Who rang the bell?"

Noah looked past George and met my eyes, turning my face into a grimace as I had a feeling I was going to get into trouble sooner than I thought. He was definitely going to add fuel to the fire.

"I did." He answered, not taking his eyes off me.

Oh?

"What was wrong?" George asked and if Noah didn't hurry up with his emergency explanation George was going to implode with all the worry.

Noah finally took his eyes off me and looked back at George. "I saw a weasel inside the building."

It was like George went through an array of emotions all at once as a wave of relief passed through him which was suddenly replaced by astonishment. "You pulled the alarm because of a *weasel?*"

Instead of an embarrassed or scared expression on his face like George and I were expecting, Noah stood there casually like he knew he had done the right thing. "Of course. What if it got close to someone and bit them with its disgusting mouth?"

I would have laughed if I wasn't hanging on to George's mercy to be forgiven for breaking the rules. Even though George had his back to me, I had a feeling he was looking at Noah like he was the dumbest guy on the planet. "Bite you with his disgusting mouth? Have you even considered how small they are compared to a tall human like you? They might feed on rodents or birds but

Weasels are harmless little creatures to humans!" By the end of his sentence, he was panting, but I wasn't sure if it was the result of all the anger or because he ran over here in a hurry. "Is that all? Nothing dangerous happening besides that?" He asked nevertheless, just to make sure.

"No, that's basically it," Noah replied casually, still unfazed by his anger somehow.

George let out a sigh of relief before pointing a finger at Noah. "You are not going to get away with this," He said sternly.

I jumped out of my wits when he suddenly turned around, his face holding an expression of extreme annoyance. He was positively pissed about the fact that he came running over in a hurry, all because of a silly fake 'emergency'. He shook his head and walked toward the door, all while I stood silently in my spot, unmoving. I held my breath, praying to be spared from his acknowledgment when he suddenly stopped beside me.

"And what are yo-" He paused, his eyes going wide as he finally realized something was not right. "What are you doing here at this time?" He looked at his wristwatch. "It's almost midnight and you're out of bed?!"

I had a feeling he was going to forget about my presence in his frantic hurry and anger, but it seems standing completely still doesn't get you out of troublesome situations. I knew he was eventually going to figure it out and come to me with his questioning, but it didn't occur to me I could have fled from the scene until this very moment.

Instead of giving him a reasonable explanation, I looked away from his demanding stare trying to think of an excuse. After several seconds of racking my brain in search of a sensible explanation, I gave up and accepted my defeat.

"I guess I am," I answered sheepishly, giving him a slight shrug.

George shook his head aggressively as he held the bridge of his nose, looking down like he was absolutely done with his job. "You both," He started as Noah left his spot at the bottom of the stairs to enter the lobby and stand in front of him. "You both are going to clean the whole lobby and common room over the weekend." He looked at the both of us, waiting for us to accept the punishment.

To be honest, I was quite relieved by the annoying but mild punishment considering that I was totally expecting to be suspended. Noah on the other hand, tilted his head back like he was offended. His 'always unbothered' expression finally breaking into a reaction.

"We have an intra-school match on the weekend." He told George.

"Then do it on Sunday," George replied simply.

"On Sunday? But-"

"I don't want to listen." George held up a hand. "You should have thought of that before you pulled the alarm for a freaking weasel."

I wasn't even going to try to argue or negotiate the punishment because I was content with not being suspended. As far as I was concerned, this punishment ensured that Asami wasn't going to be notified about my post-curfew date and I was planning for it to stay that way. I could already imagine the sick smile she would have if she found out I was caught breaking the rules, and how she would be overjoyed to finally have a reason to kick me out of the team. As I was trying my best to hide the Asami-related anxiety on my face, Noah took a glance in my direction and his strained expression suddenly softened a little bit. He quickly ran toward the door, grabbing George's arm to stop him before he left.

"Can you please not tell anyone about this? Especially the teachers?" I heard him ask George and a river of thankfulness unleashed in my heart as I felt like he read my mind.

George considered it for a second, like snitching us out to the teachers might compensate for the sudden and false distress he went through. But now that we were already cleaning over the weekend as punishment, I doubted he would take it out on us further than that. Another sigh of relief went through me as he finally nodded slowly. "Fine. I won't mention it to the teachers. But I better not see you causing trouble next time."

Noah and I nodded enthusiastically, like he could say anything and we would agree without any resistance.

"Now go back to your rooms before I change my mind."

Noah and I quickly ran in opposite directions at his final command- him towards the staircase and me towards the door. As I walked back toward my dorm building, it occurred to me that I didn't happen to see Liam at all after the alarm went off. He didn't even come downstairs to walk me to my room, which brought my attention to the fact that he didn't even check on me to make sure if I even reached the lobby safely. I found out soon enough that there was no real emergency, but Liam didn't know that. How could he just leave me hanging when there was a damn alarm going off in his building? The building that *he* told me to visit, making me risk my own identity by going out of my building past curfew. After calling me for a date, he didn't have the basic decency to check on me? To make sure I reached back alright?

Maybe Leah was right, leaving me to fend for myself was indeed a douchey thing to do. But is it really that bad? Or am I just overreacting? Maybe he had a genuine reason for not showing up and I should wait for an explanation before judging him like that.

As I reached my room, the lights were off and Mia was long asleep, the sight of her comfortably snuggled beneath the blankets made me crave the warmth of my own bed. I decided to shake the night off my head and settle inside my cozy bed, losing myself in a deep slumber that took me away from the complications of romantic relationships.

"I'm *so* glad Noah pulled the alarm before Liam could put his filthy lips on you," Leah said as we were sitting in my room on the floor, completing some assignments. The sunlight filtered through the curtains onto our notebooks, the warmth of the sun making us stay close to the window.

"He didn't even walk you to your room, what a jerk," Mia added.

"I told you he was no good. I'm still Team Noah," Leah said.

"There *is* no Team Noah, he has no part in this story!" I retaliated for the millionth time. "And by the way, he pulled the alarm for a little weasel, he's a loser."

Mia looked up at me suddenly. "*He* pulled the alarm?"

"Yes," I said in a tone that would confirm her suspicions of him being a loser.

"Are you sure he was the one who did it?" She asked again.

"Of course he was, he said it himself!"

"And you say he has no part in this story?" Mia started laughing, doubling over her notebooks.

Leah and I exchanged glances, not following the reason for Mia's laughter.

"What's so funny? Is he weasel-phobic?" Leah asked, just as clueless as me.

Mia paused in between her laughs and patted my thigh. "Girl, I think he likes you."

"*Excuse me?*" I put my hand to my chest as that was quite an offensive thing to say.

"When did you say the alarm went off?" She asked.

"... when we were about to kiss."

"And who did you run into before going to the roof?"

"Noah?"

"Connect the dots!" Mia exclaimed.

"Oh my God!" Leah said, finally understanding the connection. "He saw you guys, got jealous, and sabotaged your date!"

I rolled my eyes. "I think you're taking it too far, he was clearly scared of a weasel."

"You said he looked casual and unbothered." Leah pointed out.

"When is he not?" I told them.

"Seriously Avery, you have to be blind to not see it." Mia shook her head, still snickering as she continued scribbling in her notebook.

"You guys are delusional." I went back to writing my assignment with a dismissive shake of my head but there was a little part of me that almost believed their theory. Almost. Could he really get jealous? Over me? To the point that he would sabotage my date? Normally, this would be a situation that was supposed to piss me off, because he just ruined my amazing kiss with Liam over his stupid unreasonable jealousy. But somewhere inside my heart, I felt a hint of satisfaction. Just a hint. The unbothered casual Noah, getting so riled up that he would willingly get himself into trouble, all because of something that *I* did? I didn't know if it was true, but if it was, I knew I wasn't going to be mad about it. I didn't understand where that pleasure was coming from, maybe it was just because I liked the idea of him not being able to get something he wanted.

Whatever it was, if what Mia said was true, I was going to simply bask in the power I had over him.

If not, well, then he was still a loser with an irrational fear of weasels.

23

NOAH

"Should we go make the teams?" Mason looked up from his Nintendo after an hour, finally dropping the console on his bed. We were hiding away with our gaming consoles in our dorm, tired from the intra-school match we had yesterday. Intra-school matches took all the hype up until the inter-school matches started, and then the whole school came together to support its very own athletes. We were still a week away from our first inter-school match, which meant the pressure was now looming over our heads, and we were desperate to ignore it with a bunch of video games.

"For what?" I asked without looking up. He might have gotten bored but I was still in the middle of a deadly virtual dual.

"Cricket?" He asked, sitting back on his hands.

"Aren't you tired of playing? We already play every single day of the week." I had almost struck the enemy with my best shot, but I pressed the button just a second later and he ended up attacking me first. My character died and the words 'game over' decorated my screen. "You made me lose!" I yelled, as responding to his lame suggestion had distracted me enough to lose the timing in my game.

"You weren't gonna win anyway." He got up and started going through his wardrobe in search of a shirt.

"I was!" Defeating 'Saintbroseph' in the game was the only thing on my to-do list this afternoon, so losing the match made me lose all interest in the game as well. I considered Mason's offer one more time. "So you're actually gonna gather the teams?"

"Hell yes, I haven't played Cricket in so long." I never understood where he got the constant energy and passion to play sports 24/7, but I wasn't gonna pass on a good game of Cricket either. Football surrounds my life but sometimes even I get the urge to play something other than that. Before I even got up from the bed, he was halfway out the door.

"Let me put on my shoes!" I scrambled my way to the door and put on my shoes before running after Mason as we knocked door-to-door to assemble the players.

We were on the sixth door with three other guys behind us when we ran into George who was standing on a stool in the corridor to clean out the cobwebs. The building was cleaned every two weeks but somehow the cobwebs always made an appearance by then. With one look towards George, the incident from two nights ago flashed around my vision, as I realized I was supposed to be on cleaning duty today. It seems he had forgotten about my punishment, but I was sure if he laid his eyes upon my face he was going to remember everything and hand me a broom as well. Trying not to gain his attention, I slowly squeezed past his stool in the middle of the corridor, as silent as an ant taking a walk at midnight. George was positively busy looking up at the spider families in their spider homes and I ducked a bit, making my height less noticeable and my steps extra quiet. I was almost past him, reaching to cross over to the other side befo-

"Hey, George!" Mason exclaimed, making me jump out of my wits as I hurriedly stepped past his stool. My quick step shook his stool in the process, and he started wobbling around trying to save himself from the fall.

This freaking idiot.

George let out a shriek as the stool stumbled before Mason and two other guys caught the stool and George stabled himself holding their shoulders for support. He was panting, his eyes still closed from trying to catch up to the rush of the past few seconds. I froze in my spot behind him, desperately trying to be ignored as I realized I had once again created the same trouble he asked me not to create.

"Can't you see I'm standing here?!" He finally opened his, yelling at whoever was standing in front of him.

John Wilson raised his hands in innocence. "It wasn't me." He suddenly pointed at me. "He did it."

Annnd busted.

George turned around, and the moment his eyes laid on me, he almost sighed in defeat. "Why is it always you?"

I wished I had the answer to that question as well, but the silence I left was filled by Mason who had unintentionally made sure I wasn't getting off my duty today. "Always? What else did he do?"

Mason didn't know about the whole emergency bell story, but even if he did, I'm sure he would be asking that question anyway.

"He pulled the emergency bell the other day," George said, not taking his annoyed eyes off of me. The memory of the incident was finally resurfacing and I could tell he felt a fresh surge of annoyance

"That was you?" Mason turned to me, baffled. "But you said you didn't know who did it." Mason looked betrayed by my act of disloyalty.

"Well, yeah. It was me." There was no point beating around the bush and I admitted my defeat

George suddenly pointed at me, "Wait, wait, didn't I tell you to clean the building today?" So he finally remembered. "And where's the other girl? Avery?"

"I don't know where she is, but I was just about to ask you what I should start with."

George put his hands on his waist and tilted his head. "Were you really?"

"Okay, no." His face told me he wasn't going to believe my bullshit anyway so there was no point in wasting my lies.

"Go and call Avery, you guys are cleaning the common room first," George grumbled and went back to his duty, pushing more cobwebs out of the ceiling.

"I have no clue how you even manage to get yourself in all these troubles," Mason said, as the rest of the incomplete Cricket team went ahead, knocking on the rest of the rooms to get more players. "Now we lost our wicketkeeper."

I patted his back, as he genuinely seemed upset to be playing without me. "Sorry man, I'll see you at dinner."

And with that, Mason and company went the opposite way, as I started running towards the staircase to find my cleaning partner for the day.

"I was coming anyway, I'm not a slacker like you," Avery said with her phone in one hand and a water bottle in the other.

"Well, George asked me to bring you, or I wouldn't have come all the way just to ask for your annoying presence." The only reason I wasn't complaining about the cleaning duty punishment was that Avery was forced to do it with me. I would have found any reason to ditch it otherwise, but doing anything with her never felt like a waste of time. There was never a dull moment when she was around. I could have sat with her in a garden of nothingness and I would still be happy. Also, the fact she was not on a date with Liam at this very moment was enough to be grateful for. Who knows what would have gone down if she was free on a Sunday afternoon?

"Well, you did and I am here, so let's go." We went down the stairs of the girls' dormitory together, walking all the way to the place where the incident happened- the boys' dormitory.

"Really embracing the cleaning aesthetic, aren't we?" I glanced in her direction as she walked beside me. She was wearing a pair of denim overalls with a mustard yellow shirt inside. I had a feeling it was originally a pretty simple pair of overalls before it met Avery's eye and she handpainted a bunch of sunflowers and lilies on the bottom. There was a bunch on the front of her overalls as well, the sunflowers on the motif matching with the yellow shirt she wore inside. Her hair was rolled up in two buns on her head, and a few short strands of hair fell over her face lightly. With the soft charm and subtle elegance, she was easily looking like the cutest cleaning lady in the history of cleaning ladies.

She looked down at her outfit, feigning innocence. "What's wrong with it? It's better than your plain old mop and bucket fashion statement."

I looked down and truly enough, my outfit was just a plain old black T-shirt along with a pair of denim pants. "That's true." I chuckled. "But hey, at least my outfit doesn't scream 'I'm about to scrub the floors'."

She simply rolled her eyes, unbothered by my teasing. "Well, since we're stuck with this punishment, we might as well make the best of it. And by the way, sunflowers are in."

I loved how unapologetically she carried her own personality, and how no one could ever bring down her charm from shining no matter how much they tried. She knew what she liked and she never took any criticism of her choices. There was a part of me that had secretly started liking her uniqueness.

"Whatever you say, Captain America," I replied. "How come you were totally okay with working on a Sunday? I didn't even see you complain about it to George." I asked, still confused by her 'no issues' attitude that night.

"As long as I stay out of Asami's radar, I'm good." She said, taking a strand of hair out of her face. "This is nothing compared to your ambitions getting trampled by her."

After a good walk, we reached our building and went inside to assess the job. Our common room was simple- a few couches on the left side of the room, a fireplace and three sofas around it, a coffee table and chairs, and then a big circular table with eight chairs around it. We needed to sweep the room, mop the floors, dust the tables- and whatever was on it- and then finally set the furniture back to where it belonged. With two people working on it, it might only take an hour or two.

We had plenty of equipment for the job- brooms, dusters, a mop, and a cobweb duster. For our first task, Avery and I decided to divide the surfaces. She was in charge of sweeping the floors and I was in charge of dusting the ceilings (Because I'm a human tower, according to her). The rest of the work, we could share.

I had just stood on the step ladder to dust the ceilings when Avery pulled on the hem of my shirt while standing on the ground. "Clean the coast first, you doofus, how am I supposed to sweep with all this in my way?" She gestured toward the chairs, and how their misplaced positions were proving to be a messy ground for sweeping.

"Can't you do it yourself? I'm not in charge of the ground." I replied, turning back toward the ceiling. I knew I would step down to help her shift the chairs eventually, but would I ever willingly do something without annoying her about it first? Nope. If she asked me one more time, maybe I would think about it.

"Then get off the step and float in mid-air to clean the ceilings!" Boy, she gets mad easily. "If I'm in charge I'm making all the rules, and that means you can't stand on *my* ground." She added, trying to shake the step ladder. Despite her tiny hands doing the job, her effort wasn't futile because I let out a shriek, stumbling on the step and almost falling over on my butt. I held the ladder with all my might, trying to regain my balance as she stood there with a satisfied grin. Guess karma found me soon enough for almost making George fall down his step before.

"Fine, gosh you're such a witch." I jumped down from the ladder, following her lead to the other end of the room. She gestured her head toward the chairs around the big table, and I started picking them up to put them on the table upside down.

"I could be having a good shawarma in London right now if you didn't get absolutely petrified by a *weasel.*" She was hauling the chairs up, her whole body going backward as she lifted a chair to put it on the table.

Honestly, it was quite embarrassing to carry on with this story, the belief that I would pull the alarm over a little harmless weasel. But to admit that I did it because of her would be humiliating on a whole different level, so I decided to play along. "Why were you in our building in the first place? It wouldn't have affected you if you weren't breaking the rules already."

"Well," She raised her eyebrows, trying to think of an excuse. "Something important came up." She finished putting exactly three chairs in the time I did the other five, and now she was dusting her hands, completing her first task.

I was about to ask if the 'important' task was actually snogging a guy when the guy himself walked into the common room and I shut my mouth immediately.

"Hey, I got your text." He walked straight up to Avery, ignoring my presence like one would ignore the terms and conditions of a website. "I'm so sorry you had to do this."

Avery seemed glad to see him, but at the same time, there was a hint of annoyance on her face. "Where did you go when the alarm went off?" She asked him and it occurred to me that I really hadn't seen him after that. Avery seemed quite pissed at the fact that just left her that night, and rightfully so. I was ninety-nine point nine percent sure he must have run away and hid in his room because 1. Either he was too scared to come across an actual emergency and decided to take shelter alone or 2. He didn't want to be responsible for calling Avery after curfew when George came in. Both of these were incredibly selfish reasons to abandon her because he was the one who had called her over in the first place and if he really liked her, he should have been concerned about her safety as well. The other point one percent would be the off chance that he fell from the stairs while catching up with her, injured both his legs, and was unable to walk Avery home like a true gentleman. But since he was standing here with both his legs working just fine, that option seemed improbable.

"Uh, I-" Liam let out an embarrassed chuckle, looking down and touching the back of his head. "Henry called me over, I had to run over to our room to help him."

It was the most crappy and fake excuse I had ever heard, and as I glanced towards Avery, I was pretty sure she wouldn't-

Wait what?

She looked rather convinced by his story, but the knitted eyebrows told me she hadn't completely bought his story yet. *Come on Avery, don't believe his bullshit.*

"Help him with what?" She asked.

"Uh, the emergency. He was scared."

Avery nodded slowly, her eyes narrowed. "It must have taken you about ten minutes to realize there was no actual threat. Why didn't you call me later?" Not gonna lie, I was quite proud of her for asking the real questions, and at the same time, it was entertaining to watch Liam lie through his teeth. I folded my arms over my chest and waited for his response, totally invested in the conversation.

He looked towards the window as if trying to come up with a fictional story. "It wasn't the emergency alarm, I ran to Henry's room because he needed help with..." He thought for a second before looking back at her. "A cramp. I got busy stretching out his legs, he was in so much pain." He ended the sentence with such genuine empathy, that I almost believed his story for a second there. "I did text you later."

It was an obvious fact that they were on a date that night and that there was something between them, but when he said that part out loud, the reality of their relationship hit a little bit closer. I didn't even have Avery's number and here they were, texting each other over the nights like they were in a relationship or something.

"Oh," Avery said, looking down and feeling a bit embarrassed. "It's fine. I guess I overreacted for no reason."

And with that, the smile on Liam's face blossomed at the same time as my drastic eye-roll. Why are girls so naive to the lies of guys like him?

"It's okay." His smile was so oily it almost made me nauseous. "I would help you out but I actually have to help another friend with his homework."

I scoffed. The only homework he'll be doing was flirting with another girl probably.

"It's fine, Noah is helping me anyway." She gestured in my direction and his eyes finally landed on me. I gave him a stoic expression, hoping that my 'bored with your bullshit' face was reaching him in its truest form.

Luckily, he seemed to have received my message. "Ah that's good, you guys will be done quick." He turned back to her. "You look cute by the way, I like the sunflowers."

Avery looked down at her outfit like she forgot what she was wearing and then smiled. "Thank you, I painted it myself." Her cheeks had a touch of red tint, and I was quite sure she felt cold all through her body because she held her arms together like she was hugging herself.

"You're so talented." He replied and she blushed some more. I wish I could ask for a sick bag because this was definitely making me want to puke.

"I'm okay I guess." She tucked a strand of hair behind her ears. Liam seemed quite satisfied by how it worked out and how Avery went back to liking his deceitful ass.

He checked his wristwatch. "I have to go now or I'll be late. See you at dinner?"

"Sure." She chirped before he walked out the door, utterly satisfied by his lies.

"I'm okay I guess." I mocked her voice and her lovestruck smile immediately turned into a glare in my direction before she turned away to pick up the broom. I went towards the coffee table as well, picking up the chairs to put them on the table like I did with the round table. "What do you even see in him?" I asked her and she turned to look at me, broom in her hand.

"What?"

"Why are you dating that buffoon?"

Her hands went up to her waist, the broom now pointed at me. "What do you mean buffoon? He's a nice guy."

"What's so nice about abandoning his date in an emergency?"

"You heard him, he just got busy." It felt more like she was defending him to herself instead of me like even she could see how pathetic his excuse was. Well, at least somewhere inside her heart she knew he didn't deserve her and I was glad to see that she was at least a little bit embarrassed about liking him.

"And you believe him?" I deadpanned.

She might not have an answer to that but I might have pushed the right button because she seemed immediately offended. "You're just jealous because you're alone." Her eyes narrowed as she spit the accusation. "Mason got busy with Mia and now you don't have anyone."

"How would you know that?" The urge to tackle her accusing remark won over my logic and I blurted out the most unreal sentence. "I'm actually seeing someone."

The momentary wave of satisfaction took me in all its blissful glory before it died a sudden death when Avery responded with the question I *should* have seen coming. "And who's that?"

Well, shit.

I mentally ran through the list of girls I had liked in the past, but it was a very short list consisting of about three girls and none of them weren't anywhere near my dating radar currently. I was still trying to come up with a name when her expression changed in the slightest.

It seemed she took my silence as a need for privacy, thinking I didn't wanna share the name. "Is it that girl Everly? You guys were dating before, right?" Her eyes held a contrast of curiosity when you matched it with her nonchalant attitude. She wanted to know who it was but she didn't want to seem interested and ask.

"Yes," I answered immediately, grateful to have a name, *any name*, to make up for my lost self-esteem. The need to gloat won over plain simple logic, and for a moment, I didn't believe I had actually admitted to that. Considering how I didn't want to use a fake name, or how I didn't want to use any of my friends or start a stupid rumor, going along with Everly was my best bet right now.

"I mean we aren't together anymore. But yeah, we aren't exactly over either. Somewhere in between you know?" It wasn't a complete lie because Everly genuinely wasn't over me yet. I would never bring it up to her personally, because I didn't want to give her any false hope but the news wasn't leaving this room so I didn't mind saying that to Avery. "How did you know we dated before?"

"It's all she talks about in the common room." She read the question on my face before I even voiced it and quickly added. "I wasn't eavesdropping! I just overheard a few times."

I nodded, desperate to let this subject fall down into the pits of darkness. "Anyway, I hope that clears the concern you had about my loneliness."

"I wasn't concerned, but I guess you're not as pathetic as I thought you were." She said and turned around, starting to sweep the dust from under the tables.

That's it?

I told her I was seeing someone and that is the response I get? Cold, unbothered, and ignored? I'm not sure where this was coming from but I wanted it to bother her just as much as Liam bothered me. I wanted to see that she enjoyed my company as much as I did. I'm not saying she should be jealous, but she could at least care a little bit. She could at least feel a little bit surprised, if not possessive. If Liam mattered to her so much that she didn't even care if I was here or not, did I ever mean anything to her at all?

We spent the next hour sweeping, mopping, and dusting the whole room as I tried to ignore the nagging in my heart. The more we cleaned the room, the more dust went floating around the room and soon the sound of our sneezing was the only sound echoing over the walls.

"We should have taken Benadryl before coming here." She said, sneezing again right after.

"I'm more tired from the sneezing than the cleaning," I replied, rubbing my extremely itchy eyes. It was like an endless cycle, the more I rubbed my eyes the more I couldn't stop.

"We're almost done. What's the time?" She asked, rubbing her eyes as well.

"05:24 P.M." I glanced at my watch.

"Then it's almost dinner time! I heard they have fish and chips today." She said, happily returning to fix the cushions on the couch.

I settled the chairs back to their original places and then shifted back all the furniture that we moved to mop the floors. Once I was done, Avery and I went back towards the entrance and took a long hard look at the shining floors and the cobweb-free ceilings.

"That's so satisfying," I said, looking over the clean room proudly. Everything in the room was perfectly arranged, unlike the usual messy scene I was used to witnessing.

"We make a good team." She smiled and I almost fell over from the cuteness of it.

"Good thing we are teammates." I held my closed fist in her direction and she hit it with her own.

"Are you guys done?" George walked in, his hair a mess and his clothes full of dust. Not much different than us. I found a newfound respect in my heart for his hard work and efforts as I first handedly realized that this stuff was not easy at all.

"See, we even dusted the shelves and the books." Avery ran over to the front wall, showing George how seriously we took our jobs.

"See, this is why I don't rat you kids out. You guys are actually not bad." George seemed happy that a day's worth of his work had already been done in a perfect way.

"You're welcome." I beamed at him. Seeing him happy about getting off work early honestly made me feel happy as well.

"I seriously need to take a shower now." She came back towards the door, giving me a smile as she walked out of the room. "See you at dinner!"

Long after she left our building and went on her way toward her dorm, a realization slowly crept into my heart as I walked toward my room. The way we spent the last two hours bickering and cleaning together against our will, I should have been feeling relieved about finally parting our ways. I wanted to feel happy about finally getting off the hook and spending my time enjoying the rest of the Sunday alone. But there was a part of me that almost felt sad about not having any reasons to spend time together. I looked forward to seeing her at dinner, but I knew we weren't friends enough for me to join her table like Liam does. We weren't exactly friends, but I wanted us to be. And more than that I wanted her to crave me as much as I craved her.

But it seemed the universe wasn't willing to give it to me right now. It had finally decided to make me go through the experience that every teenager goes through. It was late in serving me this virtue, but now that it was right in front of my face, it was hard to ignore or cancel it out with something else.

The realization hit me like a lightning bolt.

I liked Avery. More than just as a rival or a friend.

It was a truth I hadn't been ready to confront until now. I'd been successful in ignoring the signs, the subtle hints that my feelings were evolving beyond the surface. But today, as I saw the spark she held in her eyes for Liam, the undeniable truth had caught up with me.

It wasn't just about the soccer field anymore; it was about the warmth I felt when she was around, the way her smile seemed to light up the room. I cared about what she thought, not just on the soccer field, but about me as a person.

I couldn't deny the pull I felt towards Avery anymore, but with it came the humbling truth — the possibility that this was how it felt when you are not important to someone who is important to you. It was a revelation that lingered in the air, leaving me with a mix of emotions as I grappled with the newfound complexity of my feelings.

Is this how it feels to truly like someone?

And is this how it feels when you realize they don't like you back?

The shower was long and cold, even though the weather wasn't exactly ideal for a cold shower. I washed my face a dozen times to get the dust out of my eyes and nose before I washed my hair properly, not leaving any bits of dust behind. Finally, I put on my dark green sweater with my loose-fitting black pants and went towards the ground to find Mason and company. Any distractions I could manage to get right now would be welcomed with open arms.

"You missed an amazing match dude," Luke said as I came across twenty-something people leaving the ground.

"For real, we played twenty overs each," Mason added.

"Jack dropped a catch TWICE," Henry added, ignoring the glare from Jack.

The conversation was followed by five of the people talking at once, telling me all the spectacular details of the match they played and how much I missed out. We were halfway to the locker room when Mason excused himself from the group and caught up to me, resting his arm around my shoulder. I ducked and swatted his arm away. "Ew, I just took a shower. Get your sweaty hands away from me."

"So discourteous." He said with a dramatic hand on his chest and fake hurt on his face.

"I'll be courteous when you take a shower first."

"Hmm." He studied me, reading every line on my face. "Either your cleaning date went really well or really shitty," Mason said in a low voice, careful about anyone overhearing our conversation.

"What date? It was a punishment."

"Sure it was," He shrugged. "But judging from how unbothered you are, it doesn't look like you feel that you missed out on a good match. And that only happens when you've been doing something *better* than the original plan."

If I thought about it, he wasn't wrong. Normally I would have lost my mind about missing a good cricket match because of some stupid cleaning duties, and I would have especially screamed into oblivion if my friends told me how fun it was. We rarely had enough time or players to play Cricket in school, let alone play for twenty overs non-stop. If I consider that, it was quite a special day for me. But somehow, missing out on all of it wasn't bothering me that much. Yes, I wish I could have played, but spending that time with Avery made me feel like it wasn't a waste of time.

"Does it matter though?" There was a hint of disappointment in my voice, enough to show him how upset I was. "She's dating Liam."

"Not really." He replied confidently and for a second it did lift my spirits up. "They aren't official yet. From what I have seen, I think she just likes him but isn't sure about dating him."

"What difference does that make? The fact is still that she likes him- not me." My head hung low in defeat.

"There's no way to know for sure." He said. After a brisk pause, his excited voice came through again. "Unless..."

I looked at him with my eyebrows raised, because Mason's 'unless' was never straightforward. He looked back with a smug expression as he pushed the door open and we entered the locker room.

"You know how Mia was always telling me how I'm not her type? But then the minute Lily started flirting with me, she was suddenly clear about her feelings?"

I saw where this was going but he didn't know that I already dropped the jealousy bomb. "I already told her I was seeing Everly and she gave me NO reaction. Not everything works out the same way."

He nodded. "Sure, not everything works out the same way and maybe that's because you guys have such a... uh complicated relationship." He took his sweaty shirt and threw it in his duffel bag. "I say don't give up yet, I have a good feeling about this."

Making Avery jealous didn't feel like the right thing to do, but the way Liam lied to her face made me feel sick in my stomach. He wasn't honest with her and he wasn't sincere about her either. To just sit and watch her date a douche like him was messing with me every single time I saw them together. But using Everly to get back at Avery was also incredibly wrong. As ostentatious as she was with our whole relationship, I still didn't think it was okay to hurt her for my own benefit.

"Anyway, I'm going to shower now. You better run to the dining hall and save us some seats before our table is hogged by the seniors again." Mason declared before heading into a stall, the sound of running water jerking me back to the present.

I walked into the dining hall as lonely as a neglected houseplant and noticed Avery's table straightaway. Her hair was still damp from the shower and she had a fresh change of clothes. Instead of the country girl look in the morning, she was now channeling a dark winter look. A loose green cardigan over a black shirt, I wondered how she pulled off each look so effortlessly. However, the pleasant sight was quickly ruined by the presence of a certain brown-haired boy, who was sitting close to her as they discussed something. Liam was at their table every single time without fail, and it was starting to get on my nerves a little bit. No actually, a lot.

Our usual table was still empty so I grabbed a tray and started piling up on my plate: fish and chips, some greens, and a pudding. The seniors were probably out on a day trip to the city and haven't returned yet. The warden will be calling them non-stop once they hit the seven O'clock mark.

Alone at my table, I was still thinking about what Mason said. Would it be okay to make Avery jealous? Moreover, wouldn't it be downright evil to break some random girl's heart so I can get back at her? Just when I was busy considering a fake girlfriend- it was like the Universe heard my thoughts and decided to execute my 'make Avery jealous' plan because Everly spotted me from the buffet area. She smiled at me as usual and I smiled back, not realizing what that would lead to. She started walking in my direction and when I looked around to busy myself with some chatter, I remembered I was the only one here.

The realization settled in that I was stuck here alone as Everly came at me with every intention to get back together. I took one last look at Avery's table, but she was still busy talking about something- using her hands way too much in the process. She didn't care if I was here or not, so I decided to return my attention back to our table where Everly was sitting down.

"Hey, Noah." She smiled with a tilt of her shoulder.

"Hey." I half-smiled back.

"Are you okay?" She sounded concerned like she was going to leave everything right this moment until she made sure I was- in fact- okay. Too bad I knew that concern wasn't actually sincere.

"Yeah, why wouldn't I be?" I started cutting into the fish with the knife and fork, desperately waiting for the rest of my friends to show up.

"Then why are you sitting alone? Where are your friends?"

"Well they're all taking showers, they will be here in a few minutes." I started shoving the food in my mouth, unsure of what to say or do. This was the first time in months that I had been alone with her, and it was awkward as hell.

"Can I say something?" Her voice went small all of a sudden, like she was preparing herself for a very emotional speech.

"Uh, sure." Shoving more chips.

"I miss you quite a lot you know?" She looked down, playing with the fork in her salad bowl.

Now *this* was awkward, because I hadn't missed her a single second ever since she spewed that nonsense about immigrant kids behind my back. "You... do?" Asking her to confirm her previous sentence was the best reply I could muster. At least it would give me time to think about what to say next. Or maybe enough time for my friends to get here.

"Of course." She said, her lips going into a pout. "I miss being in the stands and cheering for my boyfriend to score." Her face was sad but her words were empty of any affection. *Of course*, that's what she missed- not our dates, not my presence- just the matches where she got to be the popular girlfriend.

"Sometimes I also miss... the London trips we used to take." It felt like a necessity to add the actual meaningful parts of our relationship, so maybe she realized our relationship wasn't just a public stunt. "Remember how we always used to go to the same Cafe and the barista started giving us free muffins."

"Of course. Everyone thought we looked so cute together." There was a sparkle in her eye like she was flattered by the praise all over again. "I wish we could have that back."

I nodded, not sure what to do now that she had singlehandedly taken the initiative to bring our relationship back from the dead. "Um... are you sure about that?"

"Of course." Her silky blonde curls fell over her shoulder as she leaned forward to emphasize her willingness. "Inter-school matches are about to start, don't you think it would be cute to go to the matches together?" There was a glint in her when she thought about all the things we could be doing together. "And oh, the New Year's ball! It's just two weeks away and we can go as a couple!" And of course, none of those things included me or our quality time, just a bunch of public appearances.

The New Year's ball had completely left my mind in light of our first interschool match coming up, but if there was one thing I remembered, it was that I didn't want to go with Everly. "I'm still deciding on a partner." Truth was, I didn't want any other partner except Avery, but admitting that to Everly would be too embarrassing so I left that detail out. Even if Avery wouldn't go with me, going solo was still a better option than going with Everly.

"I hope you decide soon, or I might get snatched away." Before I could tell her that I wasn't worried about that since I wasn't holding on to her anyway, she looked past my shoulder and a frown formed on her face. "Anyway, I guess I'll see you later." Her frown turned back around in a millisecond, and she got up with her tray, the big sweet smile taking over her face again.

I wasn't done thanking the heavens for the interruption when Mason sat down beside me. "Did we ruin your date?"

"Of course you did, I was just about to ask her to marry me."

Despite trying my best not to, my eyes went in search of Avery, who was still finishing her food while everyone around her was already done. Their table seemed to be quieter now, compared to a few minutes ago when Liam and Avery seemed to be neck-deep in some intense conversation. Now that Everly brought my attention to the New Year's ball, I wondered if I would ever be able to take her with me. Now that she was falling deeper and deeper for Liam and I was getting left behind.

24

AVERY

Sitting at the table with some delicious fish and chips on my plate, I was seriously reconsidering my choices. Liam was sitting with us as usual, and Leah was busy telling Mia what she ate in London today. And then there was me, whose infatuation with Liam was dying a slow painful death every time he opened his mouth.

"So that's why my family went on a trip to Dubai last year, we just needed a moment of change after the robbery." He said after taking a sip of water.

I made the mistake of telling him how I love shawarma, and now he was busy telling me how you can only get real shawarma in Dubai. Then he started telling me how there was once a huge robbery at his insanely expensive and luxurious mansion- and that is why they decided to take a trip to Dubai for a 'change' to bring them out of their feeling of loss. Crazy rich people confuse me sometimes, how can you go for a whole damn trip after just getting robbed of a few hundred pounds?

"There's a good shawarma place in the Borough market though," I told him, since I didn't have any grand stories about my spontaneous vacations. "There's a sweet old uncle there who makes the best Arab food." And suddenly, the memories of our London trip fogged my vision, the thought of Noah's happy face bringing a smile out of my own.

Surprised by my own act of smiling at Noah's thoughts, I shook myself out of my trance and zoned back into Liam's conversation. "And don't you like Boba as well? I remember I went to Tokyo for a vacation with my siblings and we had the absolute Boba over there."

Physically, I nodded. But mentally, I was busy picturing the time I went to the Cafe with Noah and how he remembered to ask the barista for decaf. I don't know if it was the absolute best frappe I ever had, but it sure was the one I had with the best company. That whole day started flashing before my eyes and I found myself smiling at the memory again.

What is wrong with me?

I just spent the last two hours cleaning a dusty room with my annoying teammate and somehow he was *still* here to take up space in my head? I decided to act on my impulse and my eyes went around the hall for a second before they landed on Noah sitting at his usual table all by himself. I looked at my digital wristwatch- it was past 06:30 P.M. Why was he sitting alone at peak dinner time? Where are his friends?

"And have you been to Italy?" Liam asked after a rant about something I wasn't bothered enough to hear.

"No, didn't I tell you it's my first time in Europe?" Once again an alarm went off in my head, telling me I was driving down the wrong road. Noah- who was barely my friend- remembered something as little as my caffeine sensitivity and here I was with my 'almost' boyfriend who couldn't even remember that I was in another country for the first time.

It was like the more I paid attention, the more I was discovering reasons to dislike him. The rose-tinted glasses were finally fading off and I was seeing him like he was for the first time. A lot of the initially attractive qualities were now starting to piss me off. Being conversational was now annoying because all he did was talk about himself. Being sweet was now starting to show up as being pretentious because he was only ever sweet to you on your face. I had heard him say nasty things about someone he had just met nicely two minutes ago and it blew my mind how he could change his demeanor in a flash. Having a coy smile was now starting to offend me because he gave this same flirty smile to a dozen girls a day.

Honestly, he had been causing some serious traffic in my heart even before all this. It was like I was refusing to let go of my crush on him just because he was the first guy I liked after coming here, and it was a very nice meet cute. My crush on him reminded me of the time when I was new and clueless, and he helped me with a lot of stuff in settling in. He noticed me when people didn't recognize me. Maybe also because he had been showing me interest as long as I have. I wanted it to be something, instead of just being a short meaningless crush. But now my feelings for him were fading away, and I was left utterly confused. Ever since that night on the roof, I had been feeling a hint of irritation toward him and I thought it would get better when he apologized for it. And he did, he did apologize but despite accepting his apology, I was rethinking my decision. Noah thinks I shouldn't trust him and even though his opinion might be the last one I care about, I was starting to think he was right. There couldn't have been an emergency bad enough that he couldn't call me for a day, and now he was back here talking to me like a complete snob. How did I miss any of this before?

Liam's - more insufferable by the minute- conversation was escalating, and somewhere during his rant my eyes wandered towards a certain table. A table that was previously occupied by a single inhabitant, and was now gracing the presence of two people. A boy and a girl.

Noah and Everly.

From where I was sitting, I could partially see Noah's face but Everly was in my full view. I could see every pretty smile, each cute flutter of her eyelids and if I watched really really close, maybe I could even read her lips. Her hair was perfectly silky and the red tint on her cheeks was visible even from over here. I narrowed my eyes to understand what she was saying and immediately realized lip reading wasn't for everyone and definitely not as easy as they show it in the movies. It was incredibly hard to judge what she was saying just from the movement of her lips, but I think I did catch her saying the words 'New Year's ball'.

Suddenly, my brain went back to a few days ago when Mia had mentioned the ball coming up. She was telling how she finally had a partner to go with, and how this was the first ball she was happy to attend because she also had a best friend this time. Could it be that they've decided to go together to the ball? With the match coming up, I had completely forgotten about it, but could it be that he had already decided on a partner for it?

He did say he was seeing Everl-

"Avery? Ave? Weren't you in that class?" Liam repeated, leaning down to my eye level to make me look at him.

"Hmm? Yeah, of course, that was so cool." I faked a response, surely anything he says can be met with that same sentence.

"Huh? You think Mrs. Jones' accident with Liquid Nitrogen was cool?" Liam was visibly confused, probably wondering why I was not showing any signs of empathy toward the cold burns she received.

"What? No, I-" I quickly zoned back to our table, trying to come up with something that wouldn't make me sound like a sociopath. "I was just saying Liquid Nitrogen is so *cool*, like you know, it's so cool it can burn your skin." I was talking and nodding quickly like I never lost a single part of this conversation.

I tried to ignore the peculiar stare Mia was giving me, a mixture of amusement and concern. The amused part was more dominant though, like she just won a round of poker and won thousands of dollars. I noticed none of my friends around the table were eating anymore and then I looked at their plates which were all empty and clean. I looked at mine- only halfway done. I was so busy trying to figure out what was happening at Noah's table that I completely forgot I was sitting here with the intention of having a meal. I picked up my fork and started finishing the leftover food.

"It's okay, sometimes Avery even surprises herself with the things she says," Mia said. Technically she was saying a very casual thing, but at this point, I knew her better to know what she meant. She looked at Noah's table and then back at me, connecting the dots better than a toddler with their coloring book.

A chuckle left my mouth as I picked up some fries on my fork, acknowledging a silent conversation between me and Mia. After accusing Noah of being jealous, this felt like an instant karma slap the Universe threw at me. I wouldn't have admitted this a few days ago, but dammit the whole situation was starting to get on my nerves. After Mia, it was my turn to connect the dots. He did tell me he was seeing Everly, that it wasn't completely over for them. And now they were sitting together like a couple, probably having a cute dinner date. The words 'New Year's ball' were certainly spoken so that means he was probably taking her with him as his date. In a way, I was glad I forgot about the whole ball thing, or I know I would have impulsively asked Liam out as my date. Going solo would be far better than having a boring pompous date cling to you for the whole evening.

The table was quiet now that I was focused on finishing my meal, the silence amplifying my internal monologue. I thought about how I would feel when Noah walked in with Everly at his side, officially confirming her as his girlfriend. He would get back together with Everly, they would become the popular school couple and I would be left on the side wondering what would have happened if I was brave enough to make a move.

I had been so wrapped up in denial, in the idea that Noah and I could never get along when in reality, he had been a source of comfort for me all along. *Did I realize it too late?* It was almost as if the universe had conspired to make me recognize what I had only when it was slipping away.

I took a deep breath, trying to steady myself as I grappled with the emotions that had finally come to the surface.

Why am I always late for everything?

"You don't even complain about the extra hours of practice anymore, are you okay?" Mia asked me as I was standing in front of the mirror parting my hair so I could make my usual French braids.

"I'm going to play my first match for the school this week!" I momentarily paused my braid to deliver the news as enthusiastically as possible. "I mean only if the coach lets me play, but I'm still so excited about it." I was careful not to jump too much, holding my half-done braid tightly to not mess it up.

"I'm so happy for you Ave. Who are you playing against?" She had a happy smile.

"Oakwood High," I told her, resuming my braid and looking back in the mirror.

"Oh, that's quite far. It's way past London, somewhere before Reading." She was calculating how long the imaginary journey was, and I turned around to look at her with a sad pout. "But that doesn't mean I won't come! It's a charity event so our school would be taking extra buses anyway. Of course, I'll be there!" She reassured me and my frown quickly turned into a full smile.

"Look who's early," Noah called out from near the net, stopping his juggle and waving at me.

"Why are you always here first?" I walked towards him. It's crazy how I wouldn't willingly have a conservation with him during practice two months ago, but now it came naturally.

"I like to appreciate the silence of the ground before Coach arrives with his shrill whistle and loud orders." He was now holding the ball in his hands, shaking his head to get some wild hair away from his face.

"Fair enough."

"Is your ankle doing better now?" He asked, his eyes wandering over to my foot.

I lifted it up, moving it in a circle to see if there was any pain. "It doesn't hurt anymore but the sensitivity is still there." He nodded. "It will be fine by the end of the week if I just continue the exercises."

"It better be. I hope Coach picks you in the starting line-up." He went back to juggling the ball between his feet, unaware of the sudden heat stroke he sent through my body by saying that sentence.

"You want me in the line-up? Quit joking." I tried to cover up the fact that I was absolutely flattered by his thoughts.

"No seriously. I really want to win this match." He momentarily glanced up to look at me before returning back to his feet.

"And how is that connected to me?" I asked, just to make sure. It seemed like he implied I would be a great help.

"We can play better?" He said it like it was obvious, but it came as a surprise to me. "I wish he benches Jack. That guy just gives me extra stress."

"And I don't?"

He missed the touch with the ball and it suddenly went past his feet, rolling onto the ground. He seemed disconnected from his juggling way before that, and now he finally looked at me without any distractions. "Yeah, you get on my nerves too but your playmaking is quite incredible."

My eyes went wide for a second before I managed to blink back, my cheeks heating up suddenly. "You think? I thought you said tiny girls don't scare anyone."

He laughed his charming bright laugh. "Well, if you managed to scare me, you can scare any defender out there with your sneaky runs."

I chuckled, feeling both pleased and shy to be praised by him.

"I really hope we win this." He said, looking up at the sky. His sharp jawline was breathtakingly visible, the Adam's apple in his throat adding to his boyish charm. "It feels so good to have your team's name on the cheque that goes into a charity, knowing you contributed. Not with your own money, but at least with your skills."

I took the liberty of that moment to look at him, taking in the sincerity of his voice. His perfectly tousled hair gave him an irresistible allure, his long eyelashes adding softness to his handsome face. He was still looking up at some bird flying by and I was so grateful for this moment I had all for myself. Where I could just look at him and not have him say something sassy about it. Not being caught admiring those cute lips, the way they were in an absentminded pout at the moment.

Every conversation with Noah had something so meaningful it was almost impossible not to admire his mind for a minute before he went back to his usual sass and sarcasm. "The charity is going to an NGO that serves child education services you know?" He looked back at me.

I quickly switched my awestruck gaze to a normal one. "How do you know?"

"I looked it up online. Last year it went towards hygiene and winter necessities during winter for the needy, this year it's going towards education." He was smiling, really happy about the prospect of helping less fortunate people.

"It means a lot to you huh?" I asked softly, my tone empty of any riposte.

"Yeah." He went to pick up the ball again, walking a few feet away and I unknowingly followed. "I'm lucky that my dad is able to pay for my tuition and football now, but I know how it feels to be uncertain about your finances." He was talking casually but I knew it wasn't just a casual conversation for him.

"Really?" Was all I could manage to say, as I failed to conjure up the proper words that would let him know I wanted to know more about him but I was just too scared to ask.

"Yeah. When we first came to England, my dad couldn't find a decent job for like six months. It delayed our admissions for a little while before my dad put all his money into investing in a shop that now stands as a Turkish supermarket in Liverpool."

"A Turkish supermarket? That sounds like it has lots of tasty stuff." Inside, I appreciated every single thing he was telling me about his experiences. Outside, I was struggling to find the right words to respond to his heartwarming conversation.

"Yeah, I'll get you some Turkish snacks from his shop someday, you'll love it." His voice was sincere, without any hint of sarcasm. He picked up the ball and then looked at the far end of the field. "Oh, the Coach's here."

A handful of students were following him into the field and I realized with a bit of disappointment that our little pre-practice heart-to-heart was over. "Practice like crazy, we *have* to win the match okay?" He was smiling as he held the ball on his side and we walked toward the team together.

His eyes were bright and sincere, and it was apparent this match meant a lot to him. It wasn't just the thrill of winning the first match of a new season, but rather it was the benefaction that made him happy. It was the fact of donating to a charity that helped children get a proper education despite their financial inadequacy. I wondered how his virtuous qualities were always hidden behind his sarcastic mouth and how he was slowly building up a place in my heart.

Building up? No, actually, it was already built weeks ago without my knowledge and now I was stuck with the consequences of falling for your rival and not realizing it sooner. After the practice and my hot water shower, I was walking into our common room when I saw Everly happily having a conversation with her best friend. The New Year's ball snapped back into my head and I realized I was probably going to die of jealousy when he eventually ends up taking her as his date after the match. Even though the feeling was nagging away at my heart every waking moment, I rushed to my room and tried to brush it off. I needed to focus on the match first and if I kept picturing the image of Noah and Everly dressed up like royals and slow dancing to a romantic song, it was going to send my nerves into overdrive. I imagined the day of the match, thinking what it would be like to represent my school for the first time. Maybe a call with Ella was what I needed to get my mind off things and set them into perspective.

"I wish I could attend the match Ave, I'm so sad I'll miss it," Ella told me through the screen.

"Mia will be there, she'll send you all the videos." I looked over at the other side of our room where Mia was busy texting someone. "Right, Mia?"

She looked up, half listening to our conversation and half replying to Mason. "Huh? Yeah, of course, I'll be there and I'll record everything."

I smiled back at the screen. "I will be playing with new teammates now. It's kind of weird playing with the people I played against, but I guess I'll build the team spirit when I see total strangers playing against us."

"Isn't that guy in your team as well? Noah?"

The mention of his name made my heartbeat rise up but I tried to act natural. "Yeah, he's with us." This was different than all the other times I ranted about him, this time I had conflicted feelings about him and I wasn't sure enough about them to let her know.

"That sucks. Don't ever give him the chance to bully you okay? You deserve the spot on the team and don't let him tell you otherwise." She sounded genuinely concerned about my teammate situation but little did she know her advice was a little too late, considering we had already become friends.

"You think I'd let anyone do that?" I asked her, instead of explaining how Noah and I found ourselves hanging out together more often than not and were way past the bullying phase.

"Of course not, you're the same Avery that trashed Ian Taylor's car because he implied that girls should stick to softball and leave football for the guys." She laughed loudly.

"He was so pissed he tried to imply my actions were fueled by racism." I was laughing now too.

"Where was he from?" Mia asked, always interested in our conversations.

"He was a third-generation Japanese," I told her and then she was also doubling over, laughing at the fact that someone accused me of being racist against my own race.

And just like that, the night ended on a good note- laughing and sharing stories with my own little girl gang before we all signed off and fell into a peaceful slumber.

25

NOAH

"Are you actually gonna man up and ask Avery out or just sulk during the ball too?" Mason was on his bed texting Mia, and it was safe to say I had been sulking during the last hour.

"I can't ask her, she obviously likes Liam." I rested my head on the mattress, lying down in my shorts and comfy T-shirt.

"Did she tell you she's going with him?"

"Not really. She didn't mention anything about the ball at all."

"Then you have all the right to ask her out. The worst she can say is no." He was simultaneously texting on his phone and responding to my crisis.

"Do you even know her?" I sat up leaning on my elbows and looked at him. "There's probably a whole list of the worst things she can say."

"Wow, you really have no idea how to deal with rejection. If she's going with Liam then you should go with Everly." He suggested.

"Nah." I laid back down and stared at the ceiling. "I'd rather go alone than take her with me."

"Good luck going solo but don't bother me with your loneliness that day because I already have a gorgeous date." He smiled at his screen.

I sighed. "Guess I'll be spending the ball in the corner of the room, eating all the fancy food alone."

All of the Summerfield Football Club was standing at our bus stop, waiting for the Team bus to arrive. It was 09:00 A.M. currently, and we were all prepared for the one-and-a-half-hour ride to Reading. I was well packed with my earphones, gummy candy, some Jaffa cakes, and my team kit. Our team bus was big enough to accommodate some extra people from our school as well, and that usually meant that the players could bring their friends or partners along for the trip. The school usually sends three more buses to take the other students to the match as well, but if you were one of the people to take the extra seats on our bus, it meant you would arrive earlier than the others.

I looked around the bus stop, subconsciously looking for two specific people. Mason was obviously here with Mia, our captain Kyle had brought the most popular senior girl- Julie, and almost all of my teammates were paired with someone else. Where's Avery? My eyes scanned the bus stop again and realized I skipped her the first time as I found her standing right beside Mia. Her two French braids were falling over her shoulders and she was also holding a bag on her side. No Liam in sight. Was he late?

After a few minutes of listening to some songs, the team bus came rolling around the corner and the fact that Liam still hadn't shown up made me realize Avery hadn't brought any extras for the trip either. The bus halted in front of us and I took out my earphones to listen to our Coach give us the last-minute discipline talk.

"Focus on the match first before you guys get too happy about your dates cheering for you." He said in a bored voice. "As you all know it's a one-and-a-half-hour ride to Oakwood High. We are going to stop at a diner for a light lunch at twelve, upon reaching the city. The match is scheduled to start at two, and you guys are supposed to go straight into your locker rooms the moment we enter the school. No trash talk, no disrespect, I want to see all of you on your best behavior."

There were constant nods coming from the team, as we registered the same speech we get before every match. "The people who are not part of the team are supposed to stay with Miss Green. You can go to the stands and take your seats early. The match will likely end before four, and then all the players can go to the locker rooms for a fresh shower. It's a long ride back so I will be expecting everyone to file back in line for the bus at five. You are going to take the same bus on your way back, no changes are allowed."

All the players and their partners nodded. "Make sure all of you are on time for everything, because I'm not going to wait for anyone." He always threatened to leave us behind if we ever ran late, but we all knew he would never actually do that. "Alright, start boarding." He gestured toward the door and moved aside, letting all students file into the bus.

Since every single teammate had brought their plus ones, there were only two seats left at the end of the bus. I looked behind me at Avery and she gave me a look that said 'hurry up' so I quickly dipped down into the last seat as she sat down beside me. She noticed my earphones and took the right one off my ear before putting it on herself. She took a second to register the song and then nodded appreciatively. "You have good taste."

I didn't know when we crossed the line of friendship where we didn't even need to ask before sharing our earphones, but I wasn't complaining. *'Okay, we've sat together on a bus before, chill.'* I told my heart but it was already busy working up a hurricane in my chest.

Let's just make a casual conversation.

"You didn't bring Liam?"

Casual conversation I said! My brain yelled at me as I just blurted out the first thing on my mind.

Nevertheless, she came out of her music-induced daydream. "Huh? No, I didn't want him here." Wait, what was this strange thing spreading through my chest? Oh yeah, it's happiness. "It's my first match for this team, and I want to focus on this with all my brain capacity. If he was sitting here with me, I'd be listening to his boring talks for the whole two hours of our ride."

"One and a half." I corrected her.

"Same thing."

I was glad she was not here with Liam but if there was a part of me that wanted to ask her out, it died right on the spot. I was overflowing with my feelings for her but I knew saying anything like that before a match would only distract her a great deal. This is the first time she was playing with us and I didn't want to ruin her focus by mentioning how I have been unable to think about anything else except her these past few days. Maybe it was fine before, but ever since I watched her on the roof with Liam, it was like a switch was flipped, confirming my suspicions about liking her.

But right now, we weren't a pair of high schoolers. Right now, we were teammates, going to the arena for an important match. And I wanted to respect our formal camaraderie until the end of the day at least.

I opened up a bag of gummy worms and popped one into my mouth. I shoved the bag to her side, offering her some of my candy.

"You packed gummies?" She exclaimed and happily took some.

"I also have Jaffa cakes in my bag." I patted the backpack that sat on my lap and it made Avery smile like an excited kid.

"Wow, you really packed well for a road trip."

We relaxed back on the seats and finished my bag of gummy worms and Jaffa cakes one by one, listening to fun road trip songs on our shared earphones. The view outside the big window was fascinating, all green trees and cattle grazing the grass like we stepped into an old countryside movie. There was much more sunlight visible here on the vast green lands than I ever witnessed back on our school grounds.

"Can you put Waka Waka?" She asked when the current song came to an end. "I love it when she calls me a good soldier choosing her battles."

I chuckled, shuffling with my phone to put the song on. "You have good taste." I found the song and hit play.

"Of course I do." Was all she said before leaning back on the headrest and closing her eyes, listening to Shakira hyping her up for the match.

26

AVERY

I was in the locker room staring at my red jersey. A very cool logo of 'Summerfield Football Club' was decorated on the left side of the jersey with the name of our sponsor right in the middle. It was the logo of some construction company, though I wasn't sure how this was the best place to advertise construction. Slowly, I flipped it over, now staring at the back of the jersey.

A rush of warmth went through my whole body as I read the words 'Kai' written in huge bold letters just above the number 10. In my hands was the official jersey of my official school football club with an official sponsor and my official name. It all seemed too official to be true. I put it over my head and straightened it over my body, turning around on one of the locker mirrors to see how it looked. Our red and white kit was quite cool if you ask me, and it felt like a whole new reward to be wearing this after the Blue jerseys I was used to wearing at school.

"It suits you." Chloe came out of nowhere, noticing the near-emotional look on my face. "Let's get those Oakwood losers."

Coming out of the tunnel, I took my place on the bench as the rest of our team started their warmups. I looked behind the bench into the crowd and spotted Mia sitting in the front-row seat in a red T-shirt and black pants. This was the first game she was attending as Mason's girlfriend, so she was being as supportive as she could be. She gave me a big smile and a double thumbs up with both of her hands and I chuckled. She was the most adorable friend to have. Even Deniz was sitting up in the crowd with red colored stripes on her cheeks. Her wild curly hair was pulled together in two pigtails, with red ribbons securing them. I waved at her when she saw me and she waved back excitedly with a big smile on her face. Her sharp teeth were visible in her smile, just like they do on her big brother as well. Even though I was just sitting on the bench, having such genuine support from my friends meant I had won half the game already.

The moment of glory turned out to be kind of anti-climatic as I found myself sitting on the bench on the right side of the field, along with Leah and Reggie. I was wearing a yellow scrimmage vest over my majestic jersey because I was going to be gracing the bench today. Coach Martinez was standing just outside the touchline, a few feet away from me. The match had started twenty minutes ago with no goals scored yet. The crowd was triple the size of the usual that I was used to witnessing at our school matches. I had never played in front of such a huge crowd, there were never this many people who collectively cared about local soccer clubs back in America. But here, even inter-school matches were a source of good local entertainment. Of course, there were students from Oakwood High filling the stands, but many students from our school were showing their support as well.

Oakwood really was a bigger school than Summerfield and I remember how hard it was to get into the school. I had applied here when I was looking for boarding schools in England but they had rejected my application saying that they couldn't take in someone who had failed a grade. It did hurt me to hear that back then but now I was really glad I hadn't come here because the kids here seemed super snobby and rude. I don't know how Everly ended up in our school because she was definitely made for Oakwood. Take one Everly and multiply her by hundreds, that's how the crowd at Oakwood looked like.

"And the possession has dominantly been with Oakwood, the Summerfield players have been desperately trying to snatch the ball but have failed in their multiple weak attempts." The commentator was a guy named Larry, who sounded just as snobby as the other Oakwood bench players who were giving me weird looks. The Oakwood players were dressed in blue and white striped jerseys, sponsored by an artisanal cheese brand.

That is much better than a construction company I thought.

"And woah, look over there, Oliver has taken the lead in pushing the game more towards the red side, we can see a formation building up as they cleverly pass the ball toward the attack, Oliver to Archie, Archie to- oh Henry, is that right? Henry has stolen the possession mid-pass and is now passing the ball back to his teammate Fred. It seems they are not going to let us score so easily but of course, our players are not ones to back down." Larry's voice was being amplified all over the mini-stadium.

I rolled my eyes. I missed Luke's unbiased and gripping commentary.

"Would you look at that, Freya has taken possession for the fifth time, running towards the halfway line, and she has made a pass to Thomas, who has passed it on to Charlotte on the left side, the ball reaches Oliver again as he runs forward and- GOAALLL!! What a strike! That's a goal out of nothing! Just as expected, Oakwood High has broken the seal and scored the first goal of the game *and* the tournament, a spectacular instep kick by Oliver Wilson, assisted by Archie."

The crowd erupted in cheers and claps, meanwhile, our part of the stand was standing stunned and annoyed. The guy with the weird headband, Oliver, was running around the ground celebrating the first goal of the tournament. Noah was standing with his hands on his waist, shaking his head at conceding the 'spectacular' goal which was mediocre at best. When the blue and white team finally stopped celebrating, Ellie placed the ball in front of her and strongly kicked it off far away so it directly reached our forwards. Mason received it and passed it on to Noah, who was now passing it again to Mason because there were about three defenders on his back.

"And the game has started again, Noah Yildiz has chosen a bad spot to stand as he is surrounded by our defenders, Mason receives the pass and passes it on to Chloe, Chloe runs for a bit and passes it on to Harry on the other side, it seems they have the intention to charge forward but are playing cautiously to not lose possession again."

Observing the Oakwood midfielders and defenders for a while, I realized they had adapted the strategy to just position themselves right next to our players, so they could always have the chance to dive in and steal the passes we were giving each other. However, they hadn't realized it created a lot of holes in their formation, which could prove to be quite risky for their team if we just managed to go around their sticky tactics.

After the first goal, fifteen minutes went by with some casual passing and attempts at charging forward, but the game turned around when an opposing midfielder caught the ball and ran over to our side.

"A good change of events as Freya has gained the possession and she seems to be taking it away from the red shirts around her, a pass is given to Daniel who receives it just in time before Kyle Evans dives his foot in, the game has suddenly picked up the pace as there's a new charge of electricity going around the players."

I focused on each and every player from our team and I was pretty sure our strategy was to create a wall and stop them from going any forward, just like we had discussed before the match. We weren't going to focus on counterattacks or charging forward, instead we had planned to take the ball from the opposing forwards and keep passing it on to the safest midfielder until it was out of their reach for enough time until we solidified our attack formations.

"Daniel is dribbling through the ground, moving past every attempt of snatching the ball away from his talented feet, the ball is passed over to Charlotte who passes it forward to Oliver, Thomas is waiting on the side for an opportunity to strike forward, oh wait, Charlotte is facing quite a predicament as multiple defenders have taken ground in front of her, the passes are hard to decide as any pass could result in a loss of goal scoring opportunity."

Charlotte was standing with the ball just a bit ahead of the half line when Fred surprised her from the back and she leaped sideways with the ball on her feet. In a hurry, she passed it on to her teammate but Jack captured the pass and ran forward with the ball. I could see Diana running parallel to him on the left side of the ground, as she was continuously calling at him to give her a pass. Instead of listening to her, he kept running, reaching the midfield and passing the ball on to Henry. The midfield turned out to be in quite a risky situation so Henry passed it back to Jack who- instead of passing it back to either Kyle or Diana where the situation was much safer- ran forward again and passed it on to Mason. I don't know if he missed seeing the other three blue shirts standing close to Mason or if he just ignored the risk, but one of them interceded and gave a long aerial pass to their own forward.

"Oh, after a momentary break-off, Thomas has received the pass from Harper, and it looks like there's a moment of- AND ANOTHER GOAL!!! The goalkeeper had no chance with that one! With that ridiculously clean pass from Harper, Thomas sends the ball into the back of the net with a clinical finish! The quick counter attack had worked in our favor as the unexpected goal had shocked the stands with its precision. In the thirty-seventh minute of the game, Oakwood High scored another fabulous goal, taking the lead on the scoreboard yet again by making it 2-0."

I held my head in my hands. If it was a momentary slip and the goal was merely a spontaneous shot, it wouldn't have been so disheartening. But the goal could have totally been avoided if we just followed our plan instead of letting a defender run forward with the ball. It created a hole in our defense and they managed to sneak in another goal right in front of our eyes. It was a totally avoidable loss, but it happened nonetheless all because of Jack's stupidity. I looked over at Coach Martinez who was shaking his head, clearly catching on to what happened on the ground.

"Did he see what happened? I don't know why he always keeps him in the starting line-up, I'm so pissed!" Leah commented and we both knew who she was talking about.

It was just a matter of time until the halftime whistle was blown out and all the players returned to their respective sides of the field. Considering the reality of the scoreboard, our side of the audience was sitting quiet and disheartened on the stands. Coach Martinez came and sat beside us on the bench, waiting for everyone to come in and form a circle around him.

"What did we discuss?" He asked one person in general.

"To defend first," Jack replied, his face or voice empty of any hint of embarrassment, like he was unable to conjure up any form of self-critiquing.

"And what did you do?" He asked Jack but he remained silent. "You cost us a goal. I think you should be benched." Coach said, but it sounded more like a threat than an order.

"No!" He finally spoke up, his voice still empty of any amount of guilt or apology. "It was just a moment of haste! I noticed there was some space right beside where Noah was standing and I was trying to get it across to him." It was quite clear to me that he was trying to gaslight our memories and defend himself because all of us were so focused on Mason's position right in front of him that I'm sure no one remembered where Noah was.

"And did you learn what happens when you try that?" Coach was glaring at Jack now, trying to get his point across. "There's a reason you're a defender. Being a forward takes a different set of techniques and skills."

Jack nodded like he registered everything but I'm sure it just went through his selfish brain. "It won't happen again, sir."

"But Coach, I don't see a point in having a defensive lineup anymore, I think we should be focusing more on equalizing for the second half," Kyle spoke up, voicing his opinion as the captain.

Coach shook his head. "I think it would still be a mistake to take Jack out, he could help us if they decide to score more goals." Coach and Kyle came to a stark disagreement.

"Maybe we should bring Avery in, we need some attempts at scoring." Kyle insisted, and I was grateful for his eyes trained on the Coach so he wouldn't see the wide smile that came up on my face. I quickly tried to hide it so I didn't seem too eager and wore my serious expression again.

Coach sighed. "Are you only saying that because she was part of your team at school?"

"Of course not, but I can't say it's not partially true. I have played with her, I have seen her skills firsthand and I can assure you she will improve our attack against these guys."

"I think that's a good idea as well, sir. She could prove to be quite a challenge for them." Noah piped in, his hand raised as he spoke.

"I second that." Chloe did the same.

As some of the teammates were agreeing with Kyle, Jack was rolling his eyes and shaking his leg impatiently.

"Listen, kids, I appreciate you guys trying to encourage her, but I don't know if it's a good idea to push her into the first match right away." Coach's hand was in my direction but he was facing the rest of the team. It felt weird being the topic of a conversation without being a part of it. "This is her first time being at an inter-school match."

"Sir, I think she's capable enough to handle it," Kyle added again. His unwavering belief in me skyrocketed my determination as always.

After the last suggestion, everyone was looking at the Coach, waiting for his decision as the halftime break was running out. My eyebrows were raised slightly and trained on him, wondering whether my time had finally come.

Coach stood up and nodded. "It's not a hard no, but I will only think about it if the situation calls for it." It seemed like he considered it for a second, but now he was just saying that to get them off his back. "There are no changes for halftime, go back in the game." Coach Martinez was quite an exceptional coach, but he failed to look past the confident façade Jack carried. He might be good at tactics and training but he was too trusting when it came to his players. Even the ones that didn't deserve it.

Jack sneered, fully satisfied to be counted back in despite his captain's disapproval as he was the first to run off and take his position on the field. My spirits which were lifted for a second, died down again and I sat back down with a slump.

"I don't know what Coach sees in him." I sulked.

"He's never been on the field with him so he doesn't know. Imagine calling after him for a pass but he races forward. If Coach experienced that he'd bench his ass forever." Leah was just as annoyed as me.

The referee walked over to the center of the ground and finally blew the whistle. "The second half begins with sparks of new energy and here I am, Larry Campbell, with my fantastic commentary. There are a few changes for Oakwood High, Elizabeth Morgan has been replaced with Joseph Bailey and George Lewis has been replaced with Amelia Hughes. As for the Summerfield Institute, there are no changes as their starting line-up has once again graced the field." Larry announced as a light game of frequent passes had started on the ground.

As Kyle said, the need for equalizing the score was high so I noticed Kyle passing the ball repeatedly across the midfield to encourage an offensive game. Noah and Mason were watching the progress vigilantly, waiting for any opportunity to bring the ball forward.

"The game goes on and a passive-aggressive aura can be seen from the Summerfield players, it's quite evident they are trying everything in their power to create an attempt at a goal. However, the new additions to the Oakwood side have already gotten to work, predominantly keeping the ball under their feet as they navigate through the field."

Tension started building up around me as we saw an Oakwood midfielder run through the halfway line, going past any attempts to lose the ball. He passed it on to Thomas and by now I could tell this Thomas guy was no joke. He was swift with receiving the ball and quickly passed it on to Oliver, another Oakwood forward I won't forget the name of. The pressure was building up and I had a feeling something was about to happen. Henry, Kyle, and Ryan were blocking his advances meanwhile Jack was running to catch up with him.

"It seems Oliver is in quite a predicament here, with three defenders blocking him, he has no one to pass the ball to, he's running forward wit-"

The audience gasped as Oliver slipped back into a fall, the ball leaving the touchline as he fell onto the ground. He was clutching his foot tightly and it was pretty clear he wasn't just diving. "Oh wait, was that a foul? Oliver has been thrown onto the ground as the ball goes out of play, I guess we'll have to wait for the referee's decision, it sure looks like a harsh foul. A professional foul, dare I say, to break up the play."

From where I was sitting, I saw the whole thing go down. Jack was running up to him but instead of waiting behind or cutting from the side, he slid his foot right through Oliver's ankle as he fell back over Jack. A planned foul I suppose, so he could also plead as the victim when he fell over him. Practically, it was perfectly executed, but ethically, it was a harsh foul nonetheless. I personally knew how it felt because he did the same thing to Oliver that he did to me back in the intra-school matches. The referee ran over to Oliver and checked on him to see if he was okay. Oliver was nodding at the referee, and the referee showed a dismissive hand to the ground staff coming over to the ground carrying first aid. On the other hand, Jack had already gotten up and was dusting the dirt off his shorts, before giving a hand to Oliver to help him up. Oliver slapped it away bitterly and got up on his own, an act that satisfied my soul even if he was from the opposite team.

"There seems to have been a scuffle with Oliver Allen and uh... Jack Wright." Larry was still reading the names from a notepad it seems, because he still hadn't memorized any of them. "Not to be biased but I'd say it was a foul, what is the referee going to do?"

Unsurprisingly, the referee reached into his shirt pocket and pulled out a yellow card, raising it high in the air against Jack. Meanwhile, Jack the actor played out a surprised look, like his benevolent act of helping Oliver up should have somehow made the referee rethink his decision. Right in front of me, Coach Martinez was standing with one hand on his waist while he rubbed his forehead with the other. He was shaking his head just like he did when Jack cost us a goal the first time, and I was wondering if he finally saw what we meant when we said he played selfishly.

"A yellow card goes to Summerfield defender Jack Wright, well deserved in return for that horrendous foul on Oliver Allen. We're lucky he isn't seriously injured or we would have gone down on one of our best forwards and it would have been Jack's fault."

The audience had started booing our team and I was feeling more awful by each passing minute. Jack was portraying our team in a very bad light and it was affecting me personally to be perceived as an unethical team in front of others. When I pictured my first inter-school match in England, I never imagined it going this way. I never imagined the audience booing my team as I sat on the bench, unable to help my team in any way. It was a sickening feeling, watching ourselves lose and not being able to contribute against it. My teammates were disappointed, any hopes of equalizing the score flickering because of the yellow card.

"Oliver has placed the ball on the ground for a direct free-kick, but honestly speaking, it's on the halfway line so we would need quite a tactical shot to get a goal from it. Oliver runs up and- oh it's not a long kick, he has passed it on to his fellow forward Thomas who was right near-by and they take the game forward passing the ball to Amelia-"

"Avery." Coach called out and all the other sounds were suddenly muted in my head.

"Yes, Coach." I ran up to stand beside him, eager to hear what he had to say. A million little sparks igniting in my body with the hopes of getting sent in.

"I think Kyle's right, you should go in."

"You think so?" He said the exact words I had wanted to hear ever since the match started, but obviously, I had to make sure of it with humility.

"Yes, we are already down on the scoreboard and we can't afford to have a player get taken out. With how reckless Jack is playing, I think it's best if you replace him and we create an offensive stance instead."

"I think that's a good decision, sir," I said as I quickly took off my scrimmage vest, barely containing my excitement to be walking out onto the pitch. I started warming up, with some high knees, side reaches, and jumps. A few yards away, Noah caught my sight and saw me warming up near the touchline without the scrimmage vest; a tell-tale sign that this particular player was going to join the game. He swiftly gave me a proud smile before returning his attention to the game and receiving a pass from Chloe.

Coach yelled at the referee to get his attention and then gestured at him to stop the play for a substitute. After several seconds of Noah trying to get past a defender, the ball went flying outside the touchline and the referee blew the whistle for the exchange to happen. A man with a big manual scoreboard stood between both the coaches and held the scoreboard high in the air. The number '18' was written in red and right beside it, the number '10' was written in green.

The owner of the number eighteen jersey was quite offended to see the board and scornfully walked over to the touchline. "It makes no sense to send her in, Coach," Jack said, still trying to negotiate his redaction.

"It makes no sense judging my decision either. Sit down." Coach's voice was firm and decisive, and Jack reluctantly sat down on the bench. I'd be lying if I said it didn't send a flood of satisfaction through my body.

I crossed the touchline and stepped inside the field, my feet finally meeting the ground in my first ever inter-school match in England. Jogging over to the center of the field, I took my position and waited for the referee to resume play.

"Welcome aboard, Captain America." Noah gave me a quick salute, smiling so wide his sharp incisor was peeking through his smile. When I looked around, our whole team was happy to see me on the ground, most of them giving me a small applause considering it was my debut school match. A mixture of excitement and nerves filled my body, lighting me up from head to toe in a surge of lightning.

"And there's a new substitute coming in, Avery Kai replacing Jack Wright in the fifty-seventh minute of the game. Let's see if the decision for a substitute would prove to be helpful in their ambition to equalize the scoreboard." The audience on the right side of the stands was now cheering loudly, with Mia clapping the loudest as she cheered us on. Leah was hooting and clapping at the same time, the sight giving me the biggest push to unleash my potential. The thrills of joining my first big game caught up with me again, giving me a rush of all the pivotal emotions that I felt when I first wore the jersey in the locker room.

After a few minutes into the game, I observed the tactical play of the Oakwood players and the way they were responding to the game; most of them were covering our goal side, while some of them standing at theirs. It seemed they were prepared for us to try scoring and were determined not to let us update the scoreboard. The ball went out of play as it went over the touchline, and the last to touch it was Henry. Thomas from Oakwood went outside the touchline and threw the ball back in towards Oliver, who started running towards their side in an attempt to take it away from our forwards.

"As the sixty-eighth minute of the game goes on, Oakwood could be seen winning the possession, as Oliver runs on with a fantastic run towards the red wall of defense and the Blues are very close to the goal- oh no, the pass has been taken over by Ryan Morris, Ryan to Kyle, surprisingly, it's a very quick display of defense from the Summerfield players, and the ball is now played by Diana Davis, a few steps ahead and then... Avery, the new substitute, has received a pass from the defender."

Diana passed the ball on to me just behind the halfway line and I quickly turned around as I judged the situation on the midfield. Oakwood players were scattered in front of me, their huge muscly bodies prepared to stop my attempts at advancing on their side. As I scanned their defense line, one of the midfielders started trying to tackle and I dribbled for about two seconds before fooling him with a fake stunt and passing it on to Chloe on my left. If I had finally gotten the opportunity to step onto the ground, I wasn't going to waste any more seconds without making an effort towards the goal. After the pass to Chloe, I kept running forward, prepared to receive more passes ahead as our formation was quickly changing into an attack.

"Chloe with the possession, and the game is getting heated up at the other side, Chloe to Fred, seems like an attempt is going to be made, Fred has passed it on to Avery who has now crossed the halfway line with her sprint- oh finally, she is face to face with Daniel and Freya, did she think it was going to be that easy? Our defenders are gonna- OH."

Larry seemed speechless when I dribbled for a bit before kicking the ball right in between them and running ahead, catching up with the ball and finding any strikers to give them the shot. I noticed Mason was standing a few feet away from me right in front of the goal and it would have been easier to give him the pass. But three Oakwood defenders were blocking my way towards him and I would be risking our close attempt if I tried it on. That was when my eyes fell on Noah, as he stood on the opposite side of the field. He was still too far for a close accurate attempt but he was closer to the goal than I was. I thought about it for a millisecond before I trusted my intuition, taking my right foot back and hitting the ball.

"Avery with the possib- and oh a long aerial kick towards the left, Noah Yildiz has received the blazingly fast ball with a- okay that first touch was perfectly executed- and the path seems clear to him but Freya is running over to him -someone stop him dammit- and he's close but the- aaandd GOAL! Okay ladies and gentlemen, Summerfield has managed to score at the seventy-fourth minute, a nice goal by Noah Yildiz with a long and far assist from Avery Kai."

Just *nice*? Needless to say, I was still very much pissed at Larry's biased and distorted commentary, but that didn't stop me from running over to Noah to celebrate the goal. He had received my pass with such perfect control I almost fell over on the ground in amazement. He was quick to dribble away from the defender in front of him and smoothly struck the ball towards the net. It went flying past Freya, who was a bit too late in reaching the scene and hit the back of the net with jarring force. The crowd went crazy over the goal, even the Oakwood fans couldn't resist the wonder and applauded Noah's strike.

"That was crazy!" Fred was crashing into Noah with a hug. Mason was by their side, patting Noah's back like a proud best friend.

In a fit of passion, I ran over to him and jumped into his arms, his body warm against mine from running for the last seventy minutes. I could feel his rapid heartbeat matching mine, though I didn't know if it was because of the goal or if it was just him. "Noah Yildiz strikes again," I said as we pulled away from the hug.

"Or maybe it was Avery Kai's perfect pass." He said and there was a spark of electricity connecting our distance. But our fiery eye contact was broken fast enough when more of our teammates came running over to offer more high fives.

"I try so hard not to overpraise but you guys always manage to make me proud." Kyle the captain said and it was safe to say we both had too much of a flushed face to say anything except giving him a happy smile.

"After that good enough goal, the scoreboard is updated to be 2-1, with Oakwood still in the lead. I think it's a bit far-fetched to assume they can still make an equalizer, but I guess we'll see how the game goes."

Larry's one-sided commentary and the lack of praise for our team were now seriously getting on my nerves, and I got a formidable urge to score even if it was just to prove him wrong. Seeing- or rather hearing- him getting embarrassed about losing or drawing the match would give me more satisfaction than winning it for myself.

"The game has started again, there's a long kick from the Oakwood goalpost towards the middle of the field and it is received by Charlotte, fantastic touch by the way, and Charlotte has passed it on to Thomas, Thomas to Oliver, it seems Summerfield has decided to park the bus after that one score, but I'm sure Oakwood is not going to give up on their scoreboard just yet."

The clock showed that eighty-three minutes had gone by, which meant we only had about seven to ten minutes left if we wanted to score another goal. I, for one, was not going to rest until our score was at least tied, so I paid attention to the person who held possession and tried to map out an attempt at another goal.

"The game is mostly happening at Summerfield's goal side, with our forwards trying their best to get through the rigid defense of the red shirts. Thomas has passed the ball yet again to Charlotte, who is now face to face with Henry Fisher. Henry tackles, and- NO! I mean Oh, Henry has taken the ball from Charlotte, passing it on to Chloe-"

For a split second, Chloe's eyes met mine and it was like she recognized the fire in my eyes. Her expression said she trusted me to make another attempt and passed the ball onto me, where it barely escaped Freya's feet and captured mine.

"Avery Kai with the ball again, she is running towards the Oakwood goal, her swift pace keeping other players on their toes. She is small but the speed of this girl is impeccable. I don't think it's a good idea letting her get too close to the goal, and yet she is advancing by the second, tackling and leaving the other players in her wake."

I couldn't believe he was actually saying something positive for once, which was probably the result of talking far too ahead of himself in the past. But it was no reason to stop, I had to show him there was more where that came from.

"Avery has crossed the halfway line and is still not stopping, Daniel taking his position in front of her- and a quick pass to Harry has made Daniel's efforts useless, Harry to Mason and Mason has- ANOTHER GOAL!" Larry's voice sounded more in a disgruntled shock than surprise, and it seemed like he was going to cry at any moment. "A well-placed shot, Mason Williams has scored a volley into the back of the net, Edward being short of just an inch as he failed to save the goal, and just like that the scoreboard is now standing at 2-2 at eighty-ninth minute of the game."

Mia was cheering from the stands like crazy, and the sentiment of our side of the audience had suddenly changed as they erupted with loud cheers and applause. The enthusiastic sounds reaching my heart as an overwhelming feeling of accomplishment filled my body. This was much better than sitting on the bench and hearing the other side boo for our team. It gave me all the satisfaction in the world to change their prejudiced views of our capability and the team spirit quickly caught up with me as the happiness of my teammates made me reach a different level of bliss. However, there was one person who didn't quite capture the joy. Instead of celebrating our goal, Jack sat on the bench with a scornful expression on his face, his eyes not meeting ours as he looked down at his watch to check the remaining minutes of the game.

With the full-time whistle going off and the referee giving us an additional three minutes, the game started again. A short game that only consisted of a few more passes between both teams before the referee blew the final whistle and the game ended with a draw. We didn't win the match, sure. But drawing the match with a team like Oakwood's was better than tasting a bitter loss. I looked at the scoreboard. 2-2 doesn't look as bad as 2-0. With how the game had started, I was more than happy with the outcome.

27

NOAH

The cheers from the crowd still echoed in my ears as we filed onto the team bus, the excitement of the match lingered in the air. Avery's performance had been nothing short of spectacular. She single-handedly turned the tide of the game, putting her heart and soul into those crucial attacks that led us to a well-earned draw. The atmosphere was jubilant, and everyone on the team was buzzing with energy. As we found our seats on the bus, I settled next to Avery, just like before. Her face was flushed with the exertion of the game, but there was a triumphant smile playing on her lips.

"Well, well, if it isn't the football maestro herself. I guess miracles do happen on the field."

She smiled, her tired eyes lighting up from my remark. "Oh, miracles and a dash of unparalleled skill." She beamed. After the determined side of Avery dominated her aura through the game, her usual playful self was back now that we were off duty.

"Look at you, turning the match into your personal highlight reel." I opened up my backpack and took out my earphones, preparing for a sweet musical ride as the bus engine started rumbling.

"Well, it still couldn't have happened without your accurate shots."

"Praising one another? I think we are crossing a line here."

She chuckled softly, leaning back into the seat and taking one of the earphones from my hand. She put them on as I played quite a slow romantic song, in accordance with the feelings that were brewing inside me at the moment. The familiar tunes of our shared playlist flowed through the shared earphones connecting us, creating a soundtrack to the quiet hum of the bus engine.

"Hey, do you mind if we switch to this song? It's one of my favorites," I asked, my voice more steady than I felt.

"Sure. You know I'm always up for some good music," she replied with a warm smile.

As the first few notes of the song enveloped us, I couldn't help but marvel at the serendipity of the moment. Her presence was both comforting and maddeningly distracting. Her legs brushed mine occasionally, sending a jolt through me every time. It was as if the universe conspired to remind me how close we were physically, yet confessing about my feelings seemed like a faraway reality. The soft glow from the passing streetlights highlighted her features as she was engrossed in the music, a subtle smile playing on her lips.

As the lyrics of a song faded into the background, the realization hit me with a force that seemed to shake the very foundation of my resolve. I wanted to tell her how I felt, right here, right now, before I lost my nerve and Liam swooped in with his annoying face again. If I saw her at the ball with Liam tomorrow, I might just combust and turn into soot. I stole a glance at Avery, her eyes closed, swaying slightly to the music.

The truth was, I was wrestling with an internal debate, a conflict between the fear of ruining our friendship and the desire to be honest about my feelings. The stakes were high, and my heart pounded with uncertainty. As the bus rolled on, the air around me seemed to thicken with unspoken words.

As I saw her peaceful form, the temptation to bridge the gap between us, both physically and emotionally, became almost irresistible. Now that I had the adrenaline from the match flowing in my veins, I thought there wouldn't be a better time to voice out what I was scared to accept even to myself. With a nod of my head, I decided to follow through with my instincts before I lost my nerve.

"Avery?" I began, the words hanging in the air between us.

"Hmm." She responded, her eyes still closed as she rested her head on the comfortable seat. The urge to tell her was overwhelming and yet my nerves were shrinking with each passing moment. *It's now or never.* Swallowing my doubts, I took a deep breath.

"I... Avery," I started, the words catching in my throat. I hesitated, my mind racing with uncertainty. "I've been wanting to tell you something for a long time now. It's just... I've been too scared, too afraid of what might happen."

The bus rumbled on, the song weaving a delicate backdrop to the vulnerability of the moment.

"But now, I feel like I can't hide it any longer," I continued, my voice barely above a whisper. "I... I really care about you. More than just friends, you know? The more time I spend with you, the more I realize how much I enjoy it. I look forward to every moment we share, the laughter, the silly jokes, and even the quiet times like this." I looked at my feet, unable to meet her eyes as I said the next words. "I've fallen for you, Avery, and it scares me because I don't want to ruin what we have."

I held my breath, waiting for her reply. The seconds stretched into an agonizing silence as doubt started to claw at the edges of my resolve. But instead of responding, Avery's head tilted slightly to the side, and I noticed the rhythmic sounds of her soft snores. I finally gathered the courage to look at her. She had fallen asleep.

A mixture of frustration and amusement welled up within me. The timing couldn't have been worse, yet there was something undeniably endearing about the situation. I turned to her side, and there she was, completely oblivious to my confession, lost in the world of dreams.

A small smile crept onto my face as I watched her sleep. The fierceness that she carried when she was awake had melted into a peaceful expression and her whole zestful aura had changed into a relaxing one. The bus continued its journey, the night outside the windows cloaked in darkness. The soft snores beside me became a comforting lullaby, and for a moment, I allowed myself to bask in the simplicity of our shared space. The weight of my unspoken feelings hung in the air, yet the warmth of the moment was undeniable.

As the bus rumbled on, carrying us into the night, I made a silent promise to myself. Whether or not Avery heard my confession, I would find the right time to express my feelings more clearly. I had never felt this way about anyone and it was driving me crazy to hold it in my heart when it kept escaping the confines of our friendship. It wasn't like I had never liked anyone before, but the way Avery made me feel was different than anyone else. She made me appreciate her even during moments when she was standing against me, and her constant determination often fueled my own.

The New Year's ball was just a day away and I really wanted to take her as my date, but since she had already fallen asleep, I decided I would have to find a better time to ask her for the ball. Preferably when she was conscious and could actually hear my words. As for now, I cherished the small, unspoken moments and let the journey unfold at its own pace.

It was the day of the ball, and there was a spark of romance in the air. It was a Sunday, which meant half the student body had gone to the city, the girls shopping for some dresses and the guys shopping for their suits. I, on the other hand, was resting in the common room as always, watching TV and sharing a huge bag of crisps with Mason.

As for my outfit for the ball, I was already set for today. Resting on my bed in my dorm was a well-ironed black dinner jacket, a cream shirt, and black trousers. It actually belonged to my cousin, Aydin, but he had no events coming up so instead of letting it sit in his closet, he had given it to me before our term started so I could wear it for school events. It was as good as new and since Aydin shared a lot of genes with me, it fit me perfectly like it was tailored for my body. Last year I went with Everly, but there wasn't any nostalgia in my heart for that memory. I was planning to take Avery, and even if she refused to go with me, I would be fine going alone.

I hadn't gotten a chance to ask her yet though, which was quite a problem considering that the ball was in a few hours. Everyone was all partnered up as they had asked their dates already and were currently preparing their outfits. Asking anyone out on the same day as the ball traditionally feels like being asked out as the last resort, and I really didn't want to make Avery feel that way. At the same time, there was no one else I wanted to go with and if I saw her there with Liam, it would ruin a good whole week for me.

As I was torn between my conflicting thoughts, it seemed the universe had finally decided to bless me with some good events because almost as if she was the result of my thoughts, she walked into the common room and looked around trying to find someone. She was holding my jacket in her hands, the one I gave her when we pulled the heist in Asami's office. She had looked so cute in my oversized jacket that night and I remembered telling her it was my favorite. For some reason, it made me feel good that she had it for so long. Holding on to each other's clothes was quite a couple thing to do and even though we were nowhere close to being one, it still felt pretty good to know it was with her all along. But the bliss had eventually ended now that she remembered and was probably here to return it.

Before she could even notice me on the couch though, an infuriating voice spoke up from the sofa in front of the fireplace.

"Well, well, if it isn't the American reject." Jack got up from his seat and approached Avery, standing a foot taller in front of her. His words infuriated me, but Avery looked at him like she came across jerks like him every day. "What are you even doing here, Kai?"

"I don't have time for your bullshit, I'm here to see Noah." The last five words caused a firework to burst in my heart. Even if I knew she was here to see me, it felt better hearing it from her as she said it out loud. The last time she was here, she came to see Liam so this time it really felt like a personal win to be the one she came over for.

Jack ignored Avery's question and continued on with his bullshit. "You think you can just waltz into our school and become some football sensation? Dream on, loser."

"Jack, cut it out," I said as I got up from the couch and joined them by the door. His lame insecurity was loud enough even before this, but I couldn't stay silent now that he was verbally taking it out on her.

"Stay out of this Yildiz, this doesn't concern you." He said, still glaring at Avery.

"Everything that happens in this team concerns me. She earned her spot on the team and you have no right to doubt her."

Now I had his attention as he turned and looked at me with a scowl. "What are you, her knight in shining armor now? She needs protection from the big bad bully?"

"She doesn't need protection, she needs respect," I told him sternly. "Something you clearly lack."

"If you want to suck up to her so bad, fine. But, you'll see soon enough how useless she is." He said, his pace angry and defeated as he walked away, leaving the common room.

"I'm sorry," I turned to her. "Don't listen to him, he's just acting out because his spot is in danger."

"It's okay, you don't have to say sorry. Compared to the bullies I came across in America, he's just mildly passive-aggressive." She said and looked down, where her eyes went to the jacket in her hands. "Oh yeah, I came here to return this." She held it forward.

"Keep it," I told her, putting my hands in my pockets so she couldn't see just how nervous I was to be speaking honestly. "It looks better on you anyway."

Her eyes raised a little bit, surprised by my response. "But you said it was your favorite."

"I know," I tried to come up with a reason that sounded a bit more casual than telling her I just loved seeing her in my clothes and managed to say something vague. "But things change. Feelings change."

It was quite a casual thing to say, but my sincerity somehow crept out nonetheless, painting my words with a deeper meaning. There was a moment where I just looked into her eyes, and I might have imagined it but there was a hint of recognition in them. Almost like she understood my point beyond words.

The courage I had somehow mustered back on the bus was starting to build up, her soft eyes giving me the hope I longed for.

"Hey, Avery. I was just looking for you," Another came in, breaking our eye contact and it was all I could do not to scream at his face for disturbing my moment with her.

Avery looked away, returning his smile. "Hey, Liam. What's up?"

Liam leaned against the doorway in all his haughty glory, his gaze lingering on her. "I was wondering if you've thought about who you're going to the ball with?"

His flirty question set my veins on fire, as the courage that was once being pumped into my blood was replaced with plain old fury. Avery was looking at him with an unreadable expression and I realized I was late in acting on my feelings yet again.

"Uh, not really." She replied, fidgeting with the fabric of my jacket.

I suddenly felt like an outsider in my own space, as if I had unintentionally stumbled upon a private moment. Two seconds ago I was close enough to ask her out and now Liam was here, stealing all her smiles like he was the only one who deserved it. I could not, for the life of me, watch this happening right in front of my eyes. Witnessing Liam ask the same question I was about to, it would probably create a burning hole right through my chest.

Trying not to show my disappointment, I cleared my throat.

"I'll, um, leave you two to it," I mumbled, forcing a smile. "I've got some stuff to take care of." The only thing I needed to take care of was my broken heart.

Avery looked up at me, a hint of concern in her eyes. "Oh, okay. We'll catch up later, then?"

"Yeah, definitely," I replied, trying to sound nonchalant. I walked out of the common room, the door closing softly behind me as I left the two love birds to themselves.

Alone in the hallway, I felt a wave of sadness wash over me. The realization that Avery might be going to the ball with Liam hit me harder than I expected. I took a deep breath, attempting to shake off the feeling, and decided I should probably start getting ready for the ball. It was five in the evening and the ball was about to start at seven. Many students had already started returning from their trips to London as well, and the hallway was slowly getting filled with students carrying bags in their hands.

I sighed. Breathe in, breathe out. *Don't punch Liam in the face.*

And with that, I started walking toward my room. At least I could look forward to the food.

The walls of the huge ballroom were covered with thick pastel pink curtains, and strings of fairy lights were coming down from the ceiling every few feet. The chandeliers and lights were so bright that the fairy lights were only giving out a sparkling effect to the curtains. Mason and I arrived quite early, as there weren't many people in the ballroom at the moment. Harmonious sounds of a Piano were echoing around the room, as a few couples danced on the hardwood floor in the middle of the ballroom. Say anything about Summerfield, but our school sure knew how to throw a ball.

"I think the girls will take a bit more time," Mason said, looking at his wristwatch. We only had to shower and put on our clothes, but I bet the girls must have dozens of other things to take care of. Drying their hair, styling their dresses with multiple accessories, or whatever things they get themselves busy with.

"Well, I'm hungry. Are you coming or not?" I tried to take my mind off the fact that Avery would be walking in here with Liam any minute, and being busy tasting all the different kinds of dips with chips and nachos sounded like something I would rather do than watch them dance together.

We walked towards the food bar, where a buffet was spread, along with a station for drinks. They obviously only had fruit punches and sparkling water since this was a school, but that didn't stop some pretentious students from acting like they were actually drinking fancy wine in their champagne glasses. The buffet had fresh fruits and salads, but for the more unhealthy eaters, they also had fried chicken, macaroni and cheese, pizzas, and hamburger sliders just to name a few. The American touch of hamburger sliders immediately reminded me of Avery, but I quickly shook her thoughts from my head. So much for distracting myself.

"Damn, this mac and cheese is so much better than our usual," Mason commented as we sat on the tables arranged beside the buffet.

"I think they put some extra fancy cheese in it today," I responded, cherishing the creamy and cheesy taste in my mouth.

I sampled each dish with genuine enthusiasm, determined to savor the flavors and temporarily forget about the complexities of my emotions. After trying out more than half of the menu, Mason suddenly paused when he saw someone standing beside our table, someone outstandingly gorgeous judging by his reaction. I knew who it was before I even looked up and the Mia that was standing beside me right now was not the Mia I was used to seeing. She was wearing a sky-blue dress that matched her eyes and her blonde hair was in a loose bun, a few strands framing her face on each side.

"Hey," Mason said softly and wiped his mouth with the napkin, getting up to greet the lady. He took her hand and kissed it, lowering himself until he was almost at the same height as her while doing so.

"You look cute." She said to him.

"And you look ethereal. I can't believe you're my date." Mason couldn't take his eyes off her, the redness on her cheeks giving a pop of color to her fair skin.

Feeling like the third wheel in a romantic movie, I cleared my throat to remind them I was still there. "Uh so... where's Avery?" I was looking around Mia, expecting to see her standing close like always but she was nowhere to be seen.

"Oh, she's out there somewhere in the buffet area. She was hungry." Mia explained.

"Oh," I responded, my mind immediately conjuring up a picture of Liam and Avery sitting at a candle-lit table, having a lovely dinner in this lovely ballroom with some lovely meaningful conversations.

"I'm sorry I ate before you arrived, I was hungry." Mason rubbed the back of his neck, embarrassed that he couldn't wait for his date before having dinner.

"Oh it's okay, I ate with Avery too." She said, and a bit of relief washed over me. At least Avery and Liam didn't get to have an actual date as she had dinner with Mia instead.

"Then shall we dance?" Mason held out his hand, and Mia took it graciously before they went walking towards the dance floor.

I looked around at all the dancing couples on the dance floor, wondering if Avery was out there with her date yet. Instead of her, I spotted Liam a few feet away from Mason and Mia. I could only manage to see his face and the girl's back from where I was sitting and my heart did a violent shake at the sight. She was out there dancing with the guy she liked and here I couldn't even afford to see how pretty she must be looking in her beautiful evening dress. He was looking into her eyes the same way he did that night on the roof, and the same kind of panic crept into my chest. Except there was no emergency bell and no restriction here, they were here as a couple and I had no reason to stop or disturb their beautiful date. I turned the other way ignoring their sight and returned my attention to the pasta in front of me, trying to fill the gaping hole in my heart that seemed to only get deeper with every minute that went by.

After ten minutes of eating alone at the table, I decided it was too pathetic to be sitting here like a loner. I looked around and noticed that Chloe and Fred were standing near the drink bar, talking and observing the people around the room. I knew for a fact they didn't bring any dates, so I got up and joined them, listening to them rate the outfits of other students like we were at a fashion show. Just as I finished my second glass of cranberry sparkling water, a rushed Mason came in front of me, putting his hand on my shoulder and shaking me out of my thoughts with a jerk.

"Did you see Avery?" He asked.

"Didn't you go for a dance?" I asked, confused by his sudden appearance.

"I did, but I excused myself for a minute. Now tell me, did you see Avery?" He repeated.

"Yes I did but I'd rather ignore that sight for a while," I replied irritably, wondering why he wanted to rub salt on my wound.

"What do you mean? Where did you see her?"

"With Liam?" He was just out there on the dance floor a minute ago, did he not see him?

Mason threw his hands up and looked around, exasperated. "Look at them." He said, holding my shoulders and shifting me sideways so I could get a clear view.

"No thanks." I looked the other way, accidentally witnessing a snogging couple in the corner. I grimaced and put my glass back down on the table behind me.

"You're hopeless." He said and made me turn in Liam's direction. He gestured towards him and I noticed something I hadn't realized before.

"That's... not Avery." My voice was strained by the weight of embarrassment when I realized the girl dancing with Liam was not Avery at all.

"No, it's not, you doofus!" He lightly slapped the back of my head. "It's Amanda Cooper."

"Then where's Ave-" Before I could finish my question, he turned me further towards the left, where she was standing beside the dance floor. Seemingly without a date because she was standing alone.

"If you don't go and ask her out right n-" Mason's voice was fading in the background as I went towards Avery, each step I took making me admire her beauty more and more.

She was wearing a satin lavender dress, her wrist decorated with pretty bracelets under the off-shoulder sleeves. The dress was completely fitted up to her waist and then it went down in a gorgeous flow around her. The soft curls of her hair were falling over her bare shoulders, half of it tied up at the back. It would be an understatement to say I was mesmerized, I was completely lost in the way she was looking over at the dance floor with her beautiful eyes and tapping her foot with the music. There's just something about a girl who is mostly clad in baseball shirts and football kits, and the way her whole aura changes when she puts on a dress and shines like a beautiful flower. Although it was still very much a nervous thought to ask her for a dance, I also knew if someone else asked her first I'd pretty much disintegrate right here. I gathered my courage and stepped ahead, towards the most charming girl in the room.

"I was expecting to see you with a date," I said, and it was apparent her train of thought was broken by my words.

She turned toward me, the sight of her beautiful face up close almost making me fall over. "Are you kidding me? It's my first ball and you thought I'd waste my princess moment by already tying myself off to a guy?"

A chuckle left my mouth. "Princess moment?"

"Of course, like Cinderella. When someone at the ball falls for her and then they dance and fall in love." She held her dress in her hands and twirled it around lightly. "I feel like a princess."

"You look like one too." My gaze was soft and my voice came out way more sincere than I meant it to. It was a bit odd to pay her a genuine compliment without any sarcasm, but it would be unfair to act like she wasn't absolutely shining in her dress.

"And what kind of man are you, not asking this princess for a dance?" She asked, pretty much jokingly. She was doing one of her self-enhancing humor bits but I loved the fact that she brought it up before my cowardly self chickened out.

I smiled and held out my hand. Her eyebrows raised slightly as she looked at my hand with a question in her eyes. *Is he really offering me a dance?* It was all I had wanted to do since yesterday, but her reaction told me she wasn't expecting me to ask.

"Would this lady care to have a dance with me?"

She laughed at my pretentious prince-y dialogue. That adorable smiley laugh. As if I needed any more reason to fall for her further.

"Hey, I'm just following the script!" I said in a fake defensive tone and she laughed even more.

"Well, of course, I'd love to." A million little fireworks burst inside my heart as she took my hand ever so gracefully and we walked onto the dance floor.

28

AVERY

The grand ballroom glimmered with soft lights, casting a magical glow on the swirling couples as the waltz played in the background. Noah and I moved gracefully across the floor, lost in the enchantment of the music and the beauty of the moment. His hand rested on the small of my back, guiding me with practiced ease.

The gentle rhythm of the waltz embraced us, and I couldn't help but feel a sense of exhilaration. As we twirled and swayed, I caught Noah's eyes, and a smile tugged at the corners of my lips. His gaze held a warmth that resonated with the music, and I found myself completely captivated. It was like after all that rivalry and holding back of our feelings we could finally open the dams and let it all flow out at least for the duration of this dance. No sarcasm, no sass, no competition. Right now it was just me and him.

But then, in a fleeting moment, my heel caught on the hem of my gown, and before I knew it, I stumbled. Panic gripped me, but just as quickly, strong arms wrapped around my waist, steadying me. It was Noah, his touch both reassuring and electrifying.

For a heartbeat, we locked eyes, caught in the suspended animation of the dance. His hand was still at the small of my back, my fingers lightly resting on his chest. I couldn't ignore the gentle beating of Noah's heart, and mine seemed to echo in response.

Noah's gaze softened, a subtle understanding passing between us. There was a moment of silence, as if the world around us paused, allowing something unspoken to unfold. He stabled me back to my feet but didn't release his hold on me. Instead, we adjusted our stance, drawing each other closer, and continued to move in harmony.

The music enveloped us, creating a cocoon where the outside world faded away. The dance became more intimate, the steps more synchronized, and our connection deepened.

"Did I mention you're looking beautiful tonight?" He said, with a gaze so soft it made me feel dainty. His eyes were warm and kind, so focused on me that I felt he could see every shaky breath I took.

There was no response I could conjure up when he was looking at me like that and a wholehearted smile was all that left my mouth. My cheeks felt hot and I wondered if they deepened the shade of blush I applied before coming here. Shying away from our eye contact came almost naturally and my eyes left his to look at our hands. My hand was comparatively smaller than his and there was just something endearing about that that I couldn't put into words.

"I didn't know you could do something as graceful as dancing," I said, still looking at our hands.

"I didn't know you could stay this long without saying an insult either." He responded with a chuckle, and my eyes went back to his face.

"Well, I won't say you're less annoying now but I guess my tolerance for you keeps increasing the more I know you."

"Many things have changed the more I know you as well." His voice was suddenly serious, empty of any humor.

I nodded in a nonchalant way, but inside I was dying to know how things had changed for him. If they have changed the same way they did for me. "Things like?"

"Hmm." He narrowed his eyes and looked away like he was gathering his thoughts into a pile and wanted to sort them out. "Things like..." He thought some more like he wanted to be very careful with his words. Like he was debating how much of that pile he was willing to share, and how much he wanted to keep for himself. "Like when I first met you, I thought you were too competitive. Too aggressive and always ready for a fight." He paused and chose his words again. "But now I understand it's because you're passionate about what you love. Now I admire your zeal because it has pushed me to do better in my own life."

His words struck a cord deep inside my heart. "I never thought about it like that."

"I'm not done." He smiled. "The aggressiveness that bothered me when I first met you, is now something I adore because it means you don't let anyone walk over you or just settle with unfairness."

Hearing just one positive thing from him was miraculous enough, I didn't know what I was supposed to say when it had been multiplied by two. But it turned out I didn't have to worry about a response because he was still speaking. "All the times you got defensive, it was only because you refused to be let down by your weaknesses, not when you're always trying to improve and work around them."

I stared at him, unable to decide what I should say. All I knew was that it felt like someone caressed my heart, found all the rough edges, and smoothed it with his hands.

"You came here after an apparent failure, but look at how you've shaped it into a new opportunity and worked hard until you came back better than you were before you ever failed. All because you never gave up."

Looking into his eyes as he was saying all this, I could see that he meant every word. Of all the people who know me here, he was the one I never tried to impress. He was the one I never paid attention to unless it was about pissing him off or getting ahead of him. And yet he saw the parts that other people in my life struggled to find. The parts that even I struggled to find myself.

"You make me sound like a hero." I laughed, not being able to truly believe anything he said. All my failures, all my weaknesses, all my faults. How can he just dig past all that and find these virtues in the rubble?

"Maybe you are." He said the words with such belief and sincerity it left no more room for doubt.

"And how can you possibly know that?"

He raised his eyebrows the slightest and shrugged gently. "Well, if fighting tells a person's true nature then no one knows you better than me."

The more he spoke the more it became hard to keep my emotions from tumbling over. Years of self-doubt and now here he was, telling me these ugly parts of myself were never wrong. That I wasn't just a dumb loser like I thought I was. All the self-loathing and diffidence seemed to wash away, even if just for this moment, because he saw in me what I couldn't see in myself. Tears flooded my eyes and I blinked quickly, careful not to let him know his words were a light that reached a dark, deserted place inside my heart. All this light was suddenly making my eyes burn with tears.

"Hey?" His voice was lighter than a feather, as he looked at me with a tender gaze. "I'm so sorry, I didn't mean to make you cry. Are you okay?"

Not being able to hold his eyes anymore, I looked down, letting my tears fall as I nodded at his question. "I'm fine. I just..." A sigh left my body. "I just never thought all those negatives could ever carry any positives."

He left my hand as his finger touched my chin, lifting it up so I was looking at him. "You just need the right perspective. Just like we can't appreciate love until we've experienced hate, we can't appreciate success until we've experienced some failures." He wiped the tear that escaped my eyes and smiled- the sweetest, softest smile that made it impossible not to smile back.

"I didn't know you were a philosopher."

"You don't know a lot of things yet." There was depth in his eyes like there were layers to what he was saying. They held a secret- like they knew something I didn't. Like he discovered something before me and I was still catching up.

His eyes traveled my face, like it was a piece of art and he wanted to appreciate every detail before they strayed down and settled on my lips. A wave of heat traveled all over my body, my mind incredibly aware of every bit of unspoken communication happening between us. And then-

He kissed me.

It was almost impulsive, like he didn't mean to kiss me but at the same time, it was all he wanted to do. The kiss was so unexpected that it took me a minute to gather my thoughts, the realization that I wanted it just as much as him. But the realization came a little too late, because he suddenly pulled away, now registering the fact that I didn't kiss him back. The kiss might have come as a surprise, but the disappointment I felt when he pulled away revealed much more.

"Oh my God." He said, looking at my wide eyes and stunned expression. "I'm sorry, I shouldn't have done that without asking you first, I'm so sorry-"

"Noah."

"You were crying and I just, I'm so sorry-"

"Noah it's-"

"If you don't even want to talk to me again, I totally get it-"

"Noah!"

"I'm just so-" I reached up and pulled him by his shirt, shutting him up and finally reuniting our lips the way I actually wanted. The lips I had unknowingly admired for so long. He was stunned for about half a second before he melted into the kiss, his shoulders relaxing under my arm as we both embraced the touch we unwittingly desired. My hand left his and wrapped around his shoulders just as his hands went straight to my waist. He was holding me close and my hand was in his hair, the always messy hair that was actually well-kept for once. It was like he had been waiting for this moment as long as I had because as gentle as the kiss was, it felt impatient. Like he wanted to grasp every bit of this moment before it flew away. He tilted his head and I tilted mine, deepening the kiss, a catharsis for every time we wanted to indulge in our feelings, but couldn't.

We pulled away to catch our breath, looking into each other's eyes with a whole new meaning between us. We were standing much closer than we were when we first started dancing and the earlier melody had been replaced with an even more romantic song, like the universe knew the sudden shift in our friendship and provided the most appropriate soundtrack. The rush of electricity that went through my body was still thrumming with the beats of my heart. Locking my eyes in his gaze, I realized there was always something precious in them, the way he carries the softest heart behind the mischief in his eyes. The revelation finally dawned upon me.

I have fallen way too hard for this boy.

But as I was still catching up with all the feelings running crazy inside my body, Noah smiled at me and chuckled.

"What?"

"You're... extremely red." A therapy session and an endearing kiss were already too much sincerity coming from him in one day, so now he had to go back to achieving his one and only goal: embarrassing me.

"Shut up." Now that I willingly took the authority to kiss him, the clarity of my feelings for him made it almost impossible to maintain my usual indifference.

"Like *actually* crimson."

Yup, not looking at him now. "Go to hell."

"Really? That's what I get after giving you the best kiss of your life?"

I scoffed. "Someone here needs to get over themselves."

Before he could respond with another cocky remark, the song ended and everyone on the dance floor froze to a halt. I looked around, which -as it turned out- was my biggest mistake because I saw Mia staring at me with a huge smirk on her face. It didn't help that Leah was standing right beside her, sharing the same grin. Mason and Mia must have stopped dancing after the first twenty minutes- because how much can you dance around really- and were now standing at the corner sharing drinks and laughter. I closed my eyes and sighed, finally breaking away from our embrace as I prepared myself for a shit ton of teasing.

As we walked out of the ballroom, Noah insisted on walking me to my dorm building because apparently, it was bad etiquette to just leave your date right after the dance. Mason and Mia were walking a few feet ahead of us, and we followed the happy couple towards our humble abode.

Taking off his blazer, Noah draped it on one hand and then loosened his tie with the other. I would be lying if I said that sight wasn't attractive enough to raise my pulse. He ran his hand through his hair a few times, his earlier formal hairstyle giving way to his original tousled hair.

"Here, take this." He passed his blazer to me but the way I looked at his offer with confused eyes must have prompted him to explain. "It's fifteen degrees and you're wearing an off-shoulder dress. I can see you rubbing your arms from the cold."

I tried not to blush over how he always paid attention to me and instead decided to ask about the more confusing temperature unit. "Fifteen?"

"You Americans." He laughed and calculated in his head. "Uh, around sixty degrees Fahrenheit, I think."

"Then I totally need that blazer." I took it from him and draped it over my shoulder, the sudden warmth calming down some of the shivers in my body.

Reaching the stairs of our building, Mason and Mia shared a goodbye kiss under the moonlight, and my heart gave me a disappointing pinch at the fact that I had to part ways with Noah as well. I was enjoying his company just like always, but this time there was a different light shining between us. A different aura that radiated from our hearts until it covered us both in its light.

"See you at practice?" He asked as I stepped on the first stair.

"Of course," I replied, before disappearing into the lobby of our building, my cheeks almost burning with the way he smiled at me.

29

NOAH

Laying in bed with eyes that were refusing to fall back to sleep, I got up to check the time. 06:54 A.M. It was way too early to wake up, but it was impossible for me to sleep now. The events of last night were flashing in my eyes, and my body was probably releasing some kind of happy chemical in my veins. First of all, Avery didn't choose Liam as her date which was an accomplishment in and of itself. But the fact that she said yes to a dance with me was a whole other miracle. I kissed her, she kissed me, and there were no punches or kicks involved. I don't want to get too far ahead of myself, but I think it's a good sign. Does she actually like me back? If I kissed her first, she probably knew that I liked her, right? All these thoughts were flooding my brain and I wasn't sure if I was actually happy or nervous to see her again today. Would she talk to me in class? Would she ignore me because the kiss was just a ball thing? Am I supposed to take it seriously or forget it like it's a normal thing that happens in every dance?

The more these thoughts confused me, the more one specific image kept popping into my head. She kissed me back. Willingly. And that's a good enough sign to know if someone likes you or not. I got up and ruffled my hair, it was still too early to get ready for classes. Mason was miles deep in his sleep, his hand hanging off the bed as he looked about ten minutes away from falling off the bed. I looked back at my bed as my stomach rumbled. Am I hungry already?

I thought back to last night and realized I had my dinner early. And then after that, I was too tired and happy to eat anything else. There had been a long gap between my meals and now I was starving. Maybe I should just go eat breakfast and then get ready for classes later.

I brushed my teeth, put on my black hoodie, and walked out of the room, leaving Mason by himself on his way to fall off the bed. The cold breezes from last night were still lingering on the campus and a shiver left my body as I put both my hands inside the pocket of my hoodie and walked toward the canteen. As anyone would expect from a school canteen before eight, it was ridiculously empty, except for the janitor who was sweeping the floors. The cafeteria ladies seemed quite shocked to see a kid visit the canteen at this time, especially on a day when there was porridge on the menu. It was not a problem for me though, I actually love porridge with a bunch of dates to make it sweet.

It was quite lonesome to eat breakfast alone, but I felt much better after I finally had some food in me. Some other students had started coming in, taking up space in the canteen- and slowly after a while, it finally looked like an actual canteen instead of a haunted one. By the time I was finishing my porridge, it was 08:05 A.M., which meant I only had about twenty minutes to get ready for the class. I was scooping up the last morsels of my porridge when Everly walked in, already all dressed up in a silk shirt and a pretty skirt. She noticed me sitting alone and waved, I smiled back because I really had no idea how to talk to her now. She would come and try to convince me to get back together with me and right now I was too happy about Avery to have any awkward conversations. But things never go according to our wishes, because Everly was now sitting down at my table, probably with the intention of having breakfast together.

"Hey, you're early." She said, her perfectly styled hair lightly falling over her face.

"I was actually way earlier, I already had my breakfast." I showed her my empty bowl, hinting that I was about to get up.

"Oh." She said, a bit disappointed but still carrying her nonchalant grace.

"And I really need to rush off now, because I haven't even gotten ready for school yet." I looked at my watch- 08:12 A.M. I could actually manage to get ready in five minutes, but since getting out of here was my top priority, I needed to act like I was totally running late.

She looked at her watch as well. "You only have half an hour to get ready then." She seemed to think it was a very short amount of time, but I didn't need to tell her that it was actually plenty of time for me.

"Yeah, I need to hurry. I'll see you later maybe." I got up, picking up my tray to put it in the dirty dishes pile. "Bye!"

"Sure, goodbye." She smiled in response.

I delayed my exhale of relief until I was out of her sight and thanked God for waking me up early so I could have my breakfast in peace. Moreover, I didn't want Avery to think I was seeing her anymore, and having breakfast together without any other friends at our table might give her the wrong idea.

As I kept my tray and started walking towards the door, I noticed Avery and Mia had already walked in, standing at the tray station together. Avery was wearing a pink and blue tie-dyed sundress that looked like it came straight out of a spring catalog. She seemed happy, her face was shining with the same charming glow as it did whenever she scores and wins a game. She was looking like an absolute angel and I-

I looked down at my clothes. I hadn't even showered yet and I was wearing an age-old hoodie. A heavy wave of self-consciousness struck me, and I thought she would probably regret her decisions if she saw me this way. Not wanting to be seen as an ugly lazy cow, I quickly dropped off my tray and went outside, rushing to my room so I could properly get ready for the day.

Getting dressed up when you have a crush in your school should be counted among the toughest decisions we ever make as a human. I was standing in my towel with two outfits spread on the bed in front of me- on one side was a pair of black khakis and on the other was a dark green polo and a Real Madrid jersey. Deciding that the pants would go better with the polo, I quickly dressed up and ran down the stairs. Even though I tried to do everything as quickly as possible, I still ended up running late as I looked at my watch and realized I was two minutes late to my 08:40 A.M. class.

The best days to train are when the sun is in no mood to shine and the whole city is taken over by a huge gloomy cloud. It was not hot and it was not cold either, which meant it was the perfect weather to be running around in our training kits, doing the drills under Coach's instructions. This afternoon was still a little different though, because there was something just a bit unusual in the air. When Avery and Leah first stepped onto the field, it felt like she brought a whole cloud of blissful joy with her, and in my imagination, the whole ground seemed to light up. Is this dramatic or is this how people actually feel when they're hung up on someone?

"Line up everybody, we are doing one-touch passes today." Coach yelled at us and all the scattered players came running to stand in front of him. "Pick a partner and pair up, all of you." He pointed a moving finger at us, and immediately our team started dividing into smaller groups. As the tradition goes, everyone always picks their best friend to pair up with them, so naturally, I looked around for Mason as we are always paired together.

But as I went up to him, the sudden betrayal came quick as a flash when I saw Mason run away from me and stand next to Leah. Both Mason and Leah had the most smug expressions on their faces as we realized that Avery and I were the only ones left without a partner. She looked at Leah with a shocked expression, as did I with Mason but both of them were determined to set up their friends with their crushes and none of them moved an inch. Reluctantly, Avery and I paired and stood next to each other, an awkward air surrounding us both.

"I want all of you to stand at least twenty feet apart at first, and with every pass to your partner, you'll have to take one step ahead." All of us were standing still and waiting for the catch because there was no way the drill was going to be that easy. "However," *There it comes.* "You're only supposed to make one-touch passes, you can't settle the ball before passing it nor can you use your other foot. Pass it the moment it touches your feet, and the accuracy should be good enough for it to reach your partner directly." As always, he seemed proud about giving us an exercise that would most probably frustrate us with the amount of concentration it takes, but all of us had too much determination to let him have the satisfaction of tiring us with practice.

"So, right or left?" Avery asked, the ball in her hands,

"Right, obviously. I don't think I can do one-touch passes with my left yet."

"Really?" She asked with a hint of patronization and I knew our competition was back on. "I think I can handle your right foot passes with my left."

"We'll see." At this point, I could already tell she was going to nail any challenge she threw at me, but creating a competition was an age-old Avery and Noah tradition and I wasn't going to back down from it.

We both ran away and stood twenty feet apart, she settled the ball right in front of her and kicked it with her left foot. I kicked it back when it reached me and took a step further, preparing myself to receive the rest. Every single one of her passes was spot on, so accurate that it actually became easy for me to kick it back to her. Feet by feet we came closer, carrying the challenge with every step we took. Around us, a lot of the people had to stop and restart because the ball went entirely somewhere else but we kept going until we were only ten feet apart. Most of them were now either looking at our game or starting over again.

"Hey, go slow!" She yelled, as I kicked the ball with a bit of force and she almost failed to control the ball.

"I thought you said you could do it with both." Nevertheless, the ball reached me at the right angle and I kicked it back hard.

"I meant accuracy, not strength." She was now laughing, her eyes still glued to the ball even as she laughed and yelled at me.

"Then you should have mentioned it before." The closest pass we could do was five feet, and then we started walking backward doing the same drill.

"Fine, I'll show you." It didn't matter if her left foot was actually not as strong as her right, if you riled her up just enough then proving herself was all that mattered to her.

"Let's see who breaks it."

After two more repetitions of our drill, Avery's passes started getting wobbly, the ball barely reaching me at the right angle. Before she could totally miss the shot, I 'accidentally' kicked it to the right, completely throwing it off and losing the battle.

"Aha! Would you look at that!" She exclaimed with a big bright smile adorning her face. The smile I lost this challenge for.

"Fine, fine, you win," I said humbly and we continued our training until the sun had set and the night sky started to be lit up by the stars.

By the time we were done half of us were laid down on the ground, completely exhausted by the new training methods Coach kept throwing at us.

"Is it just me or was the training extra long today?" Leah said, fanning herself with her hands as she sat on the ground.

"It was." Coach walked over and stood beside her, his hands behind his back in true dad fashion. "Since you all will be going for the two-day spring camp this weekend, I thought it would be reasonable to make you guys cover the loss of missing those pieces of training."

Half of our team looked at him in surprise, as if making such a decision was a horrible crime. "It wouldn't have hurt us to skip two practices, Coach, geez," Avery said.

"I think it would. No one misses a practice on my watch." Coach replied and blew his whistle. "Practice is over for today, I'll see you all on Thursday." And with that, he retreated back to the staff locker room.

"Why is he so-" Avery started, but then stopped short of her sentence as she saw someone behind me. There was confusion in her eyes mixed with something else I couldn't quite understand, but when I turned around I was sure my expression would have mimicked some of hers. It was Everly, standing in the middle of the ground after practice, her eyes showing some sort of determination in the twilight.

"Uh, hey." Wish I could straight up ask why she was here but I was afraid it would lead to an even more awkward scenario.

"I just came to see you." She noticed Avery behind me and then looked back at me with a new fire in her eyes. "Like I used to."

Hearing her mention our past relationship was actually a very uncomfortable topic for me, but it became even worse in the span of three seconds when Avery held Leah's hand and started dragging her to the locker rooms. "Anyway, we are getting late. See you guys later." Her tone was somehow not as pleasant as her words. "Enjoy."

Everly raised her shoulders and gave her a wide smile as she went away.

"So," She turned back to me when Avery stopped looking at us and went on her way. "Aren't you happy to see me here? Like the old times?"

Her question was as absurd as her showing up here as my ex but I had a feeling I couldn't honestly answer that without sounding rude and petty. "Uh sure, it was nice of you." I sat down and started redoing my shoelaces, any excuse to look away from her and find a reason to run away.

"I was wondering..." She paused, waiting for me to ask about her wonderment.

"Wondering what?" I got up but instead of looking at her, my eyes glanced all the way back to Avery. She was out of the field already, entering the locker rooms with Leah. Maybe it would sound stupid but even from all the way over here, I could tell that her shoulders tensed, like she was somehow aware of my gaze. There was a moment of recognition as I thought she would turn around but the moment was snatched away from me as Everly held my chin and moved my face back so I was looking at her.

"If you have any plans to date someone."

I was getting very tired of this game she kept playing and honestly, I considered lying to her and telling her I already had a girlfriend. But somewhere inside me, I was scared of that rumor eventually reaching Avery and I decided to change my excuse at the very last second. "Yeah, I do actually," I told her.

Maybe telling her that I was planning to date someone would finally get her off my back. Mentioning Avery's name without asking her first would have been unfair to her because I didn't want to start any rumors about her either, so I kept my answer vague and didn't name any names.

"That's-"

"Dude we're getting late let's go!" Whatever she was saying was now irrelevant as she was ruthlessly cut off by Mason, who came just in time to rescue me from this exhausting conversation yet again.

"Ah okay." She looked around, her eyes sending daggers in Mason's direction but her smile kept her feelings discreet. "See you later Noah!"

"See you later!" I said and walked off with Mason, praying in my heart that there were no more circumstances where I'd ever have to talk about our relationship again.

"You can get whatever you want from the vending machine for getting me out of there," I told Mason, who was totally expecting a fee for his work.

"Hell yes, that's why I came to your rescue." With his arm on my shoulder, we went back to the locker rooms. After our kiss last night, I was expecting to see Avery at dinner and maybe share a table, but when I entered the hall she was already done and walking off with her tray. I wished her a good night and she wished me back, but her tone was somehow devoid of any friendliness. Was it just me or had things really shifted between us- and NOT in a good way?

30

AVERY

"So what is this camping trip about?" I asked no one in particular but I was expecting a response from at least one of the two people that were present in our room right now. Mia was completing her assignment and Leah was putting on nail polish, blowing on her nails as she completed her left hand.

"Well, every year we go on a camping trip to celebrate and enjoy the bliss that touches our mother Earth during Spring," Leah explained dramatically, looking at her nails carefully from different angles. "The campsite is beautiful this year."

"You saw pictures?" Asked Mia, looking up from her notebooks.

"No, I heard someone saying they've been there before. I'm sure it'll be better than last time." They both shared a glance and started laughing.

"What happened last year?" I asked.

Mia tried to hold back from her laughter so she could explain. "The campsite was near a lake and it started raining, there was no dry place to go to so we all just kinda went through the night and took the bus back first thing in the morning."

"The whole school was down with flu and classes were canceled for a week. It was both fun and annoying at the same time." Leah added, putting her bottle of nail polish back on the floor.

While they were busy remembering all the funny details from their trip last year, my mind started wandering back to the ground, where Everly came to see Noah after the practice. Isn't that something a girlfriend would do? Why did she visit him if they weren't even together anymore?

"Avery? Have we lost you?" Leah waved her freshly manicured hand in front of me, waking me up from my thoughts.

"Huh? Yeah, of course, I'm listening." I nodded, having absolutely zero idea of what they were talking about.

"Are you thinking about what happened at practice?" Leah asked as she probably noticed the way I dragged her off the minute I saw Everly visiting him. I thought I was doing a fantastic job at being natural but I guess there was a reason I was an athlete and not an actor.

"Something happened at the practice too?" Mia was suddenly invested in the conversation, shutting her books in a flash and joining Leah on the floor. "I thought you were talking about the breakfast thing."

"Oh my God, there's something else?" Leah asked Mia who was now sitting with a cushion in her arms.

I rolled my eyes. "It's nothing. Why would I still think about it?"

"Come on, I know it's bothering you," Mia said, completely ignoring Leah who was also waiting to hear what happened at breakfast.

"It's just-" I tried to sound like I was not affected but both of them gave me such a strong knowing look, I knew there was no point in hiding my thoughts. "Ugh, fine." I caved in, leaving the comfort of my bed and joining them on the floor for the discussion. "It's just bothering me how Everly is always around, talking to Noah all close like they are still together."

"She's always around?" Mia asked, who was unaware of what I saw after our practice.

"Yes, she is. In the morning when we went into the dining hall, Noah was sitting with Everly like they were a couple having their breakfast together. I thought 'Fine, it's no big deal, maybe they're just friends.' But when I went to pick up my tray, he saw me and then he practically just ran off like he wanted to avoid me at all costs."

"He ran away?" Leah seemed quite surprised, probably because she didn't expect this from Noah just as much as I didn't.

"Maybe he was in a hurry, we can't really say he was avoiding you." Mia was voicing the reasonable possibilities, giving him the benefit of the doubt before we started jumping to conclusions.

"You don't know what happened at practice though," I said. "You know how girlfriends sometimes visit their boyfriends after practice?"

Mia nodded.

"Well, Everly visited him."

"Now, now. I think we are just jumping to conclusions here. Maybe she just wanted to talk about something." Mia suggested and Leah shook her head adamantly.

"Whatever it was, she could have said it during our meals or after class. I think visiting the field is peak girlfriend behavior." Leah said, not willing to give the boy any chance to defend himself.

"And not only that, I think they almost kissed," I added, my blood feeling hotter as I remembered the sight.

"They did?!" Leah asked, quite shocked about not witnessing the alleged kiss.

"I think so. When I looked back after reaching the locker room, her hand was on his face, like they were about to kiss or something." I don't think you could call it jealousy but every time I thought of her getting close to him, I felt the urge to punch a wall.

"Okay but did you *see* him kissing her?" Mia urged.

"Well... no." I stalled, pretty sure just watching him stand that close to her should be considered enough justification for it to be a crime. "Didn't she give me a sneer, Leah?" I asked her because I knew she would support my irrational judgments better than Mia.

"She did," Leah told Mia, convincing her to believe me.

Mia rolled her eyes. "You both should stop jumping to conclusions."

"I don't think I'm wrong about this," I told her, confident about what I saw.

"At least give him the benefit of the doubt." Mia insisted. "If something like this happens again then I'll believe you, but until then I don't think you should overthink about it."

"Ugh, this is why I hate having feelings for someone." I got up and plopped down on my bed. "Now everything he does will affect me. Why did I ever kiss him back!"

Having feelings for someone was as exhausting as sweeping during a storm. Everything they do has the power to either upset or make you extremely happy. Now that I knew I liked him, everything started affecting me and there was nothing I could do about it. My mind kept replaying the warmth of Noah's embrace and the sincerity in his eyes. It felt like we had forged a connection, something meaningful that transcended the boundaries of friendship. But now, the possibility of him dating Everly felt like a betrayal of that connection.

My mind was already coming up with multiple hurtful situations that could come up in the next few days and I didn't know how to deal with it. What if he only kissed me because we were dance partners and didn't actually have any feelings for me? I was so far deep in admiring him that now I didn't know how to go back. Like it was a trench and I fell down without any way to climb back up. He will move on from the kiss and start dating Everly again but what about me? Am I supposed to just look at them as a happy couple as I watch them from a distance, still buried in my feelings for him?

"You know what?" Mia got up as well, standing at the edge of my bed with her hands on her waist. "I think you should clearly ask him about it."

"And tell him I got jealous? Yeah, not happening."

"So you're going to sit here and let him get away with it? If he was the one to kiss you first, he sure as hell owes you an explanation." She was now tugging on my arm and I reluctantly sat up, still drowning in the deep seas of overthinking.

"What if he laughs at the fact that I like him?" The question sounded stupid even to my own ears but I had to let all my doubts out so she could tell me if it even made sense.

"This girl." Mia facepalmed. "Are you gonna go and ask him about this or do you want to overthink nonsense for another week?"

"Fine, you're right." I got up and put on a hoodie over my sweatpants. "I guess I'll just ask him why he's ignoring me so much."

"Good luck, kid," Leah said while moving on to paint her nails on the other hand.

My hands in my hoodie pocket, I was lazily coming down the stairs thinking how I'll ask him about this without sounding obsessed. Would I sound too possessive? Is it even reasonable to be mad at him even though we aren't together? Does he even remember the kiss or is he just too busy with Everly to even miss me now? I reached the common room while entertaining and analyzing these thoughts but they came to a halt as I noticed who was lounging on the common couch.

It was Everly and Amanda, sharing a bag of popcorn and talking about something vehemently. My feet halted for half a second before I reminded myself I shouldn't be getting intimidated by anyone. But before I could even think about walking past, I heard something that made my body freeze in place.

"Visiting him after practice again like his girlfriend felt so good after all this time being apart." Everly was saying and even though she didn't take any names, it was obvious who she was talking about.

"You're back together now?" Amanda asked her, barely containing her excitement.

"Of course, how long can we stay apart anyway?" Everly was absentmindedly coiling a strand of her on her finger, her voice dripping with as much pride as an Asian parent talking about their overachieving kid.

That was all I needed to know for my knees to go weak and for my self-esteem to be trampled like a flower bed after a hailstorm. There was a split second of hesitation, a single thought that crept up in my mind telling me to ignore her and talk to Noah anyway. But it was quickly extinguished by a strong gust of ego as I realized doing so would definitely end up in more humiliation for me. Everly and Amanda were still too busy to notice my presence in the room so I turned on my heel and headed back, stomping on the stairs in every single step.

This is what I was scared of, this is what I wanted to avoid when I started catching feelings for someone. So basically, he had kissed me and went on to date his ex again meanwhile I was left fantasizing about our friendship, melting over the fact that Noah actually paid attention to me all this while. I pushed the door open and stomped in, taking off my hoodie and throwing it on the floor.

"What happened?" Mia asked worriedly while Leah looked like she was too afraid to even let her presence known on the floor.

"I was right, I told you guys I wasn't just overthinking!" I tried hard to keep my voice low but the amount of anger bubbling inside me made it impossible to speak calmly. "I just heard Everly saying they're back together! Now it all makes sense. This is why he ignored me at breakfast, this is why she came to visit him after practice and I'm also sure they kissed after we left. That jerk of a guy, he kissed me at the ball and went on to date her like nothing happened, I hate him, I hate him so much!" I was now fuming on the bed like a kettle of tea on high flame.

Mia was too shocked to speak and Leah was already capping the bottle of nail paint shut and getting up. "How dare he do this to you, I'm gonn-"

"Calm down! Where are you going?" Mia held her back from opening the door, pulling her inside the room.

"To show that jerk he messed with the wrong girl."

"Or maybe we can talk to him calmly and ask why he did this?" Mia was trying to calm us down, a single force of reason among two hotheads.

"After knowing I don't mean anything to him? Nice joke."

"Exactly, I don't think she should even breathe in his direction after this, much less have a conversation." Leah was calm enough to not visit their building and kick his ass but she was definitely prepared to hold a bigger grudge than me.

"How can you still take his side?" All the anger started shifting its track into the crying lane, as my eyes filled with tears and my voice started shaking. "I don't want to be friends with someone who plays with my feelings like this."

"Fine, fine," Mia was suddenly concerned when the big fat tears started falling down my cheeks, and stopped trying to be Noah's advocate. "We don't have to be friends with him if you don't want to."

The tears kept falling down my cheeks like a dam unleashed after a heavy rain, all my emotions getting the best of me as I felt a huge wave of betrayal. The moments I shared with him, all those times I felt a genuine friendship between us despite our rivalry, all of it rained down on me heavily as I realized I probably must have imagined it. I wouldn't have been hurt if anyone else did it, but for some reason the fact that it was Noah kept drilling a hole in my heart. The image of our shared moment at the ball, the warmth of his kiss, now felt tainted by the realization that he was back with Everly.

Mia passed me the box of tissues as Leah came up beside me as well, both of them comforting me with hugs until my tears subsided and my hiccups came to a stop.

"You know what? The camping trip came at the right time. We can have a little earthy vacation before you get back into your matches and classes, forgetting all about Noah and his evil antics." Leah suggested in an attempt to get me to move on.

"But Noah would be there as well." A few more tears threatened to make their way down my face when I imagined him taking hikes with Everly.

"Exactly," Leah said with utmost fervent energy. "That means you can avoid his flirty ass and show him where you stand, which is way outside his league."

"You think so?" I asked her, eyes puffy and face red like a tomato.

"I know so. Just enjoy your time at the camp and show him what he's missing."

"Guys, I know Noah, I still thin-" Mia was interrupted before she could advocate Noah's side again.

"What are you gonna pack, Avery? Show me your closet, I'll tell you what we'll need for the camp."

Mia seemed to forget what she was saying and instantly piped up when Leah mentioned the packing. "Oh, we can also pack my binoculars! There will be so many beautiful birds to watch."

"Sure, Grandma, you can birdwatch all you want." Leah giggled and opened my closet, shuffling through my mix of sweatshirts and flowy dresses as she picked out the ones that were appropriate for the camp.

Grateful for the distraction, I wiped my tears and got up from the floor as we created havoc in our room, taking out clothes and setting them down on my bed, discussing all the things we could do at camp. Despite the fire that Noah ignited in my heart, stories of camp cheered up my spirits, and soon, I was thrilled enough to look forward to the camp, the stories of potential adventures filling my head and kicking any lingering thoughts of Noah to the corner of my brain.

31

NOAH

The sterile scent of the chemistry lab welcomed me as I stepped through the doorway. Fluorescent lights flickered overhead, casting a pale glow on rows of lab benches adorned with glassware and equipment. Mrs. Jones stood at the front, ready to guide us through another experiment.

Since my last meeting with Avery went a little off-board, I was looking forward to seeing her again so I could maybe clear the air from the previous awkward encounters. The camping trip was just a day away and I had the perfect date in mind- a good long hike that led to one of the most beautiful views in England. I knew she liked outdoor activities just as much as me, which made a hiking date the perfect location to confess my feelings for her. Her thoughts had taken up much space in my head the past few weeks, and every time I saw her smiling, I had the urge to tell her just how much she made me happy. But the foundation of that friendship had to be built first, which meant the minute I entered the lab, my eyes searched for Avery.

"Your objective is to determine the concentration of a given solution of sodium hydroxide using a standardized solution of hydrochloric acid." Mrs. Jones began explaining the details of the experiment, her words a distant hum as my attention gravitated toward Avery. Our eyes met, and for a moment, the world around me seemed to fade away. However, our short-lived connection broke soon enough when she turned, adjusting her attention back to Mrs. Jones as she told us the same precautions we had already heard a million times.

"Now, this experiment will be conducted in pairs so I want you guys to choose a partner and settle down at one of the stations." There was a shift among the students at her order, everyone going through the lab to find their best friends and settling into the stations one by one.

As nervous as I was by Avery's aloof gaze, I gathered my courage to ask her to be my partner, discounting her previous reaction to the possibility that she was tired.

"Hey," I said and she nodded politely at my greeting.

But as I opened my mouth to invite her to be my partner, I felt a shift in the atmosphere. Almost as if she saw my question coming from miles away, her demeanor changed in accordance with it. The warmth in her eyes dimmed, and a cloud of uncertainty replaced it, causing a string to tug at my heart as well.

"Mia, want to be lab partners?" She turned to Mia, who glanced at us with a mixture of surprise and concern. The sharp change in her behavior felt like a sudden twist in a story I thought I knew by heart.

"Uh, sure." Mia looked back and forth between us, her expression carrying a silent plea for reassurance.

"I'm sorry, I already have a partner." Avery turned to me and smiled politely, before getting busy with the multitude of beakers and chemicals in front of her. That's it. No other words, no other explanation. Just a polite smile and she acted like I wasn't even there.

I hesitated for a moment, masking my confusion with a forced smile. Mia glanced at me with a mix of guilt and unease, shrugging slightly as if to say she didn't understand it either.

As I walked back toward my bench, where Theo was already shuffling through the equipment, I couldn't shake the feeling of disquiet. The experiment became a mechanical task, a backdrop to the unanswered questions swirling in my mind. The chemistry between us, once palpable, now felt elusive and mysterious. *Did I do something? Was there something I had missed? Is she mad that I kissed her at the ball? But she was the one wh-*

"Noah, you're spilling it on the table!" Theo yelled suddenly and I realized the acid I was pouring into the beaker was now gracing the table in a small puddle.

"Sorry, I just- I'm sorry, I'll clean it." I quickly picked up the chemical sock from the drawer and started soaking up the acid carefully. My overbearing thoughts about Avery were now messing with my experiment so I cleared my head and decided to pay attention to the class. Maybe I was overthinking and she just wanted to do this experiment with Mia. Sure, we had studied chemistry together before, and sure, I thought she still saw me as her study partner, but if she wanted to do it with her best friend instead, then so be it. I shook all thoughts of her aloofness out of my head and told myself it was not a big deal. If something was wrong, I'm sure she would talk to me about it, and maybe now just wasn't the right time.

The experiment demanded precision, so I threw myself back into the task, hoping the scientific focus would distract me from the emotional discord brewing inside me.

"And she left you hanging?" Mason asked as he tried to stuff his sleeping bag into his backpack, a task that was beyond help.

"Yeah. I don't know if it was something I did or what, but it just seemed weird to me. Like she's avoiding me." I was sorting through a pile of clothes, deciding which ones were the most appropriate to keep. An olive green sweatshirt, two pairs of khakis, and three jackets were all I had packed until now and I still needed to decide on more shirts.

"Is it because you kissed her?" Mason asked, still trying to fold the sleeping bag further.

"But she kissed me too." A warm feeling hugged my heart as I remembered that moment, which was quickly crushed by a cold gust of her indifference today.

"I don't know, man. Girls are moody. Maybe she's just not in a good mood right now." He finally managed to put it in his backpack but now he was facing a new struggle of trying to zip up the bag with that monstrosity inside it.

"You really think so?"

"Yeah, sure, you guys can talk it over at camp. Now come on, sit on this bag so I can zip it up and get it over with." I walked over and sat on the bag, and after a few more minutes of struggle, the bag was finally closed with all its unnecessary crap sitting safely inside.

That night before sleeping as I finished packing for the camp, I carefully selected a few snacks – a pack of Jaffa Cakes, a chocolate bar, and a packet of crisps. The idea was simple; share them with Avery on the bus and talk about why she was suddenly acting like a stranger. I didn't want to lose my friendship with her over this. Even if she was avoiding me because of the kiss, I wanted her to be honest with me about it so I would know how she felt about all of this. Most of all, I just wanted to know what was wrong so I could make it right. Whatever it was, I wanted to make it right.

The brisk morning air was shuffling through the crowd of students at the bus stop, all waiting for the bus to arrive. I was standing there with my hands in my pockets, the cold air taking out almost all senses in them. As I rubbed my hands and blew on them occasionally, I scanned the crowd, looking for Avery. She had been on my mind ever since I woke up, and I couldn't shake the feeling of unease that lingered from yesterday. She hadn't talked to me during our practice either, leaving without a word with Leah when the coach blew his whistle to send us off.

As the familiar yellow school bus rounded the corner, my nerves gave out a shake as if scared about the discussion that awaited me on the bus. Our story hadn't exactly started on a good note either, but this time the indifference was prickling into my heart like a needle. This time I knew how we went along so well, how we could be honest about anything without an ounce of judgment from the other and losing that genuine connection was now laying heavy on my heart.

I boarded the bus and took a seat near the front, settling my backpack in the leg room as I waited for Avery to arrive. Mason and Mia took a seat at my back and even Leah came aboard and found a bus partner, which meant Avery had no other commitments when it came to sharing her seat, except for me.

Or so I thought.

When Avery finally appeared, a radiant smile came up on my face as I waved at her. She caught sight of me, returning the gesture with a smile. However, her smile held a different spirit, like she was smiling more out of obligation than with admiration. Expecting her to settle down on the seat beside me, my spirits lifted for an instant before they fell down to their horrible deaths when she walked past me toward the back. Struck by confusion and hurt, I craned my neck to see where she was going when my heart took another hit as I saw her sliding down on the seat next to Liam. Irritation took over me as Avery stole a glance in my direction- almost as if to make sure I was watching- before she went back to having an enthusiastic conversation with Liam, who was clearly sailing on the sea of delight with the attention he got from her.

As I sat back straight, my confusion was replaced by a sense of frustration and disappointment. Now I knew I was definitely not overthinking. Something was totally up and she was doing this on purpose. Sharing a road trip with Liam a mere days after we shared a kiss? Did the kiss mean nothing to her? Was it just a fleeting moment of infatuation that took over her, compared to the months-long accumulation of my feelings? Was I the only one taking it so seriously?

However, little did I know my moment of misery was going to be spiked up by another punch in the gut, as Everly boarded the bus and scanned it before her eyes laid down on the empty seat next to me. Not wanting to invite her over, I looked out the window, desperately hoping she gets the message. But it was Everly, and getting the message was not in her dictionary.

"Hey, Noah! Mind if I join you?" She asked, her eyes sparkling with glee.

Not knowing how to execute a rejection for no apparent reason, I managed a forced smile, "Sure, I guess."

She sat down beside me, her flowy skirt falling over my legs as she placed her peach colored handbag below the front seat. "It's nice to share a road trip, isn't it?" She piped up.

"I guess it is." I was guessing a lot today. As angry as I was with the situation, she hadn't done anything to receive a cold behavior from me. As the bus engine started with a rumble, I laid my head back on the headrest and looked out the window.

I felt a tap on my shoulder and glanced sideways to see Everly offering me one of her Airpods. "You want music?"

Since the infuriating thoughts of Liam and Avery sharing laughter at the back were taking up way too much space in my brain, I decided to push them back with some melodies. I took the Airpod from her hand, secretly grateful about the fact that they were wireless. Even though we had shared some close moments in the past, it just felt awkward to share a close space again. Shifting back and resting my head back again, I tried to lose my thoughts under the influence of the songs. Eventually, the hum of the bus engine and the rhythmic beats of the music became a lullaby, as my overworked brain fell into a slumber.

We arrived at the campsite- thankfully for me- after a quiet and peaceful road trip. I had accidentally fallen asleep the minute we hit the road, which meant that Everly didn't get the chance to bring up any topics I was uncomfortable with. Although we had only been there for about an hour, the campsite was already proving to be a delight for all our senses. The cheerful chirping of birds, the rustle of leaves in the wind, and the distant murmur of a babbling brook gave our ears a break from the hustle-bustle of cities. Gentle breezes carried the scent of damp earth and pine needles, blending with the sweet fragrance of wildflowers that carpeted the ground. As for the eyes, the valleys, trees and hills nearby were enough to make us feel safe and secure by mother nature herself.

The rustling sounds of tent canvas surrounded us as everyone was busy setting up their tents for our temporary weekend abode. Mason and I picked a spot on the corner of the clearing to set up our canvas tent, determined to make it a cozy sanctuary for the nights.

"Noah, pass me the rope," Mason said, as he helped me set our tent.

Well, more like *I* was helping *him* setting up the tent, because I actually had no idea how to set up these DIY canvas tents but Mason had a mastery in everything that had to do with the great outdoors. I was just hovering around as he did the technical work, asking him if he needed any help with the set up.

"Yeah, here you go." I handed him the bundle of rope.

"Now, hold this end, and pull it when I tell you to." Mason ordered, unspooling the rope and doing something that was way beyond my understanding. As I held the rope while waiting for his order, I couldn't help but steal glances at Avery, who was a few tents away. Frustratingly enough, Liam was still by her side, sticking to her like a fox by his own tail. He was helping her with the tent, making some seemingly humorous remark once in a while that made her laugh. That adorable laugh when paired with the sunlight was almost angelic in its nature.

"Noa-" Mason started and I pulled the rope as I was supposed to, an action that was followed by the sounds of the canvas crumpling down and wooden sticks falling on themselves. I turned immediately and found the tent collapsed in a tangled mess. I realized I accidentally pulled too early, mistaking his call by the cue to pull the rope.

Mason let out a groan from under the canvas. "Watch those ropes, man! I was just asking you to pass me the tent stakes."

"Sorry, sorry, I got distracted."

He emerged from the ruins of the tent, a bemused expression on his face. "What's got you so distracted huh?" he asked, adjusting his disheveled hair.

"Nothing. Let's just get this over with and eat something." For what seemed like the hundredth time, I tried to empty my head from thoughts of Avery and Liam and focused on the task at hand- trying not to punch the blonde guy a few tents away from me.

32

NOAH

"Gather 'round, everyone, we've got our first activity for today!" Mr. Bailey stood at the center near the fire pit, as everyone got done with their tents and started gathering around him. He was responsible for our school's extra-curricular activities, but since I never got time to do anything other than football, I only met him once a year during our camping trips.

"Are we going fishing?" Someone from the twelfth grade asked with much delight in his voice.

"Not after what you guys pulled last year." Mr. Bailey told him sternly.

"Those pirate attacks had nothing to do with us." The senior guy got playfully defensive.

"Whatever, the point is, there's no fishing." He told the guy and then turned to the rest of us, continuing his speech. "Our first activity is paintball."

The crowd of students immediately burst into a hushed chatter but Mr. Bailey cleared his throat and stole the attention back towards him. "Since some of you always create your own mobs and start ganging up on others," He said, looking at a group of seniors particularly, "This time I'm going to decide the teams myself."

"But sir, I think we ca-"

"Nah ah ah." He held a finger in the air, not willing to take any suggestions from them. "I'm going to decide the teams and it's final. As always, it's going to be a game of Capture the Flag, and I repeat, you *are not allowed* to create gangs and attack others."

The group of seniors sighed, as Mr. Bailey started sorting our group into two teams—Team Blue with the blue paintballs and vest, and Team Red with the red ones.

As he kept naming the players and creating a team on either side of him, something in me wished I would be picked in Avery's. Once upon a time, we used to be rivals and our similar competitiveness always pulled us apart like two magnets that always repulsed each other with the same poles, but now that I had experienced being in the same team as her, I realized there could be no better teammate than Avery Kai. She puts her everything into whatever she does and her determination is so contagious that you see yourself putting in the same efforts to achieve the same goal.

"Mason, Blue team. Chloe, Red. Avery, Blue." He finally came down to our class and the anticipation was now building as I unknowingly prayed in my heart to be put in the Blue team.

"Mia, Red. Noah," My heart skipped a beat. "Blue." And then resumed its beating with a brand new satisfaction pulsing through it.

Avery rolled her eyes as I walked over to join her side, her past distaste somehow still within her even if we were now playing in the same team. We assigned Mason to be our captain and then took our Blue flag from Mr. Bailey, deciding where to put it in the vast expanse of the sunlit forest.

"Fred, you are in charge of guarding our flag," Mason told Fred as he hoisted it on a random tree branch at the corner of our base. "Whatever you do, do *not* leave your spot. If you get shot, yell for someone to take your place, understood?"

Fred nodded like he was an obedient soldier as Mason threw out orders like he was the commanding officer in this battle. "Everyone else, your main objective is not to get shot. Spread out and try to find the flag's location first and the minute you've got it, inform the others without getting caught and retrieve it back to our base." Our team nodded, and all that was missing in this briefing was a salute to our captain and several chants of 'Hail Mason.'

We took our positions deep inside the forest as Mr. Bailey gave us some time to explore the paths, and then after a pause of five minutes, the sound of a whistle was blaring in the forest, ricocheting off the trees and woods as it reached every corner of the place.

Like a lion on its prowl, I stealthily started walking deeper into their base, trying to look for possible places where they might have hidden the flag. The ground was covered with dead leaves, the winter breeze ruffling them around as I tried to take gentle steps, not wanting to make any noise on my way. After a lot of shuffling here and there, I noticed Mia running through the area, like she was keeping guard or scanning the area around for any potential intruders. She didn't seem to notice me as I hid behind a tree, staying silent until she went onto a different path. I had the opportunity to shoot and count her out of the game right there, but I couldn't risk getting discovered when I was so deep in the enemy territory. My first priority was finding the flag, and then I could shoot all the enemies I wanted on my way back to our base. The real war starts when the flag is in my hands.

After looking around for any hints of a flag, I noticed Theo carefully walking toward a particular tree, his eyes fixed on something up above. Following his gaze, I realized a red flag was settled up in the branches of a tree, dangling in the middle of a particularly leafy branch. They tried to hide the allure of the bright red color by hiding it between some leaves but Theo was observant enough to spot it before anyone else. Since he was already going after it, I decided to follow him, covering him in case there were some opponents around.

Out of the corner of my eye, I saw something move. Turning sideways, I noticed Chloe carefully aiming her paintball gun toward a very clueless Theo, like a sniper positioning the perfect shot. Well, too bad I saw her sneaky acts. Before she could pull the trigger, I aimed at her jacket and pulled my own, the blue paintball hitting her right in the torso and splattering into a huge blue mark. Theo, alerted by her scream of frustration, quickly got out of there, running somewhere into the forest and disappearing out of my sight. Looking around frantically, Chloe tried to find her own sniper as I tried to hide behind a tree, but my movement was too quick and loud for her hawk eyes and she spotted me before I could save my chances of getting caught.

"THERE'S AN ENEMY IN OUR AREA! He shot me, come over quick and shoot him down!" Chloe yelled for her teammates as I took the fastest run for it, running past bushes and bushes until I reached a seemingly safe space, just a few feet on the right. The flag was still in my view but the path leading to it was now blocked by a fallen tree branch. As I ducked behind the dense foliage, I heard some rustling in the bushes somewhere behind me, followed by a faint 'Ouch!', and I immediately alerted myself to be met with a potential threat. I walked slowly toward the bushes, gun at the ready and my eyes trained on the path ahead of me as I found Avery ducking behind the bushes with her back facing me.

A dried leaf came beneath my shoe and created a crunchy sound, alerting her as she suddenly turned around and instinctively pulled the trigger, shooting me with blue paint straight at my chest.

"Hey, we're on the same team!" I protested. Thankfully, the paint was blue like my vest so it doesn't count me out of the game.

"Then why did you sneak up on me like that!" She seemed quite pissed at the possibly loud shot she wasted on me.

"I didn't-" I noticed a cut on her arm as she held the gun down, the cut deep enough for some blood to drip through. "Hey, are you okay? Some bushes have thorns here."

"Yeah, I saw that, captain obvious. Thanks for pointing it out."

"Whoa, I was just checking if you were okay. No need to bite my head off."

"Do I look like I need your pity, Noah? Save it for someone else." The way she said 'someone else' seemed a bit intentional, like she had a clue regarding who the person was.

"Why are you acting like this?" My patience was wearing thin as I kept receiving the same cold behavior without even knowing why I deserved it. "You've been acting all cold and mean and I don't even know what I did wrong?"

"You wanna know why I'm acting like this? Well, Noah, maybe it's because-" Her sentence halted when her eyes suddenly held the same vulnerability they did when she was scared about something. But then she shook her head, her eyes suddenly shifting into an empty emotion, and the last bit of unspoken communication was taken away from me. "You know what? Nevermind. You wouldn't-"

Splat.

Both of us turned toward the sound of the shot and saw Theo standing just below the flag, his jacket painted with a red splash.

"I was supposed to cover him! Stop distracting me, you idiot!" She yelled, temporarily forgetting that we were supposed to stay quiet.

Henry spotted us, a few feet to our left, and we realized he was probably the sniper behind Theo's assassination. He quickly aimed his gun at Avery, his finger touching the trigger.

"Hey, get down!" I took Avery down with me as he pulled the trigger, the paintball zipping past my ear as we dodged the bullet and lay on the ground. I quickly raised my gun and took aim at his jacket, firing off my paintball which landed square in the center of his jacket.

Another enemy down!

"Quick, go and snatch the flag!" All our disputes were suddenly forgotten as our mutually competitive nerves kicked in and she ran past me toward the flag, settling her feet on the fallen tree branch before taking a high jump. Her hands reached the flag and she snatched it off the tree, landing back on the ground like a superhero and immediately running back to our base.

I watched in awe as she pulled off the whole stunt, my mouth hanging open at the sheer level of her coolness. I only blinked out of my admiration when someone took a shot at her, but her quick as lightning steps saved her from getting hit. Her petite form made her a challenging target, and my protective instincts suddenly woke up when I realized I was still in the game. Duty called, and I shook off the distraction, resuming my role as the silent guardian. As Avery maneuvered through the field, I covered her with precision, spotting all the opponents taking shots at her and firing them down from my hidden spot.

With my precise shots and her smooth agility, she reached our base and quickly hoisted the flag on our tree, announcing our victory as all our teammates abandoned their hiding spots and came running towards the base to celebrate the victory. As I joined the celebration, she spotted me and threw me a high five, her face giving me a bright cheerful smile. Well, victories do make her extremely happy.

"We make the perfect team." She said as our hands connected in a victorious harmony.

But just as my hand touched hers, it was like the reality outside of the game settled into her and her smile quickly became diluted as she walked off, carrying her triumphant self away from me.

So I take it the mysterious grudge has still not been resolved?

The pinnacle of camping adventures revolved around campfires, so as the Sun set and the darkness of the nightfall fell upon us, Mr. Bailey taught us how to ignite a campfire before leaving us to have our fun little games as he went to sleep in his comfortable cabin. All the students let out a collective sigh at his departure, happy about the freedom of not being supervised by a teacher anymore. The high school hierarchy played out per usual as the seniors took the best spot near the campfire, sitting in a huddle while roasting marshmallows for their s'mores. The juniors were then scattered on the tree logs around, sitting with their respective group of friends and having animated conversations in the light of the fire.

There was a time when Avery would have shared her presence with mine, but those times had changed as I now had to witness her sitting on the opposite side of the fire pit, as the fire separated us on either side of its glow. Avery's attention was captured by a very enthusiastic Liam and his lively storytelling sessions. Even though his voice was faded out by the constant chatter and the crackling of the fire between us, I could just tell he was busy telling her the stories of his own mediocre experiences which he was probably greatly exaggerating.

I sighed, feeling the familiar twinge of frustration for the hundredth time since this trip started. I was sitting with Mason, Theo, and Chloe, as they talked about... damn I didn't know. I was too busy admiring the faint orangish glow that fell upon Avery, highlighting all the soft features of her face, especially her eyes. They looked like pools of honey in the firelight, the orange hue meeting her brown eyes as it gave them a very beautiful hazel touch. While listening to Liam's mediocre stories, she stole a quick glance in my direction and my heart did a somersault. Her eyes met mine for a fleeting moment before she turned her attention back to the conversation. Another pang of longing hit me as we sat in silent proximity across the fire, separated by more than just the flickering flames. My mind raced with a mixture of emotions - frustration, yearning, and a hint of jealousy. I sighed and turned my attention to the flames, attempting to drown out the noise with the rhythmic pops and hisses of the fire. Now I understood why Mason made such a big deal out of his yearning.

Just when I thought the night couldn't get more complicated, my attention was grabbed by someone standing beside me as if waiting for permission to join me. Everly. She was wearing a very chic outfit for a night out in the woods- a form-fitting, sleeveless turtleneck in a rich burgundy hue with a high-waisted pair of wide-legged trousers. I glanced at her, and for a moment, our eyes locked. There was a lot of unspoken mess in my mind that I had to clear with her, and some of it was probably visible in my eyes. She hesitated before breaking the silence.

"Mind if I join you?" she asked, a small smile playing on her lips.

I nodded, forcing a polite smile as I gestured to the empty space beside me. She settled in and the smell of insect-repellent lotion enveloped me from her side. I stole a glance at Avery, who was now deep in conversation with Liam, her laughter ringing out like a melody I couldn't quite reach.

"It's really noisy here, don't you think?" I was distracted by Everly's voice and when I turned to look at her, she was looking at me with much admiring eyes.

"I think so," I responded, not sure why I was asked to reassure the noisiness.

"Well, I think maybe we should go for a walk." She held my hand and my whole attention was now on the unsuspecting hand which had no interest in being held.

"Uh, I think..." As I tried to conjure up some polite words to decline her offer, I realized it might be the perfect setup to tell her the truth about my feelings. I don't think I can go on acting like nothing's wrong when her place in my heart has drastically changed. "Sure, let's take a walk."

The crackling of the campfire seemed distant as Everly and I walked away from the group, seeking a quieter space to talk. She had been dropping hints about us taking things further, but there was a crucial conversation that needed to happen first.

"Isn't this just perfect? I love how we're here together, like the old times, enjoying this beautiful night." She was really reminiscing about our 'old times' but honestly our 'old times' only lasted about three months.

I shifted uncomfortably, feeling the weight of a conversation that needed to happen. "Everly, there's something I need to talk to you about."

She raised an eyebrow, her smile fading slightly. "What is it? You seem serious."

I took a deep breath, trying to find the right words. "Look, Everly, I appreciate our friendship, but I can't pretend we're more than that."

Her expression changed, confusion etching across her features. "What do you mean? We're great together. Why would you say that?" The way she just decided that we were great together when she had never even asked me why I had been acting distant lately told me what I needed to know.

"Sure we are good friends, Everly, but I can't ignore certain things," I explained. I hesitated for a moment to bring up the next topic, not knowing if she even remembered that detail. "Do you remember that day when you were talking to your friend about a burglary she had?"

She seemed quite confused with the sudden change of the topic but she tried to recollect the conversation I was talking about. "Amanda? Yeah, I remember she had a burglary. Poor girl was so sad."

"And do you remember how you mentioned it could be the immigrants next door?"

She looked momentarily puzzled, but then her eyes widened in realization as she remembered her comment. "You heard that?"

I nodded. "I was sent off the practice that day because of an injury, so I thought I would share a meal with you, but when I came to see you, I accidentally heard that... conversation."

She looked taken aback, probably confused as to why I was making such a big deal out of it. "Noah, that was just a random conversation. Why does it matter here?"

"It wasn't random and it does matter to me," I continued. "Because, Everly, I'm an immigrant too. I wasn't born in England. It hurt me to know that you held such views about people like me."

Her eyes widened in realization, and a silence settled between us. She tried to search for words, her expression shifting between discomfort and regret.

She fumbled for words, her hesitation evident. "Noah, I didn't mean to offend you. It's just... I was being cautious."

"Cautious about crime or cautious about immigrants?" I asked, my frustration simmering beneath the surface.

She stumbled over her words. "Well, I didn't mean to sound prejudiced. But, you know, there are instances where immigrants..."

"I can't believe you're justifying this," I interrupted, my patience wearing thin. "I expected an apology, Everly. I can't be with someone who holds those beliefs."

Her discomfort deepened, and she tried to salvage the conversation, not understanding the impact of her words. "Noah, it's not like I think all immigrants are criminals. It's just that sometimes..."

I closed my eyes and let out a patient sigh, a wave of acceptance engulfing my anger. "You know what? It's actually fine." I gave her a close-mouthed smile. As frustrating as her attempts at justifying this whole thing were, I realized there was no point in making her understand why I was hurt. She didn't apologize and I knew she wasn't going to because she didn't even understand why it was wrong in the first place. Some people never change, and I guess we just have to accept that reality and move on, instead of hurting ourselves further in attempts of making them understand our perspective. If they don't understand, they will belittle our struggles. And I didn't want to be invalidated anymore. It's better to leave their side rather than stay in a hurtful situation by belittling and denying our feelings. "I'm not holding a grudge against you or anything. I just want you to know that I am moving on. We are not happening again."

She nodded, her eyes a little sad. "So that day after practice, you weren't... talking about me?" Her voice came out feeble and embarrassed.

I had to look back and remember what she was talking about before it came to my mind that she came to me the day after I kissed Avery and I told her I had plans to date someone. I honestly felt bad that she misunderstood my words, but I had to clear it out with her nonetheless. "No, Everly, I wasn't talking about you. I'm sorry." I gave her a sad smile and she nodded.

"Well, can you please not tell anyone about this? I mean..." She looked uncomfortable saying this. "I mean the fact that you turned me down?"

It honestly surprised me that the one thing she still cared about was her own flawless image like I was nothing more than just a social status, a trophy boyfriend.

"I won't tell anyone." Thinking I could actually have a meaningful conversation with her was obviously a mistake. She could never see past herself. "So anyway," I said casually, turning toward the camp as I decided to excuse myself from her presence. "See you around, I guess."

As I walked back toward the campfire, my eyes went in search of Avery before I could stop them and I noticed she was still sitting by the fire with her friends- with Liam. However, while listening to her friends, her eyes went toward the direction Everly and I went on as she watched her return alone from our little 'walk'. Her eyes showed a hint of confusion as she looked around, and that's when her gaze met mine. She looked a little taken aback by the fact that I just caught her looking for me and she immediately returned her attention to the friends around, although I doubt she was following anything they said. With her indifference remaining the same toward my existence, I decided I had just about enough of the emotional roller coaster I was on today and went inside my tent. I would rather sulk about my ruined friendship with Avery in the comfort of my tent rather than watch her be close to Liam again.

Mason still hadn't returned from the campfire session so I just went inside my sleeping bag and tucked myself in, closing my eyes after a -physically *and* emotionally- tiring day.

My peaceful sleep was disturbed by the sounds of the cackling firewood, as I slowly sat up while rubbing my tired eyes, my sleepy brain still confused about my whereabouts. I looked to my side where Mason was sleeping in his sleeping bag and right in front of me, the entrance to our tent was closed up. *Woodfire, tent, sleeping bags.* Oh right, we were at camp. I was so tired that the hard-hitting sleep settled into my brain deep enough to make me forget my surroundings for a second. However, the sound of the cackling firewood still confused me. Mason was in my tent and there were no voices outside our tent as well, which meant it was pretty late and everyone had already gone to sleep. *Maybe they forgot to put out the campfire.*

Realizing how dangerous an unattended campfire can be, I wore my jacket and pulled the tent's zip open, coming outside with a mission to put out the fire and feel like a superhero for saving our camp. However, as I reached the firepit, I realized it wasn't unattended at all. The reason there were no sounds was because it was attended by only one person. She was sitting with her elbows on her knees, looking at the campfire with eyes that seemed lost in thoughts.

Avery.

33

AVERY

The night at the campsite was quiet, the only sounds being the distant rustle of leaves and the crackling of the dwindling campfire. The warmth from the embers seemed to be the only comfort as I sat alone on a log, staring into the dancing flames. Tired from the road trip and paintball game, the others had long retired to their tents, leaving me alone with the echo of my thoughts. Despite the exhaustion, I was unable to sleep. During the campfire, Everly had asked Noah to go for a walk. If there was any hint of doubt left within me, it vanished when I saw him get up and leave with her. I could only watch as I saw them walking away, leaving me and my broken feelings behind.

Even though I was the one who had acted bitterly and left his company to go sit with Liam, it was still bothering me to know that he shared the road trip with Everly, an activity that we were used to doing together at this point. To make matters worse, he had gone on a nice romantic walk in the forest, and long after the incident, it still stayed in my mind as it ruined any chances for me to sleep.

As I traced the patterns of the flames with my eyes, the sound of footsteps approached from behind. Startled, I turned to see Noah emerging from the darkness, his silhouette outlined by the warm glow of the fire.

"You're still awake?" he asked, a note of surprise in his voice.

I shrugged, not trusting my voice to betray the mix of emotions within. Noah glanced at the empty spaces around the campfire, then at me. There was a palpable tension in the air, a silent understanding that something wasn't quite right.

He sat down on a nearby log, and for a moment, we sat in awkward silence. I could sense his eyes on me, his gaze searching for something in the shadows.

"So Liam left early?" He asked, a hint of a taunt underlying his voice.

I scoffed, my own jealousy bubbling to the surface. "Why do you care? You've got Everly to keep you company."

His gaze met mine, a guarded look in his eyes. "What do you mean?"

"Sharing a bus seat during the road trip, taking a walk together, you know, kinda like the stuff we used to do." I tried my best to sound aloof but my words and tone alike said a lot more than I wanted to tell.

"Funny you mention that, because you skipped the seat I saved for you." The satire in his voice was too obvious to miss. "And by funny, I mean not funny at all."

"Oh, please." I exclaimed rather unpleasantly. "You saved it for me?"

"Yes, I did and you left it for Liam." His expression tightened. "I bet he didn't pack your favorite snacks or create a special playlist with all the songs you like so we could listen to it on our way here."

My gaze softened a bit. I couldn't help but feel a pang of relief, though it was still not enough to convince me against his closeness with Everly. "Don't act like you don't know what's going on."

"I don't have to act because I really don't know. You've been avoiding me, being bitter with me, and all this while I don't even know what I did wrong."

"You don't know?" I took a deep breath, summoning the courage to speak the words that had been weighing heavy on my heart all this while. "You don't know that you kissed me at the ball even though you were still dating Everly?"

His eyes widened, surprise and confusion flickering across his face. "Dating Everly? I can't believe you'd think... what are you even talking about?"

The moment was finally here where I could unleash all the rage that had been bothering me for so long. "I saw you with Everly, okay? I saw you having a nice little breakfast with her, I saw you taking a walk with her, I saw you kissing her after our prac-"

"Wait, *kissing her?!*" There was a sudden rise in his voice.

I faltered. I should have confirmed my suspicion before voicing it out. "Yes." My voice came out uncertain.

"Have you been living a different reality or something? Are you talking about the day she came to visit me after our practice?"

I nodded.

He sighed, exhausted by the heavy dose of misunderstandings. "I can't believe you'd just assume that." He shook his head, disappointment filling his eyes. "There was no kissing. No hugging, no hand-holding, and no other couple stuff for that matter! I was just telling her I was seeing someone, that's it! How could you be so stupid to assume something like that?"

Even though I knew I was in the wrong, the tone of his voice sparked yet another blast of anger within me. "I'm stupid?! Weren't you the one who told me you were still seeing her when I asked you about it? How can you blame me for it when you told me yourself that it wasn't over?"

"I only said that because you were going on a date with Liam!"

His sudden confession hit me like a truck and my eyes went wide. "So you lied to me?"

He looked away, the light from the fire illuminating his furrowed brows.

"You lied to me just because I was going out with someone else?" I asked again, wanting him to admit his fault. "Is everything a competition to you?"

"Isn't it to you too?" He turned to me, his eyes still angry. "You hung out with Liam just because you thought I was dating Everly. You could have talked to me about it but no, you decided to turn it into a competition and made me feel like an absolute douche!"

I leaned back, as if from the force of his accusation. "I didn't even call you that."

"No, you didn't call me that but was I supposed to feel like a gentleman when you told me that you thought I ditched you for Everly?" The hurt in his voice sounded more sincere than mine. "You didn't even talk to me about it. You just assumed I'm the type of guy who goes around kissing girls and then started hanging out with Liam even though he's talking shit half the time."

His accusations hit a vulnerable corner in my heart and sparked a fiery explosion of defense. "Why would I talk to you about it? It was just a kiss, why should I get jealous after a kiss?"

He threw his hands in the air, defeated. "You know what? I can't talk to you when you're like this." He stood up, frustration coating his every action. "Talk to me when you're clear about your own feelings. I thought we had something real, but maybe it was all a game to you."

His words hung in the air, a bitter truth that pierced through the night. My eyes stung with unshed tears, and I felt a deep ache within my chest. Without another word, he walked away, disappearing into the darkness toward his tent.

I sat there, feeling the weight of my assumptions and the sharp sting of regret. The night air grew colder, and I realized that in my attempt to protect myself, I had pushed away the person I cared about. The embers of the campfire dimmed, leaving me alone in the fading glow.

Left behind after his frustrated attempt to clear things out, I felt like our friendship was slipping through my fingers, no matter how much I tried to hold it close. I always felt a strangely real connection with Noah that went past any superficial or trivial parts of an average friendship. Something about being with him was immensely liberating, like I could be my worst self and he would still choose to focus on my good parts. It was something that had kept me going when everything in my life was unfamiliar and new. Somehow, all these months, he had unknowingly made me feel better- every single time I lashed out or won against him, it gave me a huge surge of satisfaction and happiness; and every time I was around him, I found myself being so raw that now I couldn't imagine living without that genuine connection anymore.

I sat there alone, staring into the dying embers of the fire. The night air suddenly felt colder, and the last few crackling flames seemed to mock the warmth they once shared. A sudden cold breeze brought a new wave of realization to my heart as it went past. I craved warmth. I craved *his* warmth. I craved him.

I can't keep denying what I feel.

As the distant sounds of the night enveloped me, my internal struggle became more apparent. I took a deep breath and looked in the direction Noah had gone. A mix of emotions played on my mind—regret, fear, but also a glimmer of understanding.

Why am I so afraid of admitting the truth? Why am I letting my ego get in the way of something real?

So what if I hated him at first? So what if our friendship was literally based on our mutual instinct of trying to outdo the other? He was still the person who made me feel the most like myself, and the way he paid attention to me meant a lot more to me than he would ever realize.

Even though there was no one around me, I nodded like I understood an equation Mr. Becker was lecturing me about and splashed a bucket of water over the campfire. The camp's safety came first no matter how dramatic I was feeling. The air around me suddenly settled into coldness and I let out a shiver before wrapping my jacket tightly around me. I looked at my wristwatch: 01:14 A.M. It was probably too late for a heart-to-heart apology with Noah at this time, so instead of following his angry footprints, I turned around to go to my own tent, deciding to settle my feelings for today so I can convince my egoistic self to come up with a few words of apology tomorrow.

34

AVERY

The new day brought a new hope to mend my ways as I woke up to the sounds of birds and a very grumpy Mia by my side. Sunlight was filtering through the open zipper of our tent as I realized I was probably way past the sunrise- the sunrise I was supposed to catch with Mia.

"You missed it, Avery," she huffed, "the most breathtaking sunrise, and you weren't there."

I winced, guilt creeping in. "Sorry, I was just really tired. I slept late last night."

"You did, didn't you? Why didn't you come in with me?"

I faltered, not sure if she would understand all my complicated feelings. "I just had a lot in mind."

Her eyes softened and it seemed she decided to forgive me for my late rising when she saw my tired eyes. "Fine, but go and freshen up! You're going to be late for breakfast and you *know* Mr. Bailey won't take any latecomers."

Without a moment's hesitation, I scrambled out of my sleeping bag. I changed out of my pajamas, throwing on a pair of cargo pants and a black shirt, deciding to add a pop of color with a yellow suede jacket. As I rushed outside, the cool morning air embraced me, and I darted towards the makeshift bathroom area to freshen up. It was a whirlwind of toothpaste, water splashes, and attempts at fixing my sleep-mussed hair. I took one last look at my almost presentable breakfast look and headed back out again, walking toward my tent so I could use some lotion on my cold sensitive skin. A bunch of people were rushing in and out of the bathrooms as well, and it made me feel a little better to know I wasn't the only one who overslept.

However, as I reached our little abode, a surprise awaited me. There, right outside my tent flap, sat a first aid kit. I looked at the bandage sitting inside the transparent box and immediately remembered the cut on my arm that was still sitting bare inside the sleeve of my jacket. I touched my arm and the cut still hurt a little bit, but it wasn't concerning. Honestly, I had forgotten about it which meant I hadn't mentioned or shown it to anyone after the game and there was no one around me at that time to have witnessed my little injury. Confusion gripped me as I couldn't understand who could have possibly known about my cut, much less remember it.

I glanced around the campsite, students running in a rush here and there to get ready for breakfast, with some of them already seated on the log near the campfire with paper plates in their hands. As I scanned the whole place, my eyes reached the corner where Noah had placed his tent and I caught a sight of him looking in my direction. I almost flinched from the shock of him catching me red-handed as I searched for him but he seemed more nervous at our interaction as he looked away quickly, pretending to be engrossed in some campsite task. The memory of our heated discussion from the previous night rushed back – a wave of emotions mixed with a tinge of regret.

Frowning, I picked up the first aid kit and examined it. It wasn't just any first aid kit; it was the one I'd seen Noah using countless times on the football field. A smile tugged at the corners of my lips. He had found me in the bushes right after the thorn pricked me, and a whole new pack of butterflies unleashed in my stomach as I realized not only did he remember it, but he decided to give me first aid even after having an argument with me yesterday. Despite our little fight, he cared enough to make sure I had what I needed.

Entering the tent, I found Mia sitting cross-legged on the floor, waiting for my arrival.

"What are you all red and smiley for?" She asked, tilting her head.

I held up the first aid box as if she was supposed to connect the dots that weren't even presented to her in the first place.

"You're happy you got... a first aid box?" I had seen her less confused when she did her algorithms back at our dorm.

"I'm happy because Noah left it for me outside the tent." I gushed, sitting on the floor and opening it to find a bandage inside. "Even though we had an argument yesterday and he was supposed to be mad at me."

She looked at me in a surprised way and yet some of her confusion still filtered through. "At this point, I can't even follow what you two have going on." She got up, walking toward the exit, and waiting for me to follow. "I just know if Ella ever asks about him, I'm not the one explaining how you went from being enemies to literally blushing around each other like crazy."

I gently put the bandage on and got up, following her outside. "Don't you dare tell her without asking me first."

As we had our first meal of the day, I kept stealing glances at Noah, the urge to go over and apologize taking over me with each passing minute. Just as we ended our meals and threw the paper plates into a recyclable bag of garbage, I walked over, my heart pounding with a mix of nerves and resolve. I needed to make amends with Noah, bandage or no bandage.

"Hey." I greeted, trying to keep my tone casual. Even though I had meant to bring up our conversation and apologize for it, some defensive part of me wanted to act like it never happened. Talking about it would mean I have to apologize and confess, which was making me feel more nervous by the second. Nevertheless, I pulled all my guard down, determined to respect and trust our friendship more than my defenses.

Noah was holding one of his hiking boots in his hands, trying to slip in a new pair of shoelaces in the shoe. He looked up as he heard my voice, his gaze meeting mine. There was just a tiny hint of surprise on his otherwise unreadable face. He didn't say anything, merely raising an eyebrow as if urging me to continue.

Okay, so he's still mad.

I took a breath, deciding to cut to the chase. "Did you leave the bandage for me outside my tent this morning?"

For a moment, he said nothing. The campsite bustled with activity around us, a stark contrast to the quiet tension in our conversation. Just when I thought he might not respond, he finally spoke. "Bandage? Why would I do that?"

I held back a sigh, knowing this was the act he was going with today – the one where he masked his feelings with a layer of stoicism. "Come on, it was your first aid kit. You couldn't have been more obvious."

He shifted his attention to the hiking boots in front of him, avoiding eye contact. "It could've been anyone's. Why are you so sure it was mine?"

I smirked, finding his attempt at denial almost amusing. "Noah, if you wanted to hide it, maybe you should've given me a different first aid box that didn't have your name on the bottom."

He faltered, blinking fast as he made himself more engrossed in fixing his shoelaces. "I don't know what you're talking about."

"Then maybe you would know what I'm about to say next," I said and his hands slowed like he was suddenly focused on my voice and words. He was waiting for me to mention it, I could tell. "About last night."

He stiffened, his hands freezing mid-motion. It was as if I had touched a nerve, and he was suddenly on guard. The vulnerability I glimpsed last night seemed to retreat, replaced by an impenetrable barrier.

"What's there to talk about?" he replied, his tone clipped. "You made things very clear. You think I'm a douche and you think our kiss meant absolutely nothing. It's fine."

As much as my apology was making me nervous, his pouty face and sulking tone made me want to kiss his adorable face right there.

"I never said you're a douche and no, our kiss wasn't just a ballroom fling," I spoke quickly, letting the words out before my nerves could stop me.

His eyes softened slightly, but the walls around him still held strong.

I need to put more effort than simply denying his words.

"I realize I might not have given you a fair chance to explain," I admitted, my words carrying the weight of sincerity. "I jumped to conclusions, and I'm sorry for that. You're not a douche, you're actually the most thoughtful guy I've met here."

Noah's expression remained unreadable, his silence stretching between us.

"I don't want things to be weird between us," I continued, my voice steady. "We've been getting along, and I value our friendship. I should've trusted you more, and I regret not giving you the chance to clarify."

He finally looked at me, lowering the shoe in his hand.

"So, I'm apologizing, Noah," I concluded, "for not understanding, for assuming the worst, and for hiding my feelings just so I won't feel embarrassed to admit it. You were right. We have something real and I don't want to lose it."

His eyes held a lake of relief as he nodded, his mouth carrying a smirk at my apology. "So you're apologizing?"

I rolled my eyes. *He's really gonna rub it in, isn't he?*

"Yes."

"And you're saying you agree with me?" The eyes that held indifference a few minutes ago were now shining with his usual charm again.

"I guess so."

"You guess? A guess isn't good enough then, I suppose." He shrugged, getting back to his boots.

"Ugh, fine," I said, not wanting to lose his attention for even a minute. "You were right and I agree with you. What else do I need to do?"

"If you want me to forgive you," he said, his voice measured, "join me on a hike after lunch."

"We already have a group hiking activity today. Of course, I'd be there."

"Nah ah," He held up a finger. "Not with the group. With me. On a different site."

I narrowed my eyes at him. "So you can push me off a cliff with no witnesses?"

"Maybe, who knows." He shrugged, a smile playing on his lips. Just this little act of witnessing his smile after our fight gave me incredible relief. It was like finding the spark that I thought we had already lost. "Guess you'll have to come and see."

A lovestruck smile escaped my mouth before I could stop it. "I'll be informing everyone about my whereabouts, just so you know."

"Try your best, Captain America." He said with a shrug and went back to fixing the shoelaces, the joy on his face too obvious to miss.

I walked back toward our tent as a smile took a permanent place on my face. Despite his jokes, he was the one I felt the safest with, and going on a hike with him would probably be safer than taking it with Mr. Bailey, who tends to forget his own safety equipment, much less the others. As I entered the tent to prepare for a hike, I had a warm feeling enveloping me from all sides. The same warmth I craved last night was back in my life and I couldn't wait to discover new places with him as we went on our very first hike. Or should I say our very first date? Even though he hadn't mentioned it to be a date, ever since our kiss and the conversation we had last night, the tension between us was too hard to miss, and even sitting on a log ten feet away from the camp would have felt like a date at this point. I packed some protein bars, a huge bottle of water, a few insect repellants, and a flashlight as well.

Admitting my feelings and coming this far in our relationship was surely not an easy thing to do, but now that I was here, I could barely hold in my excitement as I realized I was going on a nice little hiking date with none other than Noah Yildiz.

The air was filled with the scent of pine, and the excited chatter of fellow campers buzzed around me. We were all done with the lunch and had retreated back into our camps to pack up, but since I had already packed up my supplies before lunch, I decided to meet Noah early instead. The earlier we started this trip, the better.

"And where exactly are you going?" Mia asked while packing her binoculars in a case.

"The hike?" I replied sheepishly. I hadn't been able to tell her that I had planned a different hike with Noah. I had thought that maybe she would forget I wasn't around her when she saw some fancy birds or something.

"The reporting time isn't until another fifteen minutes." She tilted her head.

I fiddled with my fingers. "I'm not going with the group."

Her eyes went wide, typical mom style. "You want to get lost in the jungle or something? You're not going anywhere alone!"

I sighed. "Not alone."

She narrowed her eyes and I hesitated. Nevertheless, if I wanted to escape her anger, I had to answer.

"IamgoingwithNoah." I went fast. I don't know if it was the shyness or the fact that Mia had been right about us all along, but I just didn't want to admit that I agreed to a date with Noah.

"You what?" Her expression became perplexed. "You're going wit-" Her eyes went wide all over again. "Oh my God, you're going with Noah?!"

As she asked me the very obvious question, I looked away, embarrassed. I looked at the binoculars in her hands, I looked at the beige shorts she was wearing that reminded me of Jurassic Park, and I looked down at my fiddling fingers- anywhere except her amused and content eyes.

"Is this the right time to tell you *I told you so?*" She said with a voice that was filled with satisfaction to the brim.

I rolled my eyes. "Whatever." I was just a centimeter away from saying 'It's just a hike' and downplay our date, but somewhere inside me, I was done with masking my feelings and trying to appear unfazed. "Yes, it's a date. I'll see you after sunset."

She gave me a teasing smile that made me roll my eyes all over again and I stepped out, my feet taking me to the corner of the campsite where Noah and Mason's perfectly made tent stood proudly.

"Noah?" I called out since knocking on the tent canvas would do nothing to inform him about my presence.

"Yeah? Come on in," his voice welcomed me from inside the tent.

I unzipped the entrance and found Noah surrounded by camping gear. His eyes lit up when he saw me, and a grin spread across his face. "Ready for the hike?" he asked, packing the last few items into his backpack.

"Absolutely," I replied, my excitement matching his. "Show me the prettiest sunset I have ever seen."

Once Noah finished securing the gear, he swung the backpack over his shoulders and stood up. "Well, the path we are taking is a bit longer than the others," he warned, looking at me with a spark in his eyes. "But I promise you, the view is a thousand times better."

"Surprise me." I said as I lifted my shoulders, our casual effortless dynamic coming back as we slowly forgot all about the little fight yesterday.

We set off on our hike about ten minutes earlier than the others since Noah insisted that we had to manage our time and reach before the sunset. As we set off in a direction different from the main group, the initially easy trails gave way to a more secluded path. The sound of rustling leaves and our footsteps created a comforting rhythm, and I slowly felt at ease in the wilderness.

"How do you know about this?" I asked. "I'm starting to think it might have been a rash decision to trust you with this."

I picked out a particularly long creeper out of my way and threw it to the side, careful about coming across any bugs or strange-looking animals. I knew England wasn't exactly known for its dangerous wildlife, but I believed you could never be too careful when it came to dense forests.

He laughed, his cheeks revealing the ever-adorable dimple. "I came here last time with my dad. He loves nature and he dragged me over to this hike as well."

I smiled. I loved it when he talked about his personal life outside of school, a cozy feeling enveloping me whenever I learned more about him. "So you didn't want to come?"

"Nah. I had just wanted to stay in and play FIFA at home but later I was glad to have joined him." He stepped on a stick and it made a very satisfying snap. "You won't be compromising with the view either."

The more he talked about how great the location was, the more curiosity it built up within me. I was enjoying every second of this long trail- mostly because Noah was with me- but also because I knew it led to a beautiful destination.

We came across a wild bunny on the way, and Noah sat on the ground, moving his fingers to call it near him. He made some little chirping noises to woo him in, but the bunny wasn't buying his non-bunny language and ran away. I laughed as he lowered his head and sighed, acting like his heart was shattered by the act.

"Bet he would come if I tried it," I said.

"Oh yeah? We'll see when we come across another bunny."

Turning a simple act into a competition was the way of our life, and it brought me a vague sense of satisfaction to slip into our old familiar habits even as we discovered new parts of our relationship. The air was filled with a sense of freedom now that I had embraced all the feelings floating inside me, and I couldn't help but be grateful for the push he gave me to stop ignoring my heart.

As we went on, we came across a little pond and I saw that all sorts of wilderness had been blossoming around it- ducks, frogs, some birds, bushes that had unique-looking flowers, and then some creepers wrapped around the trees that seemed to be enjoying the view across them as well.

"That is so cool," I said, halting my steps to stare at nature's version of a diverse neighborhood.

"Isn't it?" He stood behind me, looking at the sight himself. "I remember my dad feeding the ducks with some bread we packed last time."

"Oh, I want to do that!" I exclaimed, quickly taking off my backpack to find something.

"I don't even need to see to know you probably didn't pack any duck-friendly food." He said as I sheepishly held out a protein bar.

"Ducks can't eat those preservative-filled protein bars, you dumbo." He smacked my head playfully as we both erupted into a fit of giggles.

I put the bar back in and stood up, appreciating the small ecosystem for a while before we continued on our hike. The trees and landscapes started becoming prettier and more mesmerizing the more we went ahead. If the landscape became pretty when we were just halfway to our destination, I wondered how beautiful it would be when we finally reached all the way up.

Noah shared stories from his past hikes, pointing out interesting plants and animals along the way, which made the hike a thousand times more enjoyable and fun. In my head, the warmth of his company was illuminating the whole way- like the flowers were somehow fresher, the leaves much greener as they danced with joy in the wind and the sun shone just a little brighter. The hike was indeed long but none of it weighed heavy on me as we navigated the twisted paths. My trust in him came immensely naturally as I followed him, knowing that if he promised me something, he was indeed going to deliver that promise.

As we ascended a gentle slope, the trees began to thin out, revealing glimpses of a breathtaking panorama. Noah was right – the view was indeed a thousand times better. The landscape unfolded like a masterpiece, with distant mountains painted in hues of green and blue. The beauty of nature stretched out before us, and for a moment, time seemed to stand still.

The mountains were incredibly huge up close, and the blue skies were stretching miles and miles away until they mixed with the lakes and the ground on the horizon. The big trees on the mountains far away seemed like an assembled plate of standing broccoli, and the lush forest beneath the trail laid out behind us. I couldn't believe we actually climbed our way through this dense forest. It was a spectacular sight all around, not a single sight mediocre enough to take my eyes off it.

Noah glanced at me, a silent acknowledgment that we had discovered something extraordinary together.

"So?" He asked, one word covering all his curiosity to know if I liked the spot.

"It's breathtaking," I pronounced it slowly, like saying it slowly was the only way to do justice to the word.

"I told you this was better." His smile shone with much pride like my approval was the only thing he did this whole hike for.

"It is."

"We've got about half an hour until sunset," Noah said, checking his watch. "And that is the best part."

"Can we sit and eat something until then? I'm starving now."

Noah and I found a comfortable spot on the ground, nestled between patches of soft grass and wildflowers. I pulled out a couple of protein bars from my backpack, and we shared a quiet moment, savoring the simple pleasure of unwrapping the bars. The crunch of the protein bar echoed in the serene surroundings.

Something about the vast landscape ahead of me and the sky spreading out above me made me wander deep into my heart. I chewed on the bar as the moment took me into a reverie, filling me with feelings of gratitude. A year ago, I was miserable- I was failing my classes, I wasn't playing soccer at any commendable level, I had no real friends, and sitting at home all day was my only way of coping. Fast forward a year, and I was sitting with someone I cared about, someone who made me feel all sorts of happy things, eating a protein bar as we waited for the sun to dip lower and lower behind the mountains.

"You know," I started, chewing the last bite of my bar and putting the wrapper back into my backpack. "I'm really glad I ended up here," I confessed, breaking the quietude. Noah turned to me, a gentle smile playing on his lips.

"On this mountain?" He asked, finishing his own bar and putting away the wrapper as well.

"No," I shook my head. "In England."

"I'm grateful for that too." He replied, his voice soft. "Playing for the school, doing well in your studies—I think you achieved quite a feat here."

Noah and I leaned back, propped up on our elbows, gazing out at the horizon. The sun began its slow descent, casting long shadows over the landscape. The sky transformed into a canvas of warm pinks and oranges, a prelude to the impending sunset. I could feel the energy in the air, a quiet anticipation building as the world prepared for its nightly transformation.

Hearing him talk about my achievements, I couldn't help but remember how it was last year. How I failed, how I had to work triple hard to be selected, and how I still barely passed my exams. I glanced at Noah as his encouraging gaze made me feel comfortable in sharing my thoughts.

"It's just that sometimes, it nags at me, you know?" I finally let it out. "The way I wasted a year, the way other people in my class are about to get graduated and I'm still here studying my junior year all over again. They're all ahead in their lives meanwhile I'm still struggling to catch up. They will reach their destinations first and I will be late in reaching mine."

His expression softened as he looked at me. "So what if you're late? So what if you took a few dips in your life? Don't you see where it brought you?" I thought I was supposed to answer but he went on. "You're here *because* of your failures, Avery. You're following your passion *because* you realized you weren't made to follow the same path as everyone else. Isn't that quite wonderful?"

His words hung in the air, sinking in. But my uncertainty and insecurities welled up again, bubbling out even if he made my heart feel better with his words. "My path is taking way too much time than the others. What's wonderful about that?"

Noah shook his head, his gaze unwavering. "You carved your own path, Avery. You took the path that led you to more beautiful experiences and much better lessons. Anyone can follow the path that they're *supposed* to take, but it takes guts to shift away from the crowd and go down a path you're not familiar with. A path you never thought of taking."

His words struck a chord, resonating with the insecurities deep within my heart. "Just like this hike," He continued, lifting his chin towards the sprawling landscape. "It was different than the others- more secluded, longer, uncertain, and more tiring for sure- but look where we are now. Wasn't the journey more scenic on the way here? Doesn't this different destination hold more beauty and value than the regular one?"

Even as my heart melted at his words, I didn't know how to respond so I turned to look at the view in front of me. The mountains stood tall and proud, their peaks bathed in the warm embrace of the fading sunlight. Valleys and meadows unfolded beneath, adorned with a patchwork of greenery that glowed with a golden hue. It felt like we were perched on the edge of the world, witnessing a secret, awe-inspiring spectacle.

"Sometimes, the unconventional paths lead to places a thousand times better than the usual ones." He turned toward the landscape as well. "And *you*, Avery, took the scenic route in your life."

A smile left my lips as I nodded. Maybe he was right. It did take me a lot of lows to reach here, but now that I was here, I appreciated every single thing that led me to a life that I never imagined having. My journey was longer and more exhausting, but now that I was seeing the results blossoming right in front of my eyes, I was glad I took it. Because now, when I reach my destination, I know it will be a thousand times sweeter.

I looked at Noah with a grateful smile. "How do you always manage to make the bad things sound good?"

He shrugged. "I know I'm amazing that way."

We both laughed, a warm dome of comfort standing around us. Just like that, his philosopher side was turned off and he went back to being the casual and cocky Noah.

As the sun dipped lower, casting a warm glow across the landscape, I couldn't help but be mesmerized by the marvel that was unfolding before my eyes. Noah was right beside me, taking in the view while it lasted. The beauty of the moment was not lost on me, and I knew that this shared experience would be etched in my memory forever. A sunset framed by mountains and a connection that surpassed the depths of the valleys we stared at together.

35

NOAH

As Avery and I sat side by side, captivated by the breathtaking sunset, my eyes still somehow strayed off to her, her beauty being reflected by the warm glow of the setting sun.

The mountains seemed to hold their breath in reverence, and a tranquil stillness settled over the landscape. I had seen her hundreds of times in my life, and I was looking at this sunset just for the second time, but the beauty beside me distracted me away from the beauty ahead of me. Her eyes sparkled with a reflection of the colors in the sky as she smiled, her admiration for the scene evident.

"Isn't it so beautiful?" She said as her eyes were still trained on the sunset, thankfully unaware of my admiring gaze on her.

"Yes, it is," I replied in agreement, but she probably wouldn't know I was talking about something else. "You know what else is beautiful?"

She turned toward me, the red tint on her cheeks highlighted by the orange hues of the sun. "What?"

"The stars." I joked, knowing fully well she expected me to say 'You'.

A chuckle left my mouth as she rolled her eyes and in that moment, something stirred within me. I found myself drawn to her and an inexplicable feeling surged through me as I looked at her playful smile.

"You're such a-"

Her words hung in the air unfinished, as I leaned in and kissed her.

The unspoken desire to seize the beauty of the moment took over me, to capture it in a way that transcended beyond words. Avery responded to the kiss, a silent acknowledgment of a connection that went beyond any confession we could have made. Her hands found my shoulders and I pulled her close, not wanting to let go of this moment for even a second. Our connection deepened, amplified by the beauty that surrounded us. The last few rays of warmth from the sun touched our faces, and for a brief moment, time stood still.

No doubts between us anymore, no holding back. The kiss unfolded like a poetic stanza in the symphony of nature - the rhythmic sounds of nature provided a soothing soundtrack, and the fading daylight painted everything in a soft, ethereal glow. A pair of lovers finally let go of all the things that held them back and embraced the kiss as they realized the depth of their feelings together.

As we slowly pulled away, Avery and I exchanged a look that spoke volumes. The landscape before us had witnessed a moment that transcended the ordinary- a kiss woven into the fabric of the sunset. The sky transformed, transitioning from warm hues to cool tones as the sun finally bid its farewell. I couldn't help but think how the contrast mirrored the changing dynamics of our kiss—from the warmth of passion to the coolness of shared tranquility.

"I like you, Avery," I voiced my thoughts, looking into her eyes with a sincerity that I hoped reached her heart.

She smiled, the corners of her eyes crinkling with the effect. "I think I like you too."

"Think?"

"Let's just say a ninety-nine percent chance." She narrowed her eyes with a playful smile.

"I'll take it."

Her smile turned into a chuckle. "Noah Yildiz, you charming little prick." Her smooth hair was now slipping out from her bun, and a few strands of hair framed her face in a soft wave.

She held my hand as we laid back down, the sounds of the birds becoming quieter and quieter as our eyes watched the sky transform from an empty canvas to bright little stars taking their places in it. I glanced to my side. She was looking up, her eyes reflecting the galaxy of stars above before she noticed my gaze and gave me the most beautiful happy smile.

My heart never stood a chance.

"File in quickly, we have to leave in five minutes." Mr. Bailey said as the crowd of students started sorting out into the buses, the campsite becoming empty and quiet again as the noises and laughter were finally leaving the place.

We had quickly returned from our hike yesterday once it had gotten dark, armed with our flashlights as we navigated our way back to the camp. We reached back just in time for the nightly roll call and then had dinner before settling inside our respective tents. The hike had taken every bit of energy out of us, and nothing else could have given me the much-needed rest other than my warm sleeping bag.

We were supposed to leave for our school this morning, and surely enough, the chaos of packing and getting ready made the camp loud enough just before we left.

I filed into the bus and found Avery, sitting in the middle of the row with an empty seat beside her. I saw as she shook her head when Liam reached her, telling him that the seat beside her was taken. A warm surge of satisfaction flooded through me as she told him to take another seat. Avery was finally treated him how he deserved and it made my heart pump a triumphant beat. I walked over, put my backpack in the overhead compartment, and slumped down beside her, fully confident that I was the only one she was saving it for.

"So you saved a seat for me this time?" I said, greeting her with a smile.

"I had to return the favor." She replied with the same smile that had wrecked me over these past few months.

As the bus grumbled into life, her hand found mine and she leaned back, getting comfortable for the ride ahead. Even though I had kissed her just the night before, the gentle touch of her hand still made my heart flutter in my chest.

"So you have a thing for hand-holding?"

"Shut up." She said with the typical embarrassed edge in her voice, the subtle blush on her cheeks making me smile like an idiot.

As the bus gently swayed with the rhythm of the road, her tired head settled on my shoulder and she shifted a bit to lean on me. Her hand on my hand moved up to hold my arm, her body partly resting on me as she shuffled a bit more to find a comfortable position.

I looked down at her, a soft smile playing on my lips. At that moment, we didn't need words to express what we felt. There was a gentle warmth enveloping us, creating a cocoon of comfort. It was a simple gesture, yet it brought me great joy to know how she always rested easy whenever she was with me. All this while, she had always trusted me, even if unknowingly, and that revelation gave me a lovely feeling in my heart all over again.

Our intertwined fingers spoke of a silent agreement—this was the beginning of something beautiful, a sacred connection that extended beyond any initial hatred, fights, or crazy misunderstandings.

Epilogue

AVERY

The roar of the crowd reverberated through the stadium as the match between our school and the Crestwood Heights Academy kicked off. It had been weeks since my first match for our school, and Coach Martinez had pretty much secured me as a permanent player in the starting line-up. Things were going ahead much more smoothly than before, and I felt a unique sense of belonging in my current life. My studies were going well enough and Asami wasn't bothering me as much as before since I was always quite occupied with my training schedules and matches for her to threaten me anymore.

"The game has started with quite an electric flow, the Summerfield side is gaining ground on the Crestwood's goal side, with the ball sitting predominantly with Chloe Lewis!" Luke's voice echoed through the stadium, announcing the interesting buildup. It was a home match after what seemed like an eternity and hearing Luke's voice from the speakers after so long was surely giving me a huge dose of contentment.

As I scanned through the field, it gave me quite a nervous feeling to find the Crestwood players strategically blocking any possible chances for attack, but as Chloe sped past a defender and came parallel to my side, I knew I had to give it a chance, no matter how hard it was.

"And Chloe has given a pass to Fred, Fred to Avery, would she be able to create an attack in this array of defenders?"

The ball was at my feet and three defenders were in front of me. I had a second to decide which way I wanted to shoot when Noah ran up to a prime position near the goal. If I sent in a low pass, I would be risking the pass getting interjected by one of the defenders. The crowd held its collective breath as I dribbled past a defender and then, with a timely calculated cross, I tucked my foot beneath the ball and sent it soaring towards Noah.

All of our coordinated training sessions translated their way onto the field as he understood my tactic in a millisecond and immediately jumped up to receive the high pass. It was like time slowed down as Noah's head connected with the ball, sending it straight into the back of the net.

"GGOOAALL!! The cross from Avery is delivered perfectly, and Noah finishes it off with a stunning header! The glorious Summerfield striker with yet another acrobatic goal as he rises above the defenders and stuns the goalie, the ball flying past his delayed attempt at saving! What an incredibly clever assist by the midfield magician- Avery Kai!"

The scoreboard lit up, indicating our team's lead. The elation in the air was palpable, and I couldn't help but revel in the moment. I exchanged triumphant glances with my teammates as they patted my back, the culmination of my hard work and dedication finally manifesting on the field.

As the match progressed, the precision and agility of our team were unmatched, all the players smoothly going together like butter on a saucepan as we effortlessly challenged the Crestwood players with our synergy. Being on this field, wearing my school's jersey, and hearing the stands cheering for us, an immense wave of contentment settled into my bones- a revelation that this is what I was supposed to do all along, and this is where my life was supposed to lead me since the start. *This is where I belong.*

Amidst the action, I felt yet another connection standing out in the rhythm of the game. Noah and I shared an unspoken understanding during each match, a synergy that seemed to transcend the boundaries of the pitch. The same guy I always tried to outdo on the pitch was now the one who understood my gameplay the most, and responded to my tactics with calculated ones of his own. We worked together like a well-oiled machine, each part seamlessly complementing the other.

As the match came to an end, no other goals were scored and the stands were chanting our school's name as we won our way to a victory. All our teammates were walking back towards the locker rooms when Noah found me on the field, jogging over to pat my back proudly. The intensity of the match reflected in our breathing, but our eyes held a shared confidence.

"I'm starting to think you're not so bad at this." He said, a proud smile sitting on his face.

"Not so bad? Do I need to remind you of the first day when I nutmegged you during practice?"

He chuckled and messed up my bangs as I swatted his hand away, the sounds of our laughter echoing through the field. As we reached the touchline, Coach Martinez motioned us over. His weathered face broke into a proud smile as he gestured for us to join him. We walked over, delaying our post-match shower for his impromptu discussion.

"Avery, Noah, great game today," He commended, clapping us both on the shoulders. "And guess what? I've got some exciting news for you."

I exchanged a curious glance with Noah, and the spark in his eyes told me he anticipated Coach's next words as much as me.

"Over the past few matches, there have been scouts from a reputable football club watching our team. And let me tell you, they've been particularly impressed with both of you," He announced, his eyes gleaming with pride.

My eyes widened in surprise and so did Noah's. The realization that we had caught the attention of scouts from a football club brought a mix of excitement and nervousness. This was what I had come here for, this was my dream all along, and now it was finally materializing right in front of my eyes.

"They've been following your performances closely," Coach continued. "Your skills, teamwork, and dedication haven't gone unnoticed. In fact, they're interested in offering both of you a chance to join their youth team."

A gasp of disbelief escaped my lips, and Noah was still staring at Coach without blinking. The gravity of his words sank in as a wave of disbelief surged through me.

"They want to see more of what you can do," Coach added with a reassuring smile. "It's a fantastic opportunity for both of you to take your game to the next level."

Noah and I exchanged glances, a silent acknowledgment of the incredible turn our soccer journey was taking.

"Remember, this is just the beginning. Represent our team well, and show them the passion you bring to the game," Coach Martinez encouraged. "They'll be in touch to discuss the details. Congratulations, you two! You definitely earned it."

As he patted us on the back, Noah and I stood there, absorbing the weight of the news. The soccer field, once a familiar battleground, now held the promise of a new adventure. The constant chatter from the spectators seemed to blend with the beating of our own excited hearts.

After delivering the unbelievable news, Coach turned around and got busy talking to someone on his staff, and Noah and I were just a thought away from pinching our arms to make sure it wasn't a dream.

"Can you believe this?" Noah whispered, a wide grin spreading across his face.

I shook my head in disbelief, my eyes shining with a mix of gratitude and determination. "Ella is going to lose her shit when she hears this."

"Deniz too. Although she will probably shower you with hugs and kisses before she even realizes that I was selected as well."

"She really is adorable with all her fangirling." I chuckled.

"Well, I can't blame her. You've always been an inspiration, you know? On and off the field. Your dedication, your passion – it pushed me to do better every single time."

My eyes widened in surprise at his genuine compliment, and a warm smile spread across my face. "Really? I never thought of myself as an inspiration. I was just doing what I love."

Noah reached out, giving my arms a playful nudge. "Exactly. And that's what makes it so inspiring. Your love for the game, your commitment – it radiates from you. It's contagious, Avery. Every time I saw you giving your all on the field, it fueled my determination to step up my game too."

My cheeks flushed with a mix of humility and gratitude. "I guess our rocky beginnings weren't such a bad thing after all."

"I guess not."

As we continued our walk toward the locker rooms, he suggested a few dates for us to go on to celebrate our selection, and his overly romantic ideas made me question all of his attempts at appearing unbothered when it came to love.

"Our first official date is a picnic on the beach under the stars? Have you swallowed a romance novel or something? Do I need to call a doctor?"

He shrugged, unapologetically quoting more romantic dialogues. "Well, what can I do? I like you so much I can die for you."

I swatted his arm in annoyance, but not before a bright laugh broke my attempt.

"Of course, I'd haunt you in the afterlife but really, it's the thought that counts."

I glanced over at him, his tousled hair and bright smile giving him a flattering boyish charm as always. "Is it just me or was your face always this kissable?"

He laughed. "From punchable to kissable, I think we came a long way."

ACKNOWLEDGEMENTS

You, the reader who had just finished this book, I am forever grateful to you for not only picking my book off the shelf but also reading it until the end and finishing my first ever story. I hope you didn't regret your choice. If you are a fellow chain romance reader like me, let's just do a cheers for being hopeless daydreamers together before we dive into our next romcom.

As for the dedication, I want to dedicate this book to my parents- S.H. Abbas and Dr. A. Tanveer who supported me and encouraged me to write, did everything in their power to give me the opportunity I needed, and created a space for me at home where I could peacefully work and achieve the feat I had always wanted to achieve. This is for you.

Another huge thanks to my brother- Syed Mudassir, who made me feel irritated enough to prove him wrong. You tried giving me a challenge to achieve something and I ended up doing it just to prove myself. Although your way of encouragement was annoying, it was helpful nonetheless.

And of course, I am thankful beyond words to everyone who believed in me way before I ever believed in myself. To Amena- who had always believed in me and encouraged me in everything I did, thank you for caring about me so sincerely and bringing me up no matter how much anyone else brought me down. To Yaserah and Zunerah- the very first people to know about my dream almost a decade ago, and who supported me in my journey to this day. To Madiha- who was always happy to read whatever I wrote, no matter how small or silly, and who was always ready to help me with her much important feedbacks no matter how busy she was herself. To Mavia- who always made me feel happy with her presence and made me laugh even in times when I found it hard to smile. Even when I had nothing to be proud of, you still made me feel good about myself. You always treasured me even when I thought I was not worthy of anything, and for that, I'm forever grateful. To Yusuf- who believed in my capability to write at a time when I thought I wasn't good for anything, who trusted my dream more than I trusted it myself. Thank you for pushing me on always, even when I fell back so many times. To Tehmina and Zehra- Even though I came to know you much later in my life, you always supported me and helped me whenever I doubted my abilities, whose words of motivation always pushed me to believe in myself and never stop trying. I appreciate the genuine and sincere kindness you have shown me always.

Thank you to Rehan sir from Bluerose publishing who helped me navigate this journey of self publishing, your positive encouragement and kindness helped me a lot to understand how the process works and your patience in answering my questions was truly admirable.

A huge thank you to all of my extended friends and family as well, I really appreciate the love and care everyone has given me. Each and everyone's support always meant a lot to me and helped me achieve this milestone today.

CONNECT WITH THE AUTHOR

Email- <u>syedamariyamafreen@gmail.com</u>
Instagram- @mariyams.writecorner

www.ingramcontent.com/pod-product-compliance
Lightning Source LLC
LaVergne TN
LVHW091712070526
838199LV00050B/2360